The Prince's Highland Bride

By Cathy & DD MacRae

PUBLISHED BY
Short Dog Press

www.cathymacraeauthor.com

Cathy & DD MacRae

License Notes

The book constitutes a copyrighted work and may not be reproduced, transmitted, or stored in or introduced into an information storage and retrieval system in any form or by any means, whether electronic or mechanical, now known or hereinafter invented, without the express written permission of the copyright owner, except in the case of brief quotation embodied in critical articles and reviews. Thank you for respecting the hard work of this author.

This ebook is a work of fiction. The names, characters, places, and incidents are products of the writer's imagination or have been used fictitiously and are not to be construed as real. Any resemblance to persons, living or dead, actual events, locales or organizations is entirely coincidental.

DEDICATION

To all in search of their
Happy Ever After

Cathy & DD MacRae

The Prince's Highland Bride

Phillipe de Poitiers, a prince of Antioch, finds himself a breath away from wrongful execution. Risking everything, he leaves behind his crown, his family, his country—and a body sworn to be his by the Bishop, himself.

Free of court intrigue and drawn to Scotland by memories of a woman who once possessed his heart, Phillipe sells his sword to pay for his travels and accepts the task of guarding the daughter of Laird MacLaren.

When Maggie MacLaren's abusive marriage fails, she wants nothing more than to retire to her childhood home on the banks of Loch Lomond. Trouble follows her, putting her clan in danger, and she travels to the Isle of Hola, placing her safety in the hands of a mysterious mercenary with a haunted smile and a kind heart.

As Maggie and Phillipe struggle with their pasts, love blooms. But when a pirate's treasure offers a seductive lure, will it free them—or prove the downfall of all they hold dear?

Phillipe of Antioch, briefly king of Cilicia, would be remembered by the world as an arrogant, presumptuous man, poisoned two years after his marriage to the queen of Cilicia, accused of crimes against his adopted country. This re-imagined telling of Phillipe's life, one of court intrigue, distrust, and the lust for power, shines a different light (and ending) on the tale.

Books in the Hardy Heroines Series

Highland Escape (book 1)
The Highlander's Viking Bride (book 2)
The Highlander's Crusader Bride (book 3)
The Highlander's Norse Bride, a Novella (book 4)
The Highlander's Welsh Bride (book 5)
The Prince's Highland Bride (book 6)

Words of Interest

Armenian words:
Astvats Giti - 'God knows'
Hrazhest – farewell

Persian words:
Sardar – a title of nobility which denotes a prince, nobleman, or other aristocrat
La - No

Norman French words:
Fils de pute – son of a bitch
Le chiot – puppy
Ma belle – beautiful one
Mon ange – my angel
Mon Coeur – my heart; depicts a deep love

Norman words:
Harousse – old horse/mare (from old Norse *hross*- horse/mare)

Norse words:
Donansgeir – the rock of Donan
Eyrr – a sandbank or small spit of land running into the sea
Erryhús – House on a spit of land running to the sea – the longhouse on Hola
Fálki – falcon
Freya – Norse for Lady, Mistress
Hola – hole or cavity, hole inside rocks
Hús – house
Langskip - longship
Steðja – halt, stop, settle

Scottish words:

Bawheid – idiot, fool
Bowsterous – boisterous, fierce, rowdy
Daftie – an idiot
Dirdy-flitcher – a butterfly
Dreicht - dreary, gloomy, bleak, miserable, grey, depressing, devoid of sunshine
Gey wheen – large number
Gie – give
Guid – good
Hauld yer wheesht – be silent; quit complaining
Peelies – crabs which are molting their shells; they are vulnerable to predators at this stage.
Peerie-weerie – a tiny creature
Ramscallion – a rapscallion, a playfully mischievous scoundrel
Skaithed – hurt, injured
Skunner – a loathsome, terrible person
Snell – very cold, bitter weather you feel right down to the bone.
Sump – when the rain comes down with gusto and great strength
Tottie – tiny
Twa - two

Gaelic words:
Machair – a fertile low-lying grassy plain found on coastlines of Ireland and Scotland, particularly the Hebrides
Mar – seagull; a MacLean ship
Muinnitir – 'people' or 'folk'; used to describe 'family' in its broadest sense.
Saorsa – freedom, liberty; a MacLean merchant ship

Other:
Mazer – someone who makes or brews mead
Cyser – a blend of honey and apple juice fermented together
Maimones – a garlic soup in Malaga

Almojabana – cheesecake in Malaga
Skerry – reef or rocky island

Chapter One

Phillipe of Antioch, the son of Bohemond IV, was a real person. Chosen to play a role in The Highlander's Crusader Bride, he became more to us than an unfortunate victim of politics and court intrigue. At first glance, he was destined to meet his fate in the dungeons of Cis Castle. As we dug deeper, we wanted to know, What if . . .?

The Mediterranean coast
Early winter
1224 AD

"Halt!"

The shout from behind echoed off the rocks, punctuated by the shush of steel against leather and the thunder of the mounted pack. Phillipe urged his horse to greater speed. Surrender was not an option.

To his left and right, his guards bent low over their horses, grimly determined to outpace the men in pursuit. They were past reckless banter, beyond the boasts that they'd make it to Tripoli. All attention was on the dangerous footing ahead and in assessing the manner of men who chased them. The road from Sis to Tripoli was not often fraught with such danger, but bandits were not unknown. However, if Phillipe was placing bets, his would lie squarely on Baron Konstantin.

The darkness which had hidden their departure from Sis Castle was no longer their ally, but rather their foe as they sped over the rutted road. Torchlight twinkled in the distance, marking the city ahead, taunting them with safety.

If only Father received my missive. If he's sent men to help . . ..

But Phillipe knew help would not be forthcoming. The road ahead lay silent. Failure loomed, tightening like a physical noose about his neck.

I am the King of Cilicia! They have no right! Rage burned side by side with indignation at the injustice. Grand Baron Konstantin, former regent to the young queen, Phillipe's wife, cared for nothing but furthering his own power—and Phillipe stood squarely in his way.

Phillipe's steed stumbled, his shod hooves clattering over loosened stones.

"*Merde!*"

As if to answer his irreverence, his horse pitched forward, falling abruptly to its knees. Phillipe lost his grip and plummeted over the animal's neck, landing hard on the packed ground. With a grunt of effort, he rolled and sprang to his feet, body low, sword in hand. A swift glance at his horse told him it would prove no further use in evading capture. Its sides billowed, head low, one foreleg toeing the ground as though it could no longer bear weight.

Pain flashed through Phillipe's skull. He winced and shook his head as his vision cleared. Four men shot past. They wheeled their horses in a spray of dust and gravel. Phillipe felt rather than saw his trusted guards—Hugh and John, men who, like him, called Antioch, not Cilicia, home—align to flank him.

Cloaks swirling about them like the wings of giant black birds, the bandits—if that was what they were—circled Phillipe and his men. Moonlight glinted off the long sweep of deadly *kilij*, the weighted, curved blades of the mounted warrior. Phillipe flinched. A single downward stroke would slice through him with little effort. If either he or even one of his men faltered, they were doomed.

He made a beckoning gesture with the fingers of his left hand, lips curled in a feral grin.

The black-clad men faced Phillipe and his guard, the ends of their turbans wrapped to conceal the lower halves of their faces. Moonlight glinted dully on chainmail coifs protecting their necks and shoulders.

These were no ordinary bandits.

Damn. He resisted the urge to exchange glances with his guards. Phillipe gripped his straight-bladed sword, raising it aloft in a high guard. Hugh and John lifted their swords waist-high, clearing their saddles, prepared to strike.

The bandits charged side-by-side. Phillipe backed against John's horse's flank, sticking close as his men met the charge. John ducked a swing meant to take his head and countered with a strike that bit deep into the bandit's torso. Phillipe blocked a downward attack and rammed his shoulder into the villain's horse, causing it to veer to the side. The rider grabbed the reins with both hands, dropping his guard. Phillipe thrust his sword through his foe then pushed him from the saddle and mounted the steed.

Phillipe whirled his horse at a shout from Hugh. Sleeve darkened with blood as he valiantly fought the two remaining marauders, Hugh was rapidly losing the fight. Phillipe brought his sword up for a head strike then sliced low when the bandit raised his guard to parry. The force of Phillipe's swing unhorsed the man. He landed awkwardly on the hard, rocky ground and did not rise.

Hugh dispatched the remaining bandit then sagged forward, his wounds taking their tithe.

"John, bring wine and bandages," Phillipe shouted as he dismounted to help Hugh to the ground.

Hugh waved him weakly away. "Go, my lord. Ye expose yourself. I will just slow ye down." He grimaced as Phillipe helped him to sit.

"I'll not leave ye to die in this place," Phillipe growled. "Not after ye risked your life to protect me."

John knelt beside them, placing a stoppered flagon on the ground, along with a length of cloth. He split Hugh's sleeve, exposing a deep cut the length of the man's upper arm. Blood welled steadily from the wound and the white of bone could be seen. Already Hugh's skin appeared tinged with gray.

John shook his head. "He's right, m'lord. We should run whilst we have the chance. Antioch is but a few leagues away."

"I'll not leave him to die alone."

"Then let me tend his wounds and ye go ahead. I will see to it he makes it to your father's palace."

"Go, m'lord. John will patch me up and ye can send your father's men to escort us back."

Torn between loyalty and duty, Phillipe kicked a rock with frustrated violence then mounted the horse he'd won in battle.

"Very well. But I command ye both to follow as soon as ye are able."

"Aye, m'lord."

Phillipe guided his horse into the shadows and was only a short distance away when the sound of horses thundered behind him. Wheeling his mount, Phillipe drew his sword and raced back. A score of riders encircled Hugh and John, dressed the same as the deceased bandits, swords pointed at their heads.

A tall man, his face angular, his nose as sharp as a falcon's beak, kneed his horse between his soldiers. His eyes narrowed in the barest hint of pleasure. He jerked his head toward Phillipe.

"If he resists, kill the others."

Phillipe spat on the ground. "'Tis like ye to sit back and command others to do your work, Darius. Konstantin's actions have rubbed off on ye."

Darius fluttered the fingers of one hand in a bored manner and shrugged. "I prefer not to soil my hands with the likes of thieves."

Phillipe startled, caught off-guard by the accusation. "Thieves? Ye have the wrong man." A sneer dragged at one side of his mouth. "Crawl back to your master. Ye have no authority over me."

"Oh?" He nodded to someone beyond Phillipe's shoulder. The man held Phillipe's lame horse with one hand, a leather satchel in the other.

"I found this, Sardar." The soldier opened the leather bag and reached inside. Moonlight sparkled in his hand as he withdrew it—flashes of red and white, and a twinkle of gold.

"What . . .?" Phillipe shook his head, but the unexpected sight of the jewels befuddled his mind even more.

Darius smirked, his condescending manner infuriating Phillipe—as it always had.

"We are taking ye back to Sis to stand trial, *my King*." The title dripped acidly from Darius's lips.

"On what charge?" Phillipe demanded. A sick sensation hollowed his stomach.

"Why, theft of the Crown Jewels of Cilicia, of course."

* * *

12

Phillipe choked. Smoke filled his nose. His chest contracted violently, forcing him onto his side as he gagged. Pain lanced through his head. He squeezed his eyes shut against the agony, then slowly opened them.

Damn Darius to hell. And damn his lackeys who cracked my skull.

A pair of scuffed boots entered his vision. The stench of ancient, nameless muck rose from the rotted straw beneath his cheek. Phillipe sneezed, rolling to his back with a groan. Two men stood over him, one on either side, heavily armed, with malicious grins stretching their lips above yellowed teeth. Phillipe slowly sat then gingerly moved his limbs, the clink of chain across the floor confirming his worst fear.

He was in prison. Even had he not been beaten, he doubted his chance of rescue. The underground hellholes of Sis offered little in the way of basic survival, and none of escape. The memory of his capture was fuzzy at best, but he recalled the accusation—a preposterous charge likely fabricated by Baron Konstantin himself—of stealing the Crown Jewels. One more black mark against him in the hearts of his adopted people. He was an outsider, married to their nine-year-old queen. A marriage he hadn't wanted, but his father had given him no choice in the matter. As Bohemond IV's third son, his life was that of an expendable political pawn.

It appeared he was expendable once again.

"Get up."

The butt of a spear prodded his back, spreading agony from where a well-aimed boot had connected just below his waist. He'd be pissing blood for days. If he lived that long.

Phillipe struggled gingerly to his feet and tottered unsteadily. He caught his balance, but the heavy chains dragged at wrist and ankle, making it difficult to remain standing. A shout echoed down the stone hallway, bouncing hollowly through the twists and turns. Raucous noise billowed from the cells lining the narrow passage, increasing in volume. Phillipe winced.

A man stopped before the gate to Phillipe's cell, his heavy cloak billowing about his feet. Metal clanged as the gaoler thrust a heavy key into the lock and turned it, then swung open the door. A lackey darted inside, lantern held high. The golden glow illuminated the visitor's face, but even without the light, Phillipe knew at once who it was.

"Baron Konstantin." Phillipe inclined his head in a fraction of social mockery. "How kind of ye to drop by." He spread his hands at his waist, palms up. "I'm a bit tied up at the moment, but I am certain an appointment could be made if ye wish to return when I am not quite so indisposed."

"Impertinence." Konstantin snorted, his eyes flashing. "I have suffered your shortcomings for far too long." His black eyes cut to the men on either side and his manner relaxed as if remembering he played to a crowd of avid eavesdroppers.

"Theft of the Crown Jewels carries the penalty of imprisonment." His voice, smooth and oily, reached every eager ear. "I fear the people's tolerance of your arrogance and blasphemous actions against the Armenian Church is at an end. Despite your lofty title, ye will pay the penalty for your misconduct."

Phillipe bristled. How dare the baron besmirch his holy commitments? "I fought to protect Jerusalem before I earned my spurs. Condemn me for being loyal to the Roman Church, but do not name me a common thief."

Baron Konstantin stepped closer, the smirk on his face growing. "I have ye where I have wanted ye since the day ye arrived. Ye will not live to see the end of your sentence, this I swear." His voice hissed low, meant for Phillipe's ears only. "I will rule Cilicia, make no mistake."

Fresh anger roiled through Phillipe. He rolled his shoulders, the movement rattling his chains. "Where is Zabel? If ye have harmed her, I swear . . . ." If Konstantin knew Zabel had approved Phillipe's dash to Antioch, what would befall her?

Konstantin laughed. "Never fear. Queen Isabella is quite safe. Ye do not think I would harm my ward? She has been as a daughter to me since her father died, God rest his soul."

"She ceased being your ward when she married me," Phillipe bit out, frustrated by the power struggle he'd endured the past two years.

"That did cause difficulty," the baron agreed with a sage nod. He leaned his head close enough to whisper in Phillipe's ear. "She will be well cared for. My son, Hethum, has always had a fondness for her. I think the two of them, both of pure Cilician blood and of the Armenian Church, will prove a most advantageous match."

"She's but a child!" Phillipe growled, hands fisting impotently. Zabel had never been a wife to him, her age forbade it, but he'd loved and protected her as though she'd been his sister.

The baron shrugged. "She will not always be a child. Do not worry. We have the best interests of Zabel and Cilicia at heart. She will not mourn ye for long."

"Damn you, Konstantin!" Phillipe roared. "May ye rot in the deepest hell!" He jerked against his restraints. The guards on either side clubbed the backs of his knees with the butts of their spears and he crashed to the floor. The baron took a single step back, a mocking gesture proving his superiority.

"The people of Cilicia will rejoice at your death, Phillipe. They cry out for your blood. There is no love for ye in their hearts, no matter they once praised ye and the alliance ye brought."

Phillipe ground his teeth. "My father will avenge me."

"Oh, I doubt that." A rictus of a satisfied smile flirted with Konstantin's lips. "Though he may wish to try."

His words carried a wistful quality, as though Konstantin knew something Phillipe and his father, the powerful Prince of Antioch, did not. The baron leveled a shrewd gaze on Phillipe as he stepped away.

"Enjoy what life ye have left. Prayer and penance would be my suggestion." His voice once again drifted through the chamber, pious and regretful. With a twitch of his cloak, he withdrew. The ancient metal door clanged shut behind him.

Deep, hot rage swept through Phillipe. What had been asked of him had been outside his power—or intent—to give. No matter the flowery words and promises at his marriage and coronation, the thought of renouncing his religion for that of the Armenian Church had affronted him.

Phillipe could have been a better king, perhaps even a better husband, but even his best intentions had proven inadequate. Zabel would undoubtedly fare better without her foreign husband and his suspect ways at her side. His presence—once cheered—now only divided the people. Would Konstantin truly protect her? Would Hethum—a boy closer to Zabel's age and born and raised in Cilicia and the Armenian Church— prove a wiser choice?

Phillipe had not asked for the crown of Cilicia, but he'd pay for the privilege with his life.

Chapter Two

Bridei Keep, Aberdeen coast
Early winter, 1224 AD
Scotland

Thwak!

The bolt smacked the tree trunk with a satisfying *thunk*. Maggie shifted the crossbow point down and placed her boot in the stirrup at the front of the weapon. With a strong upward pull, she engaged the string against the nut and placed another quarrel in the groove.

She glanced dispassionately at the bolts bristling from the tree trunk and the few scattered on the ground.

How many imaginary shots at the earl would it take to blunt the edge of her anger?

She leveled the crossbow, placing one thumb in a groove to line up her sighting. The image of Richard's face hovered over her improvised target.

At least one more.

Thwak!

She leaned the weapon against a boulder and reached for her longbow. She hefted its abbreviated length, thankful for her father's armorer who had insisted she have a bow that fit her stature. Not that she was particularly short—especially for a woman—but her father's six-foot bow had proved more than she could handle.

Shifting the quiver over her shoulder, she fired all six arrows in rapid succession.

One. *Men . . ..*
Two. *Are not . . ..*
Three. *Fair.*
Four. *I . . ..*
Five. *Will not . . ..*
Six. *Be defeated.*

Four of the shafts bristled among the bolts. One lay on the ground some distance away. The sixth was lost in the underbrush.

Her shoulders ached. As did her heart. The failure of her marriage was not for lack of attention. She'd tried. Her mother's instructions on how to be a good wife even now echoed in her mind. Maggie had shied from nothing and had even tried to love her husband.

Though she'd not been fond of leaving her home in the Highlands and becoming the wife of the Earl of Mar, he'd seemed pleasant enough initially, if often a bit distant, and her father desired the connection.

But during the time they'd been married, she'd given him no children, and he'd dissolved the union. She would be sent back, used, unwanted—and childless. Forever shamed as *barren*.

* * *

Maggie's view from her window of Minfur Burn changed with the seasons, and it was once again a white sparkle of water through red and gold leaves. A year. She'd lived at Bridei Keep for a year and had naught but heartache and strife to show for it. An all-too-familiar ache closed about her heart, stopping her breath. She clenched her fists, nails biting into her palms against the pain.

Around her, yet seeming as distant as the burn itself, women busied themselves packing her belongings. Yvaine's stare fired daggers between Maggie's shoulders, but she refused to cower from the older woman's judgment. Maggie drew heavily on the knowledge she was going home. Home to Loch Lomond and her beloved Highlands where she'd once again be Maggie MacLaren, not the wife of the Earl of Mar.

Give me one good reason I shouldnae chain ye to a rock and leave ye for the tide.

She suppressed a shudder, reliving the horror of the past week when Richard had at last refuted their marriage.

Because 'tis a day's ride to the sea and ye've never done anything even slightly beyond yer own comfort. She'd wanted to fling the words at him, but had resisted. Her husband—former husband—had rarely done anything that did not provide himself instant gratification, or at least the fairly immediate promise of pleasure. And he'd proven to have an unforgiving streak. He'd likely haul her to the coast, no matter the cost to his comfort, merely to prove her wrong.

A bolt between his ribs would have . . .. She drew a deep breath against the thought. A well-placed bolt would have cured naught.

She understood he needed an heir. She felt the lack of a bairn as keenly as she would the loss of air to breathe. As disgraceful as it was to be sent home barren and unwanted, it had to be better than the life to which she'd sunk once Richard had realized his efforts in her bed had failed to produce a bairn.

A wooden trunk slammed closed and Maggie jumped, battling fear as she spun about, hating the look of satisfaction in Yvaine's cold eyes.

"My son is well rid of ye. Though why he bothers giving ye passage back to yer clan . . .." She shrugged. "It speaks well of him, do ye not think so?"

Nothing in Maggie's heart thought well of Richard de Moravia just now, so she bit her tongue against an ill-guarded reply.

Yvaine lifted her chin. "Mark my words. He'll not be without a suitable woman for long."

Nae, he's been with many, suitable and otherwise, for weeks, now. The bitter words hung silent in the air. She knew Yvaine was aware of her son's numerous dalliances, but it was clear she chose to ignore them this day. Maggie pulled herself together. He'd given her another reason to fire a crossbow quarrel . . . though at a target somewhat south of his treacherous heart.

"I wish him all he desires from this life," she murmured, forcing the words. The two maids exchanged lively glances, eagerly anticipating a battle between the Earl of Mar's mother and his former, unlamented wife. Maggie would not give it to them. She'd endured the woman's disdain for twelve long months, painfully aware she did not live up to Yvaine's standards. Maggie was too tall, too robust, to meet the older woman's expectations of a proper bride. Yvaine had wished for a dainty daughter by marriage, slender and feminine, willing to fawn on Yvaine's every utterance. Maggie, with her forthright manner and the ample curves Richard had once admired, fell disappointingly short.

Spoiling for an argument, Yvaine waved her bejeweled fingers dismissively. "Ye should have retired quietly to the abbey and lived yer life in penance for yer failure as a woman. Richard would have supported ye."

"He would have supported my silence and encouraged a vow of poverty."

"None will listen to ye, and yer return to yer family will also offer a similar lack of comfort." Yvaine peered down her regal nose. "God will neither forgive nor forget yer refusal."

"At least my family welcomes me."

Yvaine arched a brow. "Yer da willnae welcome ye. He thought to rise above his station by marrying his daughter to an earl. MacLaren is a minor chief and always will be."

Maggie's temper flared. "I would rather live as the daughter of a minor chief than the wife of an arrogant earl."

Yvaine grinned, clearly pleased to have provoked Maggie.

"And so ye shall."

* * *

The travel to MacLaren land was long and made more arduous by the almost utter silence from the three men and maid accompanying her. But silence and disdain had been Maggie's constant companion for weeks, even months, and she could not deny the thrill rising as they left the rolling hills of Aberdeenshire and approached the towering peaks of her beloved Highlands.

Home meant the mountains and the crystal waters of Loch Lomond. Bridei Keep had been the earl's home, never hers. She took a deep breath against the pang of longing. She'd tried to make a place for herself at the keep named for the Pictish king who'd built the kirk at the site more than six hundred years earlier. Its ancient history called to her, but its people had not.

The wagon creaked and bumped over the uneven trail and Maggie longed for the palfrey she'd left behind. Richard had been kind to her in the beginning, eager to please, and had showered her with numerous gifts, including the pretty black mare with white stockings. Yvaine had insisted she leave everything behind. Fighting with the woman over a few possessions had not appealed to Maggie. She did not mourn the loss of jewels and rich clothing, but the uncomfortable lurch and wobble of the wagon reminded her of the loss of the mare. Her bigger regret was the passing of the chance to make a life for herself and the children she hadn't conceived. The earl had no use for a childless wife.

By the time they left the sea near Perth and began traveling west and south to Stirling, the once-colorful autumn leaves had become dry and brittle. They fluttered from the limbs in the wind and crunched beneath the horses' hooves. By the time they entered the wooded glens and braes of the Trossachs, a dusting of snow blanketed the road and a mantle of white lay atop Ben Lomond.

"Glad I'll be to put these mountains behind me," grumbled one of the men. He hunched his shoulders forward and tugged his cloak tighter about his neck.

"Winter will have reached Bridei by the time we return," another replied, disgust peppering his words.

Maggie tamed the smile tugging at her lips. Only another day, perhaps two, and she'd be home. No longer would she fear her least movement would be reported to Yvaine or Richard. No longer would she bow her head to appease those around her. Her heart hummed at the sighting of every rise, every glen, every quiet glittering loch.

She quelled the jubilant tapping of her toes. She was grateful her escort hadn't left her—or sold her—at one of the many villages and towns along the way. It was impossible to know what their instructions were, and even if they abandoned her now, it was likely she'd make it to Castle Narnain on her own.

Her maid wriggled closer to the man driving the wagon and folded her hands within his cloak. He glanced at her, brows raised, then grinned. She giggled and pressed her cheek against his shoulder. Maggie rolled her eyes. At least someone wouldn't sleep cold this night.

She didn't care. Perhaps it would keep the grumbling to a minimum. She wanted to enjoy this homecoming. Bask in the tall shadows of the mountains and the sunlight in the glens.

And ignore the dread pooling in her stomach when her father discovered her on his doorstep and his boasts of having an earl for a son-in-law crumpled about her feet.

Men. Why did they place stock in such things? For that matter, why did women? From her earliest memory, her father had prattled about his plans for her. Despite her preference for woodland trails and skills with daggers, he'd eventually forced her into castle halls and drills with needlepoint.

Excitement and dread gripped her belly, an appalling combination producing the inability to sleep or eat. Her temper grew short as the last miles to Castle Narnain slipped slowly beneath the ponies' hooves. Maggie finally lost her battle with impatience and, grabbing her crossbow and quiver of quarrels, leapt from the wagon.

The driver looked up. "Hey! Where do ye think ye're going?"

Maggie silenced him with a flap of her hand. Head high, she breathed deeply of the crisp, cold air. It stung her cheeks, brought tears to her eyes, though whether from the bite of winter or the burn of anticipation, she couldn't say. She was no longer constrained by the weight of disappointment. Her heart felt as light as a bird on its first flight. Independence running roughshod over fear.

She hiked her skirts and hurried up the path. She rounded a bend and found the tiny village of her birth scattered in the glen below. The sight drew her onward and moments later the keep of Castle Narnian rose above the trees. Ageless and formidable, and named for Ben Narnian—the mountain of iron—it clung to a rocky crag overlooking the placid water.

The wagon creaked and clanked behind her. People glanced up from their various tasks. Visitors were a rarity in this secluded glen. Apparently finding nothing threatening in the wooden wagon and two mounted men, they seemed to lose interest.

Maggie's breath came in deep pants as she approached the keep perched at the top of a steep hill. She'd had little exercise in the past year and felt the lack acutely. She mounted the path resolutely, boots treading the packed earth.

A shout sounded from the top of the hill. Someone recognized her. A ripple of excitement fluttered in her belly. Guards peered over the walls, their numbers increasing. Maggie smiled. These were her people. They knew her and she knew them. She quickened her step, reaching the gate out of breath but happy. The door to the keep opened and a shadow spilled into the yard.

Da?

Apprehension prickled her skin. Maggie paused, striving for calm. How would he greet her? She'd not heard from him for several months.

The shadowed form stepped forward. Dugal MacLaren strode across the yard, the hem of his cloak flapping in his wake.

"Maggie?"

Her heart raced. *Damn Richard for not sending word ahead of my return.*

"Aye. 'Tis me. I'm home."

Chapter Three

Sis Castle dungeon
Cilicia, the Mediterranean Coast
Two days later

The sheen of water glistened on the dungeon walls. A golden gilding, reflecting the torchlight blazing in the hall. Shadows, angular blackness, slipped between the bars.

Phillipe's stomach growled.

The bowl which had contained the rancid stew fed to him once a day, sat to one side, cushioned in the nameless filth on the floor. From the corner of his cell, a rat poked its head from beneath the straw, nose twitching. Phillipe kicked at the rodent, but it had become used to his presence and did not scurry away.

Turning his attention from the rat, Phillipe ran cramped fingers over his temple, flinching at the tenderness that remained from the beating Baron Konstantin's men had given him two days earlier. The bump, once the size of a hen's egg, had decreased perhaps by half. Though his vision had almost returned to normal, his head ached with dull, constant pain.

Another few days in this god-forsaken labyrinth and he'd be too weak to take advantage of any plan of escape. Hunger and thirst would make him vulnerable to any number of maladies that plagued such wretched places. The wracking coughs he heard from the other prisoners sapped their strength, leaving them wasted and on the brink of death.

He'd avoided the dungeons in his father's castle because of the desperation and hopelessness he'd seen in the prisoners' eyes. How much longer until his own eyes echoed the same despair? His time was running out. Whether at another's hand or by the ravage of time and mistreatment, he would soon lose hope.

He recoiled from the idea. He would not allow his life to be discarded so easily. His foster father had taught him to use his mind to solve problems, to seek solutions beyond brute strength. 'Twas how Donal

MacLean, a Scotsman, held his small but important keep in the midst of Saracen aggression.

Despite the throb in his head, Phillipe turned his thoughts to plans of escape.

Metal clanged in the distance followed by a few half-hearted shouts. It did not appear the men in Sis prison had much vigor—or hope.

Moments later, the thud of feet on stone caught his ear. Relief and surprise washed over him as the familiar form of his manservant appeared. They waited as the gaoler unlocked the cell door and motioned Peter inside. He closed and relocked the gate then shuffled down the hall, leaving Phillipe and Peter alone.

"How fare ye, My King?" Peter whispered.

Phillipe spread his hands, the chains manacled to his wrists telling their own story.

"I am glad to see ye enjoy good health," Phillipe countered. "I feared all those in my service would be put to the sword. It does my heart good to see ye hale and hearty."

Peter shrugged. "I am but an old man, and of little interest to anyone. My Queen has been most generous in placing me in her service. My status is much reduced, but I do not yet fear for my life."

"Have ye word of my guard? John and Hugh?"

Peter shook his head. "I am sorry. I have heard naught."

Phillipe swore beneath his breath. He feared they had given their lives in the ill-fated ride to Antioch. Yet another crime to lay at Baron Konstantin's feet.

Peter drew a cloth-wrapped package from beneath his cloak. "I have this for ye."

The smell of fresh-baked bread cramped Phillipe's stomach, nearly choked him with the sudden surge of saliva in his mouth. Ignoring the drag of his chains, Phillipe thrust his hands toward the offering. Peter quickly unwrapped it and broke the loaf in half. Scarcely pausing to breathe, Phillipe consumed the fragrant offering.

He swallowed the last bite with difficulty. Peter produced a small flask and popped the cork. With a grin of thanks, Phillipe guzzled the mild spiced wine then wiped his mouth with the back of a grimy hand.

"I have only a few moments more," Peter whispered, glancing over his shoulder to the empty corridor. "I bring word from the Queen."

Phillipe stilled, the bread and wine settling heavily in his over-loaded stomach.

"Tell me."

"The rumor is ye will not live to see a trial."

Phillipe nodded impatiently. He hadn't believed Konstantin would drag him through such a public display. Not one in which his father, the powerful Prince of Antioch, would be certain to attend.

Peter leaned in closer. "She overheard a plot to have ye killed, here, in prison."

Phillipe understood. His warder and any who'd come in contact with him would simply disappear, and the details of the unlamented King of Cilicia's death would neither be confirmed nor denied. Baron Konstantin—and he was certain the baron was at the bottom of this plot—would conveniently wash his hands of the act. Even if war ensued, Phillipe would still be dead and no longer king.

"She is distraught. I promised I would bring ye word. Though I do not know what can be done."

"She is well? They have not harmed her?"

"Nae. Baron Konstantin treats her as a daughter and has striven to tease her from her worry by plying her with sweetmeats and bangles."

"She is only nine, but has the heart of a warrior. Sweets and trinkets will not suffice."

"Ye speak truth, My King. She is a rare flower."

Phillipe rubbed his chin, his short beard bristling beneath his fingers. "I never intended to leave her. I thought . . .." He gave a short, derisive laugh. "It hardly matters, for it seems I will soon leave this life, and what I do no longer affects her. I thank ye for telling me of her. Knowing she is being cared for helps somehow. Of the plot to kill me—I must think on this. Be on my guard."

"The baron spoke of poison. A violent death would pose too many questions. Poisoning may seem as many things."

Phillipe nodded. Poison could mimic many deaths, and who could say Phillipe hadn't simply died of his head wound, or of guilt over his alleged theft? Too many questions would remain unanswered. And only one person would be required to place the poison in his stew. A person who would likely not live to tell the tale.

Peter glanced down. He shifted his balance from one boot to the other as if weighing his thoughts.

"Please, Peter. Do not hesitate," Phillipe said, grimness catching his words. He cleared his throat. "If ye have more on your mind, *this* is the time to tell me."

"My King, I would help ye escape if I could. I fear the path from here to outside the castle is fraught with danger, and freeing ye from this cell and your chains is only the beginning."

A chill of hopelessness threatened Phillipe. It was only slight comfort his young wife took an interest in his welfare, for she was too easily controlled by the baron, and a nine-year-old's voice—though it was that of the Queen—mattered little. The only other person concerned for him was Peter. Phillipe wasn't certain of Peter's age, but he'd been white haired when he and Phillipe had arrived in Cilicia two years earlier, and his frail form and stooped shoulders did naught to inspire confidence.

Little more than a glance was needed to see the dungeons beneath Sis Castle were impregnable. The tunnels and steps were carved from the stone of the mountain, and echoed with the cries of those long dead. Men who had clearly been imprisoned for years populated the tiny, windowless cells lining the main passage. He had no knowledge of how deep he'd been entombed in this vast prison beneath the castle, but he suspected his cell was nowhere near the surface.

"I cannot stand idly by . . .." Phillipe broke off. His words echoed off the cold stone and his wrists and ankles felt the weight of their fetters. There was little he could do *except* stand idly by.

"*Merde!*" He rattled his chains, fists clenched. He pivoted, pacing within the constraints of his shackles.

Three paces.

Turn.

Three paces back.

"What are my chances for escape?" He shook his head to stop Peter's answer. Not the question he'd meant. "What are the weakest spots in the baron's plan? How can I use this to my advantage?"

Peter shrugged. "If the poisoner fails to do his job, if he does an incomplete job . . . ."

Phillipe cut him off with a wave of his hand. "He won't refuse. Can't. If I don't die, his entire family would be at risk."

"True enough."

He sent Peter a piercing look. "What if there was an antidote for the poison?"

"I would first have to know what he plans to use. Assuming I could do this, what would ye then do? They would simply try again."

Phillipe grew still. A voice from his youth slipped through his mind. A young woman he'd once loved—before fate forced them on separate paths. She'd been fascinated with the dark arts of the Hashashin order, relating to him the subtle art of poisons on more than one occasion.

They are tricky things, poisons. What appears to have no effect on one person can cause irreparable harm, even death, in another. We know many poisons from which no one recovers. But there are others with more sinister reputations.

The memory of black hair and almond eyes hit his gut like a direct punch. Why remember Arbela at a time like this? She'd left the Holy Land years ago, and it was unlikely their paths would ever cross again. He'd learned to put her from his mind.

Or so he'd thought.

Yet he remembered the way her eyes lit as she spoke of her findings. A passion he'd once yearned to have turned on himself before he'd learned of his fate to marry Isabella. It was his fervent wish Arbela's life took a far different journey than his.

Aconitum. A beautiful flower shaped like monk's hood. Its name comes from an ancient village in the north once called Akonai. The cave there is said to be the entrance to Hades and is guarded by a Molossian Hound, a robust and fierce animal trained for combat. 'Tis said it is from his spittle the poisonous flower grows.

How like Arbela to be fascinated with such a story.

Aconitum? Phillipe wracked his memory to recall the plant. Monkshood? Wolfsbane?

His lips thinned. He gripped Peter's shoulder. "Listen to me. I believe I may have a chance, slim though it may be. I will need your help. May I count on ye?"

Peter nodded. "With my life, My King."

* * *

Phillipe paced the floor, the rubbish worn thin beneath the trail of his bare feet. He did not believe Konstantin would waste much time putting his plot into action. Would Peter be able to do what was required of him? So much rested on the shoulders of one elderly man.

Two days had passed. At least, Phillipe believed so. Timing was dependent on the schedule of his single meal, and it had arrived twice since Peter had left. Once, between bowls of fetid stew, a loaf of bread had arrived, and Phillipe had included a request for a special blessing for the aged man in his prayers that night.

Footsteps sounded in the passageway. Someone threw his bowl at the gate to his cell, the resulting clang echoing off the rock walls. The warden shouted, an irritated command for the uproar to cease. Half-hearted retorts followed then faded.

A shadow fell into Phillipe's cell. Metal clanged as the lock disengaged, and Peter slipped inside. His eyes met Phillipe's, the tug of silent questions asked and answered. The warden's footsteps died away.

"I have what ye asked for." Peter's look grew troubled as he unwrapped a parcel he withdrew from a satchel beneath his cloak.

Phillipe stared at the small flask, the emerald green glow of the glass warm in Peter's hand. Peter closed his fingers around the vial.

"My King, if there is another way . . .."

"Without a key to my fetters and an army to help fight my way to the surface and then to Antioch, I fear not."

Peter hesitated then gave a single nod. He handed the flask to Phillipe.

"Wait a bit after I've gone before ye take this."

Phillipe nodded. He had no wish to embroil his manservant any deeper in this deception than was necessary.

"'Tis a foul concoction, though an attempt was made to improve the flavor. Do not linger over it. And I beg your pardon, but do not forget to destroy the vial once the poison is consumed."

"I will do so."

"Ye may experience nausea, almost definitely a tingling in your arms and legs. If this works, the woman Lusine will prepare ye for burial. She can be trusted, and I have given her a few silver coins to buy her agreement to help." He tilted his head, a wry look drawing his lips to one side. "A sound of surprise or distress from her once ye have risen from the dead would ruin the plan."

Phillipe drew a shuddering breath, turning the green vial over in his hand. Peter touched his arm.

"My King, if there is *any* other way," Peter begged, "please tell me. My life is yours to command."

"Nae. For good or ill, I will take this. I will not succumb to Konstantin's plot. If I die, 'twill be on my terms, not his."

"I await word, then."

"Please see to the Queen. She cannot know I live. I cannot remain here, and she must be free to pursue whatever life is before her."

"I will do what I can to comfort her, yet not give away your secret. She would insist on coming with ye, and both of ye would be killed. I will not allow that to happen."

Phillipe stared resolutely at Peter. "Thank ye. May your life be filled with peace."

Peter bowed his head. "And ye, as well. Until we meet again, my King."

He turned and called to the warden. Phillipe slipped the tiny flask into the waistband of his loose pants, tugging the ragged hem of his tunic down to cover any hint of a bulge. The warden released Peter from the cell and their footfalls quickly faded.

Phillipe eyed the bowl near the door. How long before Konstantin's assassin slipped poison into his stew? Could he risk another meal? He'd been unable to eat the food provided by the warden since Peter first told him of the plot against him. His stomach knotted. The thought of forcing down even a bite of the fetid mess threatened a bout of nausea.

Better to anticipate the assassin's strike than wait. He pulled the vial from his trousers and backed into the shadow of the doorframe. The prison was silent except for the rustle of rats in the straw and the wet hacking cough of another prisoner a few cells away.

He uncorked the bottle and put it to his lips. With a quick flip of his wrist, he tossed the contents back, gagging at the bitter flavor. His stomach roiled in protest, but he kept the liquid down. Moving as far as his chains would allow, he dropped the vial and, using a bit of fallen masonry, ground it into powder then scattered it amongst the straw.

He stood, suddenly dizzy. A numbness began in his fingers and quickly spread up his arms. His legs weakened and he gasped at the slow thud in his chest. Choosing a spot close to the gate of his cell, he sat on the bare floor. His breathing labored and his chin dropped to his chest.

Phillipe slumped to the side then rolled forward, face first, onto the stone.

Chapter Four

Castle Narnain
Loch Lomond, Scotland

"Ye poor lamb! To think what ye endured at the hands of that wretched man!" Maggie's ma clutched her hands to her bosom, dismay rounding her eyes.

The comfort Maggie had expected seemed to suffocate rather than relieve. "I'm home, now, Ma. I dinnae wish to speak of it."

"Not that we dinnae appreciate ye being . . . *home* with us . . . ." Janneth fluttered about, searching for the right words. "Howbeit, we'd expected ye to . . . *not* come home."

"I scarcely had any place else to go, Ma."

"Yer da said the earl offered ye . . . to send ye . . .. Would ye nae have been comfortable at the abbey?"

Maggie's blood ran cold. "Nae."

Her ma stared at her. Silence stretched between them.

At last, her ma took a sharp breath. "Och, Maggie, 'tis not that we dinnae want ye, but yer da put forth quite an effort on yer behalf. And now all his plans are gone. Gone!" Janneth flipped her fingers through the air as though ridding them of something offensive. She stomped to the window, shoulders rigid as she stared outward. Before Maggie could reply, her ma whirled, her face a mask of tearful disappointment.

"Ye couldnae even give me grandbairns for my old age."

Her ma's harangue sliced through Maggie. Her eyebrows shot upward in response to the band constricting her chest. Could her ma not see how much her words pierced Maggie's heart? Her younger brother Uilleam, already a dashing figure at sixteen summers and away fostering with the MacGregor clan, was certain to give their ma grandbairns one day.

"I dinnae ask to be barren." The words barely squeaked past her throat.

"Yer da put much pride in yer status, Maggie. After all the trouble he went to, finding ye a decent husband. Not just some Highland chieftain wanting a passel of bairns to fill his crofts, but a *nobleman*. A nobleman who simply asked for an heir. Ye were supposed to be a *lady*."

The accusations her ma leveled rendered Maggie speechless. Not that it was a surprise to discover her da's ambitions, for she'd known of them for years. But to learn her own dismay over not delivering the required heir to the earl was of no account left Maggie cold. Yvaine was right. She was not welcome in her childhood home. The abbey would mayhap have been the better choice.

A movement at the door to the solar disturbed Maggie's thoughts.

"Och, Janneth," Dugan MacLaren stepped hesitantly over the threshold then halted. He crossed his arms over his chest and planted a wide smile on his face. "Give the lassie a bit of breathing room. Barely home the day and ye chide her for her shortcomings—for matters beyond her control. If we say the arrival of children is God's will, is it not also His will if they dinnae?"

Both Maggie and her mother stared at the man as if he'd lost his mind. Maggie knew it was rare for him to side with her against her ma, but to find him so squarely on her side—despite his mention of her *shortcomings*—was a novelty.

He took Maggie's arm. "Come with me." He gave her hand a pat as he placed it on his forearm. The budding warmth ceased abruptly. With the sense of leaving the bubbling pot for the fire, she allowed herself to be led to her da's solar.

Laird MacLaren released Maggie and motioned to a chair before the large desk that wedged its ancient surface between a shelf filled with all manner of trifles and a window overlooking the loch. To Maggie's mind, her da's office with the books and odd trinkets passed down through generations, coupled with the grand view, was one of the best rooms in the keep.

She took the offered seat and managed not to flinch when the door closed with a snick behind her. Her da strolled past and took his place at the desk. He shuffled through a couple of parchments and rearranged the position of the ink well before he glanced up.

His thin smile did not reassure Maggie.

"I am sorry to hear things did not turn out well with the earl. Do ye have anything ye wish to discuss?"

The question clearly made her da uncomfortable, so Maggie merely shook her head.

"Nae. We dinnae suit."

Dugal spread his hands wide. "Maggie, lass, 'twas more than that. Yer husband declared ye dinnae provide a child within the year, and, as such, were an unsuitable wife for him."

Maggie's eyes narrowed. "Why must we discuss this?"

He settled in his chair. Silence dragged its feet. Dugal sighed. "There is the issue of yer dowry."

Maggie clenched her fists. "Nae. Ye worry over the *bridewealth*. Have ye already spent it, Da?"

Dugal sat stone-faced a moment before his gaze slipped to the side. "'Twas to be paid in installments. But aye, the first has been used. I've had expenses. Will he want it back, do ye know?"

"I was not informed. If ye've received no word from him, I wouldnae worry o'ermuch." *Richard dinnae miss a chance to bite a coin.*

Her da frowned. "He sent naught with his men. He's washed his hands of ye, then?"

Maggie shrugged, dislodging her discomfort a bit. Despite her lukewarm welcome, there was no place she'd rather be than on the banks of Loch Lomond. The wonderful room lost a bit of its magic.

"He would have sent ye to the church. Paid for yer living. This wasnae acceptable to ye?"

Maggie shook her head, words an impossible jumble of anger and dismay.

Her da rearranged the items on his desk. "Tell me of yer dowry. I paid a sizeable pouch to see ye wed. 'Twas to see ye through yer auld age, ye ken."

He sounded almost apologetic to broach the topic, yet Maggie understood his concern. She'd paid scant attention to the details of her return to Castle Narnain, only too happy to shake the disapproval of those around her and begin the journey home. But the topic of her dowry was as clear in her mind as when Richard had spoken the words a fortnight ago.

I willnae burden ye with returning the coin yer da sent as yer dowry. Instead, I'm giving ye the deed to an island which was forfeit to me in a game of chance in Glasgow a pair of years back. 'Tis too far away to be of any benefit to me. A rather useless bit of property—quite a fitting gift for a useless former wife.

That she was now a landowner would not soften the blow that her da was without the monies he'd paid to have her wed an earl. Especially if the island—somewhere among the Hebrides—was as worthless as Richard had said.

She raised her chin. "He has likely found other use for the coin, and instead, gave me the deed to land he owned, that I might have a place to live should my presence become too burdensome here."

Dugal's face blossomed a mottled red. Maggie thought his nostrils flared. He cleared his throat twice.

"He'd no right . . . ."

Maggie lifted her chin. "Will ye be taking it up with Richard, then, Da? The fate of a few coins shouldnae leave ye in such a state."

"'Twas more than a few coins, lass, and ye well know it. The earl drove a stiff bargain to gain ye as a wife."

"And dinnae get what he bargained for." Maggie sighed. "I fear he has done all he will, and considers me nae longer his concern." The words stung as if a swarm of bees had somehow found their way inside her.

"Where is this property ye say ye now own?" With a glimmer in his eye denoting either unresolved anger or burgeoning greed, Dugal leaned back in his chair.

"I was told 'tis an isle in the Hebrides, a bit south of the Isle of Eigg, and not too far from the coast of the Ardnamurchan Peninsula. 'Tis a place called the Isle of Hola."

Dugal's eyes shot skyward. "Isle of Hola? 'Tis a Norse word meaning *hole*. How do ye know 'tis naught but a stone plastered with bird dung?" he scoffed. "Nae land for tilling—and likely no harbor, either!"

"It comes with a small income," Maggie countered. "The Earl would not have accepted the title if it had no worth."

"'Tis no place for the Countess of Mar!"

Maggie slowly shook her head sadly at the pieces of her life scattered about her.

"Da, I'm no longer the earl's wife. I am plain Maggie MacLaren, and yer wishing otherwise doesnae matter." She placed a palm on his desk. "Da, I will never again be Lady Mar."

* * *

Was this what it was like to be dead?

Darkness surrounded Phillipe. He could not move his arms or legs, could not determine if he lacked the strength or if he was confined somehow. A coffin, perhaps? A sense of panic filled him, bubbling up through his chest. Phillipe fought against the rising scream, but a thready whine escaped despite his effort.

Instantly, a flicker of light approached, trailing a thin line of smoke. The small brazier was placed near his head and the shadowed face of a woman entered his view. Her furrowed brow cleared slightly as she glanced over him. A tiny, hesitant smile crossed her lips as if encouraging a response from him.

He gaped like a landed fish, words dying in the back of his throat in a gargle of sound.

The woman nodded, touching a finger to her lips. Her calm warning reassured him and he concentrated on drawing deep, reviving breaths.

She tapped his shoulder and his eyes flew wide. Shaky as a new-born colt, Phillipe struggled to move, his arms and legs doing little to respond adequately to his need to rise. One hand bumped against something cold and firm lying next to him. Startled, Phillipe stared at the corpse of a man of much the same size and coloring as himself.

His stomach protested and he rolled to the side, retching. He heaved until he trembled with the effort, but nothing rose from his empty belly.

Phillipe wiped his mouth with the back of his hand. "I'm sorry. Give me a moment."

He sat, head and shoulders hunched forward until the bout of dizziness faded.

"We cannot linger."

The woman's voice, barely a whisper, spurred Phillipe to greater efforts. He straightened, then shifted so his feet hung off the single-plank table.

"Lusine, is it?"

"Yes, m'lord." She handed him a bundle of clothes. "Put these on."

He glanced at the silk tunic hanging from his shoulders, embroidery filled with the glitter of crystals and gold. "'Tis a far cry from my prison garb," he noted.

"The baron was magnanimous," she replied. "The Bishop was prevailed upon and gave ye your last rites."

"Nothing too good for the late King of Cilicia." Phillipe grimaced as Lusine tugged the shirt over his head. The clothing with which he replaced his kingly tunic was of coarsely woven camel's hair. Repeated washings had softened the garment, but failed to remove the animal stench. Lusine expertly placed the embroidered tunic over the dead man's head, smoothing it past an incision that ran the length of the wasted body.

Propping himself against the table, Phillipe pulled on the loose trousers and slipped his feet into a pair of worn boots. He tilted his head in the dead man's direction.

"A wretched soul from the prison?"

"Aye. None will miss him. We are fortunate he resembles ye so much."

Phillipe stiffened. *Fortunate* because if anyone checked the coffin and the deception was discovered, Lusine would be among the first to pay.

"Has my man compensated ye well?"

"He gave me an advance."

Phillipe sent her a questioning look.

Her voice sharpened. "Further compensation is unnecessary. I wish only to keep my life." Lusine returned his look for a hard moment before she resumed her task. "Peter was not so lucky."

Phillipe's gut clenched, too late to avoid the pain of learning Peter had died because of him.

He pushed his grief aside. "I will help ye."

"Nae. I have prepared many bodies for burial. This one is no different."

Yet Phillipe noted how her hands trembled. To prepare the body of a king was no small undertaking. That the task had been given to the prison's healer and not his personal physician told Phillipe Konstantin was putting on a public face of shock and mourning, but doing little to actually honor the dead king.

"I have done what I could to change his features to resemble yours. In another day's time, even your father will be unable to recognize ye. Time is no friend of the dead."

She shoved a sturdy cloak and small pouch at Phillipe. The bag clinked dully. He stared at it a moment, then handed the pouch back to Lusine.

"Ye will need this more than I."

She waved it away. "Where would one such as I acquire such wealth? What I have been given is enough." Her eyes held his in a solemn gaze. "My life will be my reward."

Phillipe nodded and tied the pouch to a piece of frayed rope he cinched about his waist. Lusine motioned to a dark corner of the room. "Hide yourself there. Ye'll find a sword and dagger on the bed. There are guards at the door. Men will arrive upon my request to put the body in the casket. Once they have left, and the guard with them, ye must flee. Go left through the door, follow the passage to the stairs. They will lead ye to a courtyard. Someone will meet ye there. Ye have six hours 'til dawn. Do not waste them."

Phillipe stepped behind a drapery hiding a narrow bed and a table scarcely large enough to support a trencher and mug. He silently strapped the well-worn scabbard about his waist, slipping the surprisingly sturdy blade from the sheath for inspection before settling it into place. A plain gray gown hung from a peg, marking the area as Lusine's private area, an insight on the solitary life she must lead.

Footsteps shuffled in the outer portion of the room. Coarse masculine laughter sputtered amid words Phillipe could not discern. A sharp word from Lusine silenced them and Phillipe was glad to see she apparently enjoyed a modicum of respect.

Boards creaked and Phillipe imagined the men hoisting the body of the dead man from the table and into the casket. He hoped the dim light and the finery that adorned the man's body would keep his identity safe.

He recalled the gleam of gold on the fittings of the casket and wondered how much it pained Konstantin to pay for such tribute—and how long before the gold handles and embellishments disappeared into the baron's coffers.

The door slammed shut and silence filled the room. Phillipe slipped soundlessly from behind the curtain and across the floor, a hand on the hilt of his sword, the roughness of the stone noticeable through the thin soles of his boots. Hearing no sounds beyond the closed door, he pulled the surprisingly heavy panel open an inch or so. A guttering torch dimly lit the passage, but he saw no other signs of life.

After repeating a Pater Noster, he asked God to watch over Isabella and thanked Him for releasing her from their union.

I was not a good choice of husband for her, nor was I the king she needed at her side. I have been declared dead by the Holy Church, and therefore Zabel is now a widow and free to remarry. Phillipe of Antioch, the late King of Cilicia, no longer exists.

Chapter Five

"An island?" Dugal's outrage was clear. He stormed to his feet, sending his chair skittering backward. He paused, settling a belligerent gaze on Maggie.

She held firm. "Aye. An island. Mayhap I should go find what exists there. It could be worth something."

Dugal folded his arms over his chest. "Ha! The earl wouldnae give away something of worth. I doubt the *small income* is much. He has cheated me out of a grand bit of coin." He leveled a finger at her. "And ye are now without a dowry."

Maggie's eyebrows rose. "I was unaware ye wished to trot me through the market again."

"What do ye think will become of ye? As my daughter, ye have some protection, but as a cast-off wife, ye will attract all manner of men. Nae of them good."

"All manner of men?" Maggie puzzled over his words, choosing to ignore his less than flattering note of her new status. "I am not appealing as a wife if I cannae bear bairns."

Her da's finger jabbed the air before her nose. "Dinnae expect me to speak of such things to my own daughter." His face and ears reddened, the hue creeping to the very pinnacle of his sparsely-populated pate. He drew back and re-crossed his arms.

Maggie was fascinated. She'd never seen her da in such a state. "Mayhap ye *should* speak of them, Da, if ye would warn me from *such men*."

His jaw clamped shut, evidenced by the tick that leapt along his cheek and the warning glitter in his eyes.

Maggie's lips formed an 'O' of understanding as his meaning became clear. "Och, *those* men. Dinnae fash. I have no wish to become a man's mistress. Such women have an uncertain future, and, truth be told, bed play isn't sufficiently compelling to give my life into a man's hands without adequate compensation."

"Margaret Ellen MacLaren!" Dugal's eyes bulged and his lean cheeks blanched.

Maggie hid a tiny smile at provoking him to her full name.

"Da, I dinnae wish to wed again. There is nae point . . .."

"Nae point? Will ye stay here and someday be a nurse to yer brother's bairns? Grow old alone? Maggie, lass, ye need a man."

Maggie choked. "I dinnae *need* a man, Da. I require only a roof over my head. The rest I can work for. I can take care of myself."

Dugal collapsed into his chair and for a moment Maggie feared she'd gone too far. It was clear neither he nor her ma knew what to do with her. It would quickly become public knowledge she'd been sent home in disgrace—and defied the church as well. The priest's words rang in her head. *Shame on ye, woman, for refusing to obey yer husband! Women such as ye are outside the favor of God.*

Maggie wasn't certain how she'd endure the looks of pity, contempt, or calculated speculation from *some men*.

She sprang to her feet. "I willnae be a burden to ye. Come spring, I will find my way to the Isle of Hola and make it my home."

Her da remained silent a moment, then waved her back into her seat. She stepped behind the chair, hands gripping the upper edge.

"I willnae deny the loss of yer dowry puts me in an awkward spot to find ye another husband." Dugal lifted a hand, forestalling her protest. "I willnae force ye into another marriage, but ye must see the practicality of it. Mayhap there will be a man who requires a mother for his bairns and ye can be of use to him. I will keep my ears open. The MacFarlanes arenae too distant, nor are the MacNabs. The MacGregor laird is wed, though he has no bairns yet." He tilted his head. "That we know of . . .."

With a shake of her head, Maggie left him to his plans.

She skirted her ma's solar and grabbed a cloak from her room, then hurried down the stairs. Snowflakes drifted down in casual playfulness, only to melt on landing. Maggie tilted her face to the sky, smiling at the crystalline touch on her cheeks. Tugging her cloak close, she wandered the path to the loch. Rimmed with frost like the touch of a faerie's paintbrush, the edges of the water sparkled in the sunlight.

'Twill soon be full winter and the roads impassable, snow in every tree and glen.

Winter had always been her favorite time of year, but the thought of being stuck in the keep during the months ahead gave her pause. Betwixt her ma's bouts of commiseration and her da's worry over her future—and lack of dowry—she could only hope this winter would be a short one.

* * *

Phillipe slipped through the dark passageway, following Lusine's directions. Fresh air burst upon his face like the bestowing of new life as he entered a small courtyard open to the night sky. A stair in the corner led to the top of the wall. He climbed cautiously then took his bearings from the view.

Sis Castle was riddled with tunnels and little-known passageways carved into the rock beneath the richly appointed upper levels. Rooms for the Queen and her court filled with silk tapestries, dyed woven rush carpets over smooth wood and tiled floors. Colorful mosaics, intricately carved and gilded screens, marble, and semi-precious stones. Fountains, palm fans, and iced drinks. All the things he had taken for granted and now swore he would not miss.

A boy, no more than eight or nine years of age, appeared from behind a languishing palm tree. He waved a thin hand before disappearing into a shadowed crevice. With only the slightest hesitation, Phillipe followed.

The boy's step did not falter as he led Phillipe through a labyrinth of tunnels. Though still weak and a bit lightheaded, Phillipe maintained pace with the lad.

Voices and footsteps rose and faded, but they did not encounter anyone. Torches flickered in worn sconces, placed far enough apart that shadows which hid the uneven floor fell in broad swaths between them. The light ceased abruptly. Walls closed in on three sides. The ragged hem of the boy's tunic swung to the side as he pivoted around what appeared to be a thick column of stone. No light reached here, and Phillipe's instant of alarm vanished as a draft of warm air touched his cheek. He slipped through the gap scarcely large enough for the boy and encountered his first taste of freedom.

The rippling roar of torches on the wall snapped in the wind soaring up from the sea. The tramp of booted feet echoed off the stone, and an occasional low-pitched shout and murmured response drifted to his ears.

"The road lies there, Sardar," the boy said, lifting a skinny arm to point to the left.

Phillipe pulled a large coin from his purse and placed it in his young guide's hand.

"May God protect ye," he said, closing the boy's fingers over the coin.

"And ye."

Before Phillipe could question him further, the boy disappeared like a djinni.

Setting his sights on the coast, he set his feet to the faint path ahead and blended with the shadows among the rocks.

He risked pausing in a tiny village south of Sis where he found a sturdy horse in a single-railed paddock patiently awaiting his morning feed. Leaving a coin in the wooden trough as compensation, Phillipe wrapped a bit of rope about the horse's neck then quietly walked the animal to the outskirts of the cluster of huts before springing onto its unbrushed back. The unshod hooves thudded softly against the hard-packed earth, kicking small stones into the low shrubs that dotted the landscape as Phillipe urged the beast to a greater pace.

"We must make haste, *harousse*. I must be far away by first light."

As if the beast understood—or perhaps found himself enjoying the freedom—he tossed his head and redoubled his efforts. Phillipe bent low over the muscular neck and crooned encouragements into furry ears.

"I will call ye Beaudoin, which means *my brave friend*," Phillipe said sometime later as he walked along the dusty streets of the next village, munching a meat roll to break his fast. The horse trailed behind, nuzzling Phillipe's shoulder. Phillipe shrugged away from the velvety nip of the thick lips. "I will find ye a bit of grain, but not too much. We have many miles 'til we make the coast. But for now, we must appear unremarkable. Look. Here is a stable where ye may rest a moment."

He paid the stablemaster for a place for Beaudoin in an empty paddock, a bit of mash and hay, and a trough of water, then settled beneath a scraggly tree, wrapping his cloak about him. The lingering effects of the poison still plagued his body. The ride had exhausted him and if his horse needed an hour's rest, more so did he.

They reached the coast at twilight. Though the hour was not late, winter's approach had shortened the day. Phillipe dared not attempt the two weeks' journey to Batroun on his own, nor did he wish to travel in the company of a large caravan, as all roads led through Antioch. Deception pained him, but Phillipe had determined a confrontation with his father must be avoided at all costs.

After a bit of haggling, he managed to obtain passage aboard a ship for himself and the horse to Tripoli, with the stipulation he board quickly and not cause the captain to delay his schedule. He led his reluctant beast over the dock planks to the loaded ship, wood creaking as the boat wallowed against the dock. Beaudoin balked at the hollow sound of his hooves on the wood, ears back, nostrils flared. He jerked his head against the pull of the rope and skittered backward as he gathered his haunches beneath him.

"Easy, Beaudoin," Phillipe soothed. But the frightened horse paid no heed to his reassurances. With a frantic whinny, the beast reared, lifting his forefeet into the air. Phillipe clung to the rope in grim determination. Men shouted, waving their arms as though to drive the horse onto the ship.

"No!" Phillipe cried, but the men advanced, eager to help load the horse and be away from port.

One hoof slipped on the plank. He landed his front hooves with a force that shuddered the wood, and, with a panicked lunge, the beast leapt past Phillipe into the bay.

The horse bobbed quickly to the surface. He glanced about then struck out for a spit of land not too far distant which sloped to the water's edge. Phillipe shoved past startled sailors and raced down the dock. He met Beaudoin as he surged out of the bay and raised his arms to ward off the spray of droplets as the horse shook like a big dog.

"Ye do not make this easy, my friend," Phillipe chided the horse as he captured the trailing rope. "And I dare not wait for the next ship."

He led Beaudoin back to the ship then wrapped his cloak over the horse's head. The beast snorted but settled with only a single tap of a hoof against the boards. Phillipe's glare kept the sailors at bay, and he walked determinedly down the wooden plank, giving the horse no time to reconsider. With a clatter of hooves and a brief toss of his head, Beaudoin made his way onto the ship. Phillipe retrieved his cloak then tied the rope to a cleat on the wall. He made certain hay and water were within reach of the horse, then strode to the rail as the ship set sail.

The inky waters passed swiftly beneath the ship's hull. Moonlight glinted on the waves as though the hand of God had scattered diamonds across the sea. The ship had put into port twice, and the following morning would place Tripoli on the horizon. Phillipe chafed at the delays the stops had created, but five days aboard ship brought him to his destination much faster than travel by road. From the port city, Phillipe knew the road to Batroun even with his eyes closed. There, he would be safe.

By midmorning, he bid farewell to Tripoli and put his heels to Beaudoin's sides. Two hours later, the forbidding walls of Mseilha Castle rose into view. Seat of the Baron of Batroun and where Phillipe had spent several years fostering, the ancient Roman fortification was more his home than any place else he'd ever lived. The day he'd learned the baron, Donal MacLean, and his children Alex and Arbela, Phillipe's closest friends, were to leave for Scotland, was still clear in his mind. It scarcely seemed three years had passed.

Phillipe ducked his head as he rode through the castle gate, not wishing the guard to recognize him. There was only one man he trusted with his secret, and he hoped he still held his position at the keep.

It took a bit of coin to convince the guard at the door of the hall to send a message requesting an audience with Amhal, the baron's steward. Phillipe waited anxiously, pacing beneath an orange tree in a shaded area of the yard. At last, a boy hurried from the hall, beckoning him to follow. Leaving Beaudoin tied in the shade, he entered the hall, winding through familiar passageways to the windowless room where Amhal attended the household accounts. He was instructed to leave his weapons at the door, and a guard checked him thoroughly before permitting him entrance.

The castellan rose from the chair behind the desk.

"The guard says ye bring word from Antioch." Amhal's gaze raked Phillipe's tattered clothing. "I am listening."

Phillipe glanced over his shoulder to the open door where a guard was clearly visible.

"I am no threat. May I speak in confidence, Sardar?"

Amhal hesitated then nodded, and the guard closed the door.

Phillipe straightened his slouch and brushed his matted hair from his face. "'Tis I, Phillipe."

"My Prince?" Amhal stepped from behind his desk, eyes wide. "Many pardons, my lord." He halted, blinking in bewilderment. "The reports of your death?"

"Only slightly exaggerated, I fear." Phillipe's laugh bore no humor. "No one knows of my escape. May I count on your discretion?"

"Of . . . of course." Amhal backed to his chair and sat heavily, pointing Phillipe to another. "How may I be of service?"

Chapter Six

"I ask ye to guard my secret with your life." Phillipe held Amhal's rapt attention, marred only by a slight narrowing of his eyes. "I appreciate your loyalty to both my father and the Baron, but neither must know I live."

"Might I ask why?"

"My *death* has already been divulged to my sire. The Bishop himself delivered my last rites. My father is under pressure from the Saracens in power in Egypt to the south, and Kayqubad, the Seljuk Turk Sheik, to the east. Both have been his allies, but he would lose everything if the Saracens side with Cilicia—which they are in danger of doing."

Amhal nodded sagely. Alliances often changed with little or no warning, and with devastating results.

"Other than lodge a formal protest, there is naught for my father to do but attend my funeral—and I fear they will be deny him."

"Can ye not present yourself to him? In secret? My lord, consider his pain at your loss."

Phillipe grimaced. "I do not see what can be gained from it, even were I able to attain an audience with him without being recognized by others. I would incur the wrath of Baron Konstantin if he realized he had been duped, and those who helped me escape would die. Too many have already been sacrificed.

"A great war would be waged on my behalf. I would again be a pawn in the machinations of men scrabbling for more land, more wealth, more power." He shook his head. "Nae, my old friend. I am well rid of the intrigue of this land. I have decided to travel to Scotland. My sword will pay my way. I will never again trade on my position as King of Cilicia or Phillipe, Prince of Antioch. The boy ye once knew no longer exists."

Amhal fingered a quill laying on his desk. "Will ye speak to the baron?"

The question was a simple one, yet fraught with danger. Phillipe did not wish to embroil Donal MacLean in intrigues he could do nothing about, yet he craved contact with the family closer to him than his own.

"I will. Once I arrive in Scotland. But 'tis very important ye do not send word of any kind to him, or expect to hear from me once I have left here. A bit of parchment can go astray, an idle word repeated where it will do the most damage. This ye must promise."

Amhal observed him for long moments. "*Très bien.* 'Twill be as ye wish. The Sea Falcon lies in the harbor and awaits only my word to set sail. She is the ship that carried the baron back to Scotland, and her captain knows the waters well. I can have ye out of the Levant by mid-morning tomorrow."

Excitement rose in Phillipe as he allowed himself finally to hope.

"Have ye heard from them? Alex, I mean."

Amhal nodded. "I received word that Lord Alex and his father, along with Lady Arbela and their aunt, had reached Scotland safely and would be sending ships back, establishing a trade route between the two countries and with several lands in between. Two such ships have arrived and subsequently returned to Scotland since, bringing us fine wool and bartering whisky along the way. We are pleased to send spices, silks, dates, and Damascus steel in return."

He grinned. "The first missive gave a rather amusing account of pirates they encountered near Gibraltar." He leaned back into his chair and launched into a memorized telling of the tale.

Phillipe grinned, pride warming his belly at the image of Arbela and her part in besting the pirates. *Ah,* mon coeur*! Nothing frightens ye. Ye have the heart of a true warrior.*

"Any word since?" He attempted a casual question though he was desperate to know more of the girl he'd admired since the day he'd arrived a mere boy at Mseilha Castle. He and Alex, her twin, had been closer than true brothers, yet the stubborn girl with a gift for strategy and story-telling held a special place in his heart. The fact she was an accomplished warrior only added to her charm in his eyes.

Amhal nodded. "Aye. The Baron continues to build his shipping business." He leveled a look at Phillipe. "Lady Arbela has wed a Scotsman."

Phillipe's breath left him in a rush. He blinked, trying to bring his tilting world back into order.

I had no right to expect otherwise. She was ever a friend, a sister. Naught more—except in my heart.

"I thank ye for your time and your tales." Phillipe attempted a ghost of a smile. "I am certain she and Alex are embracing their new lives in Scotland."

He rose and inclined his head to the castellan. "If ye have a spare cot where I might rest, I will prepare for my journey. Might I trouble ye to care for the horse I arrived on?"

Amhal stood and bowed deeply. "It will be as ye ask. *Que Dieu soit avec vous*, my lord."

Phillipe returned the blessing. "May God be with ye as well."

* * *

Phillipe stared at the ceiling. Blue and white mosaic tiles glimmered in the pale moonlight, cool and restful. But sleep eluded him. Images of his youth looped through his mind. Donal MacLean's wisdom, Alex's subtle jokes, Arbela's brash confidence.

Arbela had wed a Scotsman.

Had she fallen in love? Or had she become a pawn much as he had? Would Donal have ensured she would be cherished, that her husband would not break her spirit?

Damn! *He* should have been the one to nurture her, encourage her, feel pride in her accomplishments. Their last meeting had been bittersweet, a parting of friends who had no hope of ever becoming more.

I am to be crowned king of Armenia through marriage to Zabel—the daughter of the man who once attempted to stab my sire in the back . . ..

Arbela's reply had meant to be encouraging. She hadn't understood the depth of his despair.

Phillipe, this could be a chance to create greater unity in the north . . . I know 'tis not the future ye'd hoped for, but 'tis a significant task yer father puts before ye. . . .. The fate of many will soon rest in yer hands.

But, Arbela, 'tis ye I love.

Only then had she realized his true regard for her.

He'd kissed her, then sent her away to face the portentous news that her father was returning to Scotland to take his place as Chief of the

MacLeans. He'd watched her choose life in Scotland among her family against the life she knew in the Holy Land.

And not once had she indicated she returned his love.

Unless he considered the fact she did not plunge a dagger into his belly for daring to kiss her. But perhaps he'd taken her by surprise.

Already his plan was changing. He did not think he could bear seeing her as the wife of another man. Still, the baron's ship sailed for Scotland on the morrow, and it was as good a choice as any. The route was plagued with pirates and other dangers, and a ready sword would be welcome on any such vessel.

Would he seek Donal MacLean when he arrived in Scotland? Phillipe had changed his mind on the matter at least a dozen times in the past hour. How could he let Alex believe he'd died, imprisoned in Cilicia for a crime he didn't commit? And yet, if he allowed himself the contact, would he be able to leave and make a home for himself where he had no expectation of seeing Arbela—and her husband—again?

What would he have to offer if she hadn't wed? The knife edge of despair slid painfully through him. He'd deceived the church. He'd lied, offering another's body in exchange for his own. The bishop had declared him dead; had released Zabel from her vows of matrimony.

Was he becoming his father? Phillipe could not control the speed of his heart. Bohemond IV had supported the church—but had skirted the Pope's displeasure only by shifting alliances as required. Phillipe's grandsire had been excommunicated after his third marriage, though Sybil had possibly bewitched him, for she was reputedly a sorceress—and certainly a spy for Saladin.

Phillipe sought the silent guidance of his once-foster father, a man who'd been a firm follower of the chivalric code, a man who'd defended the church even at the risk of his own life, warred against the Saracen, protecting his land at Batroun and the passage of pilgrims and merchants from all who preyed upon them. Donal MacLean had been generous with his wealth and encouraged the kind treatment of all who came to him in need. Phillipe couldn't think of a man who'd triumphed over evil as brilliantly. And Phillipe had, for a time, been as his son.

Phillipe had failed him. He'd used the rites of the church to achieve his freedom. As he'd stared at the rotted straw on the floor of the dungeon, it had seemed only right to fight for his life. But what had it cost him?

Streaks of pearl and pale gold slowly inched their way through the open window, and the pre-dawn breeze fluttered the tapestries. With a grunt of relief, Phillipe shoved the coverlet aside and strode to the basin where a pitcher of water awaited, pushing aside his dark thoughts. He washed his face and hands, removed the linen tunic Amhal had given him after his bath the night before, and dressed in clothing more befitting the rigors of travel.

Amhal had assured him his new clothes were similar to those the baron and Alex had worn when they left for Scotland and should cause him less concern than his accent and sun-darkened skin. Even more of a stranger than he'd been in Cilicia despite his marriage to the queen, he would be out of place, a foreigner in Scotland.

The tunic and slender, thick trousers were worn soft in the right places and fit him well. Amhal had insisted on replacing his sword with one of Damascus steel, the blade straight in the European way, not curved as was the local preference. For the first time in years, his head was covered with a serviceable metal helm, not bound beneath a turban, and his feet were shod in the sturdy leather boots of a warrior, not the brocade slippers of a man striding the carpeted floors of royal apartments.

He broke the end from a loaf of bread as he traversed the main hall and paused long enough to take a deep draught of mulled wine. A few people sat at the trestle tables, but Phillipe quickly averted his face to avoid being recognized.

He stepped into the outer yard. Wind surged around him, bringing a storm from the north to taint the morning. His cloak flapped like the laden sails on a ship. The scent of rain filled his nose, though none had yet fallen. A crack of thunder sounded just seconds behind a flash of lightning, and dark clouds rolled overhead, hiding the rays of dawn.

Amhal hurried to his side, his long tunic rippling about his lean frame.

"My lord, the weather will delay the ship. The captain will not set sail against wind battering the harbor."

"Not to mention the lightning," Phillipe added on a resigned sigh. The wind's power increased, picking up bits of sand and scattering it about the yard. Phillipe raised the edge of his cloak protectively over his neck and the lower part of his face, leaving only his eyes showing beneath his helm and no opportunity for the sand to settle beneath his clothing.

"Be at the docks as soon as the storm has passed, my lord. Captain Benicio will await ye, but he is impatient to be gone. Forgive me, but I have told him ye are a kinsman, eager to travel."

"I am not insulted ye claim me as kin, Amhal. I am forever in your debt."

"May your wait not be long, my lord. *Que Dieu soit avec vous*."

Phillipe inclined his head. "God be with ye."

Amhal bowed then returned to the keep, the marks of his sandals in the dust of the yard immediately swept away by the wind. With a crack of thunder, the skies opened up, dousing Phillipe in a deluge of rain. He darted toward the town, not wishing to chance encountering any in the keep who might remember him.

He took shelter in a doorway until the storm passed, his patience waning long before the rains ceased. He reached the docks as the sun dipped over the western horizon. Locating the *Sea Falcon*, he introduced himself to Captain Benicio.

"'Tis never a bad thing to have an extra sword on board." The captain squinted upward as dark clouds dispersed overhead. "And this damned storm cost me two of my regular crew who I was told shipped out on another vessel this morning despite the weather. Fortunately, I have been able to pick up two sailors seeking passage across the Mediterranean to Gibraltar, so we shouldn't be short-handed this portion of the voyage."

The swarthy Italian grinned, eyes sparkling, his skin dark from years at sea. "Of course, I'm inclined to do what I can to accommodate Amhal, though *El Falcone* doesn't ship many passengers these days. Ye may be called on to help when needed."

"Of course," Phillipe replied. "I stand ready to assist in any way."

Captain Benicio nodded. "Welcome aboard." He turned to the man at his side. "Prepare to cast off."

With a sharp salute, the man passed the command off to the crew with a bellow that belied his wiry frame. Phillipe stepped across the deck to the bow which was already chopping against the waves. The main sail caught the wind which had reversed course and headed out to sea.

A great weight lifted from his shoulders as the shore grew distant. Phillipe watched the blue, crystal-clear waters rush beneath the hull—and smiled for the first time in many days.

* * *

The sailor jerked his hand from the befouled lines with a curse. The lateen sail snapped in the wind as it guided the ship across the sea. Phillipe snorted. The two men the captain had substituted for his lost crew were clearly inexperienced. Their clothing might be travel-stained and worn, but the cut and cloth were expensive. Had they come by it as cast-offs? Or had they relieved the previous owners of their finery at the point of a knife?

Two inexperienced sailors are inconvenient, and I may have to pitch in sooner than I thought. But work is better than sitting on my arse all day.

Now that he was away from Batroun, Cilicia and its intrigue seemed a distant memory. Work as a common sailor was a chance to pay for his passage, though he'd hoped to earn coin as a mercenary. He hurled a handful of orange pits over the side then wiped his palms against his trousers. One of the sailors eyed him askance and Phillipe recoiled at the depth of hatred in the man's face.

Whatever has set him off? I do not know the man.

Changing his mind about helping the pair with their bumbling efforts, he strode toward the stern of the ship and climbed the aftcastle for a better view.

Sunset lit the entire horizon in a blaze of orange. Stars twinkled to the east in a velvet expanse of deep blue sky. As the sun dropped low and night fell, Phillipe returned to the main deck, intent on claiming his portion of the evening meal before seeking a place to rest.

The spot between his shoulders twitched as if anticipating the thrust of a dagger. His heart rate increased. He whirled about, dropping his weight slightly, scanning the ship around him. The watch was changing, the deck alive with shadows. A darkened form appeared before him and he retreated a pace, hands at the level of his waist, in ready reach of both sword and dagger.

"Please, help me." The man clutched his forearm to his chest. He staggered against the corner of the wall before he disappeared. A muted thud and low groan reached Phillipe's ears.

Idiot. The captain will be lucky if this pair makes it to Gibraltar.

He shook his head, hoping whatever fate befell the man and his partner did not impair the ship. Striding after the injured man, he rounded the corner, his eyes adjusting to the darkness as he spied the man huddled against the wall.

"What have ye done?" he demanded.

"Yer coin, Sardar."

Phillipe drew back, startled at the man's clear voice. "Coin? What is this? Ye are not injured?"

The man pushed to a standing position, a sneer on his face. "*La*, Sardar. I am not injured. But I cannot ensure the same for ye if ye do not part with the coins in yer bag."

Phillipe snorted. How dare the man hinder him with petty thievery? "Do not be ridiculous. 'Tis not worth risking your life for what little coin I have."

The man lifted one eyebrow. "'Tis well known the Sea Falcon does not carry common passengers, Sardar. Your hands are soft and ye carry yerself as a nobleman. Your clothing does not conceal the fact ye are used to commanding—not being commanded."

Phillipe made a rude gesture, filled with anger at the man's audacity. "Depart. I will report ye to the captain and have ye removed at the next port. But I will not give ye coin."

Footfalls landed quietly behind him. Phillipe whirled, placing his back to the wall as a second man stepped from the darkness.

"I told ye he would be arrogant," the man said. A slender blade, winked evilly in his hand. "Mayhap he needs persuading."

The first man shook his head. "Kill him and toss his body overboard."

"I think a mark to ruin his looks for the afterlife is necessary." The man lunged forward, his scimitar slashing at Phillipe's face.

Too late, Phillipe saw the attack. He drew back, but pain opened like a searing brand from his temple to the corner of his mouth. His fingers flew to his cheek. Warm blood slid over his hand. Rage eclipsed the pain.

Phillipe feinted to his right then whirled left, catching the man with the blade off-guard. Drawing his dagger, he plunged it upward through the base of the man's jaw. The tip reached the top of his skull, coming to a jarring stop, a tingle shooting through Phillipe's arm.

The other man rushed Phillipe from behind, the whistle of a blade announcing his attack. Ducking, Phillipe whirled and shouldered into the charge, grappling the assassin around his waist, using the force of the attack to lift the man to his shoulder. With a slight stagger beneath the weight, Phillipe ran the few steps to the rail and heaved the man over. He landed in the sea with a splash.

"Man overboard!" The cry from the lookout high on the mast drew a flurry of excitement from the deck.

"*Merde!*" Phillipe snatched his dagger from the deck and wiped it on the first man's cloak.

The bosun skidded to a stop before Phillipe, eyes wide as he glanced from the dead man to Phillipe.

"Guard!"

Phillipe's eyes narrowed and he clenched his jaw. Two burly sailors with truncheons gripped in their meaty hands hustled up, wary-eyed. Captain Benicio strode through the gathering crowd.

"I will handle this," he said, dismissing the group. The appointed guard waited a few steps away.

The captain stared at the man sprawled on the deck, a trickle of blood staining the wood.

"Amhal vouched for ye."

"*They* attacked *me*. I do not know them. They demanded coin."

Captain Benicio frowned then nodded. "Ye have proven yer worth as a fighter. The issue is closed. Gill, the cook, will tend your wound."

A throb as if wasps resided in the side of his face returned with the memory of the wound. Phillipe fought the accompanying lightheadedness and followed the captain below deck where he roused the cook to other duties.

"Gill is handy with needle and thread and has set more than his share of bones," Captain Benicio said by way of introduction. Phillipe stared at the enormous man's thick hands and couldn't imagine him handling needle and thread with any form of delicacy.

Gill swung his legs over the side of his hammock. "Ye could not wait until I had a full hour's sleep?" he grumbled, raising one hand to scratch his armpit. He peered at Phillipe then grunted. "'Twill not be pretty now nor a year from now. Captain, whisky for me, wine for our friend, if ye please."

Phillipe downed the proffered drink and braced himself.

Chapter Seven

Narnian Castle, Loch Lomond
Mid-April, 1225

Maggie threw back her shawl, letting the sun warm her head. Uilleam kept pace beside her as she hurried to put space between herself and the keep.

"Avoiding Ma again, eh, Maggie?" He chuckled. "Some things dinnae change."

Maggie landed a solid *thunk* with her fist on her brother's shoulder and wondered when the bony points had gained so much muscle. Or, for that matter, when he'd grown taller than her.

"'Tis good to have ye home, Brother."

Uilleam rubbed his shoulder, the familiar teasing grin on his face. "Ye have a peculiar way of showing it. Ye still pack quite a punch—for a lass."

"I can still put ye on yer arse," Maggie warned him. She sent him a sidelong look and wondered if she could. Or if he'd challenge her statement. His long-legged stride was full of strength and self-assurance, no longer the lanky youthfulness of the last time she'd seen him, almost a year and a half earlier. He might be seventeen years of age, three younger than Maggie, but he was quickly becoming a man.

"'Tis good to know." Uilleam nodded. "I dinnae like the look the man gave ye in the hall."

Maggie bit back a scathing reply aimed at the injustice of arrogant, domineering men and instead tossed her head. "I could have my choice of any man in the keep—or out of it. I'm nae in such dire straits, howbeit."

"Maggie!" Uilleam's voice growled low, and Maggie glanced at him in surprise. She halted and placed a hand on his arm.

"I'm sorry, Willie. I forget ye've just arrived. I've become used to the looks and less-than-veiled invitations. Dinnae fash. No one dares more."

Uilleam's brow furrowed, hiding the bright blue eyes which had lasses dancing to his tune across the Highlands. "I dinnae like it. None will disrespect *my* sister and boast of it on the morrow."

"Och, Uilleam. Ye arenae my Wee Willie any longer, are ye?" She smiled, pushing her heart-felt gratitude to the wide curve of her lips. "I know I make light of it, but it doesnae good to pay too much notice. 'Tis mostly those men passing through, so, gone soon enough. The MacLaren men dinnae pay me much mind. Their wives wouldnae tolerate such an affront," she added with a laugh.

Uilleam's face relaxed into a light frown and he raked fingers through his dark red hair. Maggie gazed at him fondly and wondered—for at least the hundredth time—why it had seemed fair to bestow long dark lashes and thick wavy locks on her brother while her own bright hair hung in tight curls that stood out from her head of a morning, and defied her maid's best efforts to keep it pulled back in a braid. Her sturdy frame and long legs had seemed better suited to a lad than a lass—until Willie had grown up.

"What are ye going to do, Maggie? Da seems to think ye should remarry. Ma danced all around my question—in her usual fluttery way. I love them both, but . . .."

"I love them, too. Dinnae forget they have successfully run this clan for more years than we've been alive. I . . .." She halted, a sudden catch in her throat. "I've caused a bit of trouble, though 'twasnae intentional."

She held a hand up, forestalling Uilleam's words. Despite her best efforts to find a place where she could make a difference, increasing discomfort thwarted her existence at the MacLaren keep. After she'd married, others overtook her vacated areas of responsibility. Maggie's status was now uncertain. Unmarried lasses whispered and tittered behind their hands, pretending knowledge of things beyond their ken. Married women chatted of bairns and the vagaries of men—and fell silent when Maggie walked into the room. She craved something purely her own, and the Isle of Hola called to her as nothing else did.

"I have a plan to create a home for myself and nae longer be underfoot."

Uilleam tilted his head, curiosity widening his eyes. "Tell me."

Maggie took his hand and led him to a boulder. She sat and patted the stone next to her. He folded his long legs, stretching the fabric of his trews tight across his thighs, and sat beside her.

"I have an island."

Uilleam's eyebrows shot upward. "Did ye win it in a card game?"

Maggie laughed. "Almost. The Earl of Mar won it, and gave it to me in lieu of the money from my dowry when I returned home."

The earl's parting words still stung, but time had softened them somewhat. She shrugged them away.

"'Twas a frightfully *snell* winter, and there hasnae been a chance to plan a trip. The isle is near the western coast, just off the Ardnamurchan Peninsula. But 'tis mine, Uilleam, and I mean to live there."

"Do ye know aught more than where 'tis? There's a *gey wheen* of rocks in those waters with naught but roosting places for sea gulls and puffins."

"Puffins? I'd like that."

"Maggie, be serious. What if ye get there and find naught?"

"But, what if the isle is perfect?"

"Perfect? How?"

Maggie sighed, a thoughtful gesture that brought all her dreams flooding back. "Sunshine. Grass. Trees. A place for a croft—a small one. Mayhap a tiny harbor. Porpoises and puffins."

"Ye wish to hide away."

His words evoked surprise, dismay, sympathy. Maggie's neck heated.

"I dinnae need a large clan and the attendant difficulties. I wish to live simply and nae see my failures in everyone's eyes each day." The lump in her throat returned. "I have few expectations regarding my life."

"Ye cannae live alone, Maggie. Pirates and Vikings still roam the area. Ye'll need protection."

"I can still put *ye* on yer arse," she reminded him.

"I believe ye could try—and mayhap win. But ye cannae rely on wrestling every shipload of Norsemen that stumbles upon yer island."

"I can shoot a crossbow." Her humor, sidelined earlier, returned.

"Not fast enough to pick off an entire boatload of warriors," Uilleam countered, a slight grin twitching at one corner of his mouth.

"I'm faster with a long bow."

"Why don't I go with ye?"

Maggie blinked. "Go with me?"

"Ye dinnae believe Da or I would let ye go alone?"

"*Let me?*" Maggie bristled, pushing against the stricture.

"Let ye. Watch ye. It doesnae matter if ye were a lad or a lass. Traveling alone is asking to be robbed or worse." He leveled a meaningful look. "And as a lass, there is a *lot* worse."

"Da isnae going to want ye to leave again so soon." Maggie wavered between wishing to take him with her and wanting to be free from male interference—no matter how well-intentioned.

"Och, he'll bluster, but ye need help. 'Tis right I help my favorite sister."

Maggie ruffled his hair. "I'm yer only sister, ye wee *ramscallion*. And thank the good Lord there's only one of *ye*."

Uilleam ducked out of her reach then stood. "Aye, that's what makes ye my favorite. I'll go speak with Da. When would ye want to leave?"

"Last month, though the roads then were impassable. I could be ready to go within a sennight, and 'twould be best we dinnae linger and give him a chance to change his mind."

"Good point, Sister. Ye were always the brighter one."

"And ye the pretty one," Maggie replied, repeating the litany they'd shared since the first time Uilleam as a bairn had unleashed his heart-melting smile on her young heart.

He tossed her a jaunty salute then headed back down the trail, his boots pushing the new grass flat, leaving faint imprints in the wet ground.

Maggie pulled her wrap closer. Spring found difficulty gaining hold over the winter's chill, though birds sang in the trees and flowers bloomed in profusion in the glen. Water burst from the rocks, swollen with melted snow that even in late April still capped the mountain peaks.

Men on horseback had traded throughout MacLaren land for the past month, though it would be weeks before the roads dried enough for wagons to make the trek around Loch Lomond to Narnain Castle. It didn't matter. Maggie did not wish to take much with her. The MacLean laird controlled a substantial village on the northern side of the Straight of Mull, on their route west to the Isles, and she could purchase necessary items there.

Traveling alone was dangerous, she knew, but she hadn't found anyone she wished to travel with—until Uilleam.

She raised a hand above her eyes as she noticed a falcon soaring far overhead, a dark stain against an otherwise cloudless sky. It dropped abruptly, gaining speed that left Maggie's heart racing. A bird she hadn't seen a moment before entered the falcon's path, struck with killing force before Maggie had a chance to draw breath in surprise. The two birds hurtled toward the earth, prey and predator locked together.

With a scream of defiance, the falcon smote the air with its wings. It flared above the rocks and banked toward a cliff face not many steps away from Maggie. She watched as it landed near a shelf almost indistinguishable from the crags around it. Another falcon perched on what had been an eagle's nest in past years, a ramshackle affair that likely clung to the rocks with little more than ancient bird splat and tenacity.

Maggie wanted to share her find with Uilleam, but he was too far down the path for recall. She hugged the knowledge to herself, speculating on the number of eggs in the nest and how many would survive to become adults.

A nesting pair of Peregrines. I havenae raised a chick in years. Longing rose in her, but she squelched the urge. *I've more pressing concerns, and will be gone by the time these eggs hatch. 'Tis no idle matter to commit time to training a falcon.*

With a last pang of regret, she followed Uilleam's footsteps to the keep. Humming softly to herself, oblivious to her surroundings, a man who'd stepped from the trees caught her off guard.

He halted directly before her, eyes calculating, arms loose at his side.

"Is this where ye meet yer lovers, lass?"

Maggie shook her head. "Dinnae do this. Find a woman who wishes to play. I am not her."

"I think ye can be persuaded." His grin promised her easy capitulation. Maggie wagered he'd accosted women before. He took a step toward her. Maggie countered his move, keeping her distance.

He scowled. "Dinnae back away, lass. I can be accommodating. Ye've laid with a man before. What's the difference this time? Ye know I'll not leave ye with a bairn to consider."

Anger flashed through Maggie. If he knew she was barren, he also knew she was the laird's daughter. He was arrogant, a bully—and stupid. He'd picked the wrong woman.

"My only answer to ye is to keep to yerself. I'll nae have ye." Her final warning.

Anger flushed his face. He scowled and took two swift steps toward her. His hands came up, gripped her throat. Maggie tightened her neck, bowed her head and body forward, and ducked beneath his arm and to the side, slipping smoothly from his grasp. She continued, taking several steps away before she stopped and faced her attacker.

A look of bewilderment crossed his face, his hands still before him, holding naught but air.

Maggie's breath came swift with fury. "I will report ye, and ye will hang for yer assault. Ye willnae touch another woman, I swear it."

Enraged, the man bellowed and leapt toward her. His open hand caught her shoulder, thumb in her throatlatch, driving her backward two steps until her back struck the broad trunk of a tree. Maggie ignored the pain, desperate to get away before she lost the ability to breathe. His left fist drew back. She slammed the heel of her hand into the inside of his right elbow, collapsing him against her. Maggie pivoted slightly, wrapping her arm over the back of his neck, pulling him downward, pinning him to her side. She tightened her grip. He sputtered, flailing his hands on either side of her, searching for a hold. With all the force she could muster, Maggie drove her knee into his unprotected face. A crunch of bone rewarded her. He grunted, spewing blood across her gown.

He wrenched from her grip and took a step back, falling into a half-crouch. His eyes watered, blood and snot poured down his face. He shook his head and stumbled a step, but instead of giving in to what Maggie had intended to be a painful injury, his broken nose only fueled his anger. With a roar, he staggered forward, arms wavering, his step unsure. Maggie side-stepped his awkward charge. Sweeping her skirt aside, she lifted one foot and drove her boot into the side of his knee. He dropped to the ground, rolling to protect his injured leg. Curses rang in the glen. He braced on his hands, gathering his legs beneath him. Maggie stepped close, grabbed his ears, one in each fist, then drove her knee into his face once again. He howled. She shoved him away. He collapsed, landing on his arse with an audible *whoof* as air left his lungs.

Footsteps pounded the path. Maggie glanced up, fear he had an accomplice flooding her veins. Her heart raced, her breathing labored, but she relaxed her shoulders and brought her fists up protectively.

Uilleam rounded the curve and skidded to a stop. He glanced from Maggie to the man on the ground and back. The man spat a thick stream of blood and saliva and drew a dagger from his boot. Uilleam's sword flashed silver an instant before it bit through the man's neck, sending blood in an arc to pattern the grass. With scarcely a shudder, the man slumped to the ground.

Uilleam turned to Maggie. "I came when I overheard a man . . .. Never mind. I willnae scorch yer ears. Are ye hurt?"

Maggie shook her head, unable to speak as the burning in her veins became an uncontrollable shudder. She had just been brutally attacked—and her brother had just killed the man. Her throat ached and the ground dipped and swayed beneath her feet.

"Ye look a sight," he remarked as he wiped then sheathed his sword, his tone conveying both surprise and pride.

Maggie glanced at her skirt, noting the broad spatter of blood marking the front. She drew a deep breath.

"It isnae mine," she managed.

"Nae. 'Tis his. Well done, Sister. He willnae molest another woman." He stepped to Maggie's side and wrapped his arms about her. "Ye were right to fight back. His death was at my hand. Dinnae allow it to haunt ye."

Maggie absorbed his warmth and his strength. She was safe and had fought to protect herself. Her world righted, though swallowing was difficult. He held her until her shaking ceased then relaxed his arms and chucked her under her chin.

"I'm fairly certain ye could still drop me on my arse."

Chapter Eight

January 1225
La Posada del Sol
Malagar, Spain

Phillipe's gaze roamed the interior of the tiny inn before he committed himself to entering. The whitewashed walls matched the exterior of other buildings along the bay, and cheerful sunlight fell through open windows that allowed fresh air and a chirping bird inside the crowded dining area.

Inn of the Sun. My last stop on the Mediterranean. I pray my past is now behind me. The scent of fresh food and spilled ale drifted to his nose. He found an empty seat at a table, ignoring the mild looks of curiosity. One more stranger on the docks of Malagar was of little interest. Out of habit, he kept his face averted.

A serving girl placed a trencher before him. Steam rose from a dish of steamed prawns. Phillipe peeked beneath a worn piece of linen and the aroma of fresh bread wafted up. A small bowl held olive oil adrift with herbs for dipping. His mouth watered, but he resisted the urge to shove the food into his mouth, waiting impatiently while she poured a mug of an earthy-scented brown liquid.

A hand touched the servant's forearm, halting her mid-pour. Phillipe clutched the hilt of his dagger beneath the edge of the table, alert for danger.

"Vino, por favor. Blanco."

Phillipe glanced up at the bland instruction and the outrageous accent. Whoever had just saved him from drinking warm ale had only been in Spain long enough to learn how to order wine, not perfect his accent. A blue-eyed man with shocking red hair and a bristling beard of the same hue took a seat opposite Phillipe, motioning with one hand for the girl to bring him the same.

"Name's Balgair," the man said, a smile showing remarkably white teeth and a winsome manner.

"An unusual name," Phillipe ventured, still wary. The man's casual confidence did not change the fact he was well-armed.

"It's me beard," Balgair explained, ruffling the impressive mane with a flick of his fingers. "*Balgair* means fox in Scotland where I'm from. 'Tis nae the name me ma christened me with, but it stuck just the same."

Phillipe repressed a grin at the man's easy-going nature. "I am Phillipe." He nodded at his trencher. "Please join me."

"Och, the lassie'll be back with me own food in a moment. Ye sound French."

Phillipe mulled this over. The man's supposition was close enough. His family roots were the House of Poitiers which ruled much of western France. He was of French and Genoese blood—by way of Antioch, though that need not be stated. He nodded then retreated into his dinner to avoid further explanation.

The serving lass deposited a portion of seafood, bread, oil and herbs before Balgair, then added a corked bottle between them. She propped one hand on an ample hip and thrust the other beneath Balgair's nose. Without a qualm, he dug a small coin from beneath his tunic and slapped it in her palm. She peered at it then slipped it down the front of her dress and sauntered away.

Balgair motioned to the bottle. "The wine is excellent. Try it."

Phillipe poured a bit into his mug and breathed gently, catching the scent of jasmine. A sip drew a sigh of pleasure from him as the deep flavor of the grapes rolled over his tongue, leaving behind lingering citrus notes.

"'Tis very sweet."

Balgair nodded, hurriedly swallowing, and waving his knife in the air. "The grapes in this region are dried in the sun before pressing. I like it."

Phillipe eyed the man curiously. He was massive of frame and likely outweighed Phillipe by more than a couple of stones, and he ate his prawns with gusto—yet was quite conversant about the wines in the area. A warrior with a knowledge of wine and a sweet tooth?

"What brought ye to Spain?" Phillipe asked, breaking the rule he'd lived by for the past few weeks of not inviting personal conversation.

"Fourth son," Balgair mumbled around a mouthful. "Naught to do but sell my sword, and what better place than in the Holy Land, protecting Jerusalem from the Saracens?"

"Indeed." Phillipe managed another bite of buttery prawns then washed it down with a sip of the sweet white wine.

"Same with ye? A younger son with nae prospects?" Balgair dragged a chunk of bread through the oil and herbs. "Returning to France?" He bit into the bread, oil beading in his beard.

"Much the same," Phillipe agreed. A warning instinct prickled the back of his neck. He'd tarried too long, spoken too much. Though the *Sea Falcon* would not depart for another hour or two and Phillipe had looked forward to supper ashore, it no longer seemed a good idea.

Raised, angry voices erupted two tables away. The floor cleared around two men as if by magic, benches scraping the wooden floor. Pottery tumbled, spilling food and ale. Fists flew, landing with meaty thuds. Phillipe's glance slid to Balgair. A broad grin split the man's face.

"A fight!"

Phillipe rose, having no intention of joining the squabble. A man staggered against him, nearly sending Phillipe to his knees. He caught the edge of the table and straightened. Someone jumped him from behind, wrapping an arm about his throat. Phillipe ducked and stepped to the side, bringing the man partially over his shoulder. Taking a quick step backward, he reached behind his assailant and grabbed his knees. With a forward pull, he swept the man off his feet and dropped him to the ground, following him to the floor with a knee in his chest. The man's head thumped against the stone like a ripe melon and his eyes rolled back in his head.

"Och, aye!" Balgair shouted, shooting his fist into the air with approval. "Ye'll do, laddie!"

Phillipe met Balgair's gaze, the fierce surge of battle singing in his veins. With a reckless grin, he rose and, Balgair at his back, dove into the fray.

His fists scuffed and bruised, and his purse a few bits of silver lighter to help pay for damages to the inn, Phillipe leaned over the rail and inhaled the salty sea air. Gulls, their black heads a stark contrast to their white bodies and brilliant orange beaks, waddled unconcernedly among the people on the dock, pecking at anything that might prove to fill their bellies.

Balgair stood next to him. The big man stretched his arms into the air then winced and rubbed his left shoulder.

"That last laddie got in a lucky punch," he grumbled. He glanced at Phillipe, grinning, giving no further heed to his injury. "We make a fine pair, aye? Held 'em off six to one!"

Phillipe shrugged. "They were brawlers. Ye and I have had more experience."

Balgair peered at him, concern on his face. "That cut over yer eye might need a wee bit of attention. Shall I sew it for ye?"

Phillipe touched a finger to the cut and winced. "Nae. I've had enough wounds stitched lately. 'Twill heal on its own."

"A braw laddie ye are." Balgair nodded approvingly. "Yer scars will give ye a hint of danger. Lasses like a man who can hold his own in a fight."

The brawl at the inn had given Phillipe a much-needed release from anger and unease that had built since he'd boarded the *Sea Falcon*. It hadn't, however, restored his desire to be considered attractive to women—especially those he would likely encounter on the docks between here and Scotland.

"We'd best look lively," Balgair added with a nod to the ship. "The captain doesnae like to be held up."

Phillipe shot the man a curious look. "Ye travel on the *Falcon*?"

"Och, aye. I'm headed back to bonnie Scotland." His cheerfulness turned thoughtful. "If ye've a mind to sell yer sword, and havenae a yen to linger in France, being a mercenary in Scotland isnae a bad thing."

"I am uncertain where my path lies."

Balgair shoved his meaty hand at Phillipe. "Join me, laddie. Ye willnae regret it."

Phillipe gripped the man's forearm. "I am happy to join ye insofar as our paths lie together."

"We'll come guid, laddie. A sword in one hand, a lassie in the other—and a bit o' coin in our pouches. What more could a man ask?"

* * *

Late April 1225

Firth of Lorn, near Oban
Scotland

Phillipe hunkered on his haunches on the hill above the tiny port town. Lights from two ships in the bay and six tiny houses lining the coast winked in the dusk. On the far side of the firth, mountains rose on the spit of land protecting Oban Bay, blocking his view of the Isle of Mull—and MacLean Castle on the northern side of the strait.

The horse he'd purchased in Morvern, the bustling seaport which gave rise to the impressive MacLean fortress, nibbled the grass behind him. The magnificent beast showed its Turkoman Horse heritage in its long legs and shimmering pale gold coat, though it was clear from her thick neck and placid manner she was not a purebred daughter of the desert. She had cost him nearly all he'd earned on the trip from the Levant, but he thought her worth every piece of silver.

Balgair approached, murmuring soothingly to the horse as he passed. Lines fanned from the corners of his eyes, the bridge of his nose sunburnt after weeks at sea. He lowered himself toward the ground, resting comfortably on his heels.

"There is still time. We can return to Morvern if ye wish."

Phillipe shook his head. "Nae. I will move forward."

The blood of innocents is on my hands. I sacrificed others to save myself. Even with the wisdom and kindness Donal MacLean showed me every day as a youth, I was unable to extend the same to those who looked to me as king.

Phillipe cast one more look where he and Balgair had come ashore an hour earlier. *Ye were more than a father to me, Baron. Mayhap someday I will return. When my actions do not shame ye.*

He idly rubbed his thumb over the thick scar that bisected the left side of his face. He hadn't realized his streak of vanity until the wound had become the focus of women's curious looks and men's speculation. He'd at last grown a beard to help hide the knotted scar.

He rose. "The sun will be gone soon, and there's enough snow on the ground to make finding firewood and shelter troublesome. Let us put a few miles behind us before we halt."

Balgair inclined his head in acceptance and followed Phillipe's motion. Phillipe gathered his horse's reins and checked the saddle's girth before mounting. Together, he and Balgair turned their horses to the path leading into the hills.

Melting snow dripped from the branches shadowing the glen where they halted for the night, drawing a cold trail beneath Phillipe's cloak. He adjusted the set of the cloth against future forays and edged closer to the fire.

"Takes a bit of getting used to," Balgair remarked. "'Tis naught like the hell-baked lands near Jerusalem."

"I am more used to the heat," Phillipe agreed. "Though the snow is beautiful and ye seem to find the cold bracing enough."

Balgair inhaled deeply. "Bred to it, I am. In the past year, all I dreamt of was snow in the mountains."

His gaze fell away and Phillipe did not press. They each had secrets, and perhaps it did not pay to peer too deeply into the past.

"I met with a man in Morvern whilst ye bartered for yer beast." Balgair nodded at the horse, her pale golden coat reflecting the moon's light, a dark stripe within the silver mane and tail. "I'll admit ye have a fine horse, and clearly from MacKern's stable. Likely the only good thing to have come from the Holy Land, leastways as far as I can tell. His wife brought one of those Saracen horses with her that's put his stamp on all MacKern foals these past few years."

"Turkish horse, and yes, they are magnificent animals. But tell me of your meeting."

Balgair gave him a confused look then shrugged. "This man's sword is well known in this part of Scotland, and he mentioned the need for help near the Trossachs—a mountainous region east of here." He broke off, silent for a moment as he turned his gaze to the sky. "Near my home."

"Is this not a good choice for ye?"

Balgair's half smile ghosted across his face. "'Tis time I was back on Graham soil."

"The Graham laird needs help?"

"Nae. The MacLaren does. His land lies north of the Grahams. A small clan, easily pushed about by the Buchanans and MacNairns." He snorted. "Though few get along with the MacNairns."

"'Tis a sound plan."

"Then we'll be away at first light." Balgair stood and stretched, his joints popping. "I'm glad to be on solid ground, laddie. Verra glad."

* * *

Narnain Castle

Maggie strode purposefully through the hall, meeting the covert looks from those gathered about with a raised chin. In the fortnight since her attack, she'd noted the shift in peoples' reaction around her. Some women sent her looks of grim admiration for standing up to the man, others eyed her with disdain, as though she'd been at fault, perhaps led him to believe his attentions would be welcome.

Men appraised her as if she was a prize worth taking—if any had the bollocks to try. Thus far, none had, though she was uncertain if it was the fact she'd fought back, or because of Uilleam's firm stance at her side. Whatever the reasons, she'd had enough, and her father's reticence at helping her travel to her isle had continued far too long. They were overdue for a talk.

She hesitated at the door to her da's solar, drawing a steadying breath against the tears of humiliation prickling the backs of her eyes. Brave face or not, the peoples' reactions stung. The guard at the door looked away, chin in the air as though he'd noticed nothing.

Voices drifted through a crack in the door. The ancient wood had aged poorly, leaving a small space between door and post.

"Who is with him?"

The guard glanced at her from the corner of his eye. "A man on behalf of Lord Buchanan, m'lady. Mayhap 'tis best ye dinnae disturb them." The skin of his neck darkened above his tunic and he looked away.

"Why?" Maggie did not wish to interrupt an important meeting, but couldn't imagine what embarrassed the guard. At least Lord Buchanan hadn't sent his man to ask for her hand. The laird was almost twice her age and already married, though his wife was a harridan who spent much of her time shrieking orders from her bed—which she took to at the least sign of misconduct from her spouse.

Maggie leaned her ear against the crack. The guard's chin jutted higher. His ears reddened. The messenger's nasally voice rang clear.

"'Tis a good bit of coin to offer ye, MacLaren. And ye'd have peace on our borders as long as yer daughter is agreeable."

The man's words struck her like a blow to her gut. What did he offer? It was clear whatever it was depended on her acquiescence, but . . .. Her temper soared as she came to the only possible conclusion. The Buchanan wanted her for his mistress and was willing to pay her father for the right. The emissary's voice continued.

"'Tis a pity she is barren. Howbeit, the earl assured me she was willing and inventive—worth my laird's coin."

He discussed . . . me . . . us . . .. The bastard! Dark webs formed on the rim of her vision and the air seemed too thick to breathe.

"M'lady?" The guard rested a finger on her shoulder. Maggie shook her head, declining his concern. She pressed against the door.

"I have received ye and listened to yer master's words." Dugal MacLaren's voice growled with warning. "Now, *get out!*"

Maggie drew strength from the anger in her da's voice and whirled as footsteps crossed the floor. The door opened and a thin man stepped through the doorway. He caught sight of her and halted, his brows arching as he gazed at her.

"She's a fair piece and not a bony knob on her. The earl was accurate in her description, at least."

Maggie pulled her shoulders back, flexing her hands as she realized she sought the grip of her dagger. "Ye are a *skunner*, m'lord, and a blight on humanity. Tell yer master I am *not* interested in his offer. Not now. Not *ever*."

The Buchanan's man inclined his head. "As ye wish." His footsteps faded down the hall.

Dugal stepped to the door and motioned Maggie inside. He heaved a sigh. "Ye heard."

Words failed her. She nodded.

"I willnae sell ye, lass. He was an emissary for the Buchanan, and I thought he was here on border policy. I dinnae know . . .."

"Let me go to Hola, Da. I'm tired of the speculation and whispers here. I want to start fresh. Narnain was once my home, but even the loch no longer calls to me."

"I cannae send ye alone and I need Uilleam here. The MacNairns move on our northern border and yer brother leads what few men I have to keep the crofts safe, though chasing the MacNairns is much like trying to grasp a handful of minnows in the deep end of the loch."

Maggie's heart skipped a beat. Her da had spent more coin than he should to see her wed to an earl. She bit her lip against a surge of guilt at what had been expended and lost on her behalf. She hadn't wished to marry nobility. But reminding her da his excess affected the clan served no purpose. 'Twas in the past.

"I dinnae wish to be a target of men with deep purses and shallow souls. How many other such offers have ye received?"

Dugal rubbed his chin and dodged the question. "I will find two men to send to the isle and discover what is there. Can ye await their word?"

Though she chaffed against the delay, Maggie nodded. "Aye. 'Twill do for now."

Chapter Nine

May 1225
Narnain Castle, Scotland

Maggie's spirits lifted to have her brother again by her side. "Thank ye for taking time to walk with me, Uilleam. I imagine ye'd rather be stretched out on yer bed, resting." She touched his shoulder. "I'm glad ye are back and unscathed."

"Having a few moments without constant watching over my shoulder is relaxing enough. 'Tis good to see ye happy, Maggie."

Her smile widened, taking firm root in the bit of freedom her brother's presence gave her. Though she'd learned she could fight back if necessary—and with solid results—the idea of having to continually guard against unwanted attention left her with little desire to venture outside the walls of the keep.

"Ye used to vanish for hours along these paths," Uilleam remarked, motioning to the mountainous trail. "Watching the birds, picking flowers, making up stories to entertain yer wee brother. The land is awash with spring flowers, yet ye remain inside the keep. Ma is worried. Care to speak of it?"

"And ruin a perfectly good walk?" She shook her head. "Nae. Ma always looks for things to worry over. We'll find better things to discuss."

A thought captured her attention. "There is a nesting pair of peregrines just along the way. Their chicks should be big enough to see by now. They're in the auld eagle's nest on the promontory ahead."

Uilleam nodded encouragement. "Lead on, Sister. Be as silent as ye can so we dinnae disturb them. Last night's storm may have left them unsettled."

"Och. Telling me to walk quiet in the forest? I taught ye to be a shadow when ye were but a wee lad."

"Silence is more than yer feet, Sister. *Hauld yer wheesht.* They'll hear ye from fifty paces."

Maggie rolled her eyes at her brother's scold, but she remained silent as she led him to the foot of the cliff where she'd seen the falcons a fortnight earlier. Uilleam halted at her side and followed the sweep of her arm as she pointed out the nest halfway up the cliff. Small white heads bobbed above the level of the twigs framing the nest.

"I see two," Uilleam whispered. "Ye think there's more?"

"Let's get a bit closer." Maggie gathered her skirts and stepped around a few small boulders and through the brush. Several large stones streaked with white bird droppings marked the spot directly beneath the nest. She halted a few feet away.

"Can ye see better from here?"

Above, a falcon began its *kak-kak-kak* of alarm.

"We've been spotted," Uilleam warned, bracing a hand above his eyes as he stared upward.

"Dinnae fash," Maggie replied. "They merely warn us away. Peregrines arenae verra territorial, but they do protect their chicks."

A sound like the flap of a sail startled her. Something flashed past then vanished into the sun.

"What was that?" She turned wide eyes on her brother.

"I thought ye said they werenae territorial. Mayhap we should retreat."

"They may chatter warningly, but they dinnae attack humans. Unless . . . ." Maggie cast her glance about, scanning the rocky ground near her feet. The falcon screamed past again with a sharp rustle of wings. Maggie ducked. Uilleam cursed.

"Let's be gone, Maggie. The bird's daft. It's getting closer and I dinnae wish to feel its talons or beak."

"Wait . . .." Maggie moved the branches of a small shrub. "Look." She pointed to a pile of white downy feathers. Dark beady eyes stared back at her.

"A wee falcon." Uilleam searched the rock overhang above their heads. "I cannae reach the nest. And 'tis too far below the ledge above it to drop the chick into it."

The baby bird, its pin feathers bristling through the soft down, looking like a stuffed rag toy that had been left out in the rain too many times, tilted its head to the side. Maggie's heart ached for the nestling.

"'Tis too young to be out of the nest. 'Twill fall victim to predators soon."

"Ye raised one once," Uilleam mentioned.

Maggie shook her head, the urge to travel to the isle warring with the difficulty of raising a chick. "He should be with his parents."

Uilleam tilted his head. "He appears to be four or five weeks old. His feathers are coming along nicely. 'Twould be a couple of weeks before he'd be ready to fly. Mayhap he will then return to the wild."

"'Tis wrong to leave him here. Fend the falcons off, will ye?" Maggie crouched in the shrubs, tucking her skirts about her feet so they did not lift in the gentle wind and startle the bird. She inched closer, murmuring soft words. The chick shrank into the brush.

With a sweep of her arms, Maggie reached for the nestling. It squawked in alarm and waved its wings to make itself appear larger. Raising up on its ridiculously large yellow feet, it attempted to leap away, but couldn't clear the brush.

"Dinnae fash, wee one," Maggie said as she folded the chick's wings against its body, stilling its frantic motions. "Naught will harm ye."

"Och, he'll be cosseted and fat as a hen in no time," Uilleam chuckled. He ducked as the distraught parent falcon made a third pass. "I only wish we could make his da understand."

* * *

Phillipe gazed across the lake. *Loch*, he reminded himself. With the spittle-producing end to the word as Balgair pronounced it.

"I do not believe I will ever grow weary of the sight of overmuch grass—and *trees*," he said, not caring if his friend heard or not. "And water that isn't the sea."

"Och, the Levant doesnae have a tithe on Scotland for beauty," Balgair replied. "I felt as if I'd died and gone to hell with all the heat and sand."

"'Tis not always so. There is much about the land that is beautiful. But I will make this place my home—for a time at least. The Holy Land is behind me."

"Ye've spent a *gey wheen* of years more in that blighted land than I." Balgair nodded amiably. "I expect ye had a better chance of seeing the good there. I only remember the loss of six of my closest companions fighting the Saracens, and nearly died of thirst myself before I made it back to Christian-held territory." He closed his mouth abruptly, ending the reciting of his time in the Levant where he always did.

"'Tis Loch Lomond," he said, taking up a different subject. "MacLaren land lies on the other side."

"The wood and stone keep there?" Phillipe indicated stones visible through the trees.

"Aye. There are numerous cottages at the foot of the motte the castle is built upon, the whole of it protected by the mountain at its back."

"The laird will welcome us?"

Balgair nudged his horse forward with his heels. "Aye. For whatever coin we spend in his village, and for our swords."

Phillipe reined his mare behind Balgair's sure-footed mount, the trail not wide enough for two abreast.

"This doesn't seem like much of a road," he commented, swatting a dangling limb away.

"'Tis a game trail which will cut an hour or so from our ride."

"Ye know this land well."

Balgair was silent for a moment. "I grew up here."

Phillipe did not reply, giving Balgair a chance to continue or not.

"One of the friends lost in the Holy Land was the laird's nephew. His name was Alasdair Graham."

"I am sorry, my friend. This will not be a good homecoming for ye."

"I could have returned home any time in the past two years. It hasnae been an easy decision. Mayhap if things go well with the MacLarens, I will finish my journey and settle with the Grahams once again."

"'Tis often difficult to let go of the past. A time will come when holding on to it becomes less important than seeking the future."

"Och, now ye're sounding like a learned scholar, not a mercenary." Balgair cast a look over his shoulder, teeth glinting through his beard. "MacLaren willnae care how ye speak, only if ye can wield a sword."

He shifted in his saddle and raised an arm. "There's the road to Narnain Castle. The gates are up that hill."

They joined the few people on the path past the tiny village, then continued up the curved road to the keep. Phillipe noted with satisfaction the apparent well-being of the people and their homes. His attention shifted to the castle, wishing the wall around the stone keep was more than ancient timbers.

"Ye have much woodland here. Is that why the walls are of wood?"

"Aye. They've stood for many years. Laird MacLaren keeps them in good repair, though I thought he'd planned to rebuild with stone." Balgair shrugged.

A flash of red caught Phillipe's eye. A young woman with hair unlike any Phillipe had seen before walked past, something resembling a white chicken in her arms. A tall, muscular youth kept pace.

"Striking," he commented, wondering who she might be.

Balgair glanced past Phillipe. "Och, there cannae be two lassies with the same hair in this clan. Must be the laird's daughter, though why she isnae married and away is a curiosity. I prefer my lasses a bit more on the dainty side, but none can say Maggie MacLaren isnae a beauty."

Phillipe grunted, a half-smile crossing his face.

"Ye should look elsewhere for companionship, lad. The MacLaren is ambitious, a status-climber of the worst sort. He'll nae have less than an earldom for his lass."

What of a deposed king? Phillipe shook his head, dispelling the urge to know the lady further. Though his bonds to Zabel had been dissolved by the Bishop, he did not seek marriage. And he was certain Laird MacLaren's daughter would not be the dallying kind.

The young woman gasped and jerked as if something had startled her. The creature in her hands gave a *kak-kak-ka*k of distress.

A falcon! Interest instantly piqued, Phillipe thrust his mare's reins at Balgair. His long stride carried him quickly to the woman's side. A trickle of blood ran down her arm, but her grip on the falcon appeared firm. The young man at her side glanced up and moved as if to shield her.

Phillipe spread his hands wide. "Please, I can help."

Her companion jerked his chin, his brow furrowed. "Leave her."

"Dinnae fash, Uilleam. 'Tis well."

Uilleam's scowl deepened, but he moved aside. The young woman's eyes widened hopefully. "Ye ken falcons?"

"I have been around them, yes."

Her hands clasped the young bird around its girth, pinning its wings to its body, but its beak had apparently inflicted a small wound. The bird thrashed again, pecking at her hand. The woman bit her lip but neither dropped the bird nor changed her grip.

Tearing a strip from the hem of his tunic, Phillipe carefully wound it over the bird's head, covering its eyes. The chick immediately settled. The woman's bright blue gaze lit with gratitude.

"Ye've saved my hands and likely this *ramscallion's* life."

"'Tis called *al burqa*, a head covering, and serves to calm the bird."

"We forgot about a hood, Maggie," Uilleam said, a dose of exasperation coloring his voice. "Could have saved ye a pecked arm."

Her grin was rueful. "I only took him because he couldn't be returned to his nest, and this is how he repays my kindness."

"He is young. 'Twill be some time before he thinks of ye as his master."

"Och, nae. I willnae keep him. I only wish to feed him until he can fly and return to the cliffs where he was born. I have . . . other things I must do." Her voice faded awkwardly and she glanced away.

"As ye wish, my lady, though there is much to be said for a good hunting falcon."

"I raised one a few years ago, but it fell prey to a golden eagle."

"Ye have a falconer here?"

The woman's face fell. "Nae. He was elderly and dinnae live through this winter past. We havenae had falcons in the mews in three or four years."

Phillipe smiled. "Ye do now."

Her answering smile was hesitant, but it went straight to Phillipe's heart.

"Might I check on ye later? The welfare of the bird, that is."

Her look became guarded and Uilleam's hand came to rest on the handle of his sword.

Phillipe took the protective gesture for what it was and merely let his hands hang loose at his sides. "I mean no disrespect, my lady."

Maggie and Uilleam exchanged glances. "Ye may ask about the chick," she said.

Phillipe nodded. "I will not keep ye. He is in need of a nest and likely a meal."

Her smile returned. "I do remember that part. Thank ye for yer help."

"Be certain your healer takes a look at your wound."

Maggie nodded and hurried away, skirts swinging gently, bright red hair bouncing over her shoulders.

But all Phillipe saw was the memory of her smile.

Balgair appeared at his elbow. "I remember telling ye she's the laird's daughter, aye?"

"I wish only to help her." Phillipe glanced at his friend, startled at the skeptical grin showing through his beard.

"The last time I heard those words, the laddie spent a sennight at the pleasure of the Graham laird." He cuffed Phillipe on his shoulder. "Come. Let us see what the MacLaren's captain has to offer."

Chapter Ten

Phillipe stood atop the battlements and leaned against the wall. He lifted a mug of ale to his lips. He couldn't shake the memory of the red-haired young woman. Daughter of the laird. It wasn't to his benefit to think about her, but since he'd met her, warmth had blossomed in his chest and refused to budge.

Maggie MacLaren.

Why couldn't she have been a blacksmith's or crofter's daughter? Not that he'd intended to settle here—he'd the whole of Scotland to explore—but . . .. He shook his head. He was not worthy of any woman's interest beyond a moment's pleasure. The things he'd done would forever bind him. It did him no good to wish otherwise.

Streaks of amethyst and rose darkened the sky as the sun melted behind the trees surrounding Loch Lomond.

Balgair strode the length of the planks placed an elbow between the pointed timbers. "'Tisnae much in the way of coin, but the travel shouldnae be arduous."

Phillipe roused from his thoughts. Balgair held a coin between his forefinger and thumb. He tossed it to Phillipe who caught the gold piece and slipped it into a pouch at his belt.

"I did not think ye wished to travel farther. Your family is not so far away."

Balgair shrugged. "I'll make another few miles. The laird wishes a report on the Isle of Hola and is willing to pay. Mayhap this will turn profitable."

"When do we leave?"

"Tomorrow, first light. Laird MacLaren offered to send a supply wagon, but Gunn, his man in charge, declined. I agree 'twould only slow us down. We can load our bags and mayhap a pack horse or two. Hunt along the way."

Phillipe nodded, though he regretted not getting to know Maggie better. Mayhap 'twas for the best. "I have little to prepare. But I'll bid ye good e'en and get some rest." He shifted away from the wall.

"Best seek out Lady Maggie now. There willnae be time in the morn." Balgair's blue eyes danced merrily.

"I'll keep that in mind," Phillipe replied, though he had no such intention. To do so would only invite more regret. He descended the steps into the yard. A small stone building, its thatched roof in obvious need of repair, nestled in the far side of the grounds, surrounded by a wall nearly the height of the building. Against his better judgement, Phillipe angled up the overgrown path. He stepped through the opening to the mews yard where three perches still stood, silent reminders of the past. Looped tethers, the leather stiffened from the weather, hung from the bars.

He strode to the door to the mews. Naught but darkness and the aroma of dust and rodents greeted him.

A shadow fell across his path.

"She isnae here."

Phillipe whirled. The voice suggested no threat, but he recalled the protective manner of the young man with Lady Maggie earlier. The youth was no friendlier now, but he appeared relaxed, and clearly did not view Phillipe as a danger.

"The mews havenae been used in years. Since the chick needs protection as much as feeding, she's taken it to her rooms. Ye'll find her in the hall in the morning."

"I thank ye, though I will not be here in the morning."

The young man nodded and pivoted on his heel to leave. "She rises early."

* * *

Maggie slipped through the hall, wishing wee birds didn't eat so much. His cries had roused her before dawn, and he'd accepted bits of dried meat hungrily.

Where the tottie *bird puts it all is beyond me.* She entered the kitchen, then, picking up a basket of bread and a mug of cider, wandered back into the hall. The room was nearly empty, the few people awake at this pre-dawn hour huddled in small quiet groups. With a start, she recognized the man uncovering a platter on the center table.

The man who'd helped with the chick. Curiosity pulled her away from her accustomed chair and toward the stranger.

He chose a small loaf of bread fresh from the oven, tossing it from hand to hand to help cool it. A serving lass sent him a cheeky grin. Pouring cider into a mug, she set it before him then hurried off. He chose a bench and straddled it, angling his body in such a way to easily view the room. He caught her look and lifted his chin, his lean body straightening as a slight smile tilted the corners of his lips.

His eyes shone, causing Maggie's breath to deepen. *What a ridiculous response toward a stranger. He likely wishes to ask about the* tottie *bird. He certainly seemed knowledgeable yester e'en.* She took a step closer then halted as Uilleam entered the hall. He caught sight of the stranger and crossed the room to take a seat across from him at the plank table. Maggie frowned, unsure if she wished to contend with *both* men this early. She took a sip from her mug, gazing at Uilleam over the rim.

Her brother carved a slice of cheese from a wheel on a platter next to the bread. "I am Uilleam MacLaren." His words drifted clearly to Maggie. "Ye are traveling to the Isle of Hola?"

The man shifted his gaze to Uilleam. "Aye."

"'Tis my sister's dowry." Uilleam frowned and waved a hand. "'Tis nae important. We wish to know what is there, though I'm certain Da has already told ye this." He took a bite of cheese, washing it down with a swallow from his mug.

The man shrugged. "I know little of your family. I am here for the coin." He cast a look over Uilleam's shoulder at Maggie. She took another sip.

Uilleam cocked his head to one side. "Yer speech is odd. I've known men who traveled far from Scotland and returned sounding different. But ye also dinnae look much like a Scot."

The man returned his gaze to Uilleam. "My family is from France, though I was born in the Holy Land. My father was there to defend Jerusalem."

"A Crusader." The words slid from Uilleam reverent as a benediction. "What is it like? The Holy Land?"

"Hot." The man ducked his head. "I am glad to no longer be there."

Uilleam seemed to take the man's dodge as a sign he'd prefer to not speak of it, and after a moment of silence, changed the subject.

"I dinnae catch yer name."

"I am Phillipe."

"Do ye wish to return to France?"

Maggie pushed away from her stance near the head table. She dropped her basket amid Uilleam's breakfast and slid onto the bench next to him.

"Good morn, Uilleam. 'Tis good to see ye up." She turned a welcoming smile on Phillipe. "Welcome to Narnain Castle. I am Maggie, Uilleam's sister. I'm sorry to hear ye willnae linger. I'm certain I have questions ye could answer about my wee falcon."

"Thank ye, m'lady. I have accepted a duty to travel . . .." His gaze slid from her to Uilleam and back, clearly connecting Uilleam's previous words to her. "I understand the isle is your dowry. Certes, 'tis as lovely as are ye, and our report will be all ye hope."

Maggie's face heated. Though her father loved her, he did not understand her. Uilleam teased her, and the earl had vacillated between empty flattery and scorn. The warmth of Phillipe's words was unexpected. She swallowed and summoned a response.

"I wish to live there and I am anxious to travel." To her surprise, her voice trembled. Uilleam placed a reassuring hand on her shoulder.

"Would ye have advice about the wee falcon before ye leave?" Uilleam adroitly turned the conversation back to the chick.

Taking the change without question, Phillipe nodded. "'Tis a young bird. Try not to form a close bond with it or it may become prone to challenging ye."

Maggie blinked in surprise. "Oh. I hadnae thought of that."

Phillipe continued. "Have several hoods made to fit him as he grows and have him wear them often once he is feathered out. He must become accustomed to the hood." He peered upward, as though gathering his thoughts. "Whate'er ye wish him to become accustomed to—be it dogs or people or horses—do it now. And choose a sound to call him when ye feed him—a whistle is good. 'Twill help with his training later."

Maggie sighed. "I've started remembering some of what our falconer taught me, though 'twas two years ago and knowledge I dinnae expect to use again. Ye have given good suggestions, Sir, and I thank ye."

A man strode to the table, his bristling red beard marking him as Phillipe's companion from the evening before.

"My lady, Sir Uilleam." He gave them each a brief nod then turned to Phillipe. "'Tis time we were gone. The horses await and the guard is opening the gate."

Maggie rose. "We will walk with ye."

Uilleam leapt to his feet, taking a final bite of cheese before hurrying to catch up. They stepped into the yard, cold mist enveloping them. Maggie pulled her shawl closer about her shoulders.

Six men, including Gunn, her da's second commander, already sat their mounts. A mare, her coat gleaming gold in the torch light, nickered as Phillipe approached. He allowed her to sniff one hand as he rubbed her neck with the other. She nibbled his palm gently with her thick lips.

He laughed. "I neglected to bring ye a treat, Avril."

Maggie stood entranced. "Avril? 'Tis French for the month of April, is it not?"

Phillipe glanced up. "Aye. The month I acquired her."

Maggie stepped close and touched the mare's glistening hide. "She is beautiful. I havenae seen a coat such as hers. Where did ye get her?"

"She is from the MacKern stables. They have stood a Turkoman horse at stud for several years. His name is Voski. I'm . . . told 'tis the Armenian word for *gold*."

Avril's ears pricked forward and she shifted her attention to Maggie. The horse's warm breath reached her in short bursts as she collected Maggie's scent.

"Armenian? I only speak Scots and a wee bit of French. And Gaelic."

Phillipe smiled and Maggie's heart skipped a beat.

"Not many choose to learn other languages. Ye are a rare woman, my lady."

He gathered his reins and stepped into the saddle. "*Hrazhesht.* 'Tis Armenian for farewell."

"*Hrazhesht.*" The word fell stiffly from her tongue but Phillipe gave her a pleased smile before nudging his horse forward.

The horses moved through the gate accompanied by the soft squeak of leather and the gentle jingle of harness. Maggie followed, ignoring Uilleam's admonition to remain inside. One by one, the horses disappeared into the mist at the forest edge, as completely out of sight as if they'd never existed.

The sky paled slightly to the east, though the sun would not top the trees for another hour or more. Maggie breathed deeply of the crisp air, dispelling the last of her unexplained reaction to the mysterious Phillipe of France and the Levant.

A shout from the wall slid into a cry of pain. A body thudded to the ground at Maggie's feet, a thick-shafted arrow bristling upward. Maggie's eyes widened as fear winged through her, stealing her wits.

"Maggie!"

"Close the gate!"

Booted feet trampled the parapet and the yard as men rushed to claim their positions at the wall.

"Maggie!"

Dark shapes rushed past her, piling through the open gate. She flattened against the wall, blending into the shadow of the barbican's tower. Timbers groaned as the guards struggled to close the gate against the men spilling from the forest to flood the keep. A wagon careened past, piled with stones and pulled by a single laboring horse.

"Maggie!"

A hand grasped her shoulder, jerking her from her feet. An arm encircled her waist and hauled her up, skimming a horse's shoulder. She kicked and squirmed, but the man dragged her before him, placing her firmly on the horse's withers. The saddle's pommel pressed painfully against her thigh. She pushed away from the horse, but the man's grip tightened.

"'Tis I, Phillipe. Do not jump."

The words rasped in her ear. She blinked in disbelief. He was with the attackers? Fury raced through her. She slammed her head backward, catching Phillipe a glancing blow on the side of his head. He grunted and settled his arms close on either side of her. To Maggie's surprise, she realized he headed into the bailey. Did he mean to produce her as a bid for her father to surrender?

"He willnae ransom me," she warned. Gaining no response from the Frenchman, she grabbed the horse's reins and hauled backward. Avril tossed her head against the punishing grip and skidded to a halt.

Phillipe grabbed Maggie's shoulder and forced her to face him.

"I am not the enemy!" He tore the reins from her hands and kneed the horse across the yard to the relatively empty ground near the mews. He pulled the horse to a stop and dumped Maggie to the ground. "Hide there. I cannot get ye closer to the hall. Do not come out."

Released, Maggie darted through the opening into the mews yard. Phillipe whirled his mount and charged into the battle. She drew back until she was certain she was hidden in the shadows then peered cautiously through the leaves of a heavy vine that climbed the stone wall and swept across the opening.

Men shouted, metal clanged. Torches flared red in the darkness, giving men the appearance of those already damned. Arrows rained from the parapet, finding targets and peppering the ground.

Maggie glanced down the side of the keep to the kitchen door. Partially open, it spilled golden light onto the flagstone path. Hoping the attackers had not yet breached the door into the hall, Maggie gathered her skirts and dashed the short distance to the kitchen. Plunging through the keep, she ignored the pleas for reassurance from those huddled within and bounded up the stairs to her room. She grabbed her crossbow and quiver then raced back down the stairwell.

I willnae stay put. The thought of meekly hiding where Phillipe had dumped her firmed her determination. *But, the door to the mews is a place where I can be of some help.*

The kitchen was now empty, the servants fled. The morning fire burned unattended in the hearth. Maggie stepped to the doorway and peered into the yard. She blinked, adjusting her eyes to the glare of torchlight. Men stood on the walls, firing arrows beyond the keep. A few bodies lay on the ground, but she could not determine who they were. An overturned wagon, stones spilling from its bed, traces trailing empty on the ground, lay across the gateway, fouling the attempt to close the gates.

Keeping to the shadows, she darted to the mews, slipping past the concealing vines. She placed her foot in the stirrup at the front of the crossbow and drew back the string, then fitted a quarrel in the groove atop the stock. The weight of the weapon was familiar and her hands found their accustomed spots. Maggie stepped into the yard, keeping the wall at her back, finger close to the trigger.

A man's head appeared over the top of the wall. Wielding a sword, he struck one of the MacLaren guards. Maggie raised her crossbow to her shoulder, her thumb lightly atop the bolt to keep it in place, and aimed at the man who lifted his sword high for a killing blow. Her arrow caught him square in the chest and with a cry, he fell from the wall.

A rain of arrows whistled into the yard. Shafts fractured as they struck stone, sending arrowheads and splinters of wood in a deadly scatter. Maggie turned away, using the doorway to the mews to shield herself from the fragments. Cries from the yard told her others had not been as lucky.

She peered around the doorframe. Men rushed through the partially closed gates, stumbling over prone and falling bodies as MacLaren swords and arrows found their marks. She lined up another shot as one dark form slipped past the narrow entrance. He fell before he took another step. Three more men dashed past, quickly lost to the shadows. Maggie edged back into the shadows of the doorway as she reset the string on her crossbow.

With a squeal of wood, the wagon was uprighted then pulled away from the gate. Voices rose in effort as the gates were finally closed.

Maggie took a deep breath and faced the yard once more. *Now to keep them out.*

Steel rang on steel, interspersed with the duller thunk of metal on wood. Cries of anger and encouragement settled into the low grunts of hand-to-hand combat. Maggie shot her quarrels where she found clear targets, hoarding the two last bolts for her own defense.

The tone of the battle changed. Fighting slowed. Men faced the door of the keep. A man appeared on the top step, another held before him. Silence gripped the yard. Torches crackled in the dawn breeze.

"I have yer laird. Surrender the keep!"

Chapter Eleven

Phillipe's sword sang. Two men fell. Torchlight battled with the earliest rays of dawn, playing tricks on his sight as shadows lengthened. Attackers feinted at the walls, drawing MacLaren arrows. The enemy slipped past the overturned wagon where the fight to hold the gates open was at its fiercest. Phillipe shrugged one shoulder in a circular motion, loosening the muscles. He worked his jaw, his tongue testing the teeth Maggie MacLaren had rattled earlier.

A crossbow bolt sang past him. Phillipe ducked, startled to discover it came from behind him. He glanced about, seeking an enemy flanking him. Movement at the entrance to the mews caused his heart to stutter, certain the laird's daughter was in danger.

Maggie!

As though summoned by his thought, a slight shift in the shadows revealed her as she stepped from the doorway, crossbow in hand. Surprise wrung a grunt of laughter from him.

The woman has warriors' skills? Even at a distance he read determination in her stance. Immediately reminded of another young woman with similar skills, he sent Maggie a silent salute, more than pleased she could protect herself, then rejoined the fray.

A hail of arrows struck the paving stones leading to the hall, shattering on impact and sending splinters of flint and wood spinning through the air. Avril squealed and flattened her ears but did not change her gait, and Phillipe hoped she had merely been startled, not injured. He dispatched another man who aimed a dagger at the mare's rear legs and glanced about for his next target.

Someone leapt from the wall, falling hard against Phillipe's chest, knocking him to the ground. He landed with a grunt as air fled his lungs. His vision darkened. He fought to regain his breath, catching sight of the dagger aimed for his throat a split second before it struck. Grabbing his attacker's wrist, he wrenched it to the side. He bucked his hips up with a twist, flinging his attacker to the ground. Scrabbling atop him, Phillipe shifted his grip on the man's wrist, bringing the hand up then sweeping the arm out to the side to land across the leg of a fallen soldier. An audible pop and cry of pain told him the man's elbow had snapped. Phillipe shoved him aside and climbed to his feet. He dodged a dagger thrust from another man aimed at his belly. He grabbed the man's shoulders as the strike went wide, and bent him over as he drove his knee into the man's chest. Shoving him aside, he grabbed his sword from the ground where it had fallen and searched for his horse.

Avril stood a few feet away, one rein trailing as she backed away from the wool-clad man reaching for her. Phillipe gripped the man's shoulder and spun him about then drove his fist into the startled face. The man staggered back and Phillipe strode past, a croon in his voice to soothe the frightened horse. Her ears perked forward and she nickered softly. He swung into the saddle then reined her in a tight circle, scattering the men who thought to close in while he was distracted.

Too many enter the keep.

The MacLaren archers kept most of the enemy off the walls. The main gate was the stumbling block to securing the keep. Phillipe's glance fell on the overturned wagon. Someone had procured a rope and tied it to the reach pole which ran the length beneath the wagon's bed. To grab the rope, men had to sheathe their swords, leaving them defenseless as they struggled to right the wagon.

Phillipe spurred Avril to the gate. "Give me the rope!"

With only a moment's hesitation, the rope was tossed to him and he wrapped it around the pommel of his saddle. Avril danced forward until the rope tightened, then halted, tossing her head. He nudged her forward and she settled into her haunches, increasing her power. The rope creaked and the wood groaned as Avril surged against the rope and the wagon pulled free. With a shout of triumph, men put their shoulders to the massive gates and forced the enemy back.

The battle renewed its vigor and MacLarens cleared the gatehouse and closed the gate.

The yard quieted, the lack of sound eerie, threatening. Heads turned toward the hall.

"I have yer laird. Surrender the keep!"

Phillipe blinked away the sting of sweat in his eyes. A burly man wrapped in a woolen cloak advanced through the hall doors and shoved a slimmer man down one step—leaving his own head and upper body unprotected by his hostage.

Setting his heels to Avril's flanks, Phillipe sent the mare charging across the yard, bending low over her side in hope of confusing the enemy long enough to gain the upper hand. The horse's thundering hooves stunned the man to inaction, clearly not expecting a counter to his challenge. He grabbed for the man before him, but Phillipe's sword sang through the air, the flat of the blade catching a stunning blow to the back of the burly man's skull. His legs crumpled beneath him and he struck the MacLaren laird as he fell, sending him staggering down the final steps into the yard. Phillipe swept low and lifted the older man to the saddle before him. Within seconds, he raced away, swallowed by shadows.

He drew to a halt near the mews. Avril pawed the ground and snorted. Maggie appeared in the door's opening, crossbow rigged for a quick shot. Phillipe lowered Laird MacLaren carefully to the ground. The older man's legs trembled but he quickly recovered and stood.

"Step away, Da." Maggie eyed Phillipe over the top of her crossbow.

The MacLaren captain rushed to his laird's aid, pulling up short at the sight of the tableau. He lifted his hands, palms out.

"Does he threaten ye, m'lady?"

"I'm a bit worried the attack came on the morn our gates were opened earlier than usual." Her lowered brow clearly indicated she was not convinced Phillipe had naught to do with the attack.

"Aye," Phillipe agreed, voice steady to avoid being shot by Maggie's crossbow. "Though 'twas not by my hand."

Balgair stepped close, dried blood plastering his beard on one side of his face. "I can vouch for this laddie." He indicated Phillipe with a jerk of his chin.

"Balgair is known to me," Neacal, the commander added.

Maggie slowly lowered her crossbow, though she sent Phillipe a wary look before turning her attention to her father.

"Are ye *skaithed*, Da?" She leaned her weapon against the wall and strode to her father. Gathering his hands in hers, she raked her gaze over him from head to toe, as if daring him to deny an injury.

"I am a bit shaken, Daughter, but whole—thanks to this man." His gaze fell upon Phillipe. "I owe him my life."

90

Maggie's sharp gaze slid to the Frenchman. He sat quietly atop his horse, neither acknowledging nor denying her father's claim. The golden mare was flecked with sweat and she champed her bit, blowing great breaths in the aftermath of battle. With both Neacal's acknowledgement and her da's declaration, Maggie carefully disarmed her crossbow, though she was slow to relax her guard entirely.

Men surrounded her—more likely surrounded the laird. She searched their faces, noting with relief many she knew.

"Uilleam? Where is he?" She tensed, glancing into the yard, her gaze lighting on covered forms that would move no more.

"I will find him." The Frenchman dismounted and led his mare away, pausing to speak to men, sparing each fallen form a quick glance. Maggie soon lost his tall, lean shape in the milling crowd. Her breath quickened as fear threatened to consume her.

Where is Uilleam?

Three more soldiers approached their group. One gave a short bow to her da then spoke in a low voice to the commander. Neacal nodded.

"The man who attacked ye has been taken into the hall under guard," Neacal informed her da. "Do ye wish to question him, or shall I have him placed in the tower?"

"I will question him." Dugal peered at Maggie. "Come with me."

At her nod, he waved for his commander to accompany them. She gathered her crossbow and reluctantly followed the heavily armed group into the hall.

A stocky man sat in a chair in one corner of the room, scarcely visible through the soldiers surrounding him. He held his head in both hands, face toward the floor. Donal's personal guard stepped closer, clearly reeling from their laird's kidnapping minutes earlier.

"Who sent ye?" Dugal's voice rang authoritatively.

The man groaned and swayed. A soldier grabbed his shoulder and jerked him back in his chair.

"Answer the MacLaren."

The man's head lolled to one side, the dark centers of his eyes huge. He blinked then squinted. His mouth worked, gaping open and closed like a fish out of water. Spittle drooled from one side.

"Ma . . . Mac . . .M'Nair . . .."

"The MacNairn?" Dugal's brows shot together in a scowl. "I thought we'd kept them on our border."

The soldier prodded his captive with the butt of his spear, but the man gave no further answer.

"I have found your brother." Phillipe's low voice startled Maggie. She whirled, his relaxed mien calming her racing heart. "He is injured, but I think not too severely. The healer is with him now."

"Take me to him," she demanded.

Phillipe gave a nod of acquiescence and led her into the yard.

Dawn had at last broken over the trees, bathing the air with peaceful light. Those who had fallen had been removed from the yard, leaving only those who awaited the healer's care. Phillipe headed toward a small cluster of men who stepped aside to admit Maggie to the man in the center.

Uilleam spared her a half-grin, but his jaw clenched tight and his eyes were over-bright. His pallor and the sheen of sweat on his brow spoke of blood loss as well as pain.

"Ye spared us some losses with that crossbow of yers, Sister," he rasped.

Maggie's eyes misted. "Och, ye would do the same for me." She sought the healer's gaze, needing encouragement.

The older woman gave a curt nod. "The lad has a great gash on his arm, fortunately 'twas nae his sword arm. 'Twill heal with time and care. I have stitched the wound closed. Make certain he doesnae use it for at least a sennight and report to me immediately if he becomes feverish."

The woman gathered her things and moved to the next person awaiting her care.

"Ye will do as she says," Maggie stated, raising her brows for emphasis.

Uilleam waved his other hand briefly to indicate he'd heard her. Maggie was well aware the gesture did not mean he would heed her.

"Help him to his room. I will tend him there."

Two men lifted Uilleam, arms about his waist as they gave him a moment to gain his feet.

He beckoned her close. "Ye must take care."

"I always do, Willie." Maggie nudged a lock of hair from his forehead and stroked his head as if he were six again.

Uilleam grabbed her hand, his look fierce, chest heaving. "Nae. Ye dinnae know . . .. The man who did this, who led the MacNairns here."

"Dinnae fash, Willie. Whatever it is will wait."

"He wasnae simply reiving."

Maggie stilled. "What was he after, if not our sheep or cattle?"

"He was after ye, Maggie."

Her head whirled, suddenly full of the insults she'd endured since she'd arrived home.

Da was right. No offers of marriage, but proposals to establish me as mistress—or worse—seem to be in abundance. Despair warred with anger. *I willnae sit idly by, unable to walk outside the walls of the keep for fear of being spirited away. And I willnae bring a battle to the doors of Narnain Castle again.*

She glanced up, meeting Phillipe's gaze. He waited several feet away, but the look in his eyes told her he'd heard Uilleam's words.

"Will ye be leaving soon for the isle?" she asked.

"Aye. Unless your father changes his mind, I see no reason to linger."

Maggie gave a short nod. "Good. Give me a few minutes to pack. I will be going with ye."

Chapter Twelve

Rain dripped from the canopy of leaves overhead. Maggie shrugged deeper into her plaide. Droplets beaded on the thick wool and joined together in rivulets that ran across the weave. The falcon chick huddled silent beneath the covering on the cage Maggie had fashioned from lashed sticks. Its leather bottom was easily removed for cleaning, the structure sturdy enough to provide protection as they traveled.

Satisfied the wee bird was as dry and comfortable as possible, Maggie shifted her gaze to her traveling companions. Gunn and five of the original six who'd set out for Hola the day before formed her guard. The sixth had fallen in the fight at the castle. Dawe, a childhood friend, easygoing and with a watchful eye to her care, was one of the five. His da, Callan, one of the MacLaren's own bodyguards, had been added at the laird's insistence when Maggie had refused to back away from her decision to travel to Hola. She doubted much escaped his eagle-eyed gaze, and wouldn't be surprised if he had established some means of communicating with her father at Narnain Castle.

Her maid, Leana, only a year or so younger than Maggie, had tossed together a bag of her belongings with alacrity, eager to tread beyond the shores of Loch Lomond. Maggie suspected there was a broken heart amongst Leana's reasons for the journey, but Maggie had not pried the information from her. 'Twas enough to have the woman along as a chaperone. Maggie knew her reputation lay in tatters, no need to flaunt the issue by traveling as a lone woman in the small party, though she was perfectly capable of caring for herself and was certain anyone showing her undue interest would be met by MacLaren swords—and an invitation to harass their laird's daughter at their peril.

Balgair, she had learned, was a Graham, and as such was an ally and could be trusted. Phillipe, the Frenchman, was a complete mystery, though he had proven himself by saving her father's life and helping repel the attack from the hated MacNairns.

Maggie sat alone, the men giving her plenty of space as they had the past two days. Leana huddled beneath her plaide only a few feet from

Maggie. The drumming of the rain and misty shadows separated them as much as if they'd sat on opposite sides of the fire. A fire that smoked and sputtered beneath a crude leafy shelter that kept some of the rain at bay. Poor it might be, the shelter allowed them a bit of warmth. Maggie hoped the rain ceased soon—for both her own comfort and to avoid the prospect of languishing in Oban until a boat could be hired to take them to Hola.

They would reach Oban Bay on the morrow, and from there by boat enter the Sound of Mull—and then to the open water between Mull and—hopefully—her new home.

What would she find? A large rock devoid of soil or plants, suitable only for nesting sea birds? Or a varied, fertile land of mountains and valleys, sandy beaches and plunging cliffs? Surely the deed to a barren rock would not be worth a nobleman's wager. She wanted to envision a haven suitable to raise sheep and plow a bit of land for a garden, with porpoises in the bay and sea birds crying overhead. But the name *Hola* was Norse for *hole in a rock*, and no amount of wishing could disperse the image of a monolith rising from the waves, white foam beating against the forbidding, unforgiving, inhospitable stone.

The rain pattered to an end. Maggie sighed and pushed her plaide away from her head. Phillipe rose and, shifting his cloak more firmly about his shoulders, stepped around the men sitting near the fire and halted next to Maggie. She glanced up, startled to find him close. His short, black beard glistened, wet from the rain, and his dark eyes glimmered above an almost hawkish nose.

"May I join ye?" He swept a hand to one side, indicating the end of the fallen tree she sat upon. Maggie stared at the wet, crumbling bark a moment then, gathering her wits, cast a swift glance at Leana who appeared to pay them no attention.

"Aye."

He gave a slight nod then seated himself upon the trunk, leaving a space between them. He unfolded a small bit of cloth to reveal three chunks of meat.

"I sliced these from the hares before they were spitted over the fire. Your *eyas* will not benefit from cooked meat."

"*Eyas?*" Maggie battled the tremors racing just beneath her skin. She sat poised on the edge of the tree trunk, leaning a bit forward—and toward

Phillipe. Folding her hands beneath her plaide to banish the temptation to trace the scar partially hidden beneath his beard, she settled, hoping he hadn't noticed.

"An *eyas* is a chick taken from his nest for training." Phillipe motioned to the covered cage, his attention on the bird. "Has he been fed today?"

"I caught a mouse early this morning. I am teaching him to step to my hand." Maggie uncovered the cage, leaving a corner of the cloth partly shielding the box. The chick fluffed his feathers, droplets of mist glistening on his downy coat, then shook the moisture away and fixed Maggie with a beady gaze.

"Very good," Phillipe acknowledged. "Each thing ye teach him should lead to another."

As if scenting the bits of meat in Phillipe's hand, the fledgling falcon perked up, tilting his head as though to catch the scent. Phillipe handed one piece of rabbit to Maggie.

"From your hand only."

Maggie placed a leather gauntlet on her left hand then untied the opening to the cage and carefully picked up the trailing end of the jesses attached to the wee bird's legs. After working the leather straps between her fingers to secure them, she placed the meat in her fist, leaving only a small portion protruding from between her fingers. She gave a low whistle. The bird cocked his head in response and gave a demanding cry. Placing her hand through the open door, Maggie held the morsel a few inches away from the chick and whistled again.

He bobbed his head and lifted his wings, a motley collection of down and partially unfurled pin feathers. His big orange toes gripped the perch lashed the width of the cage, but he overbalanced forward, his tail too stubby to provide adequate counterbalance. He beat his wings and righted himself, then carefully stepped from the stick to Maggie's proffered glove. Catching sight of the meat, he grabbed it in his beak, shielding his action with his wings, a posture meant to keep other animals from stealing his food.

"Ye are doing well with his training," Phillipe said.

Maggie glanced up, uncertain if the warmth around her heart began with the wee bird's acceptance of her or with Phillipe's words of encouragement. His dark eyes glowed.

"There . . . there is much I dinnae remember, things I must learn."

"Do ye plan to keep him, then? 'Tis not a bad thing. Many chicks die their first year because they are not good hunters. Giving him a year to prepare himself could save his life."

Maggie worried her lower lip and dropped her gaze. "I would like him to fly free. But that willnae be for some time. Mayhap later. If the isle . . .."

She hesitated. If the isle was hospitable. If the isle did not disappoint. If, if, if.

"Ye have not seen the isle?"

The words fell soft, gentle, hardly even a question. Maggie hazarded a look at the man beside her. His dark eyes rounded with sincerity, deep pools of warmth—and not a hint of derision or impatience. Her heart sped, her breathing shortened.

She shied from the unfamiliar sensations sliding through her. "I was told it provided a small income, but I dinnae know more."

Phillipe's eyebrows rose slightly.

Embarrassment slid through her at her lack of knowledge. Yet, how could she know more of the isle when the earl had told her so little? To tell the Frenchman of this was something she could not do. "Mayhap some time ye could tell me of the Holy Land?"

He blinked and a hooded look fell over his face. Before Maggie had a chance to regret changing the subject, his lips tilted up. "Mayhap, if time permits, we can exchange stories."

Maggie blanched. "If time permits." The words choked her, but she could scarcely decline. She would simply avoid raising the subject again.

The falcon shifted his weight on her glove and gave another demanding cry. Maggie flinched and stared at the bird. "Och, he's finished this bit. Should I give him more?"

Phillipe handed her a second piece, slipping it to her with his hand turned palm down in a fashion to keep the keen eyes of the chick from realizing where the food came from. She quickly tucked it into her fist, poking a bit through her fingers, and whistled the alert for food. The bird dug in as though famished.

"Feed him what he wants now. When 'tis time to train him to fly and hunt, ye will not feed him so much."

"I call the bird *he*, though I dinnae truly know," Maggie mentioned, keeping her gaze on the falcon. The Frenchman's gaze warmed her overmuch.

"Ye are likely correct. Males are considerably smaller than the females, and he is old enough his size should tell us. Will ye name him?"

She shrugged. "I havenae thought of it."

"Fleeing your home and fighting a battle does take up time."

Maggie flashed a look of surprise then grinned to see the gentle humor on his face. "Aye, that it does. Give me an Armenian name for him."

Phillipe appeared as startled as she at her request. She knew her question would draw an unfavorable response from him. Why *did* she wish to know more about him? 'Twas unreasonable. They would part in a matter of days, and she would not prove the gossips correct and engage in an affair with a man to whom she was not wed.

"*Hakan* is a common name in the East meaning *one who rules*." Phillipe answered as though her request did not dismay him, but she saw his eyelids narrow in the instant before he glanced away. He shrugged. "Mayhap ye would consider *Colyn*? 'Tis French meaning *one who brings triumph*."

Embarrassment heated Maggie's cheeks. She would in the future steer clear of his past in the Holy Land. She grabbed the suggestion of a French name as if he'd offered a rope to a drowning swimmer. "Of course. *Colyn* is verra nice. Thank ye."

Phillipe settled his gentle smile on her then rose. "Balgair has built two small shelters for ye and your maid. May they keep the rain from disturbing your sleep. Get some rest, my lady. We've a long journey ahead."

Phillipe made his way to the picketed horses, his mind on the red-haired young woman by the fire. Avril lowered her muzzle into his cupped palm, her breath warm on Phillipe's chilled skin.

"'Twas never this cold or rainy in the Levant," he confided to the horse. "And yet . . . I wonder if I would find this weather the same in France? There is something here I have not encountered before. What about this place calls to me?"

Avril snorted and shook her head, clearly uninterested in his rhetorical mood, and moved a step away to nip at the grass beneath the picket line.

Satisfied the mare was unperturbed by the recent rain, Phillipe strolled deeper into the forest, his footsteps no more than a whisper against the wet leaves.

He halted at the edge of a low cliff. A bubbling brook—a *burn* Balgair called it—glimmered silver below. Raindrops glistened like costly diamonds on every leaf and stone. He leaned his back against a broad tree trunk, dismissing the beauty before him. Maggie's bright blue eyes instantly sprang to mind. Her cautious smile, face framed by unruly hair. Something drew him to her, and he did not believe it was a chance to tutor her in falconry.

The thought sobered him. He had no business spending time with Laird MacLaren's daughter. Women, in his experience, often took the wrong inference from such actions. His attentions would be seen as less than honorable, for his future did not include marriage.

The crack of a small branch alerted him to another presence.

"'Tis I." Balgair spoke clearly.

Phillipe's hand relaxed, moving away from the hilt of his sword.

Balgair stepped to the edge of the rocks and peered over the edge. "Considering the view, or something else?"

Phillipe grunted. "'Tis likely something else."

"Something—or someone—with flaming red hair and the look of a wounded angel?"

Phillipe glanced up sharply.

Balgair shrugged and placed one boot on a low boulder and leaned his forearm across his knee. "I dinnae know the lass's story when we first arrived, and once I did, I thought it best left alone. Since she now travels with us, mayhap ye should hear it."

Sympathy tugged at Phillipe's heart. He nodded.

Balgair's glance slid to one side and he sighed. "Her husband of a year, an earl no less, sent her home a few months ago, dissolving their marriage on the grounds she dinnae gie him a bairn."

Blood boiled in Phillipe's veins and his teeth ground tight in his jaw.

Balgair continued. "'Tis all the men around here are interested in, beyond the fact she isnae a virgin and isnae likely to draw a serious marriage proposal as the MacLaren clan is small and of little military use. Their land is beautiful and moderately prosperous, but nae enough to give her much to look forward to. It seems there has been more than one randy bastard willing to take her to bed—her willing or nae—and one serious bid for her services as a mistress. The MacNairn attack was the last straw."

Phillipe drew a deep breath, but his anger spiraled upward. "And how did an earl interest himself in a young woman from such a small, unimportant clan?" His words spat like the first icy drops of sleet before a storm.

"She was his third wife. The first died in childbirth, though 'twas rumored the child wasnae his, and her death wasnae a misfortune but mayhap something more sinister. His second wife packed off to a nunnery without producing a bairn nae too long after the nuptials." Balgair lifted his hands palms upward as if offering up his thoughts. "Mayhap he thought a braw lassie like our Lady Maggie would prove of more robust stock than the delicate lasses his ma dangled before him. But I only repeat what I've heard. I've nae proof."

"It sounds as if my lord earl is the one lacking, not his wives." His fingers clenched tight. "'Twould be best if I did not learn his name."

Balgair's teeth flashed in his beard. "Aye. I believe ye would lose yer civility in his presence. And there's naught but a hangman's noose to be gained by the man's death, whether deserved or nae." He straightened. "I'll leave ye to yer thoughts, but remind ye we've an early start in the morn, and ye wouldnae enjoy giving me the pleasure of rousting ye from yer slumbers with the toe of my boot."

Phillipe smiled grimly at his friend's quip. "I'll return to camp with ye. As lovely as the lady is, I have naught to offer her, and I have accepted coin to keep her safe."

Balgair clapped Phillipe's shoulder. "Aye, ye have. I believe ye have the second watch this night. Best ye get what sleep ye can. We've a ship to catch."

Phillipe glanced over his shoulder, the hair on the back of his neck prickling. He found naught but the darkness and the knowledge of where the journey would take them. Dread pooled in his belly like an untried lad on the eve of battle.

Across the water lay Loch Aline and the village of Morvern—and the reminder of what he'd lost.

Chapter Thirteen

"He's a wee bit peculiar, dinnae ye think so?"

Maggie glanced up as she settled the falcon chick—Colyn—into his cage. His low-pitched chirps told her he wasn't entirely happy with the transfer, but he was becoming used to the routine and allowed her to place him inside with little fuss.

Leana smoothed her skirts as she sat upon the fallen tree next to Maggie. She leaned close, canting a look at the men who settled near the fire, plaides over their shoulders.

"The Frenchman likes ye."

Maggie shook her head, refusing to be baited. "He is interested in the falcon, naught else." She latched the cage and pointed to the two shelters of lashed branches a few feet away. "I wish to catch a bit of sleep—dry if possible."

Leana rose and followed Maggie, then perched on the edge of the pine boughs keeping Maggie's blanket off the cold, wet ground. "Why do ye think he knows so much about birds? Falcons are the mark of nobility."

"And the mark of someone who hunts for his food," Maggie rejoined. "Mayhap they do things differently in the Holy Land." She sat, gingerly testing the gentle spring of the pine boughs. Not a feather bed, but comfortable enough—and mostly dry.

"But he's nae crofter," Leana insisted. "Ye have only to see the way he stands, hear his voice . . .." Leana sighed. "I could listen to him all day. He isnae brash nor rude, but polished and confident."

Maggie peered around Leana, catching sight of Phillipe as he strolled into the meager firelight. His chain mail glinted gold and black, reflecting the flames, his skin a dusky hue. Broad shoulders lay beneath his cloak, and she knew her head would reach his chin if she stood next to him. The memory of his strong arms pulling her atop his horse as he rode back into the keep warmed her—startling her with the unexpected sensation. She sat back into the shadows of the small shelter.

She waved Leana's words aside with a frown. "He is a mercenary. There is naught unusual in what ye say. They oft times form elite guards."

Leana scoffed. "Och, ye cannae fool me with yer dour look. Mercenaries are bold, mayhap a swaggering lot, but rarely carry themselves like . . . like a prince."

"Ye are being fanciful," Maggie replied. She peered around Leana again. Phillipe's close-cropped black beard blended into the shadows, a dark slash across his firm jawline, partially hiding a scar which ran down one side of his face. How had he received such an injury? She flinched to consider his pain. Did she wish to know the truth of his past? Did it matter?

Phillipe glanced up, catching her gaze. Maggie jerked back, using her maid as a shield against his questioning look.

Embarrassment fluttered in her belly—and lower. Maggie scolded her body's traitorous response. She was no young lass to find herself a-twitter at a handsome man's look. Nor was she an untried maid eager for his touch. The earl had at first stirred her passions, but long months of disappointment as she did not quicken left her husband's attentions merely a thing of duty—and distaste.

"It doesnae matter. He is here for the coin, and I willnae become a way to relieve the boredom of the journey."

Leana drew back, her eyes wide. "I dinnae suggest becoming his lover, m'lady. Though I cannae see how that could be a bad—or difficult—thing. 'Tis only that ye have been too quiet, too withdrawn since ye came back to us. How could ye ignore an opportunity to speak with a man who clearly likes—and respects ye?"

Maggie gave Leana a skeptical look. "Ye dinnae want him for yerself?"

Leana fluttered her fingers. "Och, he hasnae glanced at me more than twice since we left Narnain Keep. If I thought he was interested, I'd let him warm me this night. But he hasnae offered, and his eyes dinnae stray far from ye."

"He watches the bird," Maggie insisted even though her cheeks heated to think on Phillipe's steady gaze.

"If 'tis what ye believe . . .." Leana leaned close. "Ye waste an opportunity ye willnae have on yer island, I fear. There cannae be many people there." She cast a glance over her shoulder then back to Maggie. "Nor young men like yer knight."

"Mercenary."

102

Leana rocked to her feet. "Call him what ye wish. I choose to believe he is a member of a noble house, lost to his family through a mysterious tragedy." She laughed softly. "Of what matter is his past when all ye know of him is good?"

She moved a few steps away to her bower. Maggie set her wee falcon's cage near her feet where she would provide some protection and be alert to its early morning cries. She pulled her plaide about her shoulders, flipping the hem several times until it covered her feet.

Who was Phillipe? Was there more to him than a sword for hire? Leana spoke true, and Maggie had been neither blind nor deaf to his actions and voice. His words bespoke a life of courtliness—she'd heard enough from nobility visiting the earl—and of an advanced education. His sword-play far exceeded any she'd previously encountered. He *did* carry himself with masculine grace and assurance and rode his horse as if born to the saddle. Maggie sighed, recalling the gentle cadence of Phillipe's voice. He spoke French, English, Armenian, and whatever language her heart longed for.

Her curiosity was piqued. But what would be the cost of her questions?

* * *

The Sound of Mull
Next day

The small vessel slipped through the water with little effort. Wind filled its single sail and its bow slapped gently against the mild chop of waves. Verdant shores lined both sides of the water, glinting gold in the evening sun. Maggie and her maid hovered at the rail, but Phillipe's gaze pulled to the distant northerly shore.

The land parted where Loch Aline emptied into the sound. Fishing boats and larger, two-masted ships rocked gently at harbor a short distance away. He felt the boards shift beneath his feet as the boat's captain ordered the vessel north, into the channel.

His teeth clenched. Dear Lord, how did he get himself into this? He had spoken against stopping for the night. They had little need for supplies, yet the varied markets in Morvern held more attraction than those in Oban, and Maggie had decided to purchase household items she deemed necessary from the busy port before sailing to Hola.

Mayhap none at the dock will know me. Mayhap I will remain aboard ship.

Yet he knew he would not. Maggie had already engaged his help for hauling her purchases back to the ship. She would have only a few hours to shop before dark, and the captain insisted on being on their way at daybreak. Though there were others she could have asked, she'd chosen him, and he hadn't known how to deny her request. Even though the thought of treading the streets where his closest friend lived tied his gut in knots.

Is my shame so great? I cared for little more than extricating myself from a fate I did not entirely deserve. Yet, honor says not all charges leveled against me were lies.

The ship slipped smoothly against the dock, rocking Phillipe gently on his heels, his knees taking the brunt of the movement. Maggie waved excitedly to him. He ignored Balgair's grin and followed Maggie and her maid across the hastily laid plank to the dock.

Skirting sailors beating a tattoo on the wooden slats from their ships on their way to the village, Maggie and Leana, with Phillipe and Dawe in tow, hurried to the shops. Phillipe and Dawe waited patiently as the two women amassed several lengths of woolen cloth, two bags of oats in a barrel lined with cloth oiled on one side to protect the grain from the weather, numerous kitchen implements piled into a large cooking pot, and a box of sundry goods including a parcel from a wizened wise-woman whose small shop reminded Phillipe violently of the herbs he'd taken in prison not so long ago.

He stood transfixed by the scents of the shop, his stomach empty and complaining in an embarrassing manner as Maggie paid the healer.

Maggie then faced him with a smile. "I dinnae know when our next cooked meal will be," she said, handing him a silver coin. "Would ye see to a bit of food tonight for all of us whilst Dawe begins transporting the purchases to the ship? I'm fair certes Callan or a pair of sailors can assist with the rest."

Phillipe automatically held out his hand, even as his mind hesitated to accept the task.

Maggie wrapped his fingers closed over the bit of silver and gifted him a sweet smile. "It shouldnae be too difficult. I saw an inn just two streets over, and there are likely other vendors if ye'd care to search for skewers or bits of sweetmeats. Dinnae fash. Whatever ye choose will be well-received."

Phillipe gave himself a mental shake to pull himself together, accepting the coin with a ghost of a smile. "As my lady wishes." He offered a brief bow. Her cheeks pinked. As Maggie collected her purchases, Phillipe strode down the street in the direction she'd indicated.

A polished sign bearing the likeness of a hunting hound, a rabbit gripped in its jaws, jutted over the street. Taking the closer—and therefore easier—option, Phillipe ducked inside.

"Welcome to The Hound, m'lord." The cheerful voice belonged to a rather stout woman, her assets modestly covered by an apron pinned to her ample chest and tied about her waist. Her smile beckoned him to a wooden bar that glowed warmly in the light from a massive fireplace in the corner of the room.

"How might I help ye, sir? If ye require a room for the night, all I have left is a spot in a chamber which sleeps four. Three of the pallets are already taken, but they're good lads and willnae give ye trouble."

Phillipe shook his head. "I thank ye, madam, but I only require food for six that I might take with me."

"Och, madam, is it?" She leaned across the counter and poked Phillipe's chest in a playful manner. "Ye have the manners of a lord, and the voice of an angel. Whereaboots do ye hail?"

"I am new to these shores, but I have traveled far. My family is French."

The woman straightened, one hand on her hip as she gave a satisfied nod. "I thought so. We hear many accents here. Laird MacLean's shipping interest brings novel people to our doors." She waved him to a stool a few feet away, at the corner of the hearth. "Sit. I'll have Coira prepare ye a basket of meat pies and a few of my berry pasties." She dimpled. "They're famous, ye ken."

Phillipe inclined his head, a smile creeping unbidden at the woman's friendly charm. "Many thanks, madam. I am certain the meal will be greatly relished."

"I am Moibeal. Ye ask for me if ye need aught else." She disappeared through a wide doorway, clapping her hands and shouting for Coira.

Phillipe glanced about from beneath a lowered brow before taking the offered seat. The hairs on the back of his neck prickled and his muscles tensed.

The room was packed, giving credence to Moibeal's mention of full sleeping chambers. However, in this prosperous village servicing an active sailing line, an inn likely kept very busy. Good-natured shouts and guffaws erupted from a spot at the other end of the hearth where a crowd gathered about three men seated on the floor. Phillipe could see the tops of their bent heads and guessed they played a game of dice. Serving wenches wove in and about the tables, platters held high. A couple of them sent Phillipe speculative looks, but a shake of his head kept them away.

Something bumped against his lower leg then grabbed the hem of his cloak. Startled, Phillipe glanced down, snatching his garment away. Counter-weighted firmly, his cloak ripped as a rotund body tumbled across the floor. The puppy slid to a stop, furry butt in the air, chin on the worn stone. He blinked his dark round eyes then plopped his hindquarters to the floor and lifted his head until he sat, a comical look on his face. Phillipe chuckled.

"Ye must be more careful, *le chiot*," he chided. "Attacking strange cloaks is not how ye win friends." He bent and ruffled the puppy's ears, eliciting an expression of delight from the creature, tongue lolling out the side of his muzzle from between sharp baby teeth.

Phillipe inspected the damage to his cloak. "I've no needle and thread to repair the rip. Mayhap I should see if m'lady has such in her purchases."

The pup yipped as if in response. A shadow fell over them as Moibeal stepped near.

"Awa' with ye, laddie," she scolded, waving a hand at the puppy. "Ye'll nae bother the guests." She turned an apologetic half-grin on Phillipe. "He's the last of my husband's bitch's litter, and a wee terror for all the attention he gets here. I'd be happy for him to find a home where I'm nae tripping over him all the day."

Phillipe eyed the pup. His chunky body was clad in a dense coat of medium brown with a dark mask over his eyes. A white muzzle, boots, and tip to his tail completed the picture.

"What sort of dog is he?"

"Och, his dam is a coley dog—a right braw hand at herding sheep. His sire, howbeit, is whatever the laird's son brought with him from abroad. Something useful for protecting sheep. I daresay this one'll turn out to be a right good dog, but for now, he's just a wee pest."

Phillipe stilled. An Aidi. *Alex and Arbela brought their dogs with them.* His heart stuttered at the reminder of how close he was to the family he'd lived with for more than half his life.

The door to the inn opened and closed and booted steps brushed through the rushes on the floor. An arm wrapped familiarly around Moibeal's sturdy shoulders.

"How's my favorite landlady this eve? Any chance I could beg ye to part with a pastie or two? I see ye still have one of the pups. Trying to talk this man into taking him home with him?"

The air darkened around Phillipe, and he struggled to draw a breath. No matter it had been nearly three years since he had last seen Alex MacLean. He would know his voice anywhere.

Chapter Fourteen

Phillipe's skin tingled—from anticipation or dread he couldn't say. He'd talked himself into not connecting with the MacLeans, yet fate had intervened. He forced his muscles to relax, drawing on years of preparation for battle to steady him for this important engagement.

"Alex?"

The tall, lean man's jaw dropped. His arm slipped from Moibeal's shoulders and he stepped forward, clasping Phillipe's arm in a vice-like grip.

"Phillipe?" Alex's voice, hoarse with surprise, strengthened. "Phillipe! St. Andrew's teeth! 'Tis a pleasure to see ye. Why did ye not send word?" He glanced about the inn. "Why do ye wait here? Come to the castle! Da will be overwhelmed to see ye!"

Phillipe shook his head, resisting Alex's enthusiastic tug toward the door. "I cannot." His gaze met the other man's puzzlement. "Please. May we speak in private? Here?"

Alex's gaze lingered a moment before he turned to Moibeal with a smile. "Would it be possible to gain a table where my friend and I could speak?"

She waved a hand. "Och, take the innkeeper's office through that doorway. I'll see to it ye arenae bothered."

Alex nodded his thanks. Phillipe rose, hindered as the pup once again attacked the fluttering hem of his cloak. Phillipe bent and lifted the puppy, pulling the cloth from its teeth. The door to the inn opened again.

"There ye are! I'm fair starved and wondered if ye needed help. Och! Look at what ye've found!" Maggie crossed the floor, eyes on the puppy. She placed a hand on Phillipe's sleeve, apparently oblivious to Alex's curious look. The pup bounced in Phillipe's arms, wiggling furiously in his attempts to smother Maggie with kisses. She laughed and fended the squirming creature off with raised hands.

"It isnae coming with ye, is it?" Skepticism colored her voice.

Alex's questioning gaze settled like a shroud.

"Nae, the pup remains here." Phillipe set the wee dog down and for a heart-stopping instant considered introducing Maggie to Alex. Changing his mind, he gave her a smile. "I will bring supper soon. They are packing a box for me." He motioned to the door. "Is Dawe or Callan with ye?"

"Aye. 'Twas our last trip for supplies. We're headed to the ship now."

"Go, then. I will be with ye soon."

Maggie bent and gave the pup a farewell pat then strode across the room to where Dawe held the door. Phillipe drew a breath and faced Alex.

* * *

Maggie glanced over her shoulder. Something was wrong. She'd seen the strange man's grip on Phillipe's arm as she walked in the door. For a moment she feared a fight was imminent, the man's stance was so intense. But he'd stepped back as she approached and her fluttering heart resumed its normal rhythm. Still, Phillipe's insistence she go back to the ship instead of suggesting she wait with him struck a sour note.

How new is he to our shores? What complications involve him?

She had not mistaken the bleak look in Phillipe's eyes. Something was wrong.

She waved to Dawe. "Go. Phillipe awaits our meal and I will help him. Dinnae fash. I'll be fine."

Dawe gave her an uncertain look. "I can wait with ye. Naught here that's in a rush to get to the ship."

Maggie shrugged. "As ye wish." She glanced at the darkening sky then nodded to the cloth and other sewing supplies wrapped and tied with twine on a bench beside the door. "Have a care to keeping that lot dry. It may rain this eve. I will wait inside with Phillipe."

Dawe sighed and hoisted the bundle to his shoulder. "Ye'll be along soon? Da'll have my hide if ye are gone long."

"Och, I willnae be long at all." She flashed him a smile. "I see Phillipe's waiting for me. Take care, Dawe."

The young man hefted the bundle to a better balance, then strode away. Maggie slipped through the inn's door and stepped inside. Her heart sped as she glanced about the busy room. Men looked up from their meals and conversations as she entered alone. Curiosity became speculation. Lewd grins evoked a shiver. Her skin prickled as though she was a lame rabbit in a den of wolves. She'd lied to Dawe. She did not see Phillipe anywhere.

A stout woman intercepted her. "Good e'en, lassie. How may I help ye?"

Relief flooded Maggie. "I seek a man who is a member of my party. He's awaiting supper."

"Och, I saw ye a few moments ago. With the Frenchman, aye?"

At Maggie's nod, the woman beckoned her to follow. "He and m'lord requested a private room, but I know he wouldnae wish ye to remain out here alone. 'Tis nae much of a place for a pretty lass such as yerself. Though ye've height and determination, some would only see that as a challenge."

"M'lord? Who is he?"

The woman flashed her a grin. "Why, Laird MacLean's son, Lord Alex, of course. He's a braw laddie, and few finer, in my opinion. He'd wish ye to be safe as well." She paused at a closed door. "Slip inside there, lass. 'Twill be a tight fit, what with the disarray the innkeeper leaves it in. Find yerself a seat if ye can. I'll see where Coira and yer supper are."

Maggie placed her hand on the wooden panel. She lifted the iron ring and pulled gently. The low rumble of voices reached her ears. Suddenly unsure of her welcome, she halted the door's progress. She gripped the metal ring firmly and held her breath. Oh, something was definitely wrong.

* * *

Alex hefted one hip onto the corner of the innkeeper's desk and folded his hands before him. "I am verra happy to see ye, Phillipe, though I scarcely knew ye with yer beard. But ye dinnae seem pleased to be here. Why did ye not come to the castle? Ye will always be welcome there."

Phillipe forced a slight smile. "Ye sound different, Alex. More like your father."

Alex laughed. "I've heard his voice all my life, and been in Scotland nearly three years. 'Twas bound to rub off on me."

Silence formed a wall between them as Phillipe struggled to find the words he wanted. He pivoted on his heel and stalked the floor, dodging a crate of wine packed in straw and a chair with one leg missing, listing dangerously to one side.

"What has happened, my friend?" Alex asked gently. "I remember our last days in Antioch. Ye were to be wed."

Phillipe came to a reluctant halt. "I did. Wed, that is. The six-year-old queen of Cilicia." He lifted his gaze, meeting Alex's concern. "Things did not go well, and my death was plotted."

Alex startled. "They wanted to kill ye?"

Memory robbed his words of strength. "I was to be poisoned. With help from those who are likely now dead if the subterfuge has been discovered, I deceived the warden and received last rites from the Bishop. A dead man took my place and I fled Cilicia." He held his hands wide, palms up. "Now I am here."

Alex's face paled. "What happened?"

Phillipe's lips twisted. "I was not a good king."

"Pfft!" Alex shot up from the desk. "Ye are a *good* man. Ye would have been an *excellent* king."

"I was a good prince of Antioch. A better knight at Batroun. But once I became king and defeated the Turks and they no longer threatened Cilicia, the people found reason to dislike—and distrust me."

"Tell me," Alex invited.

With the air of a doomed man seeking absolution, Phillipe did.

* * *

Maggie leaned against the portal. The unmistakable cadence of Phillipe's voice reached her ears.

"Only Amhal knows I am here. I could not risk war on my behalf. Nor did I wish to become a pawn in a different scheme." He sighed. "Alex, I must ask ye say naught about seeing me. I am not proud of how my life has turned out, and I cannot risk word getting back to Konstantin. As it stands, Zabel is free to marry, to become the queen she was born to be. Father would risk too much if able to use me as a rallying cry."

"But when Arbela hears . . . she will be devastated."

"Then do not tell her. Let her remember me as we parted."

The room was silent. Maggie pressed closer.

"I see the truth in what ye say, yet it grieves me to maintain my silence. My sister is . . . in a delicate condition. Ye spoke to Amhal—ye know she is wed?" A brief silence then Alex continued. "For now, 'tis best I dinnae alarm her. I will honor yer request as I am able. I willnae cause a war, but neither will I allow my family to grieve ye. When word arrives, I will take them into confidence. They willnae betray ye."

Maggie's heart slammed in her chest. What had Phillipe done? What secret did he carry?

A nudge on her leg sent Maggie stumbling against the door. It slammed shut, the slap of wood against the doorframe like a clap of distant thunder.

The puppy she'd seen earlier sat at her feet, tail sweeping the floor as he stared at her with happy anticipation.

"Ye wee skunner!" she hissed, waving the puppy away.

Taking her movements as an invitation to join a game, the pup leapt forward with a yip and sank his teeth into her skirt. He backed away, growling and shaking his head as he fought the cloth billowing around him.

Maggie dropped to her knees and grabbed the pup, holding him as she attempted to wrest her skirt from him. The door opened, thudding against her side. Maggie fell, landing on her bottom, listing precariously to one side before she righted herself. The puppy abandoned her with a happy bark at the sight of Phillipe.

Phillipe's eyes narrowed as he spied Maggie. Her cheeks heated, embarrassed to be caught at the door. She scrambled to her feet, flicking her skirt once to assess the damage. Glancing up, she caught sight of the woman who'd assisted her weaving through the crowd like a ship under full sail.

Maggie indicated the woman with a tilt of her head. "I believe our supper is ready. I'll help ye carry it."

Phillipe shifted his gaze to the inn's main room then back to her. "Are ye hurt?"

She shook her head and surreptitiously brushed the back of her skirt with a swipe of her hand to dislodge any dust or detritus from the floor. "I am well."

Phillipe's eyes followed her movements. He cleared his throat. "The puppy is a nuisance. I must request needle and thread from ye later to mend a tear in my cloak."

Maggie peered at his garment, her eyes traveling from his shoulders, lingering a fleeting moment where his belt tugged his tunic tight at his waist, then down the long length of his legs. She swallowed, her mouth suddenly dry, then caught sight of the rend at the hem of his cloak.

"Och, I can mend that. Dinnae fash." Her gaze swept upward, catching sight of the man Phillipe had been closeted with. His gaze locked with hers as if assessing her worthiness to capture Phillipe's attention.

"I'm sorry to interrupt," she said, dropping her voice to a soft murmur. "I can wait if ye wish."

"A moment only, if ye dinnae mind," he said, indicating the door with a smooth wave of one hand.

Maggie glanced at Phillipe, noting the grim lines at the corners of his lips. "Do ye wish me to go?" she whispered.

He nodded and gifted her a small smile. "All is well. I will be with ye in a moment." Phillipe nodded to the woman with the box. "Attend my lady a moment longer, please." He handed her a coin and the woman's eyes lit.

"Och, dinnae fash, my lord. She's a right bonnie lass and nae trouble."

Phillipe stepped into the room and closed the door.

Maggie's gaze lingered on the portal a moment then darted to the other woman. "I dinnae mean to interfere with yer business. I willnae move from this spot until he is prepared to leave."

The woman waved a hand. "Och, a few moments off my feet is a blessing, lass. Come. The crowd is thinning and there's a bench beneath the window where we might rest." She clucked to the pup and strode purposefully across the floor, patrons parting with respectful nods at her approach. She tucked the box beneath the bench then settled with a sigh. The puppy charged across the room, dodging feet and table legs, off on pursuit of something only he knew.

"Where are ye headed, lass? Yer Frenchman said he purchased these meals for others—aboard a ship, are ye?"

"Aye. 'Tis not a long journey." Maggie twitched her skirt, surveying the damage to the hem and delaying her answer. "I've an isle a bit to the west of here. I wish to . . . see it."

"Aye? A lass inspecting a bit of land? Rather curious." She waved a hand. "Och, dinnae mind me. I've my two feet firmly planted here and no longing to stray far from my bed."

Maggie managed a smile. "I may live there if it appeals. 'Tis something only a woman can judge, aye?"

The woman leaned close. "Tell me of this isle. I hear much here with all the sailors in and out, and may know of it."

"'Tis called Hola. I've heard 'tis a useless piece of land, but the information came to me by someone I dinnae trust." Maggie's heart clenched. Would this woman know of the isle? Would her dreams come to naught? Or was there good to be said of the land?

The woman pursed her lips then gave a nod. "I've heard of this isle, and a wee bit of legend is attached to it. 'Twas once a bit of Norse land before the MacDonnell claimed it. 'Tis small, and near the Isle of Eigg. Or mayhap Rum." She shrugged. "I dinnae remember. Howbeit, there are certes those who do. An abandoned monastery lies on its shores."

'Tis real. Maggie startled to realize she'd feared the earl had played her for a fool, giving her papers to an island which did not exist.

"Do ye know more?"

The woman tilted her head back and forth. "Only a handful of people live there. They make a small living with sheep, though their apple mead is right tasty. 'Tis much in demand here, and we cannae keep enough to satisfy our custom. They learned the making of it from the monks many years ago, and it commands a fair price."

"What of the legend?" Excitement threaded Maggie's pulse.

"The tale is one fit for any isle to the west. I wouldnae speak louder for there are too many listening ears attached to heads foolish enough to believe my tale, but once or twice, a long time ago, sailors spoke of an isle protected by fierce men with yellow hair. A place surrounded by cliffs that soared to the heavens and welcomed birds of all kinds. Porpoises played in the waters and seals lazed about on the shores. But in a hole in the rock beneath the waves, in a cavern none has seen in more than a hundred years, lies a treasure so vast, it fair boggles the mind. Though, if the legend were true, the people of Hola would do better than raise a few sheep and apples."

Maggie blinked then stifled a laugh. The woman appeared serious. "I thank ye for yer tale. I hope for little more than a fair place to live, able to support myself."

The woman patted Maggie's knee. "'Tis good ye dinnae think much on this. There is little more than sheep and mead to recommend the isle. And I'd mention ye should take into consideration others—including soldiers—who can care for and protect ye. No matter it was in the MacDonnell's possession before ye, if pirates claimed it once, they're likely to do so again."

Chapter Fifteen

The door to the inn closed, instantly silencing the din of upraised voices, tumbled crockery, and clattering bench legs. It also blotted out the light of candles and fireplace like a dark cloud before the sun. Maggie drew her cloak closer as a tendril of cool evening air drifted around her ears and down her neck.

Phillipe shouldered the box of meat pies and pasties. The savory aroma leaked from beneath the linen covering. "I apologize for my tardiness. The inn was busy, and I encountered someone." He cast a glance at her, his gaze slipping quickly away.

Questions flew about in Maggie's head.

How does he know Laird MacLean's son—on what appears to be very close terms? Who would go to war on his behalf? Is this the reason he is in Scotland? Who is Zabel?

The ramifications of the possible answers overwhelmed her. Leana was right. Phillipe was more than a mercenary. *Who, exactly, is he?*

"I dinnae know ye were friends with Laird MacLean's son." Maggie tossed the statement out, looking at Phillipe with naught more than a swift sideways glance.

"They lived for a time in the Holy Land. I knew them there."

Phillipe's answer made perfect sense, but his lifted chin and curt answer dismayed Maggie.

"I dinnae mean to pry."

His wry grin did nothing to alleviate her discomfort, but at least he glanced at her.

"Ye are curious, aye? I am a stranger with unexpected connections."

"Nae. I mean, aye, ye are different, but I heard . . . before the puppy . . .." She hesitated, not liking to admit she'd listened at the door.

Phillipe canted his head. "What did ye hear, my lady?"

"That some would wage war because of what happened to ye. Were ye wrongly imprisoned?"

"Mayhap we should speak of this later." He tilted his head, indicating the end of their walk. "We have reached our ship and are about to be met by several very hungry people. Now is not the time for words which require no interruption." He motioned her to proceed him.

Maggie lifted her skirts out of the way and stepped onto the gangway. Dawe and Leana approached, hands extended, offering help. Callan and Balgair lingered a few paces back as Maggie and Phillipe were assisted aboard the ship. The other MacLaren soldiers cast covetous eyes on the box they'd brought from the inn.

Leana glanced at Maggie from beneath slanted brows. She spread a blanket on a plank placed atop two barrels and laid out the food. "I dinnae worry. Ye were with m'lord."

Maggie bumped against her maid's arm. "Dinnae call him that," she hissed, casting a glance at Phillipe over her shoulder.

Leana peered past Maggie then finished unwrapping the pies. "Never mind. Ye and I clearly see him as different men. Or, mayhap ye dinnae wish to see him as any other than a paid sword."

It isnae true. I want to know about Phillipe of France. I want to know what drove him to our shores, why he sells his sword. 'Tis a distraction, naught more. There's no reason to let his story engage my heart.

Maggie picked up a pie and bit into the warm crust. She stepped aside as the men jostled for their food. Phillipe chose his pie then moved to a row of wooden boxes stacked against the rail. She selected a mug then moved to follow him, her heart pounding.

"May I join ye?" At his nod, she sat. Maggie managed another bite then glanced about for a bit of linen to wipe her fingertips. Finding none, she rubbed them against her skirt, wishing to ask about the conversation she'd overheard, but not knowing where or how to start.

"Have ye thought of what ye will do once ye arrive at your isle?" Phillipe's dark eyes peered at her over his mug of ale.

Maggie brushed crumbs from her lap. "I dinnae know what to expect. No one seems to know much of the isle." She hesitated then shook her head. "The woman at the inn . . .."

"The innkeeper's wife? Moibeal?"

Maggie shrugged. "I dinnae know her name. The woman who waited with me at the inn."

At Phillipe's nod, she continued. "She thought mayhap 'twas an isle she'd heard of, though 'tis most likely a mere legend."

"Tell me the legend."

"The isle—if this is in truth the same as the one in her story—is small but lovely, with porpoises and birds." She drew a breath. "And pirates."

Phillipe swallowed quickly to avoid choking on his watered ale. *Pirates?* "We will hope 'tis naught but a legend. Inheriting an isle inhabited by pirates would not be good."

Maggie shook her head, tendrils of red hair catching the torchlight. The sun had set moments ago in a burst of glory that had not been half as beautiful as the woman next to him. Her blue eyes glowed deepest sapphire in the gloaming. Something tripped in Phillipe's chest.

Protection. She needs protection.

Yet, the memory of her determined defense from the men who'd attacked the keep two days prior belied Phillipe's notion.

But she cannot defend herself against pirates on her own. Of this, Phillipe was certain. Balgair's hair-raising tale of Maggie defending herself against a single assailant whispered in his ear—*she needs no man's protection.*

Phillipe scowled. I *wish to protect her.*

He set his mug aside. "We are here to guard ye on your journey. Yet, who will care for ye once ye arrive? Ye have accoutrements for your household, yet ye do not know if adequate lodging exists. Who will build a suitable home for ye if this is what ye need?"

"I dinnae need much." Maggie's chin lifted slightly. "Rich appointments and a display of wealth dinnae interest me. A small cottage, snug from the winter storms, is all I require."

"Ye are unlike other women of my acquaintance," Phillipe admitted, though he was certain she would waver once she discovered her isle was little more than a large rock set amid crashing waves. Or was it?

"Tell me," Maggie said. "Tell me of these women."

Her gaze lingered. What to tell her? Certainly not the truth. Or, at least, not all of it. What could he say that would satisfy her curiosity?

"Women of the court are soft—any court." Though, not every woman. *Not Arbela. Not Zabel.*

Phillipe frowned at the whisper in his head.

"They are accustomed to servants and fine food." The voice in his head was silent, no accusation for this statement. "Rich clothing."

"Do the women of the Levant look like me—like the women of Scotland?"

Phillipe stared at Maggie, her flaming hair, her woolen gown, serviceable and warm. His gaze drifted over the curves rounding her bodice. Muscles slid beneath the tight sleeves of her gown, capable of drawing the string of her crossbow and holding it steady.

"Nae," he murmured. "Ye are nothing like them. And I am glad of it."

Her cheeks darkened and she ducked her head. "I'm neither slender nor dainty. The earl's mother reminded me of my shortcomings often."

"Ye have no shortcomings save those ye choose to believe exist. Do not let others' ideas overtake your own."

Her gaze lifted to his and Phillipe lost himself in her uncertainty. "Ye are the first woman I've met with hair the color of the purest flame. The first with the height to nearly be my equal. I know of only one other with weapon skills similar to yours, though she used a Turkish bow and sword, not a crossbow." His lips curved in remembrance. "There were other skills she was not allowed to demonstrate. Her father did not approve."

Maggie's eyes widened. A shocked look spread across her face. Phillipe quickly caught his error.

"Nae. I do not mean to scandalize ye. She learned of poison and other subtle weapons one summer when visiting her uncle's castle. He sheltered men of the Hashashin order and she followed their training until her father learned of it."

Maggie's face cleared. "What is the Hashashin order?"

"Fanatical, disciplined men who engage in subtle warfare with often terrifying results. It is said a man targeted by the order can be convinced to do anything by simply finding a dagger and a threatening note on his pillow."

"I havenae heard of such." She shivered. "'Twas good her da put a stop to it."

Phillipe laughed. "Little could stop her. She continued practicing scaling walls and studying the effects of poisons whenever she thought no one watched. Arbela pursued her goals almost as fanatically as the Hashashin."

"Arbela? I have heard her name. She is Lord Alex MacLean's sister?"

"Yes. Ye know her?"

Maggie shook her head. "Mere rumors. Her marriage to Laird MacKern three years ago formed an alliance between the clans. 'Twas shortly after she and her da . . .. Och, it makes sense now."

"What does?"

"Laird MacLean had died." She fluttered her fingers in an impatient gesture. "The old laird. His sons had died also, the last one of the fever that took many in the area. Too far away to affect us, but we waited to see who would take his place. 'Twas rumored the youngest son had followed King Richard on crusade to the Holy Land. He became a baron there, but he returned when his clan needed him. There were whispers his daughter was . . . er, different."

The description warmed Phillipe's heart. "'Twould not be untrue." He drew a breath. Perhaps he could learn more of Arbela from Maggie. "I wonder why she married so soon after they arrived in Scotland."

"I heard 'twas an alliance, but naught else. I left Narnain . . .." Her voice trailed off, then she lifted her chin. "I was married to the Earl of Mar a year or so after Lady Arbela married Laird MacKern. I know only hers was a ceremony the likes of which are only heard in faerie tales. She was said to wear a fabulous gown the red of dragons' blood, and a ruby the size of a goose egg hung from a necklace ablaze with diamonds and pearls."

Phillipe hazarded a grin. "I distinctly hear a bit of envy, my lady."

Maggie's eyes widened. "Och, I've worn gowns where no expense was spared, and been bedecked with priceless heirloom jewels. And I was accounted of lesser worth, for when my use was determined to be at an end, the diamonds and velvets were returned to their chests and 'twas myself which was discarded."

Phillipe frowned. "I have no use for men who do not value their wives."

"Have ye married?"

How by Saint Andrew had he lost control of this conversation? He'd wished only to hear of Arbela, perhaps acquire some acceptance for the paths they each trod. He had no wish to revisit his past, had been relieved Alex had allowed him to leave without satisfying every aspect of his tale.

Maggie's gaze lingered. She'd apparently overheard more at the inn than she'd admitted so far. It was clear she would parse the information from him unless he answered with care.

"I was. Death severed the union."

He regretted the wording. It enabled a lie, though the result was necessary. Phillipe, King of Cilicia, *was* dead, rites spoken by the Bishop himself. Phillipe, Prince of Antioch, was the only part of himself he clung to, yet even that person little resembled the mercenary he'd become.

He also regretted the distress on Maggie's face. She did not deserve the guilt riding in her lovely eyes, the sorrowful rounding of her exquisite lips. But some secrets he could not part with, and he did not deserve her sympathy—or her trust.

"I am so sorry. I dinnae mean to bring up such memories."

"Ye could not know. But the wound is still fresh." *Betrayal is as much a wound as one inflicted by a physical blow.*

"I willnae speak of yer past again."

Phillipe weighed his words carefully. "There are things I cannot speak of. I appreciate your understanding."

Maggie glanced away then tilted her mug to her lips, draining the last drops. When she lowered the cup, her smile did little to hide her lingering unease.

"I thank ye for the company. And for the thoughts on how to proceed at Hola. I'll be glad to arrive and put knowledge to this idea I have."

Phillipe nodded. "Aye. 'Tis the not knowing which offers the biggest stumbling block. Ye may count on me to assist ye however ye need."

She rose with a small nod, then carried her mug to the basin and rinsed it before placing it with her belongings. Phillipe followed her movements until she vanished into the shadows.

Balgair appeared from the gloom and propped a boot on the box Maggie had vacated. "'Tis a sight better to spend yer evening with a pretty lass than with a rowdy soldier such as myself." He angled his body so his words fell on Phillipe's ears alone. "She is curious. Ye tweak her interest."

Phillipe raised a brow at his friend's solemn tone. "Not two days ago ye thought I should pursue her."

"I dinnae know yer past, and do not ask to know more. 'Tis clear ye turned yer back on the Levant as completely as have I. And ye are nae common mercenary." His gaze narrowed. "Yer speech, the way ye carry yerself, bespeak a man of some lineage. I dinnae care what drove ye from ycr home, for I have found ye to be honorable and I am pleased to have made yer acquaintance in Spain."

"What is your caution, Balgair?"

The Scot's red beard bristled, gold-tipped in the torchlight.

"My caution is this, Phillipe. Ye are no longer in the Levant. Begin a new life. Dinnae look back."

The impact of Balgair's words swept over Phillipe. "Ye think I should marry the lady and settle down? Her rank is far above what a mercenary could aspire to."

"Aye, but what will happen when the former Countess of Mar is known to have set up house on a small isle with possibly little or no fortification? She was sought after whilst under her da's protection. There are none to save her on the isle."

Chapter Sixteen

Purple, pink, and pale gold streaked the sky above the dark stone. Waves sprayed white and silver atop amethyst seas at the base of the Isle of Hola. Maggie gripped the rail as though she could will a harbor to appear. Rocky cliffs high above her head loomed upward, affording no place to dock.

"We have just enough light to make landfall, m'lady," the captain assured her. The birlinn tacked to starboard, following the coastline as close as possible. The steep rock face descended as they rounded a spit of land, spilling at last into a wide, sweeping harbor. Foaming waves crept onto the sand, pulling back to roll into small waves that broke upon the shore once again. Large rocks lay scattered near the mouth of the harbor, protecting the opening. A pair of small boats were beached on the shore, nets strung onto frames to dry.

A few of the rocks moved. Raised their heads. Maggie gasped. "Seals!"

Leana leaned over the rail, her lips rounded into an 'O' of surprise.

The ship edged into the channel as a sailor tossed a lead line into the water.

"Twelve feet and closing. Bottom is sandy," the man called.

"Bring us in closer," the captain replied.

Butterflies danced in Maggie's belly. Her island had a harbor—and she would soon set foot upon its shore. The waves gentled as they sailed into the inlet, and the ship rocked smoothly forward. Her heart raced.

"Ten feet," the sailor sang out.

Maggie's booted toe tapped impatiently against the wooden deck. In the failing light, a broad sweep of land emerged, stretched between two great cliffs. A short pier made of rock lined one edge of the harbor. A long croft settled top a small rise set a short distance from the beach. Smoke rose through the thatched roof. Firelight twinkled on the shore. A shout rang out and dark forms spilled from the doorway.

People. Hostile or welcoming? At the very least, somewhat suspicious, for the isles lived and breathed tales of Viking conquest and pirates. Maggie couldn't wait to meet them, reassure them.

I want them to like me.

With a braking shudder, the ship settled against the fenders hanging over the edge of the pier. A seal barked across the water. A breeze, born of the evening, lifted a curl of hair against Maggie's neck.

"My lady?"

Gunn's questioning voice pulled Maggie's attention from the shore. She turned her head, eyebrows raised.

"Aye?"

"I do not think it wise to send ye ashore until we test the mettle of our welcome. How do ye wish to order the landing party?"

Maggie ignored his warning. "I will go with ye, Balgair, Phillipe, and two others. The rest may follow later."

The man bowed, sweeping his arm aside. "As my lady wishes." He addressed Callan. "Ye and the rest of the soldiers follow immediately, but remain on the pier until my command."

Maggie settled her cloak about her shoulders with a shrug, its length kept from the ground with a belt about her waist. Her small crossbow rested in its sling over one shoulder, a supply of quarrels tucked into a quiver. Colyn rested quietly in his cage, its cover pulled tight to ward off the chill evening breeze off the water.

Leana gripped the handle. "I will bring him ashore as soon as 'tis prudent." She grinned though a shudder ruffled her shoulders. "I cannae believe we've finally arrived."

Maggie nodded, anticipation tensing her muscles. "Aye," she breathed. "We're about to start anew."

Phillipe stepped to the rail. "Is my lady ready?"

At Maggie's nod, he helped her over the rail, and released her to Gunn's care.

She strode the length of the pier, her gaze on the sight before her. Black rock lay everywhere. Grasses waved gently in the breeze. The long croft to the right appeared a mix of black and dark gray stone and turf. The roof rose to a high pitch and looked much like the upended keel of a boat.

Light from the open door spilled onto the ground. There was no sign of a protecting wall or fort.

A fire flared on the beach. Six men stood abreast between the hut and the beach. Maggie's heart raced.

They reached the end of the pier. Gunn stepped onto the sand. Balgair joined him, stepping between Maggie and those on the beach.

Gunn spared Maggie a glance. "Wait here." His lowered brow brooked no refusal and Maggie sighed. The six men at the bonfire did not appear armed, nor willing to approach.

"Dinnae frighten the people, Gunn. I wish for a chance to speak to them. We are friendly, aye?"

Phillipe stepped close. "I will await your word." He brushed aside the edge of his cloak, revealing the hilt of his sword in a gesture known to soldiers everywhere. Maggie understood, though she resented the implication she required protection, and hated the idea of being coddled simply because she was a woman. She pulled her crossbow from her shoulder and dropped it and the quiver to the stone at her feet.

"I will wait also."

Phillipe checked his look of surprise. He'd not gotten past his shock that Gunn had allowed Maggie from the ship before peace could be ascertained. The small party on the shore did not appear threatening, but with Maggie's talk of pirates and treasure, he would take nothing for granted. He stood ready to protect her at all cost.

Her acquiescence to await word was unexpected. He glanced at her, but her gaze followed Gunn along the beach. The six men at the fire did not advance. The evening deepened. The blaze brightened, revealing faces taut with concern.

Gunn, flanked by two armed soldiers, halted.

"I speak for my lady, the Countess of Mar."

The six men exchanged looks. After a moment, one stepped forward.

"I am Asatrus. We are peaceful. We arenae prepared to fight."

Maggie bolted forward. Her boots sank into the soft sand and one ankle twisted beneath her. Phillipe caught her arm.

"'Tis not wise to leap into soft footing," he admonished in a low voice. "Nor is it wise to charge onto shore before your captain has finished his speech and assessed the danger."

She sent him a slanted look but held her ground. She scowled.

"I'm *not* the countess."

"Ye were. 'Tis important for the people to know why ye claim their land."

She blinked. "I dinnae think of it as such. I dinnae wish to run them from their homes."

"Then let Gunn reassure them."

She dipped her chin in a short nod. The men of Hola gave their attention back to Gunn.

"The Countess has received title to this isle. Ye owe her yer allegiance."

Maggie's chin lifted. Nobility flowed through her posture, but Phillipe still saw the kindness on her face. The people of Hola would not come to harm under Maggie's protection.

Her protection. Phillipe glanced at the croft. There was no protection here. The building was of stone and cut turf, the roof thatched with dried grass. No wall surrounded it, no fort commanded the hillside. Did pirates truly visit this isle? What would draw them here?

Maggie stepped forward. Gunn faced her expectantly. The MacLaren soldiers formed about her. Balgair landed next to Phillipe and nudged his arm.

"I will wait here against unforeseen actions if ye wish to go with her."

Phillipe moved to Maggie's side then slipped a half-pace behind where his view of the men and the isle was unrestricted. He trusted Gunn to have ensured the men were unarmed, but he could not refrain from watching for surprises.

A woman stepped from the longhouse and moved to stand next to Asatrus, her gaze on Maggie.

Maggie halted next to Gunn. "I am Maggie MacLaren. I hold title to the Isle of Hola."

The woman inclined her head. "I am Ingrida, Asatrus's wife. We've lived here for generations, my lady. We are honored to have ye on our shores."

"Thank ye, Ingrida. I am pleased to be here."

Maggie drew on her recollection of protocol from her da and from the earl as she spoke to the people of Hola. After a time, she and the others were invited into the longhouse, the holding shared by all who lived on the isle.

The odor of sheep, smoke, and fish greeted Maggie. She swallowed against the heavy onslaught of scents. Faces expressing varying degrees of interest, expectancy, and apprehension followed her as she entered the crowded space. A dog barked. Sheep bleated. Maggie noted the pen at the far end of the house held a number of fleecy animals. A black and white dog slipped through the crowd and sniffed Maggie's boots.

"*Steðja*, Gerdur." Ingrida waved the dog away. "Kleppr, return Gerdur to the pen with the sheep." She motioned to a fur-covered bench. "Please sit here, m'lady."

Maggie sat. The seat was warm, as if recently vacated. She glanced about. Small fires glowed at intervals down the length of the room. Benches much like the one she sat upon lined the center aisle. To either side lay sleeping areas, raised beds piled with furs shrouded in comparative darkness. Low bits of shelves with bowls and other bits of pottery divided the spaces. An old woman, her chair tucked beside a post near the fire, bent over a piece of cloth, plying a needle. Her sparse white hair hung about her. A cat curled atop her feet.

Ingrida waved a hand about the room. "Welcome to Eyrrhús. Whatever we have is yours."

"Thank ye, Ingrida. I wish to learn to know ye and yer ways. What ye do here. How ye make yer living. 'Tis of great importance to me that ye live well."

Ingrida's eyes flashed, but she maintained a calm expression. "As ye see, we are few in number and poor in the wealth of the world." She settled a hand atop the head of a young girl who slipped from behind her skirts to peer at Maggie. "But we are quite blessed in other ways."

Maggie's heart swelled. She would make this place her home.

Phillipe shook out a woolen blanket and spread it near the fire on the beach. "The captain will maintain watch aboard the ship. We will set a watch here as well."

Balgair passed close, his shoulder brushing Phillipe's. He halted, drawing a deep breath as he surveyed the area. "This isle isnae the inhospitable rock I envisioned. Even in the moonlight 'tis a fair place."

"I believe there is a legend attached to the isle."

"A legend? Of what?"

Phillipe's lips twisted in a grimace. "Pirates."

Balgair's eyebrows shot upward. He glanced at the two MacLaren soldiers readying their sleeping pallets then jerked his head to the side. "Come with me."

Phillipe cast another glance at the longhouse where Maggie, Leana, Gunn, and three other MacLaren soldiers remained for the night. No hairs prickled on the back of his neck. Nothing seemed amiss. After a slight hesitation, he fell into step beside Balgair.

They strode into the darkness, boots hissing softly on the wet sand. They swished through grass that reached their knees as their path took them inland, their eyes adjusting to the moonlight guiding them past boulders and to the sweep of mountain beyond the huts.

They climbed the steady slope, the wind rising as they ascended to a promontory point overlooking the northern shore. Far below, their ship rocked at anchor, a dark smudge against the water. Moonlight lit the white-crusted peaks as swells dropped into ebony depths.

Balgair halted. "There is a pirate legend of this place?"

Phillipe shrugged. "Would ye find it less usual to learn a pirate legend had *not* been attached to this isle?"

Balgair's grunt acknowledged the probability. "When did ye hear of this?"

"Maggie spoke of it yester eve. The innkeeper's wife at The Hound in Morvern mentioned it to her, though she could not recall if the tale was of this isle or another."

Balgair nodded thoughtfully. "The Norse claim many of these isles, though most owe allegiance to the Lord of the Isles or the King of Norway himself. Asatrus and his clan appear to be undefended and left to their own charge. However, their names and home suggest at the very least a Norse heritage."

Phillipe quirked a brow. "I know naught of the Norse."

"If memory serves, Asatrus means *faithful to God*."

"The lands may have a tie to Norway, but Maggie's late husband won possession of Hola in a game of chance. 'Tis now a Scottish possession."

"Late husband?" Balgair chuckled. "Makes it sound as if he has passed into the afterlife."

Phillipe considered this. "'Twould not be an unwelcome happenstance. I will refrain from killing him myself, but only as long as I do not knowingly meet the man."

"Ye mean to remain here long?"

Phillipe shrugged. "I do not have a clear thought on remaining. I only know I cannot leave her unprotected."

Balgair slanted him a look. "She has eight MacLaren soldiers."

"Eight soldiers her father could ill-afford to send. How long before he recalls them?"

Balgair shrugged. "I dinnae know. Ye make a valid point. Ye and I are the only ones not tied to MacLaren. Yet, I have little desire to remain on a tiny isle in a longhouse packed with people, waiting to see if pirates come ashore."

"I would ask ye to remain only until we have some manner of fortification built."

"A fort? Ye are talking months if not years of work, laddie. I've nae the skills for it."

Phillipe scowled. "Something should be done. She cannot remain here unprotected."

"Why do ye think her da allowed her to come?"

"Allowed?" The question caught Phillipe off guard. He chuckled softly and stared over the ocean. "Though I do not believe my lady is overly reckless, I am well aware she is stubborn. After what has happened in the past weeks, mayhap she was right to move away for a time."

Balgair nodded and shifted position, placing his back to the stiff breeze. "If men sought her as fair prize after her marriage was dissolved, she was right to be concerned."

"Concerned?" Phillipe's voice rose with indignation. "Offended, mayhap? Angry? She has survived actions from men that would leave another woman reeling." Phillipe examined the tide of fury sweeping through him. What would he contemplate if such had befallen Arbela? Zabel? Murder? War?

Guilt pricked him. Did Zabel enjoy Konstantin's protection—and that of her rank? Or had calamity befallen her? He would likely never know, and there was naught he could have done to protect her once his death was demanded. 'Twas in God's hands now.

Balgair sighed. "I shall help for a time. Mayhap on the morrow we should check the length and breadth of the isle. Mayhap there is more to this isle than a longhouse, a few fishing boats, and a small flock of sheep."

Chapter Seventeen

Wind whipped across the promontory overlooking the harbor, shredding the morning mists. Pale sunlight pierced the clouds. A small crowd included two men of Hola, two MacLaren soldiers, Phillipe, and Maggie clustering on the edge of the cliff. Maggie's skirts whipped about her legs and her hair, strands pulled free of its braid, danced wildly about her head. Ignoring the disarray, she held her breath as the mysteries of Hola were revealed.

Far below, fat seals wallowed on the rocks, their barks rising on the wind. They wrestled their ungainly bodies into the sea with a splash. Birds reeled against the blue sky, their cries echoing above Maggie's head. Distant blurs of white and gray roosted in nests tucked in precarious perches up and down the edges of the cliffs. Waves crested white, dashing foam against the black rock. Tiny pink and blue and yellow flowers bloomed at her feet.

"'Tis beautiful!"

Asatrus ducked his head against the wind. "We have little use for this bluff, as the soil is verra thin, and the wind buffets everything relentlessly. However, 'tis a strong look-out site and ye can see the seal cove from here. We hunt them when necessary, but the sea rarely gives us easy access to the rookery. 'Tis dangerous waters on that side of the isle with the rocks rising from the sea. Currents are strong as well. Though the seals dinnae seem to mind and their cove is well-protected from predators."

Maggie could not imagine hunting the rollicking, funny beasts, yet remembered the seal hides in the longhouse. In the cold months, the hides—and meat from the seals—could mean the difference between life and death for the people of the isle.

Asatrus turned and headed back down the slope. The others followed. Maggie caught sight of several giggling children as they scampered ahead.

"Get back to yer chores," Asatrus shouted, though with little heat in his words. "Without bait for the fishing, we willnae have supper."

The children scattered to the shoreline near the longhouse, laughter fading in their wake.

"What do they seek?" Maggie asked.

"Peelies, m'lady. Fish cannae turn them down, and flatties are easily caught near the shore."

Maggie blinked. "Peelies?" She glanced at Phillipe. He shrugged.

Asatrus halted. "Crabs as they begin to shed their shell and grow another are called peelies. They're soft and attract fish. If the shell is hard, the fish willnae bother."

"And flatties?"

"Flat fish. I dinnae know another name. They live close to the beach and the bairns fish for them. The men use nets farther out to sea to catch saithe and haddock."

"Thank ye. I have much to learn."

Asatrus sent her a curious look then continued down the path.

They walked the length of the isle. Seals and cliffs on the northern shore, marshland to the south. The beautiful harbor swept across the western beach, framed by cliffs. A few trees dotted the landscape. Short and twisted by the wind, they clustered near the foot of the cliffs. One tree clung to a ledge at a seemingly impossible angle, its seed dropped there many years ago with just enough soil to take root.

Sheep grazed the hillsides to the north and south. Ewes due to lamb were kept close to the longhouse, some had even shared the space inside the night before, and the flock likely would return to the shelter of a nearby shed or even the longhouse when the winter storms came. Lambs frolicked in the waving grass, leaping small stones with clumsy grace.

"What lies there?" Maggie pointed to a path that wound east beyond the longhouse. A swell of land hid the eastern shore.

"Saint Martin's Abbey, m'lady. The monks are nae longer there, but they grew apple trees and made mead. We still use their trees and recipe."

"Show me."

The path meandered over a hill, then down to a wide, wind-swept area. The abbey's ruins lay to one side, mere feet from the edge of cliffs which fell a short distance to the sea. Its ancient stone walls encircled an orchard of perhaps thirty trees, protecting them from the winds that seemed to never die. On the leeward side of the abbey walls, a well-designed garden grew. Large red and green cabbages lined the edge of the long rectangle and vines trailed against the wall. Tufts of what were likely carrots and turnips sprouted from the ground. To one side, an herb garden grew.

Sheltered against an upsweep of rock were a half-dozen bee hives. Insulated against the wind and rain with a wattle and daub mixture, they resembled tall, muddy, upturned baskets.

"Ye have a beekeeper?"

"Aye, m'lady," Asatrus replied. "To make mead."

Phillipe appeared at her shoulder. "I know of mead. May we taste it?"

Asatrus inclined his head. "Come with me."

They entered the abbey ruins through a wide opening in the courtyard wall. The height of the wall blocked most of the wind. Maggie instantly noticed a change in the air. Peace fell in soft sunlight in the protected garden. The apple trees swayed gently, their upper branches extending above the wall and caught in the wind. White flowers flashed among green leaves and carpeted the ground beneath the trees with fallen petals.

Wide, shallow pottery bowls sat along the wall. Maggie approached, halting at Asatrus's cry of caution.

"The honey was recently harvested, m'lady. 'Twill remain here until 'tis blessed and must remain untouched."

"Blessed?" Maggie glanced at Phillipe who arrived at her side.

"When the honey begins to ferment, which is necessary to produce mead," Phillipe replied.

Asatrus bobbed his head. "Each bowl is stirred once with the blessing staff, then it must be allowed to rest undisturbed until the fermentation begins. If 'tis interrupted, the flavor will go bad."

"Blessing staff?"

Asatrus nodded to a gnarled rod leaning against the wall. "It has been used for generations and the mead couldnae be prepared without it."

"How long does this take?"

"A night or two, mayhap longer. We harvest the honey thrice yearly, but only create mead twice per year. The apples are picked before Samhain and stored over the winter to ripen the flavor. Some are pressed in late winter, another batch in late spring."

"I see. Thank ye." Maggie stepped carefully away from the open bowls of golden honey, and the entire abbey seemed to breathe a sigh of relief. She followed Asatrus into the building. Sunlight fell through the open roof and windows long open to the elements, making patterns on the swept floor.

They continued through the vaulted main hall and into a series of separate rooms.

The storage room was dark, but not terribly cold. Thick walls protected the multitude of vessels which lined the floor, shoulder to shoulder, from the changes in the weather.

"The pots are beautiful." Maggie gently touched her fingertips to the decorative grooves. Each pot, flat-bottomed and wider at the top than at the bottom, held a different pattern. Most appeared to be very old, grooves and raised portions worn almost smooth in places.

Asatrus removed a lid and set it aside. A narrow ridge just inside the neck of the jar held the lid in place when closed. Using a wooden dipper, he carefully withdrew a measure of clear, golden liquid from the jar and offered it to Maggie.

"'Tis ready to bottle. It has ceased bubbling and any impurities have settled to the bottom of the amphora."

Maggie accepted the dipper and gently inhaled the aromas wafting from the liquid.

Apples. Crisp. Sweet. Her mouth watered in anticipation. She took a cautious sip. The mead rolled across her tongue with a hint of honey sweetness blended with a full range of the bright flavor of apples. Heat blossomed in her belly when she swallowed, warmth tingling into her arms, fingers, and toes. She made a note not to over-imbibe lest she lose her senses. This was a potent drink.

Phillipe quirked an eyebrow. She handed him the dipper. His nostrils flared at the scent. His eyes widened appreciatively at the taste. Then widened more as the impact of the alcohol landed in his stomach.

"'Tis amazing. My father has offered meads at his table, but naught to compare to this."

Maggie flicked a startled gaze at him. Who was his father? Phillipe appeared not to notice. He took another sip then handed the dipper to Asatrus.

"What do ye do with your mead?" Phillipe glanced about the room. A quick calculation put the stock at thirty to forty amphora of varying sizes. Perhaps eight to ten gallons each.

"A ship from Morvern will arrive in a few weeks and purchase our entire stock." Asatrus waved a hand over the pots. "God has been good to us."

Morvern. He flashed a glance at Maggie who responded with a questioning look. He gave his attention back to Asatrus.

"This is how ye tithe to your liege?"

The man's cheeks flushed. "Aye. Some years are better than others. Two years past, only a third of the trees bore fruit. Many were planted by the monks over a century ago. It took us several years to raise trees to begin to replace the ancient ones. This autumn, the young ones bore fruit."

"The earl wouldnae have appreciated only a few gallons of mead," Maggie murmured.

Phillipe gritted his teeth. He could see to it the people of Hola received fair payment for the mead—but he would be forced to trade with Donal MacLean, Alex's father—the Baron of Batroun and once his fostering lord. His self-imposed exile risked exposure.

He could help Maggie and the people of Hola. But he would be required to bare his soul to the few people on this earth he cared about. People to whom he did not wish to make his past conduct known. He wanted to speak the words, to assure Maggie her island with its ancient monastery and orchard was definitely of worth—and with careful curating, could increase in value.

But the words would not form. He forced a smile.

"I am glad ye have restocked your trees. My lady, ye shall do well here."

Coward. Keeping services from her impinges upon honor. Honor I abandoned more than a year ago.

He pivoted on his heel and strode from the room. Entering the vaulted hall he halted, hands at his hips, breathing deeply to clear his head. Maggie's footsteps sounded behind him. He bolted forward, forcing his stride to an even pace. Maggie grabbed his arm.

"What is amiss?"

He allowed her to stop him, the worry on her face shaming him further.

"Naught is amiss, m'lady. I have things I must tend to." He inhaled deeply and stared over her shoulder. "I will go back to the harbor and help Balgair off-load the remaining supplies. Asatrus will finish his tour."

He gave a curt nod. Her hand fell away. Confusion drew her eyebrows together and a frown tugged at her lips, but she did not reply.

Phillipe's boots beat a rapid tattoo over the uneven ground. He followed the path between the cliffs, absently noting the narrow passage created an area easily held against attack. At least until a way was found over the cliffs. Was that why the monks had built their abbey on the eastern edge of the isle rather than closer to the harbor?

His steps slowed. Perhaps this was another way to help Maggie. She needed a defensible shelter. As Balgair said, it would take months, mayhap longer, to build a wall about the longhouse and place defenses around the harbor. But the abbey was already standing—most of it, at least. How long to repair the wall and roof?

Men and tools from Morvern would make the task easier.

Phillipe halted, closing his eyes against the surety that he held the key to safety and prosperity for Maggie and her people. The only cost would be to his pride.

Chapter Eighteen

Phillipe shoved his tunic sleeves above his forearms, allowing the air to cool him after his exertions. A pile of supplies sat on the beach, women sorting through it with cries of delight.

"Who thought a new cooking pot would be such a prize?" Balgair chuckled. "Ye could have allowed the sailors to unload the ship, Phillipe. Or some of the MacLaren soldiers. 'Twas nae yer job."

"It matters not. 'Tis finished and the captain will sail on the morning tide." Phillipe cast his gaze on his friend. "Will ye sail with him?"

Balgair sat against a boulder and crossed his arms. "Aye. As glad as I am to nae longer be fighting in the Holy Land, this isnae what I envisioned." He stared across the water, silent a moment before he continued.

"'Tis peaceful here. Too peaceful for my liking. I'll see where the next bit of work takes me."

"What if there was work here? For a time."

Balgair grinned, one eyebrow adrift. "I know naught of sheep beyond how to spit one, and dying when a langskip of pirates lands on this unprotected shore isnae the future I'd planned."

"We can help them protect the isle."

"Ye know 'twill take months to build a defensible structure, and we lack the men to see the work done."

"We won't need to build from the ground up. The abbey needs repair, but mostly a new roof and reinforcements to the wall. One side is protected by cliffs dropping down to the sea, two other sides by numerous rocks and protrusions."

"And the fourth side?"

"A path between the cliffs. It provides the only easy access to the abbey."

Balgair's gaze turned thoughtful. "Mayhap I could take a peek at yer abbey and see if yer plan is sound."

"Come with me." Phillipe beckoned over his shoulder as he strolled up the beach. They passed the longhouse and continued to the trail that led up a small hill and to the plateau beyond. In the darkness of the previous evening, they'd noticed nothing but the sheer cliffs, hadn't known to look upward from the ship to see the abbey silhouetted against the sky.

Phillipe halted where the path opened to the abbey grounds. Balgair observed the ruins, his beard bristling as his lips pursed in thought. He paced left then right, eyes taking in the scene before him.

"We could mayhap place a gate here, though 'twould be better if we had a form of murder hole, mayhap machicolations in a protected bridge stretching from one side of the path to the other. I have no expectation of these people becoming warriors, but given a walled area from which to fire arrows or drop stones . . .." He pivoted, his glance covering the rocky cliffs. "Stones of which we have aplenty."

"With some repair, the abbey should be defensible, do you not agree? And remodeled into a suitable manor for Lady Maggie."

Balgair rubbed his beard. "I'd want to walk through it before I spoke, but for now I agree. The walls should be added to, both height and breadth. A slate roof for the abbey would be best, but mayhap a thatched one for now. And I dinnae know what the interior is like, or what m'lady would want."

He turned to Phillipe. "I can gie ye suggestions on defense, mayhap stack a few stones. But the work willnae get done with just the twa of us. We'll need more men, and supplies I dinnae see on the isle. Iron and wood for the gate, for instance. The trees here willnae gie ye the boards, and there is nae smithy for bars and hinges."

Phillipe drew a sharp breath. Balgair was right. They would need help. To ask the MacLeans for help was almost more than he was willing to bear.

Damn! There was more than knowledge of his failure in Cilicia he wished to keep hidden. His very life depended on his escape never becoming known. Obscurity had seemed a reasonable refuge. Had it become his prison?

Alex, heir to the MacLean Barony, had pressed him to return after his service to Maggie ended, reassured him he could ask anything of him and his family. Alex would not deny him men or supplies. But Phillipe would not go behind Donal MacLean's back. If he chose to ask for help, he would do so in a forthright manner. And entangle his former foster lord in the deception that had saved his life.

Was Maggie worth the cost?

Voices pulled his attention. Maggie, among the group of MacLarens and men of Hola, exited the orchard, her red hair flaming in the sunlight. Her head bent at a listening angle as Asatrus spoke, canting a glance to one side as Gils the bee-keeper added to the conversation.

Already the people of Hola warmed noticeably toward her. They saw her kindness, her interest in their land, their lives, their needs. What would be her fate if he did nothing? How long before pirates or men seeking the former countess of Mar arrived?

She lifted her gaze. Caught sight of him. A faint smile played about her lips. Phillipe's blood warmed. She had been used by her father to claim social standing, only to be cast aside by her husband who should have protected her. He would not be the man to fail her this time.

"I must go to Morvern." Firm. Determined. A weight lifted from his shoulders.

Balgair nodded. "We could request workers from the baron. But how will ye pay for them? 'Twould beggar ye to use what ye received from MacLaren."

"'Tis of no matter. I will see it done."

"The lassie has ye bewitched into being her champion. Yer time as a mercenary is at an end."

Phillipe hazarded a ghost of a smile. "All things are as God wills. But I will not allow her to be harmed again."

The sight of Phillipe and Balgair drew Maggie's steps to a halt. She waved Asatrus and Gils on. The soldiers and men of Hola hesitated only a moment at her bidding then vanished down the trail between the cliffs. She set her gaze on Phillipe. Balgair pushed away from his stance against a rock and sent her a respectful nod.

"M'lady."

He clapped Phillipe's shoulder then followed the others down the trail. Phillipe's gaze lingered on Balgair a moment before he faced Maggie.

Her heart raced. "Is aught amiss?"

Phillipe shook his head and ventured a brief smile which did not reach his eyes. "Not at all. Balgair and I have assessed the defenses of the isle and I wish to offer a proposal. Will ye walk with me?"

Not for the first time did Maggie note the sorrow in his eyes, at odds with the reassurance he offered. She bit her lip, halting the impulse to draw her fingers over the short beard covering the long scar running along the side of his face. To smooth the lines of worry on his brow.

"Aye." She sent him an encouraging look and paced at his side to the opening in the abbey wall where he halted.

"Ye must have a way to defend yourself and the people of Hola. The people of the isle are not warriors, and I have no desire to change them. But I would have ye safe." He lifted a hand, indicating the path they'd just trod.

"'Tis the only easy access to the abbey. Though it winds between two cliffs which are not overly tall, the narrow passage allows no more than two men to pass through abreast."

Maggie glanced at the path, framed by the tall stones. "*That* 'tis helpful."

"If ye had archers to pick the enemy off as they came through the gap, 'twould be enough. But ye do not. We suggest ye build a gate that can be closed and locked. 'Tis possible to bolt it into the rock. Also, bridgework spanning the path could be put into place to offer a protected way of dropping stones or even hot water or heated sand onto an enemy."

A shiver ran down Maggie's spine. "What do we have that would invite such men? Apples?" Her lips twisted with scorn. "Is the *cyser* made from them such a beacon?"

Phillipe's lips thinned. "I know why ye fled Narnain."

Heat rushed through Maggie. Anger. Embarrassment. "'Tis behind me. None will follow me to this isle." Alarm rose. She raised her hands as if to ward off his words. "They could no longer have interest in me."

Phillipe took her hand, his thumb running a gentling motion across her skin. "I wish I was wrong, but word will soon filter out that the former Countess of Mar has taken residence on the Isle of Hola."

"I am *not* the countess." Maggie hissed, fresh pain sliding through her. "That title is nae longer mine."

He frowned. "I wish I could spare ye, but 'tis certes unscrupulous men, men who choose to see ye as a challenge, will come."

"My past will follow me here?" Her skin blanched cold with shock, then blazed with anger. "I am nae a *challenge*! They willnae cross the sea on some manly whim."

Phillipe peered at her, his gaze roaming her face. "Aye, *ma belle*, they will."

His choice of words startled her almost as much as his certainty her presence would bring dissolute men to Hola.

He thought her beautiful?

What would the presence of such men do to her isle?

Panic swept over her. "I could rebuild the monastery. Create a nunnery. I would be safe there."

Something—sorrow?—crossed his face. "Ye have no wish to remarry? A man with a powerful name could protect ye."

Scorn swept away her fears. "I *had* a powerful name. I *had* a husband. Neither protected me."

"Please accept my apology, m'lady. I knew this, yet I thought . . .." He sighed and stepped away, lifting an arm to the abbey's walls. "We could strengthen the walls, raise the height, also. Replace the roof. Tile would be best, though mayhap a job for next summer." His voice took on an impersonal tone.

"I would ask ye to inspect the interior, create a plan for the rooms within. New buildings or additions would also need to be addressed next year. There are not enough weeks left before harvest to do more than fortify what is already here."

Maggie inhaled sharply. She liked Phillipe when he spoke to her as an equal, but not in this aloof tone that built a wall between them.

"Thank ye. Ye have put a great deal of thought into this. 'Tis clear we are in need of a way to protect ourselves. I willnae keep running. This will be my home."

Phillipe's muscles relaxed. His eyes softened. "I did not think ye would run. That would not be the woman I have come to know."

Maggie's lips curved. "Your suggestions are sound ones. But I have nae means to pay for supplies. I dinnae know what the income from the cyser will be. I doubt there is surplus wool from the sheep to sell. There are fewer than ten men on the isle. Each seems to have his own responsibility. I doubt they could spend much time rebuilding the abbey. I would need to hire workers."

Phillipe grew still. A muscle twitched in his jaw as if he wrestled with his next words. "I will speak with Baron MacLean and his son. 'Tis certes something can be arranged. May I speak for ye?"

Maggie studied the man before her. She trusted him to arrange good terms with the baron on her behalf, but something made her hesitate.

Three children ran excitedly up the trail. "Freya! Freya!"

The mix of languages from the children amused Maggie. She'd been addressed as *Lady* most of her life, but the Norse equivalent fell strange, though not unpleasant on her ears. She laughed as the three bairns danced about her.

"Freya, Ma says to bring ye home. We'll have a feast this e'en in yer honor!"

The youngest, her pale gold hair floating about her shoulders, silken strands slipping free from two long braids, tucked a hand in Maggie's and leaned close.

Maggie tilted her head to the child.

"Narfi caught a mouse," the little girl whispered, brown eyes wide. She slipped a thumb into her mouth.

"A mouse? Whatever for?"

"To feed yer falcon!" The lad propped his fists on his hips. "Svala doesnae like mice."

The little girl shook her head violently and more strands of hair escaped the frayed plaits.

The other child stepped between Narfi and Svala. "Leave her alone. Ma said we mustn't fight in front of Freya."

Narfi sent her a scowl then gave a one-shoulder shrug.

"'Tis verra kind of ye, Narfi," Maggie soothed. "But teasing lasses isnae how ye prove yer worth as a hunter. Come with me and I'll let ye watch as Colyn eats."

"Narfi isnae his real name," the elder girl stated. "Narfi means skinny."

Maggie tilted her head thoughtfully. "Then I suppose it suits him. But I see him as wiry and agile. He's been a grand help to me."

Narfi's cheeks flushed. "Can I feed him this time?" Excitement lit the lad's eyes.

"Nae. Colyn is my bird, and only I can feed him. But ye may watch and learn, and mayhap one day a falcon will come to ye and ye will know how to care for it."

Narfi accepted Maggie's decision with a reluctant sigh. "I can get more mice."

"'Twill soon be time to teach him to hunt, and yer help in the meantime is greatly appreciated. But we dinnae wish to keep yer ma and the others waiting."

Chattering excitedly, the girls grabbed Maggie's hands and pulled her after them. Maggie cast a helpless look at Phillipe.

"May we speak later?"

A thoughtful look crossed his face and he smiled. "Of course, m'lady. I am ever at your service."

Chapter Nineteen

Lit by firelight in the longhouse, Maggie's hair fell about her in a glittering shower. Her eyes glowed, delicate skin crinkling at the edges of her eyes and lips as she laughed. Phillipe imagined there'd been little to encourage her laughter of late.

He sipped warmed apple mead, the flush of heat through his veins from more than the drink. He set the mug on the floor beside his seat, out of tempting reach. He'd imbibed enough of the heady elixir.

"'Tis a fine cyser they brew." Balgair bumped Phillipe's elbow. "Yer lass may be on tae something."

"M'lady is not *my lass*, but ye may be correct about the mead." Phillipe moved his elbow from Balgair's range and reached for his mug. He took a thoughtful sip. "'Tis somewhat dry, yet the flavors sparkle on the tongue and linger in the nose. The apples are bold yet fleeting. A very imaginative honey wine."

Balgair drained his cup in three noisy gulps.

Phillipe arched a brow. "'Tis drunk the same as a fine wine. Not like a cheap ale on tap at a public inn."

"'Tis good." Balgair belched then wiped his beard with the back of a meaty fist. "I want another."

Phillipe grinned. "'Twill be your last, my friend."

Balgair lifted his empty mug in a salute as he stomped across the floor of the longhouse to the tables groaning with food and drink. Men slapped his shoulder, plying him with more mead.

Phillipe's gaze pulled back to Maggie. Three women and two men beckoned her to the center of the room where benches had been moved aside to create space. A grizzled man, long hair pulled back in an intricate braid, strands twined with clay and silver beads, blew into a hornpipe, and a willowy young woman drew slender fingers across the strings of a small harp. The wild skirl of the pipe punctuated the soft, sweet ripple of the strings. A roar of approval rose as Maggie lifted the hem of her skirt and joined the dancers.

Hand claps as fast as the beat of her heart urged Maggie's feet to a brisk tempo. She dipped and swayed, spinning as hands passed her from one dancer to another. This was no stately, courtly dance, suitable for the earl's hall, but one filled with the untamed soul of the isle. Laughter as bright as the ripple of water over black rock spilled from her. Her skirts and hair whipped about her as wild as the storm-swept seas. Music screed in the air, devastating as the absence of breath when it halted.

She stood in the middle of the longhouse, panting, heated, alive and carefree for the first time in months. Smiling, she shook her head as the music began anew. She accepted a mug of chilled mead, relishing the crisp flavor. Emptying the mug, she set it aside, still overwarm from her exertions. A cool breeze beckoned from the open doorway, and she followed the desire to feel its touch.

With a shake of her head, she declined Callan's silent offer to follow. He'd placed a guard among the revelers on the beach and the ship remained at the pier. Though the sailors had been invited to the feast, the captain maintained a watch over the harbor. There was nothing to fear.

Mist lay low over the tidal pools, like steam rising from scattered cauldrons. Waves in the harbor reflected a thousand moons. Foam slid up the beach to form a rippling line in the sand, retreated, then formed again. Maggie inhaled the salt air. She loosened the laces at the side of her gown, allowing the coolness of the night access beneath the cloth. Fingers of a breeze lifted her hair and trailed beneath the neckline of her kirtle. The heat of the longhouse disappeared.

She stepped carefully across the sand, aware of a curious buzzing in her head, a tingle in her arms and fingers. Like the bubbles in the mead, the sensation raced just beneath her skin. She grinned.

The mead is even more potent than I thought.

Water seeped into her footprints then disappeared in a flurry of froth. Choosing a gently rounded boulder, Maggie perched atop, tucking her skirts close to keep them from the teasing waves. Bending her legs, she rested her cheek on her knees, shoulders rounded, fingers trailing in the water pooled at the base of the rock.

Her gaze moved from the stretch of sand to the clifftops rising above the harbor. Stars twinkled in the dark blue sky, mingling their white light with that of the moon on the gently waving grasses, glistening stone, and rippling water.

Mine. This was given to me by a man who has no idea what real riches are. I have been here scarcely a day and already feel ties to this bit of land and water. Naught could entice me to leave.

Warmth swept through her.

And the people accept me.

They like me.

She hugged the thought to her, joy welling. Laughter and music drifted from the longhouse. The sea called from beyond the harbor.

"May I join ye?"

A spurt of annoyance flashed through Maggie at being disturbed, but Phillipe's voice soothed the displeasure. She was too content to fuss, and she discovered she wanted to share this perfection with the Frenchman.

"Aye. Choose a seat."

Phillipe's hawk-like eyes glittered, his beard a shadow in the moonlight, hiding the lower half of his face. He propped a boot atop a boulder a few inches away. He met her gaze.

"Ye are enjoying yourself."

A simple statement. Neither censure nor disbelief marred the words. A smile of delight slid across Maggie's face. Lifting her head, she unwound and braced her hands to either side. She arched her back, face to the stars. "Aye. This will suit me well."

Phillipe cleared his throat, a low rumble of sound that ignited a pleasant shiver over her skin. "Have ye thought of the suggestions I spoke of earlier?"

"Aye. Or, nae, though I dinnae know what else to say but to thank ye." She admired the stars then let her gaze drop to the man next to her, seeing much to admire there as well. A faint bubble of laughter rose along with a sense of utter well-being.

The mead. I drank too much mead. The thought both appalled and amused her.

Her gaze followed the lines of his tunic stretched taut across his shoulders, then to the rolled cuffs which revealed strong forearms. He'd removed his chain mail, and she realized she'd never seen him without it before.

I like ye better without the mail. Her eyes flew open wide. Had she spoken aloud?

She drew a soft, shuddering breath and glanced away. With an effort, she forced her attention back to his question. "I see the merit in yer plan, and though I dinnae know where the funds will come from, I will do all in my power to pay in a timely manner." She cast a furtive look at him beneath lowered lashes.

Phillipe's lips twitched.

Damn! She pinched her lips together between her teeth to hold the words back. *Saint Finnian's beard! I willnae drink mead again.*

"I did not wish to add salt water to the list of grievances when I next clean and oil my armor."

"Of course." Butterflies did somersaults in her belly. She *had* spoken aloud. "I cannae imagine brine improves the quality of steel."

"It does not," he agreed solemnly. He studied his hands a moment then glanced up. "I like ye better with yer hair tousled and laughter on yer lips."

Maggie's breath failed her. Words danced out of her reach. She swallowed. "I like dancing."

"Ye should always dance, m'lady. It becomes ye."

"I . . . I believe we are past *m'lady*. I am plain *Maggie*."

"Never plain . . . *Maggie*."

The bottom dropped from her stomach. Her name had never sounded so beautiful, so elegant—so sensual.

The mead. 'Tis surely the mead.

Heat rose, spreading up her neck and cheeks. Embarrassment. Longing.

He is a mercenary. He will be gone soon, and I have much to do here. Spending time in the arms of a man nae my husband would be ill-advised.

Her heart twisted against the words. She closed her eyes and fought her attraction to him.

Phillipe remained motionless, asking nothing of her. Had she imagined the drop in his voice as he spoke her name? She swallowed. She would not embarrass herself further by acting like a swooning lass.

"When will ye speak with Laird MacLean?"

Maggie's voice squeaked. She shivered lightly as if touched by a cool breeze. Blood flowed thick through Phillipe's veins, deepening his voice, thickening his cock. He didn't dare move for fear of drawing her attention to his state of arousal. How had his intentions veered so far off course?

I like ye better without yer mail. Sweet Jesu! Had she really said that? Or did the sight of her affect his ability to think? Thank God he hadn't spoken the first words that rose to his tongue.

I would like ye better without your clothes, flushed beneath my kisses.

He reined his thoughts back to the original conversation.

"I will sail with the birlinn on the morrow and make landfall at Morvern by evenfall."

Did she frown? What flashed in her eyes?

"I do not know when to expect an audience." *Other than immediately when the Baron receives my request.* He did not think he would be kept waiting. Their relationship had been too deep for political posturing between them. Whatever was taking place at MacLean castle, Phillipe did not imagine the baron would shunt him to the end of the line.

"Do ye trust me to form an alliance with Baron MacLean?"

With Maggie's thoughtful nod, his reservations of the task faded, replaced by the sight of the woman before him. 'Twas nigh impossible to look at her and not be overwhelmed by the urge to care for her, to sweep her into his arms and press his lips against her hair.

But he'd given up the privilege of caring for another, of offering himself without restraint. Atonement was not something he found within his grasp. He would not drag her into the sins of his past. He would see to it she had as bright a future as he could arrange for her. That would have to suffice.

A deep ache wallowed low in his belly, carving an empty place only Maggie could fill. His hands twitched, restrained from touching her only by the force of his will. His body leaned forward as if swayed by the wind. A little closer and he could smell her—kiss her.

No. He drew back, muscles resisting. He managed a small smile. "Thank ye for allowing my help."

Maggie blinked owlishly. Her lips parted and closed. He glanced away, gathering strength to treat her as a business partner, not as the woman he wanted more than any other before. He'd once been in love with a woman he could not have, then married against his will to a child whom he'd protected and cared for rather than loved. Maggie—lovely Maggie was completely different and touched him as no other woman had.

"For now, ye should have some funds available after the sale of the cyser. Ye should consider enlarging the orchard and increasing the production of the bee hives for more mead in the coming years. 'Tis a fine brew and I believe ye can create a demand for it beyond Morvern's shores."

Maggie clutched her skirt, fingers kneading the rough cloth. What would she look like draped in fine silks with jewels to match the fire of her hair? Once, he could have given her such things.

"I will speak with Asatrus and Gils on the morrow and see what must be done." She stared at him, longing on her face, bared by moonlight. "Ye will return?"

Hesitancy rode her voice.

"Aye, m'lady. Ye have my word."

She frowned. "I dinnae wish ye to call me that."

"The children call ye *freya—lady*."

"They are bairns." She lifted her chin. Her eyes flashed. "Ye arenae a bairn."

"Nae, sweet Maggie. I have not been a child for many years." He smiled at the challenge she offered. Did she know how little restraint remained in his control? "Upon my honor, I will return."

Chapter Twenty

Phillipe reached deep within, seeking calm buried beneath a jumbled mass of fear, destroyed expectations, and anger. Each slap of a wave against the ship's hull reminded him of his flight from Cilicia and the life he left behind.

All is as God wills.

He'd spoken to Balgair as if this were the holiest truth. Yet, he'd lived his life as it suited *him*, not always in the service of others as he'd been taught. His vows as a knight and as a king had sworn self-sacrifice to those in need. If his imprisonment in Sis Castle had been punishment for neglecting the good of the people of Cilicia, then it was on *his* head, not God's. He rather doubted The Almighty had a hand in Konstantin's demand for his death.

Helping Maggie could be a step toward atonement. One step in whatever time was granted him to do some good with his life. His narrow escape from death had to be for some greater purpose. To achieve this goal, he would be forced to face something that disturbed him more than Konstantin and his assassination plot. He would reveal his inadequacies and failures to the man who'd always been like a father to him. Phillipe was not certain he could survive the sorrow and disappointment in Baron MacLean's eyes.

A thousand ways to speak to the baron of the past three years paraded through Phillipe's mind. Starting. Stopping. Tempting him to abandon the task. Telling him how much easier it would be to travel north. South. Anywhere except Morvern. He stepped to the rail, gripped the wood until his knuckles whitened.

I will do this.

It helped to remember he'd already spoken to Alex, who'd encouraged him to return to Morvern.

Ye are more a brother to me, Alex, than any my father sired.

For a time, his thoughts returned to Maggie. She'd been tipsy on mead the previous night, her normal restraint delightfully absent. He smiled. It had led to an interesting conversation.

She likes me without my mail shirt. His smile widened. Her blunder showed plainly on her face, cheeks flushed with embarrassment when she realized she spoke aloud. He'd struggled to keep from responding— keeping the words to himself nigh impossible.

I would *love to see her naked. The statement would not have been a lie. Though, 'tis not the thing to say to a woman such as she. Such words make me no better than the men who pursue her.*

She was completely unexpected, her sweetness mingled with a strength of spirit that captured his heart.

If life had been different; if he hadn't followed his father's decree and married Zabel; if he hadn't once given his heart to Arbela . . ..

Had he not done those things, he would not have left the Holy Land. Would not have traveled to Scotland. Would not have met Maggie.

Evening wind swept through the strait, pushing the birlinn faster. It skimmed the tops of the waves, making short work of the distance to Morvern. Tall masts appeared as the boat rounded the point, each rooted within the bowels of ships resting at the quay. Birds wheeled overhead, fighting for the discarded bits of fish from the vessels that had returned from fishing. The birlinn shouldered between two larger ships and bumped gently against the protective camels, empty barrels lining the pier. Sailors hurried about, securing the vessel. Not waiting for the boarding plank to be placed, Phillipe leapt across the narrow space and stalked up the pier.

He retrieved his horse from the stable near the docks, delighted with her welcoming nickers and the gentle nudge of her nose in search of a treat. He pulled a bit of carrot from the pouch at his waist and she took it daintily. Her golden coat shone in the evening light, an indication of the care she'd received in his absence. After checking the girth on her saddle, he mounted the horse and rode up the winding road to the castle.

Torchlight flickered on the walls of MacLean Castle as he approached. Darkness would fall soon. People hurried about, the end of their day beckoning them homeward. The guards at the gate let him pass, but their scrutiny followed him like the warning tip of a blade against the back of his neck. He handed Avril to a stable lad, slipping him two coppers to assure she had extra oats, then strode to the imposing double doors of the great hall.

Maggie's face rose before him, reassurance for his next steps. One of the doors swung open, disgorging several people who spared him a curious glance as they passed. Aromas of roasted meats, the spice of cinnamon and cumin rose from platters on the tables in the hall and escaped the still-open door.

Instantly, Phillipe felt at home.

He stepped through the doorway, scanning the room, gaze settling on the people seated at the high table. Alex and a woman Phillipe did not know, her face drawn and thin. Two young boys, one perhaps two years of age, the other a handful of years older, sat between the woman and a man seated in a carved wooden chair, mid-table.

Baron MacLean.

His dark hair was shot with strands of silver, the once-red beard losing its battle to gray. He laughed at something a woman to his left said, the sound creating a swell of remembrance.

How many years did I enjoy at Baron MacLean's table? How many years of hearing his voice as I grew from a green youth to a knight?

He clenched his fists, warding off the pain of loss, bracing against what was to come.

Phillipe strode, chin up, shoulders square, to the head table. The baron half-rose from his seat, his chair legs scraping against stone. Silence fell.

Alex rose to his feet, his grin wide. "Welcome, Phillipe. 'Tis good to see ye."

The baron braced his hands on the table. His gaze questioned, faltered. "Phillipe?"

Phillipe dropped to one knee. "I beg your blessing, my father."

A fire blazed cheerfully in the hearth. Golden light danced on the walls of the baron's solar, highlighting shelves filled with books. Paintings hung in heavily carved frames. A costly rug of a design Phillipe recognized softened and warmed the stone floor. A tray of food and drink lay on a small, ornately worked table on one side of the room, the level of whisky in the flask lowered to a comfortable level. Donal MacLean, Alex, and Phillipe sat in cushioned chairs before the fire. Phillipe's confession left him hollow, drained. Exhausted.

Donal's low rumble broke the silence. "The only grief is that ye dinnae come to me sooner, Phillipe. And that I wasnae there to help ye. I question yer decision to nae speak to yer da, but . . .." Donal raised a hand, quelling Phillipe's attempted protest, "I understand how close to death at the hand of the Regent ye came, and I dinnae know if I would have acted differently."

Phillipe stared into the glowing coals at the base of the fire. "I should have done more to prevent their hatred."

Donal raised an eyebrow. "'Tis an important lesson, lad. People react when their families and religion are threatened. The church split a hundred and seventy years ago and never reconciled. Should ye change yer beliefs to suit others? 'Tis the larger sin, I believe. I willnae say ye are without fault, but 'tis past, and ye will learn from it. Come." He rose and strode to his desk then motioned Phillipe to follow.

Curious, and a bit lighter of heart, Phillipe stood and moved to the baron's side. Donal sorted quickly through a stack of scrolls. With a grunt, he pulled one to the center of his desk. Unrolling it with care, he weighted the corners, holding it open. Phillipe studied the map over the baron's shoulder, but it was of a place of which he had no knowledge. Scotland?

Donal tapped a spot in an area marked as the Sea of the Hebrides. A land mass lay to the east, a scatter of islands to the west and south.

"Lady Maggie's isle lies here." He pointed to a dot scarcely discernable on the map. "'Tis just south of Eigg . . .." His finger slid to the right. "And west of the peninsula." Silent a moment, a thoughtful tilt to his head, he mimed an arc along the northern edge of the land mass protruding into the sea then halted.

"Why did ye join her entourage, Phillipe? From all accounts, she is a fair lass, but to claim an isle—especially one such as Hola which is little more than an inconvenient bump in the sea—and attempt to hold it on her own?" His brow furrowed. "A few warriors and a ruined abbey arenae enough to protect her. She'd have been safer under her da's eye surrounded by high walls and scores of warriors."

"She chafed under the judging eyes and whispers of her clan and wished to claim her dowry, the one thing she believes she has control of. The isle is largely worthless, sir. Other than the notoriety of casting for the once-Countess of Mar, what would draw men to the place?"

Donal shrugged. "I know only that the entire region is riddled with pirates. We've routed them from our shores, but 'tis akin to chasing rats from the pantry. There are skirmishes from time to time, and if they'll brave *my* wrath, what keeps them from Hola?"

"'Tis why I asked for your help restoring the abbey . . .."

Alex rose and joined them. "'Twill be some time before the abbey is adequate, Phillipe. Even then, ye will need more soldiers to defend it." He tilted his head. "Is Hola capable of supporting such a force? How long will ye remain on the isle?"

"As long as Maggie . . .." Phillipe hesitated.

Alex and his father exchanged looks. "Another damsel in distress, eh?" Alex's voice teased.

Phillipe's neck heated. "What do ye mean? I've seen her skill with a crossbow and know she is cool-headed in battle. Lady Maggie is capable of taking care of herself."

Alex scoffed. "Ye've always had a heart for those who need yer help. Remember the cobbler's daughter? She was, what, twelve summers to yer seventeen?"

"Her father was ready to sell her to put food on their table." Phillipe's gaze narrowed. "Her entire family was starving."

"And so were ye until we realized ye took yer own food from the table—and what ye could wheedle from cook when she heard yer rumblin' stomach—and gave it to the lass." Alex glanced at his father. "Da was happy to assist once he set the man straight about his daughter. And what of Zabel? Ye've said ye did everything ye could to ensure she was protected *before* ye escaped." He shrugged. "Lady Maggie may be older, but she is in dire need of protection whether she will admit it or nae."

Phillipe glanced between the two men. His heart thudded in his chest. What drew him to Maggie? Was it naught but sympathy? No. It was something else. Something he'd dared not think too much upon, never mind speak aloud.

"I . . . 'tis more than that. But I cannot offer more than my friendship and protection. I have no name to give her, and no means to care for her. 'Tis certain the church will not support marriage on my behalf." He drew his shoulders back. "Before I leave her, I will see she is well-protected. I will find a solution."

"Lad." Donal's soft voice wavered between admonition and agreement. "The church isnae likely to support either of ye. A second marriage when both spouses yet live?"

Pain shot through Phillipe's chest. "'Tis not fair. She deserves more. She did not deserve to be set aside after only a year of marriage."

"Yet, none will give her fairness. Until she is safely bound to a strong man's care, she will remain vulnerable, prey for men who would see taking a former countess as proof of their strength." Donal peered at Phillipe. "Ye will ever be the son of my heart, Phillipe of Antioch. Ye have divested yerself of yer past life with just cause. I would help see to yer future if ye've a mind to humor an auld man."

Phillipe tilted his head. "What are ye considering, m'lord?"

"'Twould ease my mind . . .." He studied the map a moment. "Aha!"

Alex leaned against the table, an eager look on his face. "We need someone we can trust at our northern shore. MacDonnell hasnae proven loyal."

Donal nodded. "Aye. Land, men, and supplies are yers if ye would provide this service, Phillipe. Deeded to ye and yer heirs, bound to the MacLeans as family in truth, making ye and yers as though ye were blood."

Phillipe exhaled sharply. "I do not deserve this. I am now, and will forever be, outside the church—the very center of my honor. I have lost my way. I have no place in your house. There is much for me to do before I am reconciled—if ever."

"I claim whom I wish, Phillipe. Ye have always been as a son to me. 'Twould please me to recognize ye now. I know yer heart—have known ye from yer time as a lad fostering at Batroun, through yer knighting and more. I am an auld man, but I am not yet in my dotage."

Phillipe leaned heavily against the sturdy desk. "What ye offer is beyond . . . I am content with your blessing as I am beyond my sire's. This is far too much."

"I will determine the justness of my offer, lad," Donal admonished. He pinned Phillipe with a stare. "Will ye accept my offer—take my name as yer own and become my son?"

* * *

Rain sluiced over the stones and collected in puddles on the abbey floor. Maggie wrapped her arms about her waist, hugging her cloak close. The roof of the storeroom had been maintained with thick thatching to protect the mead, and from her vantage point in the doorway to the great hall, she was dry enough. Colyn sat on a perch Narfi had lashed together so she could take the falcon with her when she was at the abbey. Giving the post two extra legs allowed it to stand almost anywhere, and Maggie had been pleased with his thoughtfulness.

Narfi had blushed when she'd hugged him.

The scent of mud hung heavy in the air, overpowering the delicate aroma of honey and apples. Behind her, men from Hola checked the final batch, preparing it to be moved with the rest to a stone building near the harbor to await shipping to Morvern. The ship was due to arrive in two to three days, and though the rain hindered their ability to transport the mead to the harbor, she doubted the *dreicht* weather would cause the ship to be late.

At a corner of the abbey, opposite where a fallen slab created shelter from the rain, Dawe and Gunn maintained guard. On the promontory, two other men had built a small lean-to, their view of the waters surrounding the isle spectacular—and an easy point from which to keep watch. The other pair were likely sleeping, or perhaps eating. They would be expected to watch through most of the night. They were as safe as six men-at-arms could make them. Soon, thanks to Phillipe's efforts, their jobs would be easier.

Leana flounced onto an ancient bench that had likely sat at a dining table when the abbey was in use. At some point, the accoutrements of the hall had been either dismantled, taken to the longhouse to be used, or—in the case of the bench—set out of the way and forgotten. She scooped her skirts off the damp, dusty floor and tucked them about her feet.

"Do ye miss him?"

Maggie wanted to tell her to not be presumptuous, but she had struggled the past fortnight to make even the barest headway against being called *countess*, and to be accepted as one of the people of the isle. Was it fair to use her status only when Leana provoked her?

She pretended, instead, not to understand. "Who?"

Leana faced away, but Maggie still imagined the young woman rolled her eyes.

"He favors ye." Leana didn't bother to chase down Maggie's stalling tactics. "I've said it before, and now he's off to magically produce supplies and men to turn this pile of rocks . . ." she waved a hand about to indicate the ruined abbey, ". . . into a home worthy of ye."

"Into a home capable of protecting us all if necessary," Maggie corrected. "And 'tis money, not magic, that will bring them here."

Leana tilted her head. "The earl did ye nae favors—neither in marrying ye, nor in sending ye home with naught but an isle in exchange for a year of fillin' his bed."

"That's quite enough, Leana!" Maggie's face flamed, though the anger was divided equally between Leana for bringing up the past in such a manner, and the earl for making her words naught but the truth.

"Phillipe risks much for ye."

Curiosity—and a small measure of dread—overrode her pique. "How so?"

"'Twas something Balgair said." Leana's tone was flippant, daring Maggie to ask for more information.

"Tell me. What did he say to ye?"

"The twa met in Spain. In a brawl, actually." She sent Maggie a look from beneath her brows, eyes dancing. "He's a braw man, Balgair is. Talks a lot when he's relaxed."

"Leana!" Too late, Maggie realized how Leana had come by her knowledge.

Leana laughed. "I told ye Phillipe hadnae eyes for me—but Balgair does." She tossed her braid over her shoulder. "'Tis a shame he's gone. The men here . . .." She gave a one-shoulder shrug. "They arenae warriors."

"Sometimes that is a good thing. Not all men . . .." Maggie stopped her scold. Why should she rebuke Leana for wanting a man she felt could protect her?

"Phillipe was attacked aboard ship on his way to Spain. 'Tis where he got his scar. *A lucky strike from a middlin' fighter.*" Her voice dropped low to mimic Balgair's rumble then slipped back to her normal tone. "He says there's more to Phillipe than meets the eye. He's a well-trained warrior—as Balgair attests."

"I knew that. We've discussed this before."

"But something drove Phillipe from the Levant, of this Balgair is certain. He willnae say what, but Balgair said there is something in his recent past that has given him much sorrow."

Something was wrong at the inn. He wasnae happy when I found him speaking with Alex MacLean. Her heart leapt into her throat. *He's gone back to meet with him again—for me.*

Leana twisted to face Maggie, one eyebrow raised. "I'd bet ye a day of leisure this will become a place of beauty and service dedicated to its new owner."

Maggie frowned. "Mayhap I intend this to be a nunnery. In that case, its owner is still God."

Leana shook her head and settled again on the bench. "He will not like it if ye take vows." She gave a one-shoulder shrug. "'Tis yer life, but I still believe the Frenchman would share it with ye if ye offered."

Maggie shook her head. She'd declined a lifetime at an abbey with the earl's support. She'd scarcely take vows now. "'Tis much to think on. When he returns . . . ."

Will he return? A sharp pain stopped her breath. *He promised.* She turned her face to the sky and murmured a silent prayer for Phillipe's safety.

The rain ceased, becoming little more than a heavy mist. The dark orange of sunset pulsed just behind the silver veil. Maggie placed her forearm at Colyn's breast and he stepped from his perch to the leather bracer. She moved from the doorframe and stepped in a puddle turned gold by the last rays of evening. Men bustled about, hauling the heavy amphora on low sleds that slipped easily over the stone floor, leaving them massed at the doorway to the yard.

Gils paused, head drooping slightly with an apologetic air. "We will leave these here tonight and hope the morrow brings fair weather. Sloppin' these great pots through mud is difficult, as well as dangerous. Much more likely to drop one or two when the goin's rough."

His gaze caught hers then slid to one side. What did he not wish to tell her?

When he said naught else, Maggie nodded. "So be it. Half are already at the harbor. We've still a day or two until the ship from Morvern is expected." She ignored the fluttering in her chest at the thought of Phillipe's return. "Mayhap a better path could be constructed which would be easier to travel in all weather."

Gils sent her an encouraging smile and a bob of his head.

Recognizing the silent request for permission to leave her presence, Maggie waggled her fingers at him. "Let's see what Ingrida has created for our supper."

She tied the hood about Colyn's head then linked arms with Leana. Together they trailed the men through the path leading between the cliffs. Smoke rose, thick and heavy in the water-laden air.

It was not a cooking fire. She smelled only wood and peat, not the savory aroma of meat or fish. She dropped Leana's arm, glancing wildly about for a suitable perch for the falcon.

A bedraggled form loomed ahead, skinny arms flailing as he fled down the path.

"Halt!" Tears blended with the mists, creating rivulets that ran down his face.

"Narfi! What has happened?" Maggie's heart tripled its speed. Colyn squawked and gripped her arm, wings spread to counter her movements.

The lad glanced at her as the men from Hola bolted toward the longhouse. Dawe and Gunn reached for Maggie, but she stepped to Narfi and placed a hand on his shoulder.

Narfi's eyes were wide with worry and fear. "A ship approaches, freya."

"A ship? The ship isnae due for three days."

"Nae the one from Morvern." Narfi pulled Maggie's crossbow and quiver from his slim shoulder and his voice dropped. "Pirates."

Chapter Twenty One

Gunn swore. Dawe's hands hovered over his weapons. Maggie instantly deposited Colyn on an upright boulder. He squawked a protest as his talons skittered across the rough surface. She stripped away the leather bracer and slipped it over Narfi's forearm. As he'd seen Maggie do many times in the past fortnight, the lad quickly used it to retrieve the falcon. Maggie grabbed her crossbow and settled the quiver strap over her shoulder.

"M'lady," Gunn barked, "ye will go with Dawe to the abbey. We can secure ye there."

She sent Gunn a quelling look. "I willnae be *secured*. Ye may, howbeit, help me ensure the safety of the people of Hola."

Gunn swore again.

Maggie's eyes narrowed. "A woman and child are present. Mind yer tongue."

Gunn glanced at Leana and Narfi. A muscle in his jaw twitched.

Maggie's gaze slid back to the lad. "I thank ye for yer warning. Take Colyn and go to the caves with the others. Ye will be safe there."

"I can come with ye. Ye'll need my help."

Maggie blanched. She would not allow this child to be harmed. "Nae. I need ye to care for the falcon. Dinnae fail me."

Narfi scowled. Colyn batted his wings. White pin feathers fluffed with the movement, mingling with the long gray flight feathers that would soon cover his wings. Determination slanted Narfi's brow.

Gunn gestured to the lad. "M'lady, we dinnae have time . . .."

Maggie frowned her impatience at the man's insistence then spoke to the boy. "I must count on ye to care for Colyn if something happens to me."

Narfi gave a reluctant nod of acceptance, but Maggie wasted no time gaining further assurances. "Go to the caves. Take Leana with ye."

Narfi wheeled about and raced up the path, Leana at his heels.

Maggie offered the MacLaren soldiers an arch look. "Coming?"

They hurried down the trail, hesitating only long enough at the entrance to the field near the harbor to ensure no boats had entered the protected waters. A large bonfire lit the beach, crackling in the gloaming, sparks reaching high. Three men of Hola stood near the fire, eyes fixed on the harbor. Two MacLaren soldiers ranged farther distant, their gazes covering the cliffs. Gunn and Dawe approached one of the MacLaren soldiers who had been at guard on the promontory.

Maggie joined them. "What news, Gawan?"

The three soldiers sent each other questioning looks but did not challenge her right to be there. Callan arrived with a nod of apology for his lateness, his breath slightly quickened.

"Baen and I spotted a ship some distance off shore to the south." Gawan snorted. "Naught but MacDonalds and pirates that direction. This ship has a tall prow—and a striped sail. As soon as Igor caught sight of it, he scampered down to the longhouse and raised the alarm. Evan and Paden remain on the point with one of the older lads. They will send him with any further news."

Maggie clenched her fists, drawing on the pain as her nails bit into the soft flesh to slow her racing heart. "Where are the women and children?"

Callan jerked his head to one side. "They've gone to the caves." He glanced quickly about then lowered his voice. "There's somethin' goin' on. They dinnae bother fleeing when our ship approached. Why now?"

"We came from the north," Maggie mused. "And our birlinn carried a white sail."

Callan nodded. "Aye, but still, 'tis somethin' amiss."

The sun melted into the horizon, turning the sea to molten gold edged in sable. The bonfire on the beach burned brighter. The MacLarens kept away from the flames, their gazes on the harbor. Tension hung in the air.

Maggie glanced at each man, noted their stern faces. Hands hung loose, lightly flexed at their sides. If their ears could have moved, they would have swiveled to catch the sounds of the evening, parsing the bleat of the sheep on the far distant hill and shush of wind over the cliffs from the slap of water against the rocks—and against the hull of the ship sliding into the harbor.

Callan stepped before her, shielding her from sight of those aboard the birlinn as it glided ashore with a soft crunch of wood against stone. Maggie took a step to the side, but remained within Callan's shadow.

A red and white sail stretched across the ship's yard, casting a shadow over the rippling water. A man stood at the bow, legs splayed to counter the roll of the ship. Two men leapt over the side, boots clattering on the pier, then parted as the first man—possibly their leader—joined them.

The three men of Hola shrank back. Callan tensed. Maggie restrained him with a touch to his arm. "Nae. If they keep secrets, let us discover what they are. Give this a moment to play out."

"I estimate ten to twelve men aboard," Dawe murmured.

Callan's shoulders relaxed. The odds were fair. Maggie removed her hand and rested it lightly on the stock of her crossbow, reassured by its solid, familiar form. She breathed deep, settling into a watchful state, every muscle alive, sight sharpened.

Flanked by his two comrades, the first man reached the shore.

* * *

Phillipe glanced at the wooden crates stacked to one side of the merchant ship, tied fast with sturdy rope to create a makeshift stall for Avril. She tossed her head, silver mane flowing like silk over her golden neck, and Phillipe felt a jolt of pride.

A beautiful reminder of a friendship renewed. Baron MacLean had been pleasantly surprised to discover Phillipe had purchased the horse and withdrawn his offer of his choice of beast from the MacLean stables. The baron's Andalusian stock was prime horseflesh—but the half-blood Turkoman horse recalled his life in the Levant. And Arbela.

I am pleased she has found a husband to love. He grinned. Alex had assured him if it was necessary to remind Caelen MacKern how to treat his wife, Phillipe would be invited to attend the lesson.

Mayhap 'tis best I do not visit Arbela until more time has passed.

His thoughts turned to the baron's generosity. Land. *The wherewithal to support a family. Would that include Maggie?* In Scotland, according to Alex, simply stating one was a husband or a wife was considered binding. It seemed untoward to join with a woman without the church's blessing. Would Maggie accept such an irregular marriage?

Contentment swept over him, dispelling the mild regret which had been simmering since the past evening meal. His last meal with the MacLeans and his final words with the baron.

Tend to the isle, Phillipe. I count on the shipment of mead. Donal MacLean's grin attested to whose table at least part of the mead graced. *Take what time ye need. The land will be waitin' for ye.*

He had a chance at a new life with people he loved. What more could he ask?

The hollow clop of hooves on wooden planks caught Phillipe's attention. A flash of bristling red beard passed with a murmur of gentle encouragement to the sturdy horse crossing to the ship's deck.

"Balgair?"

The man peered over the horse's neck. A grin split his face. "Aye?"

Phillipe fell into step as his friend led his horse to a second make-shift stall. "Ye were heading back to Oban, mayhap your home." He did not frame the statement as a question, simply let the implied query dangle.

Balgair tugged the knot securing his horse inside the stall then waved a dismissive hand in the air. "Och, why linger for weeks in search of a bit of work that may or may not be suitable? I have a friend who needs me help." His grin returned. "Dinnae fash. I'll be out of yer hair before ye grow weary of me."

Delighted to learn the sturdy Scot would be accompanying him back to the isle, Phillipe shot an arm about the man's shoulders and gripped him tight before releasing him.

Balgair staggered two steps across the deck, fingers splayed in either mock surrender or half-hearted warning. "I cannae leave ye to muck up what promises to be a striking new fortification—or a beguiling new romance."

Phillipe drew up short. He blinked. "What do ye mean?" A thought struck him. "Ye and Leana?"

"Och, ye are such a *bawheid*. Leana kens she has nae hold on me." Balgair fixed Phillipe with a stare. "I speak of ye and the lovely Countess."

Shock washed over him, tempered by the swell of truth and new purpose to his life. Phillipe rubbed his jaw. "I will not pressure Lady Maggie." He leveled a frank gaze on his friend. "Howbeit, ye should know one thing for certain."

"What is that?"

"She is no longer the countess—and will thank ye to remember it."

"Och, I but jest. She owns the isle and its people—who have given her their hearts. She's a lady and a bonnie lass, for certes. Ye couldnae do better—though ye havenae her rank. Still, ye'd be a right *daftie* to nae pursue her."

Phillipe mulled his friend's words. His mind caught on the memory of her before he'd left the isle. Bright red hair tousled by the breeze and her exertions in the dance. Perched atop a small rock, the surf lapping near her feet. Her lips parted as she studied him.

I like ye better without yer mail.

Pleasure welled inside and he could not stop the grin which spread across his face.

The boarding plank screeched then clattered as a sailor shoved it to the deck. A pair of sails flapped above, stretching to catch the wind. The merchant vessel creaked as it rocked against the waves pushing the ship. Phillipe bent his knees slightly to absorb the gentle rise and fall beneath his feet. He and Balgair stepped to the bow.

The *Saorsa* slipped from the harbor and entered the Strait of Mull, catching the current in earnest. Waves grew, shoving the ship between the isle and the mainland as if it had sprouted wings.

Sailors' voices rose in a chant, a solitary voice joined by others on the chorus.

One day when I was on the misty mountain, I saw a wonderful sight.
Far al a leò ro ho bhi ò
Hoireann is ò ho rò bhi o ho
Hi rì ho ro ho bha ò hug ò ro

The Clan MacNeill's ship passed by; away from MacLean country,
Far al a leò ro ho bhi ò . . ..

Toward joyful Kisimul where the feasting takes place,
Far al a leò ro ho bhi ò . . ..

Drinking wine from night to day . . ..

Balgair leaned against the rail then nodded to the stores and the eight men seated upon the crates. "MacLean approved of yer venture?"

"Aye." Memory of the baron's enthusiasm over Phillipe's request lightened his heart further. "I feared for a moment he would head the project himself."

"How could this be a bad thing? The Baron is influential and has deep pockets."

"Truth. Howbeit, I need to clear my head and accomplish this on my own—or as near to it as I can using MacLean materials and workmen."

"Fair enough." Balgair's voice trailed off, inviting further explanation.

"I fostered with the Baron as a youth. When he and his family returned to Scotland, my life took on a shape of which I feared he would not approve. Though I have left that life behind and I sought this land as solace, I kept from his household as a form of penance."

Balgair's eyebrows broached his hairline. "Fostered? Lad, I've never mistook ye for a crofter, but to foster with a baron would mark ye a nobleman's son."

Phillipe grimaced. He hadn't intended to expose so much. "My father is, or was, of some consequence," he admitted. Choosing to place his father in the past aligned with the fact he never would hold a conversation with him again. In every respect, he was dead to his father—and his father to him. Baron MacLean's friendship now made all the more dear.

Balgair's lips twisted thoughtfully. "Many Frenchmen have traveled to the Holy Land to defend Jerusalem from the Saracens."

"Aye. With varying degrees of success. Some made homes there. I chose to leave and follow the MacLeans here. His son and I were once great friends."

"I have heard the baron is a fair man."

"Indeed. My fear of his reception was ill-founded."

Balgair clapped his shoulder. "I am pleased for ye, my friend. I look forward to working alongside a man who nae longer wears such a long face." He braced his forearms over the rail. "Ye are a braw fighter, but moody enough when ye grow silent."

Phillipe laughed, and a bit more weight fell from his shoulders. "'Tis what I like best about ye—ye say what ye mean. 'Tis a good trait in a friend."

Balgair shot him a grin. "'Twill all work out, now that ye've a bit of humor about ye."

Phillipe nodded to the horizon. "Heavy clouds may indicate a bit of wet weather ahead. I hope 'tis not enough to bother the horses."

"Och, dinnae fash over the weather. 'Tis a fine ship and she'll nae tip us into the sea. We'll be at Hola in a few hours. The only thing the captain has to worry about is pirates." Balgair shrugged. "Who would challenge a MacLean ship?"

Chapter Twenty Two

Dusk overtook the beach. Asatrus stood his ground as the three pirates stepped from the rough pier. Igor moved closer, aligning with his leader. Maggie and the MacLarens kept to the shadows behind the men of Hola, beyond the glow of firelight. Maggie lowered her crossbow from her shoulder and drew the string, the gentle creak of wood lost in the soft crunch of sand beneath the men's boots. She settled a bolt along the groove atop her bow and nocked the end of the bolt against the string, keeping her fingers well clear of the trigger. She stroked the feather fletching and waited for the coming conflict.

The strangers halted within the light of the bonfire. Orange light licked at them, casting dark shadows along the ridges of brow and nose. The one in the middle, his hair a tangle of long dark strands decorated with tiny beads that glittered in the firelight, crossed his arms over his chest, planting his feet in the sand with a confident swagger.

"Where are the barrels, auld man?"

Maggie's gaze cut to Asatrus who shuffled his feet in a moment of seeming indecision. He peered from side to side, but the glare of the fire would have stolen his night vision, and he gave no indication he could see the MacLarens. He gave a slow shrug.

"'Tis been a poor year, Arrick."

Poor year? Maggie's ire rose. What was going on? How did he know the man's name? How often did pirates reach these shores?

Arrick waved a hand. "Pah! I dinnae care what yer harvest is like. We are here to collect our tithe. One tun of mead—or would ye rather we make free with yer other property to make up the loss?"

A *tunweight*? 'Twould be half their brew for this season! Small wonder Hola was considered of no account from a monetary viewpoint.

Without gold or precious gems—that she knew of, and she was beginning to wonder what secrets were left to uncover—Maggie did not linger to wait for the man to explain further. She knew, even with the women and children tucked inside the caves, they would become the *tithe* these men sought. Slavery was not unheard of and it would not take long for their hiding place to be discovered.

Dodging Callan's grasp, Maggie stepped into the edge of the firelight, the tip of her crossbow angled toward the ground.

"The property here—is mine."

Callan and Dawe moved to flank her, drawing the strangers' attention. The leader of the pirates shot a look over his shoulder then back to the MacLarens—weighing the odds?

The odds were against him. Though he did not know of the MacLaren soldiers still outside the reach of the firelight, his own men were several seconds away aboard their ship. Seconds in which he and his two comrades would likely die. They clearly had not expected any hindrance to their plan.

"Who are ye?" He tried for bluster.

Maggie raised her weapon, her grip steady. "I am the woman with a crossbow aimed at yer chest. This isnae open for discussion."

More looks were exchanged. Boots shuffled against the sand. Hands hovered close to weapons, not ready to spring an attack, but not willing to give way to a mere woman's challenge.

The leader—Arrick—scowled. "MacDonnell owns this isle."

"And lost it in a game of chance to the Earl of Mar more than a year past," Maggie replied, her tone dry. "Move yer hands from yer weapons, or I will pin ye to yon ship."

Callan and Dawe stepped closer, adding their support to Maggie's command. Firelight danced over half-drawn swords. Two other MacLaren soldiers shifted behind them, silhouettes in the darkness. The pirates again exchanged looks.

Arrick jerked his chin toward the men in the shadows. The gold beads in his hair flashed. "We've nae come to harm anyone." He opened his arms expansively, showing empty hands. "The good people of the isle set aside a wee bit o' mead for us each year, 'tis all. We're here to collect."

"There'll be nae more collecting," Callan rumbled. He nodded to the ship, its hull a stain in the darkness, its shadow a blot against the water sparkling in the rising moonlight. "Ye arenae welcome in this harbor."

"'Tis a sad day when a man cannae visit a friendly isle," the pirate remarked. "Mayhap the change in ownership wasnae a good thing."

"*Mayhap* 'tis nae yer concern," Maggie replied. "'Tis nae a fight ye can win. I am responsible for this isle and its people." She tilted her head to Callan. "As he said, ye arenae welcome here. Find harbor elsewhere."

The pirate bowed deep. "As ye wish, m'lady. Until better times."

The three spread hands waist-high then plodded across the boards back to their ship. Their boots thudded on the deck as hands reached over the rail to help them aboard. Moments later oars slipped free and slapped the water. The ship pulled away from the pier.

A shout rang from the pirate's ship. A lad raced around the corner of the longhouse, skidding to a stop with a gasp at the threat of Gawan's sword. Maggie's attention swept from the harbor to the lad. Gawan lowered his weapon and shoved the lad into the midst of Callan's small group.

"Evan and Paden have spotted another ship."

Phillipe chafed at the lateness of the hour. The sun dipped into the western seas, leaving the isle of Hola silhouetted against the pale gold and amethyst sky.

He stood at the bow, anxious to see Maggie. Had she thought of him? Might she have missed him? Would she still be awake? The sun lingered late this time of year, and most people would likely be abed. Would the watch on the promontory alert her, or leave her to sleep?

Balgair joined him at the rail. "Wonderin' how she made out with ye nae here?"

Phillipe wasn't certain if the Scot teased him or if it was that clear what was on his mind. He shrugged. "'Tis certes she is well. She is protected by her own soldiers."

Balgair's low hum of response could have been anything from agreement to speculation. Phillipe didn't ask.

His friend shifted to lean his back against the rail. "How long before 'tis known the former countess is in residence?"

Phillipe frowned. "We will see to it the rumors and any foolish actions are quickly quelled."

Balgair offered a one-shoulder shrug. "I like yer confidence, laddie." He nodded to the MacLean men scattered about the ship. "We'll put these men to work at sun-up on the morrow. 'Twillnae take long before we have m'lady a new manor house and better protection."

A voice rang from aloft. "Ship in the harbor!"

The captain of the *Saorsa* joined Phillipe and Balgair a moment later. "A ship has been sighted, under weigh to open water. We shall wait until they clear the mouth to the harbor. The lad aloft has sharp eyes to catch sight of them in the gloaming." He nodded in satisfaction of a job well done.

"Do ye recognize the ship?" Worry nudged the back of Phillipe's mind, setting up a whirl of alarm in his belly.

The captain grunted. "In this light and at this distance, I wouldnae know me own ma. As the ship approaches, I will take a look."

Phillipe understood, yet chafed at the lack of information. The strange ship angled through the mouth of the harbor, its sail turning to reveal red and white stripes. It's long, low hull skimmed the waves. The drumbeat keeping pace of the oars rang across the water, quickening its tempo. A tall man, long tendrils of hair lifting in the breeze, stood amidships.

"Damned pirates!" The captain turned from the rail, shouting to the men on the *Saorsa*. "Look lively, lads! We'll nae be sittin' ducks for the likes of them!"

Phillipe glanced to Avril, reassured she was still safely ensconced in her makeshift stall. He wore his chain mail beneath his cloak and his weapons were all to hand, but he fingered them swiftly, lightly touching each to ensure their proper positions and that none had settled too deep in their sheaths. From the corner of his eye, he saw Balgair following the same ritual.

MacLean soldiers hustled about the deck, drawing bows and quivers of arrows from deep chests stored aft. Sailors manned their stations, climbing rigging with the graceful ease of long practice. The *Saorsa* pulled hard to larboard as the other vessel rounded the tip of the harbor to the right. Tension swirled through the salt air. Phillipe tore his gaze from the pirate ship and peered into the darkness, straining to see around the rocks protecting the harbor. A golden glow warmed the night.

Fire.

Balgair nudged him. "It may only be a bonfire."

Phillipe swallowed past a knot in his throat. "'Tis not . . .."

Balgair shook his head. "Give it a moment. We will know for certes in a moment or twa."

A cold sweat broke out on Phillipe's brow. He fingered the pommel of his sword, lightly tapped the grip. His jaw clenched and it took physical strength to relax his muscles and steady his breath.

The pirate vessel cleared the harbor. The *Saorsa* sat just beyond the entrance, lingering outside the enclosed waters.

Impatience flashed through Phillipe, though he knew the captain was cautious, likely worried about a trap.

"The longhouse doesnae appear to be aflame," Balgair grunted. "They've a gey bonfire on the shore."

Phillipe nodded jerkily, relief flooding him, setting up a fine tremor in his muscles.

What had happened? Did the people of Hola partner with the pirates? Had they welcomed them—or did they have reason to fear them? How long had the pirates remained on the isle? What had caused them to leave?

He slammed his fist down onto the rail, needing the pain to distract him from the things he could not control. He could not put the *Saorsa* and her crew in possible danger in order to reach shore faster. He could not change what had already happened between the pirates and the islanders.

But if Maggie was injured and he wasted a single moment . . ..

Balgair settled a palm on Phillipe's shoulder, startling him from his dark thoughts.

"Ye will be ashore anon. Dinnae fash. Ye left good men here to protect her, and a plan for her safety should the need arise."

Phillipe grunted. "Ye believe she went to the caves with the women and children when the pirates were sighted?"

His friend sighed. "Nae. At least, nae willingly. She's a braw lass, no denying. But she's got a good head on her shoulders, as well. Believe the best, lad. Dinnae waste yer energy on worrying on the worst."

"I know better than to despair over something I cannot change."

"Aye. When ye care for someone, things are different."

The deck shifted beneath their feet. The boards groaned as the ship entered the harbor, angled somewhat across the waves as they approached the small pier. Gulls launched into the air, shrieking their usual demands. The fire on the beach grew brighter. Two men Phillipe recognized from Hola stood closest to the flames. Four burly MacLarens marked a forbidding line in the sand.

In their midst, crossbow angled slightly down and to her left, stood Maggie. Tall, strong, clearly unharmed—yet . . .. Phillipe gritted his teeth. He had no authority over her. No right to tell her she should have gone to the caves with the women and children. Yet, he wanted to yell at her to not be such an idiot as to face down pirates with a crossbow.

His breath escaped in a snort of anger. Anger which had no other convenient outlet. He spoiled for a fight. He clenched his fists and rocked with the roll of the ship as it bumped against the pier. Men hurried about with their tasks. Phillipe stalked to Avril's stall. She snorted and rolled her eyes, ears flicking back and forth. He waited until she settled, aware his anger had upset the horse.

"'Tis not your fault, Avril," he murmured, stroking her nose as she calmed. "Let us depart this ship and place our feet on solid earth."

He tugged gently on the lead rope. With only a token resistance, the mare followed him. Men lit torches along the path, pushing back the darkness.

Hylnur met him at the end of the pier. The boy's eager face glowed. "Might I care for her? I've a good hand with animals."

With a nod of agreement, Phillipe handed Avril to Hylnur then strode across the sand, closing the distance between himself and Maggie with hard, sure strides.

"'Tis good to see ye, Phillipe," she murmured. She removed the bolt from her crossbow and placed it into her quiver before releasing the string.

Phillipe stared at the weapon, remembering another time and place—another woman who would have done the exact same thing. Pirates would not faze Arbela, either.

"M'lady. Baron MacLean was most generous in men and supplies to rebuild the abbey." He nodded to the crates as men carried them to the store house just beyond the pier. "Foodstuffs as well to feed the extra mouths. Wood for floors and for support timbers. Tools. We will offload what we can tonight and finish in the morn."

The words fell stiff and formal. He couldn't help it. If he gave a single inch, he feared he would crush her in his arms, telling her with his body how much he'd feared for her, and how grateful he was she lived—or scold her like a parent with a particularly unruly child—or both.

With a jerk of her chin, she led him away from the others, where they would not be remarked or overheard.

"Ye are angry."

"I did not expect to see ye challenge pirates."

Maggie blinked. "Why not? Hola is my responsibility."

Phillipe scowled. He glanced down, only to snap his gaze back to hers. "Ye are not mine to command." He drew a deep breath then sighed. "And if ye were, I would worry over your safety as I proudly watched ye stride into battle."

"Ye arenae vexed with me?"

He lifted a hand, his fingers tangling gently in the strands of hair curving about her chin. "I am vexed with not being here or having fortifications in place—leaving ye unprotected. Yet, even though my heart nearly expired at the thought of ye threatened by pirates, and I almost leapt from the ship when I saw ye on the beach—instead of sheltering with the women and children—I admire your honor and courage."

A smile softened Maggie's mouth, relaxed her shoulders. "I thank ye for understanding. 'Tis not my intent to have others fight my battles."

"I wouldn't have it otherwise, *mon coeur*. Though I do not wish to see ye facing down a band of pirates again. Let us hope they do not return."

Her brow dipped and her smile vanished. "I dinnae believe ye will get yer wish. From what I gather, the pirates have made Hola a regular stopping point for years. If I were to make a prediction, I would say they *will* return—soon."

Chapter Twenty Three

Fine wisps of clouds brushed the sky, fading from pink to white as the sun climbed. Rocks dotted the hillside that formed one edge of the field. The grass, cropped short by grazing sheep, crunched beneath Maggie's feet. Phillipe's mare and Balgair's gelding stood apart from the wooly sheep. The MacLean ship rocked gently in the harbor. Thin trails of pungent peat smoke drifted from the thatched roof of the longhouse, the scent faint on the salt-laden breeze. Colyn's shriek rode high in the clear air.

"Have a wee bit of patience, laddie," she chided, struggling to keep her mind on her task. Men traced the path from ship to shore where a growing stack of supplies marred the landscape. Sunlight winked on a bit of metal before Phillipe's cloak shifted in the breeze to cover his mail, reminding Maggie of the pirates' visit the previous evening. Wearing the armored protection meant he did not believe the danger was past. She considered the three daggers hidden in sheaths at her waist, forearm, and thigh. Neither did she.

What will happen if they return before our defenses are ready?

Colyn shrieked again. She shifted the bird to the twisted branch of a low tree, careful to tie his jesses before removing his hood. The slender leather creance trailed from one leg, though the training lead would soon be removed and the bird allowed to fly free. Her heart sped at the thought.

"Ye've grown apace, me *tottie* bird. A beauty ye are, even if ye havenae quite all yer feathers in. Soon, laddie, soon."

She pulled a hunk of raw meat prepared with a twist of brown feathers from the pouch at her waist and deftly tied it to the lure, her back to the falcon so he wouldn't see her actions. Quickly hiding a second, featherless piece in her gloved fist, she tossed the lure to the ground. Colyn cocked his head and ruffled his wings, gaze intent on his prey. Maggie tugged the string attached to the lure, making it twitch. Colyn crouched. Maggie dragged the lure, flipping it across the ground, inviting him to chase it. With a flap of wings, he leapt from the low perch, tottering a bit as he swept through the air. He struck the lure with a snap of sound, curving his wings forward for balance and to hide the food he'd just caught. His beak tore at the meat and he gulped it down.

Maggie knelt beside the bird and gave a low whistle, offering her glove. Colyn stepped to her arm as he had so many times in the past weeks. He quickly sought the meat hidden in her fist and she wound the trailing ends of his jesses through her fingers to keep him from leaping from her hand once he'd finished.

Footsteps warned of an approach. Maggie glanced up. Phillipe halted a few feet away, a question reflected in the tilt of his head. She stared at him hungrily. His leine was made of wool so fine it fell elegantly over his broad shoulders and moved with every breath. Trews wrapped his muscular legs, disappearing into boots which rose to his calves. The memory of his return the night before swept through her. The reason she'd scarcely slept. He'd called her *my heart*.

"Ye have done well with the falcon." His voice rumbled, warm velvet.

"Thank ye." She stroked the soft feathers on the falcon's breast, searching wildly for something else to say.

I am verra glad ye have returned.

I counted the days.

Please say ye willnae leave again.

She caressed the supple leather lead dangling from the bird's leg. "He is almost ready to allow off the creance." *Coward.*

Something flickered in Phillipe's eyes. He nodded and moved closer. "Aye. The first time will be the most difficult. Not knowing what will happen. Will he return to ye or will he discover his freedom?"

He touched her cheek as he had the night before. Heat blossomed over her skin. His hand fell away and he took a step back. "Come. Show me the caves. I did not expect to need them so soon and wish to know if they are defensible."

"Give me a moment to place Colyn in the sheep fold and ask Narfi to keep an eye on him. I'm using the shed as a mews whilst the sheep are at pasture." Maggie hurried down the path, Phillipe matching his stride to hers. "Not that we've many predators on the isle, but the occasional company keeps him attuned to people. Narfi has been a lot of help."

She bit her lip to slow her rambling speech. Her step faltered and she glanced at Phillipe. "I missed ye."

Better.

His lips curved upward and the skin crinkled at the corners of his eyes. "I missed ye as well."

Happiness swept over her and she ducked her head to hide her smile. He shouldn't affect her so. He was a mercenary—albeit a well-spoken one—pledging his sword where he willed. She was a cast-off wife who had failed to give her husband a child. A pang lodged mid-chest. She swallowed and cast a glance at Phillipe. He knew why she was here—likely knew the entire tale as it was no secret. The church condemned her. Even other women found her lacking. Yet, when he looked at her, he smiled.

The knot in her breast unraveled, then vanished. The sun shone a wee bit brighter, the salt tang in the air sharpened. A gentle breeze kissed her neck and teased an errant strand of hair. A weight lifted from her heart and she settled Colyn in the make-shift mews with a smile she couldn't seem to control.

She shielded her eyes as she exited the dim interior of the shed and immediately caught sight of Phillipe chatting with Narfi.

The lad gave her an amiable nod. "I'll keep an eye on the wee bird, freya. Dinnae fash."

"I thank ye, Narfi. We're going to take a look at the caves."

Her attention could not linger on the lad. Phillipe tugged at her awareness, banishing the presence of all others. His dark, hooded eyes, his lean cheeks and close-cropped beard, nose slightly hooked—beckoned her. He was mysterious and exciting. And he'd set aside the pain of his past to help her.

They followed the path the women and children had trod the day before seeking safety. The earthy scent of decay rose from the mud. Maggie slid on the trampled, rain-slicked grass. Phillipe caught her elbow, steadying her as she regained her balance.

"Thank ye." She sent a glance to the silent man at her side. He gave her a brief nod and set her back on her feet.

Maggie indicated the cliffs a short distance away. "I've been to the caves only once—to learn where they are should the need arise." She frowned. "I dinnae expect . . . pirates."

Phillipe's hand lingered on her elbow. "The people had not mentioned them. Asatrus's explanation last night was unsatisfying. I understand I was not on the isle long enough to learn everything, yet I felt we had gained their trust—or I would not have left ye."

"The pirates have apparently forced them to their bidding for a number of years, without recompense. No one beyond the isle queried their safety, only their ability to tithe to whomever claimed ownership. Though I admit I find it troublesome to realize after a fortnight here, they had not confided in me."

Phillipe released her arm. "Mayhap they hoped we would provide protection before the pirates arrived this year. Asatrus and his men seem to know little of defense, and the fact they rely on retreating to a cave to protect themselves . . .." He shook his head. "They are not warriors."

They rounded the point without further mishap. The sea lapped noisily against the shore, slapping against boulders before sliding upon the rock-strewn sand in a lacy froth. Seals eyed them from the finger of coastline a short distance away, safely tucked in their rookery. Gray coats splotched with white blended with the dark cliffs streaked with bird droppings. Their coloration would have made them unremarkable on the rocky shore, but their barks of warning and ungainly movements drew Maggie's attention.

"They should give birth in the next month or so," she said. "Then the breeding season will start and I've been told we'll hear the males fighting clear on the other side of the isle."

Phillipe chuckled. "Males brawling over females is never a quiet affair."

"'Tis a *gey wheen* of seals making enough noise without there being squabbling males," Maggie quipped. Her merriment slipped. "Narfi said they'll wait until the pups are weaned before hunting the seals for meat and skins."

"This troubles ye?"

"A bit," she admitted. "I understand the need and they have always done so, but my sympathy lies with the seals."

"Mayhap ye can offer a different solution. Bring in looms to help weave the wool the sheep provide. Import wool if necessary. Simply because they have always hunted the seals does not mean 'tis the only way." He nodded to the rocks. "'Tis dangerous for the hunters as well."

"I had focused on the orchard and mead production. There is much I need to learn. So many things to accomplish."

"I am pleased to offer any assistance ye need."

Maggie sighed and leaned against a boulder. "How long before the abbey is completed?"

Phillipe's steps slowed. He faced her. Stopped. "We should discuss this."

She tilted her head, a frisson of alarm sending warning tingles down her spine. "Why? What has changed?"

He stepped close. He took her hands, lifted them. Gently squeezed her fingers. "My lady, when I left the isle, my only goal was to see to the rebuilding of the abbey, to give ye a place to live and to ensure ye were protected when 'twas time for me to leave."

Maggie's heart lurched. She did not want to listen to his concerns, his misgivings. That he would someday leave. Her fingers curved, gripping his. His thumb moved gently over the backs of her hands, soothing. She sighed, easing her grip. Phillipe caught her gaze, held it as he drew her hands upward. He kissed the backs of her hands, his breath warm on her skin. Her breath fluttered in surprise. With deliberate slowness, he lowered them, not relinquishing his hold.

"I lied to myself. And, therefore, to ye. 'Tis my desire we have truth between us. Are ye willing to listen?"

Phillipe turned her hands over, opening her palms to his gaze. Callouses lined the soft skin at the base of her fingers. Another protected the thick muscle beneath her thumb. She believed in working hard for her dreams. He loved this about her.

The pulse quickened in Maggie's throat, the blue line clearly visible beneath her pale skin. Her lips parted. Closed. She lifted her chin. "Aye. I would hear what ye have to say."

"When I arrived in Scotland, the prospect of explaining my presence to Baron MacLean overwhelmed me. 'Twas cowardly, yet I chose to not approach him or his family, though they had been more than my own kin to me for many years."

"Ye approached them for my sake." Appreciation warmed her voice.

Phillipe ghosted a smile. "Aye. Though I gained much more than help for ye." His smile broadened, remembering the baron's welcome. The unexpected peace. And hope?

"Tell me," Maggie urged.

"I did not receive the censure I deserve. The baron listened and offered the wisdom he has always shown. When I spoke of your needs, he proved more than willing to assist ye." Phillipe drew a deep breath. He was fairly certain Maggie wasn't going to like what he said next. "But he does not believe this is a good plan."

Her scowl wasn't as deep as he'd feared, and she did not pull away from him. Her gaze, however, threatened mutiny. "I willnae return to my da."

"Ye should have walls and warriors to protect ye." He spoke the words, seeing them unexpectedly from her view. *Walls to cage ye. Warriors to see that naught ever touches ye again. Not fear or hope. Neither hatred nor love.* That was not the life he wanted for her.

He placed both of her hands in one of his. He drew the fingertips of his free hand across her cheek, sweeping slowly across the flush spreading from her neck to her ears. He touched a strand of flame-red hair, startled when the coil did not burn.

"All my life I've studied warfare, and I agree with the baron. If I design a heavily fortified keep, ye would need more than a score of men to defend it. For a time, the outer defenses would suffice. But sooner or later, someone would decide breaching the walls is a challenge he could not resist. And ye would not be able to outlast the siege, for there is not enough foodstuffs and water to feed the warriors needed." He studied her face, the subtle denying shake of her head.

"Maggie, *mon coeur*, without ye here, 'tis likely the pirates would be the only threat. A problem a handful of warriors can manage. Your presence is another matter. Ye cannot remain on Hola."

Her lips thinned, bitterness furrowed her brow. "Ye ask me to give up my freedom, my chance to make a new life."

"Nae, I ask ye to change your plan, protect the people of Hola, exchange your dream for another."

"Without Hola, there is naught for me."

Her despair tore at his heart. That she did not rant against his words told him she knew he told the truth. "I know ye would give your life for the people of Hola, though ye know little of them."

"But if I remain, I ask them to give their lives for me?" Anger flickered in her eyes. "Where do I go, Phillipe? What must I do to escape the curse leveled against me when the earl cast me aside?"

"Marry me, Maggie. Become my wife and I will protect ye and give ye new dreams."

Chapter Twenty Four

"Marry ye?" The words spilled in a whoosh of disbelief before she could stop them.

Phillipe raised a brow. "'Twould not be the hardship ye seem to envision."

Maggie swallowed, pulled her hands free. She flattened them against the cold stone at her back. "I dinnae know what to say."

"Might I hazard the thought ye care for me a bit? Ye did say ye'd missed me."

A teasing glint lit his eyes.

"I willnae deny it." She glanced down, then back to him from beneath her lashes. "There is something between us that speeds my heart. Compels me to listen for yer step."

"And what else, *mon coeur*?" Phillipe eased closer until the hem of her gown fluttered intimately about his feet.

Maggie's skin tingled. Her lips parted, silent words pouring forth.

It pulls me to yer presence—yers and none other's—begs for yer touch—for yer kiss.

As though he'd heard all she hadn't said, Phillipe's head lowered until his lips skimmed hers. Rough silk. Coarse hairs of his beard lightly tickled her skin. The sensation was exhilarating—and completely unsatisfying. Maggie leaned closer, needing the fullness of his touch, the heat of his mouth. His lips firmed beneath hers, parted slightly. Their tongues touched, polite query, then tangled in a flurry of passion.

She pressed against him and his arms encircled her waist, pulling her tight.

A moment later, he released her. "This . . . this will require more honesty, Maggie. A story ye must know before ye answer me yea or nae."

Reality flooded Maggie in an icy wave. "I must tell ye, Phillipe, I am certain the church wouldnae bless us if I accepted yer offer. The church stood firmly on the earl's side when I was told I should retire to a nunnery and live my life in penance for my failure as a woman. Because I refused, I was assured I am outside the favor of God."

Phillipe's jaw clenched. Damn! Damn the earl and damn the people who'd convinced Maggie any failure was hers alone to bear. The smiles and laughter he'd witnessed from her since they'd landed on Hola were more precious than he'd ever known.

He tucked a crooked finger beneath her chin and raised it with gentle insistence. He touched his lips to hers, lingering until she drew a shuddering breath before he released her.

"*Mon coeur*, do not doubt your worth based solely on your ability to bear a child. 'Tis far more likely the earl is at fault for the lack of children than are ye. Despite what ye were told, bearing the earl's child would have been more along the lines of a miracle than fulfilling your duty. 'Tis not always the woman's fault there are no children, whether the man believes it or not."

Maggie's face whitened, the pink touch of the wind vanishing from her cheeks. "'Tis heresy to speak such."

He quirked a brow. "Ye do not believe men are somehow infallible, that women are only as honorable as their husbands?"

Phillipe was gratified to see the flush return to her skin. He leaned an elbow against a bolder, setting a small space between them.

"Nae. But . . .." She shrugged, a wry smile tugging at her lips, adding irony to her words. "'Tis every woman's lot to obey."

"I am pleased to see ye do not subscribe to that particular view. Otherwise our paths would not have crossed, and I would not have just kissed a woman who makes my heart leap with joy."

Her smile widened. "In Scotland, if one declares he or she is married, and the other agrees, 'tis binding. But I cannae marry ye without ye knowing my past. I would bring naught to the joining but this small isle. Neither power nor money. And certainly nae social standing. Alliance with the MacLarens is a good thing, though ye ken the state of my da's holdings."

"Maggie, I care naught for these things, least of all social posturing. Baron MacLean has assured me of a living in return for my help keeping his northern border. Howbeit, ye should know the church will not sanction this marriage—because of me."

Maggie's brow furrowed. "There is nae caution against remarrying after the death of a spouse."

"Nae, *mon coeur*, though I must tell ye, my young wife is very much alive."

Maggie blinked. Her stomach knotted. Anger sliced through her, sharp with betrayal. She wasn't certain if she wanted to hit him or simply walk away. She flexed her hands. "Ye told me she died."

He shook his head. "Nae. I said death severed our union which led ye to believe she had died. I am sorry for the deception, though it seemed the correct wording at the time. 'Tis a long tale. Will ye hear it?"

Muscles stiff with shock, Maggie jerked her head.

He motioned to a flat rock nearby, sheltered by the cliffs. "I think we should be comfortable there."

They sat side-by-side, close enough to touch, her skirt billowing gently in the breeze, fluttering lightly against his leg. Maggie stared out over the water, wanting to reach the end of whatever he had to say and flee to whatever sanctuary could protect her from the past and the tenuous future he proposed.

"I was born a prince of Antioch and fostered in the home of Baron Donal MacLean." Phillipe began his story, then hesitated.

She startled, catching his gaze. "Go on."

"The defense of the church, of pilgrims, trade, and Jerusalem, was my life. Protecting the innocent. Honoring those who stood in authority over me. I spent ten years fostering with Baron MacLean, who had remained in the Levant after King Richard returned to England, and entered my father's service. His bravery, loyalty, dedication to God and the church, and his canny gift for strategy earned him my father's favor and the barony of Batroun. He treated me as his son and I foolishly gave my heart to his daughter."

"Arbela?"

Phillipe nodded. "She was as a sister to me, and I a foolish lad, yet I hoped more could exist between us. She did not return my regard, and though we parted on good terms, I never saw her again. She and her family left for Scotland, and, as my father's third son, I was required to marry the Queen of Cilicia not long after."

"Required?" The roil of anger and distrust faded. Maggie understood what it meant to face a future not of her choosing.

He leveled a gaze full of regret. "Cilicia—known to some as Little Armenia—our sometimes ally to the north, was under attack by Seljuk Turks on one side. They faced my first cousin, Raymond-Roupen, on the other who claimed the throne of Cilicia after the death of Zabel's father. 'Tis my belief I was considered young and malleable enough to be of little threat to Baron Konstantin who was the young queen's regent. Cilicia desperately needed my father's support. There was no question *if* I would marry Zabel. I was merely a political pawn."

Maggie nodded. An urge to touch him rippled through her fingers. A need to reassure him. She bumped her knee against his. "I am sorry things dinnae turn out as ye hoped."

He ghosted a smile. "I wed Zabel—she was six at the time—and fought off the Turks. For a time, I was lauded by both my young wife and the people of Cilicia."

"What happened?"

Phillipe's gaze drifted away for a thoughtful moment. "I was required to abandon Papal authority and join the Armenian Church." He frowned. "'Twas a pledge I made at the time of my coronation and failed to uphold."

"What divided ye? I dinnae understand the differences."

"There are many points on which Rome and the Armenian Church disagree. Upon deep reflection, they are not likely enough to condemn either, but the schism has never repaired, though they have agreed to disagree.

"There were also many decisions poorly made on my part—or at least with poor results—during my time in Cilicia. Singly, they were enough to estrange the people who'd once cheered me. Together with Baron Konstantin's innuendo and subterfuge, they were enough to sign my death warrant."

Shock stole her breath. "In my worst days—and there were a *gey wheen* of them toward the end of my marriage—I never believed my life was truly at stake." Maggie snorted. "He threatened to tie me to a rock and leave me to my fate, but I dinnae believe he'd bestir himself to actually harm me."

Phillipe's head slewed around, his eyes blazing. "He threatened ye?"

184

"I dinnae take him seriously. Neither should ye."

His gaze promised retribution, and Maggie was glad it was unlikely he'd ever encounter the Earl of Mar. "Tell me how ye escaped."

Phillipe relaxed slightly and resumed his tale. Horror simmered in Maggie's belly as he brought his tale to a close, recognizing how he came less than a faerie's wing away from death.

Phillipe's fingertips tapped against his knee. "This has been difficult. I did not wish to die—fought against Konstantin's plot as hard as I could. By falsifying my death, I abandoned all I cherished, determined to start anew, though I knew not where my path would lead. Then I discovered ye, and I fought against forging a relationship with ye, as well, for I could give ye naught. Baron MacLean has given me a chance to become someone new, someone—I pray—better than I was, and the opportunity to wed with ye."

"I cannae believe . . . cannae fathom what ye've endured," she murmured. "Despite rebelling against marriage to the earl simply for social recognition, the early days were surprisingly idyllic. I was accorded all privileges of my rank, and treated well." She hesitated as a shiver coursed through her. "Once I was nae longer beneficial, that changed."

Maggie inhaled a refreshing breath of sea air thick with the earthier scents of mud and seals. She smiled. "We are quite the pair. Cast aside as soon as our usefulness was at an end. Now outside the covenant of the church and overshadowed by spouses whose vows to us have been broken, though they both yet live."

"I did what I could to ensure Zabel was free to pursue her life in whatever form that takes. I regret the grief I cost her. She loved me enough to send my manservant to me with warning, risking her life to do so. I believe Konstantin is canny enough to keep her alive, even if only to manipulate the throne through her. Zabel is beloved of the people so he'll risk no harm to her. She is young and will in time put aside her mourning."

Maggie chuckled softly. "Leana insisted ye were a prince."

Phillipe blinked. "She did? Why?"

"Yer mannerisms, yer voice—and she is a fanciful lass. She wanted to believe ye came from a noble house."

"What do ye believe?"

"I believe what ye *were* doesnae matter as much as who ye *are*."

"Does that mean ye will marry me? I am no longer a prince, for that is forever in my past and must never be spoken of. I will take the MacLean name and become someone new. Dedicated to my new country—and my new wife, should ye accept."

Maggie stared into the distance. White birds wheeled against a blue sky. Emerald waters plunging into the depths of the sea.

"I wanted . . . I wanted so much to be free. How will I know if I succeed . . .?"

"If I am there to help ye? Why should this lessen your success? Why can I not help someone I love?"

"Love?" Maggie's gaze snapped back to his. "Ye speak of protection and alliance . . . and attraction." She tilted her head. "Love?"

"*Mon coeur*, I respect ye, admire ye, and, yes, love ye. Though that may show many transformations as time passes. I do not expect well-tended love to be a passive thing. Would ye agree?"

Sunlight fell full on Maggie's face. "I dinnae understand love. I desire it, my heart longs for the elusive dream. But I dinnae know how to recognize it or nourish it."

Phillipe placed his palms on either side of her face, gentle as the wakening morning breeze. He touched his forehead to hers. "Like this, Maggie, love."

He kissed her temple, feathered kisses along her cheek. His fingers wove through the tangle of her hair, the light tug against the strands sending sparks racing beneath Maggie's skin.

"I promise to honor ye, place your needs above mine, and give ye every inch of my heart."

Tears slid from beneath Maggie's closed lids and pooled beneath Phillipe's thumbs. He hesitated, uncertain of her thoughts, then pulled her into his lap, tucking her head beneath his chin. She drew her knees up like a child and rested against him as her stuttering breaths eased.

"Can ye tell me what made ye cry, *mon coeur*? I do not wish to cause such again."

"'Tis not ye, Phillipe. No one has ever desired me for myself before. All I have is myself and a tiny isle that brews good mead."

"Excellent mead, if I recall."

She laughed and Phillipe's heart sighed.

"They are happy tears," she said. "Ye told me I am precious to ye without asking about a dowry or other compensation. I dinnae know what to do with this other than say, aye, I'll marry ye."

"Ye'd be a lackwit to deny me, aye?"

Maggie jerked, a bark of laughter exploding from her lips. Smug with the knowledge she'd bound herself willingly to him, and that he'd made her laugh in the bargain, Phillipe grinned. She placed a hand over her mouth, eyes wide with merriment. He kissed her fingers. She slipped her hand away and his lips touched hers. Her fingertips feathered through the hairs of his beard, up the side of his face. His breathing labored.

"Mayhap we should take a look at the caves before someone searches for us," Maggie whispered.

He grunted. "Give me a moment to compose myself."

Maggie's cheeks flamed and she hopped from his lap. Another giggle escaped as she perused him, so he deepened his scowl and grunted again. She danced down the trail, heedless of the wet grass.

"The caves are just over here, I think." She paused, hands on her hips as she stared at the cliffs. With a shake of her head, she moved to her right, tilting her head in concentration.

Phillipe inhaled deeply, willing his body into submission. He wanted her, and he was glad she did not appear distressed over future encounters, but the effects of her nestled against him, her willing kiss on his lips, were slow to leave.

Maggie moved farther away, pausing between two large boulders. "I dinnae see . . . .."

With a shriek, she vanished.

Chapter Twenty Five

"Maggie!" Phillipe leapt to his feet.

Birds exploded into the air in a flurry of feathers and squawks from the rocks where Maggie had stood an instant before. Phillipe's heart raced madly. Nausea roiled in his belly. He bounded across the grass, twisting to avoid the boulders in his path. Reaching the site, he peered into a narrow hole at his feet.

"Maggie!"

"Aye. I'm . . . ouch. I'm unhurt . . . mostly. Och, ye should see this!"

His heart fluttered then slowed it's racing beat. He swallowed the rise of bile in the back of his throat. *She is safe.*

He bent and peered into the opening. To his surprise, he could see Maggie. Though shadows dappled her form, light appeared from behind her and he realized the pit must also have an opening to the sea in the cliffs below.

"I'm coming." He sat and, pushing his feet past the tangled grass around the edge, slid into the hole. His boots landed softly on wet sand, sliding on stones the size of his fists or larger. Standing slowly to ensure he didn't bump his head on the surprisingly low ceiling, he sought Maggie.

She absently rubbed one hip as she stared at a column in a cave that continued beyond the reach of light. A dark splotch marred the cloth of her gown.

"What happened?"

Maggie glanced at him then down. "Och, the spot where I was standing just gave way. I twisted my ankle on those wee rocks when I landed and fell on my backside—on a bit bigger stone. Naught to fash over, though I may need help walking back to the longhouse." She waved a hand, brushing aside his concern and beckoning him close. "Look! Runes!"

Satisfied she'd taken no great injury, Phillipe stepped to her side, angling his shoulders to avoid blocking the light shining down into the cave. The pale stone she indicated differed from the black rock of the rest of the isle. Shadowed lines resembling the tracks of birds ran across the column. He touched a finger to the surface, trailing across the carvings.

"What do ye suppose they are?"

Maggie shrugged. "I dinnae know, but they must be writing of some kind. I would suspect Norse runes, though I have now told ye all I know of such. Do ye think Asatrus or one of the others might know?"

Phillipe glanced about the small chamber. "Mayhap. Though I dislike making this known to the children. 'Tis potentially a dangerous spot." Water lapped at his boots. "There is sea access." His gaze traveled across the walls. "Look. Where the stone changes color. At high tide, the chamber is flooded nearly to the ceiling."

Maggie's gasp told him she recognized the danger. She looked down. "We should be careful. I wish to explore further."

Phillipe chuckled. "I do not know how fast the water rises. Mayhap we should climb out then return with a sturdy rope to ease our escape next time."

Maggie frowned, her gaze swinging from the back of the cave to the light pooling on the surface of a shallow pool of water that hadn't been there a few minutes earlier, he was sure of it. Finally, she sighed. "I dinnae know if I can pull ye from the hole, and I wouldnae leave ye once the water begins to rise in earnest." Her jaw squared with a slight forward jut Phillipe had come to recognize as Maggie at her stubbornest. "We should leave whilst we can, though I will come back. Will ye come with me?"

"If ye promise to never come here by yourself, I will return with ye within the next full day—whenever 'tis safe to do so. Will that do?"

Maggie gave him a nod, but he saw the look of longing she cast once more at the shadowed recesses of the cave.

Phillipe braced his feet and bent forward slightly. "Come. Place your foot in my hands and I will lift ye up through the hole."

Maggie glanced from his cupped hands to the hole as though judging the distance. He grinned. "I promise to do my best to not bash your head against the ceiling. I believe ye are agile enough to do this."

She accepted his challenge with a raised brow. Drawing her skirt back, she placed one low boot in his hands, then flattened her palms against his shoulders. "Go."

Phillipe hoisted her up and her head and shoulders cleared the hole easily. "Be certain the edge is steady before ye place your weight on it."

Maggie hesitated, then pulled herself upward as he supported her. A moment later, she was free. Her face appeared above him.

"I dinnae think I can pull ye up."

He glanced about the cave. Two or three large stones lay scattered in the sand. He pushed against the largest and it gave slightly beneath his hand. He shoved harder, putting the full of his weight against the stone. It shifted a bit more before settling back to its original position.

"If I can push this rock beneath the hole, I believe I can use it to climb out."

"Use caution, Phillipe."

Her soft tone took him off-guard. He'd heard too few kind words of late. His mood lightened. His decision to marry Maggie had been a good one.

He rocked the boulder again. Sea water swirled past his boots, sweeping sand away. He stared at the floor which was now an inch or more deep in water. The wave drew back then returned, filling the chamber a little more.

Phillipe put his shoulder against the rock, timing his push when the tide rushed in again. The stone shifted then settled back into the sand with a small splash. He drew a breath and firmed his stance. And pushed once more. This time, the rock teetered to the side for a long moment before slipping from Phillipe's grasp. He leapt back, keeping his feet clear of the stone as it thudded back into place.

"Is it working?" Maggie's worried tones drifted down.

"Aye. One more push should do it." He stared at the water, catching the rhythm of the waves that now danced ankle-deep about his boots.

Closing his eyes briefly, he murmured a prayer. The tide rushed from the chamber, leaving seaweed and bits of shell in its wake. It surged inward again and Phillipe shoved against the stone with all his might. Water slapped against the rock, rushing upward to break apart in a flurry of swash. His hand slipped on the wet stone and he fell, scraping his wrist and cheek against the coarse rock.

The boulder tumbled to the side with a splash. Phillipe caught himself on one hand and knee, then pushed himself upright. Water rushed into the small cavity left by the butt of the rock, swirling about in eddies before sliding back out to sea.

"Phillipe?"

He wiped his hands with a downward swoop against his trousers. "I believe that did it. Give me a moment to see if this gives me enough height."

He placed one foot against the upper surface of the rock, then tested it with his weight. His boot slipped a fraction and he adjusted his placement. More water rushed into the cave, this time filling the small sea access, blocking the light. Only the hole above allowed rays of sun into the chamber.

Something glinted, catching his eye. He blinked and turned his head slowly to find the sparkle again. The sheen of water on the darker stones in the cave? Or something else? The waves ebbed back, sluggish now that the tide had apparently risen to a similar level outside. As it receded, the light from above caught the glint again. Phillipe stepped from the stone and squatted next to the depression the stone he'd overturned had left in the floor of the cave. A piece of wood, silvered and pocked with age and decay, poked through the sand.

Next to it lay a piece of gold.

Phillipe quickly brushed away the sand and pulled the flat, round bit of gold from its watery nest. He held it up to the light, twisting it slowly back and forth. Kufic script flowed around the margins, and five lines centered on either side of the coin.

A gold dirham? Here?

He quickly searched the indention as sand and water swirled to cover the hole. The wooden bit proved to be the top of a small box, one of six slabs once nailed together and bound with metal bands which had fallen to the side. Scattered in the sand, Phillipe discovered six more gold coins and a small cache of darkened, flat, round items. Silver coins?

He dug deeper, his hand striking other objects as the waves crept deeper. Water brushed the seat of his trousers, recalling him to the danger of the rising tide. He stood.

He shrugged out of his tunic and spread it on the rock then grabbed the coins, sluicing them in the water briefly to remove as much sand as he could. When he'd placed a large number of them on his shirt, he rolled it into a ball and tied the sleeves together to secure the bundle.

He climbed atop the rock, the top of his head clearing the opening to the cave enough he could see outside. Maggie eyed him anxiously. He grinned and handed her the wadded cloth.

"There was more in the cave than ancient runes."

Gripping the sod, he heaved himself out of the hole and rolled to his side before catching his feet beneath him. He stood and Maggie handed him the cloth, her eyes drifting over his bare chest, lips caught between appreciation and concern.

"Yer cheek. Does it hurt?"

Phillipe shook his head. "'Tis naught but a scratch. Here." He unrolled his tunic. "Hold out your hands."

She did, and he slowly poured out the coins.

Her mouth rounded in surprise. "What, by St. Andrew's crooked toe, is this?"

Maggie glanced at Phillipe—at his eyes this time, though she'd gladly linger on his well-muscled shoulders and trim belly a moment longer—or two. Maybe three. And she'd just accepted his marriage proposal . . .. Oh, my. The earl had been so much older. Maggie swallowed and reined in her thoughts.

Phillipe cupped his hands beneath hers, supporting the weight of the coins. Warmth flowed from his palms. "This, *mon coeur*, is part of what appears to be an earl's ransom in gold and silver coin."

Startled, she studied the black and silver bits in her hands. And gold. Gold glinted among the rest.

"Oh, my." She sagged against a boulder, eyes on the small fortune. She spared Phillipe a brief glance. "These are silver coins? And gold?"

"Aye. These *dirhams* are currency found from Spain to the far east, though the gold ones are quite rare—and quite valuable. They would have been exchanged all across the north for items such as fine furs and ivory."

He chose a gold coin and held it up. "See? Look at these markings." His fingertip traced the script surrounding the edge. "'Tis inscribed in Arabic, Kufic script. 'In the Name of God, this dinar was struck in Nishapur in the year 444.'"

"'Tis a Saracen coin?" Maggie stared at the silver and gold in her hands, awed at how far the coins had traveled.

Phillipe nodded. "Aye. 'Twill take a bit of cleaning for the silver ones, though they appear little touched by the interment in salt water all these years."

"How long do ye suppose they've been there?" Maggie glanced at the hole in the ground.

He shrugged. "I would not think the people of Hola would have left this fortune here if they had known of it. It had to have been buried here long before the monks came."

"Ye said there was more?"

"Aye. But we must find a better way to explore without risking getting caught by the tide. Once the tide goes out, we shall look again."

Maggie scarcely noticed the pain in her ankle or the twinge in her hip as she and Phillipe retraced their steps to the longhouse. She tried to control her excitement over the coins, but breathless anticipation of announcing she and Phillipe were to be wed kept a smile on her face she simply couldn't shake.

Phillipe had buried the coins beneath a rock near the hole—a decision Maggie approved of—then pulled his tunic back over his head—one she was less happy with. As if his proposal had given her new eyes, she found she could scarcely take her gaze away from him—and she loved everything she saw.

Casual strength in the rangy length of his stride. A quick smile with a hint of intimacy glowing in his dark brown eyes. Capable hands that cupped her elbow and gave instant assistance if she stumbled. The low, sweet cadence of his voice as he recounted his meeting with Baron MacLean.

"Once we have defenses completed here, we will see what must be done on the MacLean northern border. Are ye willing to do this?"

"Leave Hola." Maggie forced the words past the pang in her chest. "I've come to cherish the people here, but I will bring them naught but grief by my presence." She sighed as she came to a halt. "They've ruled themselves these past many years. I doubt my absence will be remarked one way or another. At least, not for long."

"Ye will be different from the others who've ruled them, *mon coeur*. They will know ye for the way ye care for them and do your best to see they have what they need to not only survive, but to thrive. We will sail here a couple times a year and ensure things meet your satisfaction." He smiled. "And to visit the friends ye've made here."

"We will help them expand their orchard and production of mead, ensure they dinnae lack over the winter, and cease being beleaguered by pirates." His enthusiasm was catching, and Maggie thought she could live with his version of her dream.

Phillipe touched his forehead to hers. "And whatever else is required. This, I pledge ye."

Happiness bubbled through her. "I had never considered marrying again—apart from deciding I dinnae wish to, I'd not given it another thought. I wish I'd met ye before the earl."

"I understand. Yet, the experiences in our lives before this moment have made us who we are—made us right for each other. I'm glad my future has ye in it."

Maggie's entire body warmed, hummed with longing. Her knees threatened to abandon their duty, and she leaned into Phillipe, accepting the support he offered. She laid her cheek against his chest, little heeding the cold damp cloth against her skin. The thud of his heart sang beneath her ear.

His hand rested at her waist, fingers warm and firm. She swayed closer and his arms wrapped about her, a solid barrier against doubts creeping in from the shadows.

I know so little of him. He is so different from me, from what I've known. Will he keep his promises?

The unknown merged with taunts from the past.

He will own me. I will be his to do with as he pleases, and I will disappear into his household and lose myself.

She inhaled sharply.

Phillipe's lips pressed against the top of her head. "What bothers ye? I would hold ye until ye are comforted, yet I would do more if ye'd allow it."

"'Tis such a big step. 'Twill be a marriage of our own consent with no binding contract, no roots in ceremony. Will it last? Are we enough alike, or will we find our expectations too different?"

He hummed low, either in acknowledgement or agreement. "I believe we are more alike than different. But, aye, our opinions will sometimes differ. 'Tis to be expected. I suggest we take the next few weeks whilst we finish matters here, and come to know and understand each other more."

She drew back slightly so she could see his face. "Ye would do this? Ye would wait?"

"Maggie, to be certain ye come willingly into this marriage, I would do many things. I do not wish to enter a marriage between two people who are ill-suited. Ye and I have wed before, and it did not yield good results." He rested a palm atop her shoulder then slowly drew his fingertips down her arm. Fire sparked beneath her skin and tightened her belly.

Maggie's breath shuddered. "I dinnae believe we will wait long."

Chapter Twenty Six

Maggie gripped Phillipe's hand and he relished the reassuring touch. Her brow furrowed lightly with a hint of regret, but the corners of her mouth tilted upward, her lips still soft and swollen from the kiss she had ended only moments past.

"If we announce our betrothal, we shall be watched, kept apart to prevent us anticipating events." A slight blush stained her cheeks and she sighed. "If we truly wish to learn about each other, I dinnae believe 'tis in our favor to be constantly looking over our shoulders, worried over what the others think."

He grinned. "Ye expect to keep everyone in the dark when I can do naught but linger in your presence, gaze upon ye as if ye are the reason for my next breath?"

Maggie's flush flared, spreading past her hairline and down to the hidden areas beneath the neckline of her gown. He loved the strength of her response.

"I dinnae know what to think, Phillipe. 'Tis the honest truth. Ye've turned my life upside down and I scarcely know ye."

"Come now, *mon ange*, ye know much more of me now than ye did a few hours past—and ye still accepted my proposal."

She studied him, eyes narrowed curiously. "Ye say the simplest things with such . . . .." She waved a hand, fishing for a word just out of her reach. "'Tis scarce a tale of sweetness and light, yet I cannae help finding ye likable, intriguing, and . . . trustworthy."

Guilt swept through Phillipe, dark memories that dimmed the morning light. "Trustworthy? If so, ye are the first to remark upon it in a long time."

Her gentle smile settled him, reminded him why he wished to bind himself to her for the remainder of his life. "Ye encourage me to be a better man than I have been these past few years, Maggie."

"I hope so," she teased. "We've a goodly number of years ahead of us, God willing." The grip on his hand tightened. "Phillipe, will it matter to ye if we dinnae have children?"

He kissed the tip of her nose. "Do not worry overmuch. I look forward to a satisfying life with ye whether we welcome a child into our hearts or nae. And now, as much as I would wish otherwise, I must make time for the men unloading our supplies. Once I have jobs allocated, we will return to the cave—tide permitting. Are ye agreed to move forward with renovating the abbey for the purpose of expanding the orchard and mead-making process rather than for use as a manor house?"

Maggie stilled, a thoughtful look on her face. "Aye, though I have a suggestion for a portion of the coins—and mayhap a somewhat different use for the monastery, if ye will hear me out."

Phillipe nodded. "Aye. What are your thoughts?"

His calm acceptance of her possible change of plans warmed her heart and encouraged her. "I was chastised for my lack of commitment to the church when I refused to retire to the nunnery at the earl's insistence."

"The abbess saw a fat purse from the earl and was less than happy to lose it."

Maggie nodded at Phillipe's wry observation. "Precisely. We have just discovered enough coins to send to the abbess to make up her loss."

"Ye would buy your way back into the woman's—and therefore the Almighty's—good graces?"

She heaved a disgruntled breath. "I would pave the way to a smoother acceptance of our marriage. Yer life is changed by yer ties to Baron MacLean. I havenae such a sponsor, and dinnae wish to be the only one of us with a mark against my name."

"'Tis your decision, my love. I care not if the abbess accepts us. I understand how her words wounded ye. She had no right to do so."

"We will set this aside for further consideration, then. The abbey, if I am to not live here, might be better put to use as housing for guardsmen. Expand a room or two for mead storage, but use the rest as intended— cooking, living, and lodging which wouldnae interfere with the lives of the islanders."

Phillipe gifted her a brilliant smile. "I believe ye have hit upon the solution. 'Tis your decision entirely, and I am honored to help in any way I can."

Maggie fairly hummed with excitement from the possibilities before her. "Mayhap I should ask Asatrus and Ingrida how this would impact them."

"It seems ye and I both have our work cut out for us this day. Meet with me at the noon meal and we shall discuss what we've learned."

Maggie gave him a quick kiss on his cheek—still awed by the abrupt turn their relationship had taken, and aware a longer kiss was inevitable if she aimed for his lips . . ..

Phillipe strode away, disregarding the breeze piercing his damp tunic, for thoughts of Maggie kept his body well-warmed. He ignored Balgair's narrow, questioning gaze, ducking his head so the man could not see the grin his look prompted. Perhaps later he would take the Scot into his confidence. With Maggie's blessing, of course.

"What is left aboard ship?"

Balgair rubbed his beard. "They are nearly finished." He canted his head toward the hoard of chests and barrels lining the dock. "We only await yer judgment as to where these items need to go."

"Our plans have changed somewhat. I'll tell ye the why of it later, but the abbey will be restored to its original form, not as a manor house. The renovation should thus be easier, or at least quicker, than we'd thought. Work on defenses for the longhouse will go much as planned."

"Shouldn't ye change yer clothes, laddie? Lady Maggie willnae like ye catchin' yer death from wearin' a wet tunic." Balgair's raised, bushy brows invited an explanation for Phillipe's disarray, but Phillipe waved his curiosity away then turned his attention to the containers on the dock.

"Och, I meant to tell ye," Balgair continued. "'Tis a box labeled for m'lady sittin' tae one side," Balgair called. "I dinnae know what's in it. The captain said it came on orders of the baron, himself."

Phillipe strode to the carved wooden chest set slightly apart from the rough-hewn boxes. Twin bands of lightly tarnished metal bound it closed, the bottom set so it was nearly a hand's breadth from the ground.

No carpenter's box, this, but a lady's chest. "I'll take it to the longhouse and fetch a dry tunic whilst I'm there." He motioned to the tools packed tightly into wooden crates. "Have these taken to the abbey. We'll move the boards once we've crafted a small sled."

He returned to the dock as four men set off toward the abbey, boxes on their shoulders. Spying the master carpenter, Munro, bearing in his direction, Phillipe awaited the burly man's arrival.

"Thank ye again for coming, Munro."

The carpenter nodded impatiently. "Aye, aye. Are ye ready to begin?"

Phillipe gave a nod. "Come. I will show ye the way to the abbey."

* * *

Maggie glanced about. All appeared normal, if busy, near the harbor—a seeming impossibility after the decisions she'd just made. The thought of Phillipe's proposal shifted her entire world. How did mundane tasks continue in the wake of such an enormous change?

At this distance men were scarcely more than dark shapes against the gray rock and sand, moving from ship to dock, stacking a large number of cases near the shoreline. Smaller forms darted among the gentle waves that lapped over the sands on the southern side of the harbor as children fished for flatties. A thin line of smoke rose from the remnants of the bonfire from the night before where women took advantage of the low embers to smoke fish the men had netted earlier.

What is winter like here? Do they ever see snow? Do storms sweep out of the sea to torment the isle? Are ships forbidden access to the harbor because of wind and ice? How do the people deal with the loneliness of long, bitter nights? She was no longer certain she'd ever know the answers.

Maggie shook the thoughts from her mind and covered the remaining distance to the longhouse. She spotted Asatrus's wife among the women smoking fish.

"Ingrida, might I speak with ye a moment?"

The woman's eyes flashed—irritation or relief—an instant before she nodded and led Maggie a few feet away where the breeze feeding the coals of the fire would sweep their words away from curious ears.

"What may I do for ye, freya?" Ingrida's carefully hooded eyes gave nothing away.

"Do ye not like me?" Maggie blurted, not at all what she'd meant to say.

Ingrida's hesitation was brief yet brought a pang to Maggie's heart. "I dinnae know ye well enough, freya. Give it time."

Maggie frowned. "Though I've been here a fortnight, I havenae convinced ye I mean well for the people of Hola. Am I much the same as others who've laid claim to the isle in the past?"

The woman blinked, her composure slipping a notch. "Nae. Ye are naught like the others. Yet, ye arenae one of us."

"Why?"

Ingrida sighed. "Ye are used to finer things, freya. We are simple people, grateful for what the isle gives us each year. Yer ways tempt the children to change, to want more than is their birthright. They love yer stories, but 'tisnae fair to speak to them of things they will never know."

"I see." Maggie bit her lip. Even with the hours spent learning the tasks and needs of all who lived here, she was merely tolerated, mayhap cautiously welcomed. How many would breathe a sigh of relief when she left?

"There have been some changes. I spoke with Phillipe this morning, and he brings word from Baron MacLean."

Curiosity widened Ingrida's eyes.

Maggie turned with a swish of her skirts, pacing as her thoughts formed into words. "I am committed to seeing Hola prosper. And to its defense. But I will no longer live here, though I will return from time to time." She faced Ingrida. "What do ye see as Hola's biggest need?"

"Protection." Ingrida's answer was prompt. "Yet we dinnae wish to host a horde of warriors who will do naught but eat and take up space."

"Until they are needed."

"Aye. Until they are needed." Ingrida spread her hands. "There lies our problem. We've no one to teach our men to be warriors—and I doubt there are many women here who wish to see their husbands and sons embrace violence. Ye've noted our numbers are few, yet, adding fighting men will stretch our stores."

"What if men could be sent here who would agree to help with the daily running of the isle, who were able to pick up arms when needed? And whose lodging wouldnae interfere with yer lives?"

"Would they not also require time and space to hone their skills?" Ingrida shook her head. "This alone would expose our children to violence—would change us. Change our way of life."

"It might keep ye from being slaughtered by angry pirates."

Ingrida bit her lip. "We have everything we need to live here as we always have, raising sheep and making mead. Change isnae welcome. If the pirates would leave us alone, we would want for naught."

"How many years have they come here?"

Ingrida shrugged, eyes tracking the distance as she considered the question. "They have come every year for at least the past ten to fifteen summers, though less frequently before that. I remember, as a lass, hearing my grandparents whisper they came for the treasure of Hola." She smiled. "Our mead was well-regarded even then."

Maggie startled. "The treasure of Hola? 'Tis what they called the mead?"

"Certainly. What else could it be?"

* * *

Maggie and Phillipe crested the hill, leaving the longhouse behind, and the push of gazes which had lingered on her during the noon meal vanished. Nothing disturbed the peace beyond the distant barking calls of seals and the soft crash of waves against the rocks as the tide receded. Wiry grass fluttered their fluffy tops in the breeze. Sunlight slanted against the scattered boulders, throwing shadows toward the east.

She sought Phillipe's fingers and his hand closed over hers. He halted, bringing her to a stop as he pulled her to him, mouth descending hungrily on hers. Her entire body flamed as brightly as a torch newly soaked in pitch. His body responded to hers, desire building as the kiss consumed her.

She forgot what she'd wanted to tell him.

Her fingers slid through the heavy waves of his hair, tugging lightly as she demanded more. He obliged, pressing against her, his cock hard against her thigh. Her breath labored, her belly tightened—and a hundred angry pirates couldn't have pulled her away.

Pirates.

Clarity sparked. She blinked and memory fanned back to life.

Pirates.

She broke the kiss, pressing her forehead against his neck as she relaxed against his chest. His heart thudded wildly, ragged breathing almost obscuring the racing beat.

"Pirates."

"What?"

"Ingrida said they were looking for the treasure of Hola, but she always thought 'twas the mead."

"The pirates thought the mead was the treasure? What of the coins in the cave?"

Maggie sighed and stepped away. "Nae. Ingrida told me the pirates have been accosting the people of Hola since before she was born. She remembered her grandma saying the pirates had once demanded the treasure of Hola. Obviously, no one here knows of what ye discovered, and they've sent the pirates away with a share of the mead ever since."

Phillipe rubbed his chin. "Why would pirates accept mead in lieu of silver?"

She shrugged. "Mayhap 'twas an old tale and none knew the exact nature of the treasure. Certainly, the mead is superior to any other I've drunk. And the color is that of pure gold."

"I suppose that is as good as any explanation. *Astvats giti.*"

"Pardon?"

"Sorry, my love. 'Tis an Armenian phrase that covers anything that cannot be explained. It simply means, *God knows.*"

"Then, 'tis apt. There are likely none here who remember exactly what happened when the pirates first arrived. Or why they accepted the mead."

"The Treasure of Hola. I am looking forward to seeing what we find. The tide is on its way out, and we must be out of the cave before nightfall. Are ye ready?"

Maggie grinned, excitement blooming. "Aye. Let us see what lies in the cave."

Phillipe shook his head. The dirhams had clearly been struck hundreds of years ago, but he couldn't imagine a treasure so ancient that the pirates more than fifty years ago had been uncertain what they sought.

Rumors. Fragmented memories. Clues hidden in everyday words to lessen the chance others would discover where the treasure had been hidden.

He and Maggie approached the hole she'd fallen through earlier. Taking a sturdy rope from a bag slung over his shoulder, Phillipe tied it firmly to a boulder near the hole, repeating the process with a second rope and boulder.

"The stones seem quite sturdy, but 'tis best to be certain at least one holds firm when needed."

Maggie sat on the crumbled edge, clearly unconcerned about tumbling into the hole once again. "The water isnae verra deep. Should we wait?"

"Unless ye wish to compete with the drifting tide washing sand back inside whatever hole ye dig, then aye." He laughed at the frustrated lift and fall of her shoulders. "We could, howbeit, take a torch and explore a bit farther into the cave if ye like while we wait for the tide to ebb completely."

"Aye! I'd like that." She slipped through the hole, landing with a splash.

"A bit deeper than ye thought?" Phillipe's chuckle was tinged with worry.

"Och, mayhap a wee bit." She was silent for a moment, then her voice drifted back to him, rich with echoes. "Verra dark. Hand me a torch, aye?"

He handed it down, along with another for himself and a waterproof pouch with a small stone hollowed out to allow a bit of glowing peat to be carried inside. With a final glance to ensure they were unwatched, he slid past the sea grass into the treasure cave.

Maggie set the ember-warmed stone atop a boulder, beyond the reach of the water. Pulling bits of dried grass and straw from the pouch, she carefully used the ember to light a small fire. The oil-soaked dry grasses fastened around the end of the torch flamed quickly when she touched them to the flames, bathing the chamber in pale light and smoke. Phillipe grabbed the edges of the hole overhead and pulled, widening the opening as bits of mud, stone, and grass tumbled into the cave.

The smoke eagerly sought the larger hole. Maggie coughed. "My thanks."

Phillipe accepted the second torch. "Lead on."

They waded through ankle-high water. He noted Maggie had drawn her skirt between her legs and draped it through her belt, keeping it out of the water and exposing her legs nearly to her knees. "Playing at being a fish wife?" he drawled.

"I'd have worn trews, but I feared 'twould draw more attention."

Phillipe considered in his mind the shape of her nether side encased in tight-fitting, supple leather—recalled his splay of fingers over Maggie's rounded rump earlier—and promptly banged his head on the lowered entry to a shaft branching off the main cavern.

He stifled a curse.

Maggie gasped. "Look!"

He hurried to her side. She halted in the middle of a small chamber perhaps twice the width of her outstretched arms. Torchlight glimmered gold on the wet black rock. Phillipe raised his torch, but the light did not penetrate to the ceiling. Maggie stepped away.

"Ouch!" The tip of Maggie's torch dipped downward.

Phillipe jerked about in alarm. Maggie pointed to the floor. "I dinnae see that."

Bits of wood rested askew in the sand along one edge of the room, wedged between three stones rising nearly knee-height from the ground.

"This appears to be the remains of a rather large chest." He handed his torch to Maggie.

The last of the tide lapped in the doorway. Phillipe squatted on his heels and gently pulled the wood from the sand. Maggie stuck the ends of the torches in the sand.

Phillipe whistled low and sat back on his haunches, forearms propped on his knees, a golden brooch in his hand. "I don't know who this once belonged to, Maggie, but 'tis spectacular."

Maggie's mouth dropped open. Blue and red gems winked in the uncertain light, pale crosses glinting across the surface of each smooth stone. The beaten gold setting gleamed with warmth in the torchlight, the rich colors pulsing with life.

She turned it over in her hand, noting the peculiar thickness of the gold and the resulting weight.

"Where do ye suppose 'tis from?"

"I would hazard a guess it 'twas stolen from a wealthy lord—mayhap spoils from a shipwreck—or possibly trinkets from a soldier returning from the Holy Land many years ago."

Maggie frowned. "Trinkets? Who carries such as this in his pouch?"

She tilted her head at Phillipe's movement and nearly dropped the brooch. His hands, cupped together, glittered with gold and colored stones.

"I do not know, *mon coeur*, but it appears *this* is the Treasure of Hola."

Chapter Twenty Seven

Maggie sat amid the wiry grasses of the overlook and stared at the hoard of jewels in her hands. The light of the setting sun warmed the gold, creating the illusion of heat against her skin. Rubies glowed the red of a heart's blood, signifying pure love and loyalty. Blue sapphires, as mysterious as the night sky, spoke the language of power and strength. Pearls glimmered pink and cream as they preened in the light for possibly the first time in hundreds of years.

"Unbelievable," she murmured, caught in the spell of the wondrous sight.

Phillipe collapsed to the ground beside her. Maggie glanced up, instantly swayed from the treasure in her hands. His shirt, open at the neck, fluttered in the breeze, revealing a scattering of black hair. He nodded to the gems. "A rather nice addition to your jewelry chest."

She dragged her gaze from his chest. "I dinnae wear jewels. Highly impractical things."

"Ye will. As my lady, ye will be privileged to wear them or not as suits ye. These are a mix of very ancient cultures."

He drew a finger through the pile. "This pendant of gold filigree is set with a glass bead and reminds me of what ladies in the Levant wore every day. As does this ring, which looks enough like the pendant to have been part of a set. This . . .." He held up a silver ring, spit on it, then rubbed the flat top vigorously against the hem of his tunic before angling it into the light.

"See the engraving? 'Tis of a lion holding a cross. A similar design is used by those who belong to the Order of the Dragon whose members are tasked with the protection of the cross."

"Ye should wear it."

Phillipe studied it a moment then tossed it in the air. He caught it with the ease of a magician's sleight of hand and slipped the bit of silver into a pouch on his belt. "Thank ye, *mon coeur*. 'Tis a meaningful piece."

Maggie smiled, happy to have been able to give him something that pleased him. "All of this is as much yers as mine," she reminded him. "I dinnae know how to find the original owner of the pieces."

"'Tis a mix that may not have one true owner. Mayhap a Crusader brought prizes home and placed the chest here, fearing capture or preparing for a long, dangerous journey, and was unable to return to retrieve it. 'Tis possible all of this is pirate bounty, though I believe these jewels are from one source, and the coins from another." He motioned to a third pile of silver items, some of which appeared broken. Some were tarnished, looking worn and unlovely. "That may yield treasure of another sort."

"What do ye suppose 'tis?"

"They will need to be cleaned to tell for certain, though their submersion in this cold water doesn't seem to have done them much harm. That larger one may be a flagon, mayhap for wine. These smaller pieces may be small silver cups."

"They're too small to drink from."

"For a ritual?" He drew a flat piece of metal from the pile, worked with flowing designs and crossed with a shorter piece a little more than half way up. "This appears to be a cross with a heavy wooden base—or what remains of it—to allow it to stand. Do ye know if the abbey here was abandoned by agreement—or by force?"

The warmth from the sun vanished. A cold breath blew across the back of Maggie's neck. She stared at the flagon and its sentinel of small cups arranged at its base with a sense of dismay.

"I dinnae know . . .. Wait. They—Asatrus and the others, back at least a generation or two—were trained by the monks to make mead." She lifted her gaze to Phillipe. "Doesnae this mean the monks left peaceably?"

"Likely. There are plenty of other places, other isles with abandoned abbeys from which this could have come. And I do not recall smoke damage to the abbey here. General neglect, but not wanton destruction."

Maggie closed one hand about the heavy gold brooch and peace flowed over her.

Phillipe was right. The altar adornments were likely from an abbey on another isle or mayhap from the private chapel of a lord. The thought of Saint Martin's Abbey—*her* abbey—destroyed, monks killed, violence on Hola—*her* isle—shocked her to her core. Abbeys weren't immune to bloodshed, their precious articles of faith not the only temptation to the greedy. But she was relieved to realize such had probably not been Saint Martin's Abbey's fate.

"What are we going to do with this—this plunder?"

"'Tis yours to do with as ye please, *mon coeur*. Howbeit, I suggest we keep the discovery to ourselves. The hunt for the Treasure of Hola has faded to a tribute of mead, and the isle would not survive if 'twas known gold had been found here. As the titular owner of the isle, all of this . . .." He waved his hand over the piles of silver and gold. "'Tis yours. Even if the children had stumbled across it whilst playing, 'twould be yours."

The enormity of Phillipe's words swept over her. "I own Hola."

"The isle, its people, the birds, the seals—and every bit of gold and silver."

She frowned. "I dinnae own the people."

"Then, they are beholden to whatever ye provide for them. Mayhap they are free to leave, but as long as they live here, ye control their destinies."

Maggie sighed. "Is this what it means to rule? It dinnae feel the same at Narnain Castle."

"'Tis because ye didn't have a treasure to dispose of."

"Mayhap." Maggie glanced at the piles, unhappy to think she would walk away with silver and gold that had been sitting under the islanders' noses and leave them with naught. Yet, such was the law. The isle was hers, and everything on it. She could, however, use the treasure for the good of Hola. 'Twas a comforting thought.

"At least, the earl gets naught." Humor twitched the corners of her lips.

"Aye. Though ye'll not get the satisfaction of telling him so. Ye should do naught that draws attention to the isle."

"Others would destroy Hola, hoping to find an overlooked trove."

Phillipe nodded. "We cannot defend this isle against such an onslaught."

Maggie sighed. "Let's pack this up. Though I dinnae know how we'll hide it."

"Baron MacLean sent ye a chest. I don't know what's in it, for 'tis bound and locked. I have a few leather sacks with me. We'll bag up the treasure and stow it in the chest. I suggest we both leave for Morvern on the morrow."

"Will the baron help us?"

"Aye. And the sooner we remove this from the isle, the better."

* * *

Baron MacLean wasn't the larger-than-life person Maggie had expected. He was slightly taller than her, but his son, Alex, and Phillipe topped his height by several inches. He'd once been a powerfully-built man, but age had softened him somewhat if the gentle roundness of his cheeks and paunch were indications. His back was straight, though a slight hitch in his gait betrayed his age and, perhaps, a wound from his youth. His dark red hair held strong against a light dusting of silver, though his beard was liberally salted, and his eyes sparkled with good humor and intelligence.

"Welcome to Castle MacLean, Lady Maggie. 'Tis a pleasure having ye here. My seneschal Grizel will take ye to yer chamber and see to yer comfort."

Maggie met his gaze boldly and declined his offer. "If ye dinnae mind, I'd rather speak to ye first."

The baron exchanged looks with Phillipe. Maggie hid her annoyance at being passed over for Phillipe's consideration. She was tired from the trip and the subterfuge of hiding the treasure. She wanted a bath and a nap, but not a pat on the head from a well-meaning baron. Her comfort could wait a bit longer.

Phillipe placed an arm about Maggie's waist. "My lady has information for ye as well as a request. Howbeit, I believe we could both use a bit of time to freshen up before we tackle the issues at hand. May we join ye in your solar in an hour's time?"

Phillipe's sense of diplomacy won her acquiescence as the baron inclined his head, his gaze lingering on Phillipe's possessive gesture.

"By all means. I will have food and drink brought, and will await ye both there." He turned shrewd eyes on Maggie. "I am intrigued, my lady, and look forward to our meeting."

She allowed Grizel to lead her to a chamber on the third floor, her legs protesting the final flight of stairs. Phillipe pressed a kiss to her temple, then continued to a door farther down the hall.

Grizel motioned to a wooden tub next to the hearth. Steam rose invitingly from the surface. "M'lady's clothing will be freshened as soon as yer belongings are brought up. For now, I've a gown in mind which should fit ye. Climb into the tub and I'll send Mòrag to help ye."

Maggie unlaced her gown and let it fall to the floor, then stepped into the tub. She slid beneath the steaming water with a sigh, her taut muscles easing in the heat. Her eyes closed as the salt spray on her skin rinsed away and the scent of roses filled the air.

I wouldnae have dreamed acquiring a treasure was such a burden. A blessing, for certain, but still a burden. 'Tis difficult to think I have such power over the people of Hola. 'Tis not my treasure to dispose of in a frivolous manner, but my duty to see it is well-spent for their benefit.

Maggie sighed, remembering the furtive hour they'd spent placing the bags of treasure within the fabulous chest the baron had sent her. The feet were carved to resemble paws, perhaps of a lion—tales of which Phillipe had entertained her with on the voyage from Hola to Movern. The rest of the cask was carved with figures drinking wine and making music. Decorating the outer rim of the top was a script unknown to her, which Phillipe told her was well-wishes for the owner of the chest.

She'd been intrigued with the cask, and pleased with the soft woolen cloak lined with fur that had been the rest of the baron's gift.

The treasure had fit snuggly into the chest, the cloak folded atop the bags. A small key had fit the lock, and broad bands of metal, locked together with a crossbar, had further protected the chest against casual intrusion.

A knock at the door revealed a young woman of roughly Maggie's age. She bustled inside as Maggie bid her enter.

"I'm Mòrag. We havenae much time, m'lady, but I think ye'd feel better for washing yer hair as well." Once the maid was satisfied with her efforts, she spread Maggie's locks over the edge of the tub, angled to catch the heat from the fire on the hearth.

Maggie relaxed, her muscles limp as Mòrag's fingers soothed away tension in her scalp and neck. She closed her eyes, stealing a moment's rest.

I was a simple laird's daughter, my dowry monies spent, and now have more gold and silver coins than I can spend in a lifetime. Only yesterday I was determined to devote my life to aiding the people of Hola—alone. Joy bubbled in her chest. *Now, I am to be Phillipe's wife—Lady MacLean.*

She snuggled deeper into the water, a smile playing about her lips. *Should I tell him I've admired him since first we met? Aside from the mistaken notion he'd betrayed us to the MacNairns.* Maggie giggled at the memory. She'd been angry and distrustful at the time. *Nae. I willnae tell him now. Mayhap later.*

The door opened and closed. Maggie opened her eyes and sat up. Water sloshed gently about her. Her eyebrows shot up as she beheld the pink and burgundy gown in Grizel's hands.

"Ye *do* realize I have red hair. Verra red."

Grizel held up the gown. "The dark burgundy will deepen the rich undertones of yer locks." She gave Maggie a shrewd look. "Few with yer coloring can wear this. Most lassies with hair the color of yers settle for green or, too often, brown. I believe 'twill suit ye for a rare treat."

The woman's words rang a challenge, and Maggie grinned as she stepped from the tub. "Ye expect me to make an impression?" She grabbed a length of linen from Mòrag and rubbed her limbs briskly before donning a soft wool robe.

"I expect yer young man will not be able to put his eyes back into his head." Grizel shrugged. "He seems kind enough, though there is a reluctance about him—nae for ye, lass, but for something in his past that tugs at him still."

"And I will change that with this dress?"

"Ye will at least take his mind from it for a time. With the right words, a touch, he will soon decide his efforts are best spent on ye, not on whatever happened before he met ye."

Mòrag placed Maggie in a chair and carefully combed her hair. The strands dried quickly before the fire and soon crackled to life in the girl's hands. She and Grizel helped Maggie into the fine wool gown, its velvet bodice sliding luxuriously over Maggie's thin linen shift. Wide bands of lace glimmering with metallic thread bound the neckline and cuffs, and at her elbows where sheer silk over-sleeves fell to points near the floor.

Under Grizel's critical eye, Mòrag created a braid on either side of Maggie's face which she bound behind her head then let fall to mingle with the rest of the coppery red curls. Grizel produced a silver filigree set with clear blue stones to nestle atop the braid.

"I am now a faerie princess," Maggie laughed. She tucked an errant strand of hair behind one ear, thrilled with the purely indulgent flow of the silk sleeves. "I'm indebted to ye, both."

"I've other business to attend, so I'll bid ye fare-thee-well. My lord baron is well-pleased tae have ye here, and looks forward tae seeing ye anon. I wouldnae rush to the solar if I were ye." Grizel cast a glance at Mòrag. "Keeping the men waiting a moment or twa willnae hurt them. They will forget to fuss the moment they lay eyes on her."

"I am more used to a crossbow as my weapon of choice," Maggie noted. "Howbeit, a pretty dress may prove the better choice in this instance."

She folded her hands before her in a studied pious gesture and inclined her head. "I am ready to speak with the baron."

Chapter Twenty Eight

The trill of doves filtered through the open window in Baron MacLean's solar. Sunlight lingered late on this summer's day, finding its way into the high-walled courtyard just beyond the baron's chamber. The delicate scent of lemons drew Phillipe to the window where he found a trio of trees with fruit ripening among the leaves.

Baron MacLean crossed to his side. "The trees are in pots so they can be brought inside once the winter winds arrive."

Phillipe smiled. "Does the scent remind ye of the Levant?"

The baron nodded. "Arbela had the foresight to bring many things with us that remind me of our time there. Our cook has learned to use spices and vegetables from the east. Zora had a time battling with Cook over the new foods. My sister by marriage left everything she knew to come here with us. She is missed." Donal paused as pain slid over his features.

"Zora ran your household well, and loved Alex and Arbela as if they were her own." Phillipe allowed a small smile. "She took me under her wing as well. She set me straight on more than one occasion, though I never made the same mistake twice in her presence. I am sorry to hear of her passing."

"She planted these trees for me." Donal hesitated again, then seemed to reach a decision. He faced Phillipe.

"Ye favored Arbela. I knew this. Yet, yer da had other visions— visions I dinnae necessarily agree with. Howbeit, I dinnae see Arbela returning more than a casual friendship with ye, no matter ye had been raised together. Mayhap that is why she saw ye only as a brother. Mayhap, given more time, she would have grown to feel differently toward ye. But, Bohemond received an offer which would create an alliance, though it bound ye to the child-queen of Cilicia." He shook his head. "By all that is holy, I'd never thought ye'd face the challenges ye did. I knew ye'd triumphed over the Seljuks and won the hearts of the Cilicians. I dinnae realize how quickly the tide would turn."

The twinge in Phillipe's heart did not distress him as it would have a month or more ago. However, he found his pride still wounded. "Do not worry, my father. All has happened as it has been ordained, to a future that is in God's hands. I am content, and I have learned from the mistakes in my past."

"Ye dinnae make mistakes, my son. Ye did as honor dictated and obeyed yer da. 'Tis my notion Baron Konstantin is far more to blame than ye." He grasped Phillipe's arm. "Know that I am glad ye are here, and I look forward to seeing ye happy in yer upcoming marriage."

Phillipe laughed. "Marriage? Ye caught on, did ye?"

Donal MacLean snorted. "Ye wouldnae touch a woman without her full willing, and never so possessively unless yer heart was involved. Maggie MacLaren has had a rough patch nae of her making, but she is a bonnie lass, and possesses a caring heart. Much like ye, she followed where honor dictated, agreeing to marry the earl because 'twas her da's wish. The earl doesnae care for any but himself. Had she borne a child, he would have most likely continued to amuse himself by treating her well enough, though I doubt he would ever have shown her a tenth the love ye carry inside ye. Ye are both lucky to have found each other."

A knock at the door drew their attention.

"Enter."

A guard at the portal admitted a serving lad laden with a tray of food and another carrying an assortment of drinks. Setting the trays on a table near a trio of chairs, they took their leave.

Phillipe tweaked the linen cloth spread over a silver tray. Scents of cinnamon, nutmeg, and paprika drifted out. His mouth watered.

"Falafal? Spiced carrots? What must I bribe your cook with to leave MacLean Castle and come with me?" He reached beneath the cloth and grabbed a small, dark ball and bit into it. He closed his eyes.

"Heaven." He dipped another ball into a creamy sauce seasoned with dill.

"Amazing." He lifted the cloth further, breathing deep of the familiar scents, then grabbed a bit of thinly sliced meat atop a small, round flatbread.

"We will wait upon Lady Maggie, if ye please." The baron's firm reprimand halted Phillipe's foray. Mouth full, Phillipe pivoted on a heel as Donal nodded to the doorway.

Maggie, hair aflame and curling to her waist, gowned in burgundy velvet trimmed with pink silk, gave him a hesitant smile. He swallowed and strode to the door, hands held out in welcome.

"I've seen ye as the red-haired young woman bravely holding a distressed falcon chick, hands bleeding, stubborn, kind. And as the warrior woman who, with her crossbow, drove back raiders who breached her castle's gates. Now, I see ye, Lady Maggie, gowned befitting royalty, outshining the best efforts of seamstress and maid."

Her cheeks flamed but she did not drop her gaze. "Which do ye prefer?"

Phillipe halted before her and grasped her hands. "I prefer the Maggie who is fierce in her passions, be it protection of the defenseless, determination to meet life on her own terms . . .." He bent his head, mouth to her ear. "Or the willingness to meet me in all purposes of our lives together."

Her fingers gripped his, tightening as her chest rose with a deep inhale of breath. Phillipe placed the proper space between them then raised her hands and kissed her fingers. Her gaze fluttered to his, exchanging a silent promise.

Phillipe pivoted to her side and faced Baron MacLean. "My lord, may I make known to ye Lady Maggie MacLaren, the woman who has consented to be my bride?"

A shiver rippled down Maggie's spine, shedding a bit of the heat and passion of Phillipe's words and touch. He made her feel beautiful. Wanted. Desired.

She drew a breath to clear her head and shifted her attention to Baron MacLean. His grin broadened the lower half of his face, crinkled his eyes, beetled his brows. Clearly the introduction pleased him.

Baron MacLean fisted his hands on his hips. "Lady Maggie, I am pleased to make yer acquaintance. 'Tis my great joy to meet the woman who has turned my Phillipe's head. Ye are most welcome here."

Maggie dipped into a curtsy. "Thank ye, m'lord."

"Och, no formalities, lass. We are about to become family. Ye may call me Donal if ye wish."

"Then ye must call me Maggie."

"*I* am Alex . . . .." A man's voice from the doorway was interrupted by the yip of a dog. "Damn, pup! Get by!"

A blur of dark fur streaked into the room, clipping the backs of Maggie's knees as it barreled past. Phillipe caught her before she did more than wobble, pulling her against him protectively.

"Serkan! Sit!"

The dark-haired man at the door and the furry pup locked gazes. The young dog tilted his head to one side, tongue lolling from his mouth as he panted gently. One ear tipped forward, the other stuck straight up in the air. His rich sable coat overlaid with black contrasted with his three white feet, and a pale tuft of fur blazed like a star on his chest. Neither man nor dog moved for several moments.

With a small whine, Serkan closed his mouth, shifted his gaze, and sat.

"Good lad." The man gave a grunt of satisfaction. He lifted a rueful grin to the others in the room. "He's a bit head-strong, but smart as a whip."

Maggie glanced at the pup. Something tugged at her memory. "Didn't he belong to the innkeeper's wife?"

"Aye, Moibeal bid me take him with me the last time I was there. I havenae the time to train him—not much, anyway. But we'll muddle through. He's got great bloodlines—half Aidi as his sire came with us from the Levant. Excellent livestock protector."

"Big paws to fill," Phillipe remarked. "I remember Toros."

"Both Toros and Garen reside with Arbela. I've placed a pup or two with our herders and they're hard workers. This laddie is large enough to be part wolf and has a bit of mischief in him, aye, my lad?"

The pup's tail beat the floor in a rapid tattoo, his lips pulled back in a canine grin.

"Ye used to be a good hand with the dogs, Phillipe. Ye should take him."

Phillipe sent Maggie a sidelong look. "We shall think on this. Howbeit, we have things of greater importance to speak of at this time." He gestured to a chair next to the table. "Please, have a seat."

Maggie took the proffered seat. Serkan sprang to his feet and padded over to her. Placing his chin on her knees, he stared at her and Maggie didn't know whether to be intrigued or annoyed.

"Ye chewed the hem of my cloak, ye rascal. Ye willnae touch this gown."

With an exaggerated sigh, Serkan collapsed against her, his body sliding down her leg until he curled at her feet. Alex sent her a triumphant grin. She narrowed her eyes at him.

"Ye willnae pawn yer *bowsterous* laddie off so easily." She scratched Serkan's ears and the pup groaned. Alex laughed.

Phillipe handed Maggie a trencher and she carefully filled it, curious and slightly anxious over the unusual fare. Phillipe's explanations did little to enlighten her, for she had no idea how fried chickpeas would taste, nor did she have knowledge of eggplant or shawarma meat. But it smelled wonderful, if odd, and tasted better than she'd imagined.

Donal refilled the goblets with a dark red wine that flooded Maggie's mouth with notes of cherry, dried fig, and vanilla, and reminded her of the casket it must have aged in.

"A fine Spanish wine," Phillipe said, raising his cup in toast. "And my compliments to your excellent cook."

"Noted. Now that we're fed and relaxed, why dinnae ye tell me what brings ye here."

Maggie set her knife aside and wiped her fingers on a damp scrap of linen. "I thank ye for yer hospitality, m'lord—Donal. May I start at the beginning?"

"Certes." Donal settled back in his chair. "Please begin."

Maggie described the ownership of the isle, but left out the fact the earl had likely cheated her da out of a great deal of money. She reasoned the baron would have—at least by now—heard of her marriage and annulment, and did not waste time giving details.

"I know of Hola," Donal said. "Damn fine mead. I would push to increase production if I were ye, Maggie."

Maggie nodded. "Aye. 'Tis foremost on my plan for the isle. 'Twas a hefty undertaking as I had nae resources when I arrived on the isle. Howbeit . . .."

The baron stretched his legs before him. "Phillipe asked for men and materials to provide a defense of yer isle, my lady, which I gladly provided. I confess I know little of growing apple trees."

"I'm nae here to request help to grow the orchard, my lord," Maggie said, finding herself on formal footing with the baron as she formed her request. "I find myself unexpectedly possessed of quite enough coin to see this done, and am willing to settle my account with ye for that which ye've already generously provided."

"Then, what do ye ask?"

"I need help storing a rather large treasure."

Phillipe untied a leather pouch from his belt and set it on the table, the clink of coins audible.

Donal's eyebrows shot up and he straightened. "What is this?"

"Phillipe and I discovered this in a cave on Hola. Pirates arrived at the isle a few days ago, demanding a tribute of mead."

The baron's eyes narrowed.

Alex slapped a palm against the arm of his chair. "Bastards!"

Donal sent him a reproving glance.

Maggie ignored them both. "It appears the pirates have done this for quite a number of years, receiving up to one-half of each season's mead. Howbeit, years ago when the pirates first arrived, they simply demanded the Treasure of Hola, which the people took to mean the only thing they had of value."

"The mead." Donal frowned. "They dinnae know of this treasure?" He motioned to the bag.

Maggie untied the strings holding the bag closed and slowly poured the contents onto the table. Candlelight gleamed on the gold coins and sparkled across the surfaces of the jeweled pins, pendants, and rings.

Donal stared at the pile then glanced at Phillipe. "These are from the Levant. They arenae Celtic in design." He gestured to the treasure. "May I?"

Maggie nodded. "Certes. There are also bits of silver broken, Phillipe suspects, into pieces for use as payment for services or goods. And a few verra old pieces which may have once belonged to a monastery or chapel."

The baron grunted. "We can have Father Sachairi take a look at those later. He has a vast knowledge of the history of the area, though his Latin translations are a bit suspect."

Donal gently spread the coins and jewelry across the table and studied them piece by piece. "This gold dirham was struck in Nishapur. Gold is a verra precious commodity, yet in verra low demand in the Levant. Too pure, and it distresses easily—see how worn the edges are? If it stands up to much use, 'tisnae likely worth much."

He fingered a silver-colored coin, a smile teasing his lips. "A Crusader coin. All but worthless. 'Tis a denier made of copper with a bit of silver. Five of these would buy ye a fat chicken." He inhaled sharply. "Och, but these are a find."

Maggie leaned forward, noting the gold coin he held aloft.

"A dinar of the Fatimid Caliphate—likely almost pure gold." He traced a fingertip over the script in the outer circle. *In the name of God this dinar was struck in Misr the year eight and fifty and three hundred.*" He placed the coin back on the table and sat back in his chair.

"Ye've a large number of silver coins which could have come from any place in Scotland, England—or France, for that matter. These gold coins arenae something ye come across every day."

He leaned forward again. "And that doesnae even address the matter of the jewelry. Most appears to be minor bits from a wealthy woman's box, for the stones are unblemished, and the weight of the pieces substantial, but without the ostentatious goose-egg sized ruby or emerald accent piece such as I have seen elsewhere."

"Arbela's wedding finery," Alex laughed.

"Does she still have the dragon's-blood ruby necklace she inherited from her mother?" Phillipe asked.

"A stone as large as a goose's egg?" Maggie was skeptical.

"Och, aye," Alex replied easily. "That and others."

"Who wears such?"

"As Phillipe said, she inherited it from our ma. She was a princess of Armenia."

Maggie went silent. It seemed incredible, yet, the men appeared unconcerned with the discussion of things she'd never dreamed of.

Even the earl's ma wouldnae know what to do with a ruby that big. And, I've never known a true prince before.

"Are ye, then, a prince, Alex?"

He shrugged. "Mayhap. Though it does me little good. Ask Phillipe. Bloodlines and successions are tricky things. His da, Bohemond IV, became Prince of Antioch because he was his father's only living son, though his cousin Raymond-Roupen was the third Bohemond's heir by primogeniture, being the son of Bohemond's eldest, deceased son." He grinned. "As for me, the barony of Batroun—Da's barony—is in Amhal's capable hands where it will remain as long as the region remains in the hands of the Roman church. I'm happy in Scotland. Despite Ma's family ties, I claim no rights to the throne of Cilicia."

Phillipe touched her hand gently. "Remember what I told ye, *mon coeur*? I have no wish to resurrect my past titles. They are meaningless to me, and I have a brighter future without their burden."

Donal cleared his throat. "Is this the whole of the treasure?"

"Nae, m'lord. 'Tis but a sample of the coinage and jewels. The rest is in a locked chest in my chamber. Howbeit, I almost forgot." Maggie slipped a hand through a small slit in her gown to a pouch hidden beneath the cloth and withdrew the jeweled obelisk she had a peculiar reluctance to part with.

"'Tis an unwieldy piece. Rather thick and awkward, I would think, for a brooch." The glimmering crosses shone clear on the smoothly polished rubies and sapphires. Donal held out his hand and she hesitated only an instant before handing him the piece.

The baron hefted it in his palm. "'Tis weighty, yet I dinnae believe 'tis because of the gold." He turned the brooch over and studied a tiny flower carved into its back. He tapped it then flicked it with a fingernail. The brooch gave an answering click and shifted on hidden hinges to reveal a crack running its perimeter. Donal opened the locket. A clear, rather dull stone nestled within winked in the candle light. The baron stared at it, mouth ajar.

"By the saints! 'Tis a reliquary!"

Chapter Twenty Nine

Phillipe shot to his feet, his chair scraping across the wooden floor. "Are ye certain?"

Fingers visibly trembling, Donal carefully plucked the stone from the center of the brooch and held it to the candle light. Something long and slender rested within.

"What do ye suppose 'tis?" Maggie murmured.

Phillipe glanced at the baron who slowly, carefully, placed the shard back inside the brooch and clicked it shut.

"There was a rumor many years ago of a relic of the cross—a splinter of wood with the healing power of our Lord. To keep it from being worn from the touch of many hands, 'twas embedded in a piece of crystal, the process of which is unknown to me." Donal shook his head, eyes on the brooch. "As with many legends, the details changed over time, and the relic was hidden away for fear of it becoming lost or stolen, placed in a container of great beauty though of little value except for the precious treasure within."

Maggie touched the brooch reverently. "This contains a piece of the cross?"

"It appears it somehow made its way to yer isle, and now belongs to ye."

"It . . . it soothed me." She glanced at Phillipe. "I was upset to think the abbey at Hola had been attacked in the past, and as I closed my hand over the brooch, my worries vanished."

He smiled. "Ye hold the true treasure, *mon coeur*. The rest is pretty coins and trinkets. The reliquary is a great responsibility."

"Should this not be relinquished to the church?"

Phillipe hesitated. It was a good question, yet . . ..

"The brooch has come to ye, though we do not know for what purpose," he said. "'Tis a piece meant to be worn, to be accessible to any who need it, even when the request has not been made. Not hidden away or used only for those deemed worthy. We have other pieces we have pledged to return to the church. If ye agree, this will become an heirloom of our house."

Maggie stared at the brooch then closed her fingers over it. "Aye. I dinnae know how to allow others to benefit from this, yet I will do what I can."

Alex shifted in his chair. "Do others know of the treasure?"

Maggie glanced at Phillipe. "I dinnae truly know. We did our best to place the bags within the chest without being seen. Howbeit, 'twas nae a simple job, for all the care we took."

Phillipe frowned. "'Tis one of the reasons we came directly here. There is but one longhouse on the isle, and all share its space. I did not like the thought of leaving the chest alone during the day. 'Tis well known a locked box invites curiosity."

"Ye discovered the treasure yesterday, and came straight to Morvern today?" Donal's glance traveled from Phillipe to Maggie. They both nodded. "What reason did ye give for yer sudden departure? And with the chest?"

Maggie blushed. Phillipe thought the color became her and he lingered on the sight a moment before replying. He placed his hand atop Maggie's, squeezing gently.

"We told them we were traveling to Morvern to wed."

Maggie returned Phillipe's reassuring grip. She swallowed, her throat suddenly dry. The baron beamed. Alex pushed his chair back and rose to clip Phillipe's shoulder.

"Congratulations! I'm verra happy to hear it." Alex glanced between them, his grin as wide as if he'd brought them together himself. "Shall I call for Father Sachairi?"

Maggie stifled a gasp. *So soon?*

At her feet, Serkan shifted with a whine. She dropped her free hand to the pup's head, giving him a soothing pat. He licked her fingers then shoved his head into her lap.

Phillipe inclined his head. "'Tis up to Maggie. Do ye trust this priest? Neither Maggie nor I are overly fond of the self-righteous arm of the church at the moment."

Her eyes widened as a chill shivered through her.

The baron chuckled. "Ye have scandalized yer bride-to-be, lad."

"Nae." She shook her head. "We've each explained our pasts. What he said is nae lie, though I wouldnae have spoken it aloud."

"Dinnae fash. Despite a propensity to conjugate Latin verbs incorrectly, Father Sachairi takes his vows seriously. He is a fair man and willnae speak of anything ye tell him in confidence." Donal rose and crossed to the door. Opening the portal, he spoke to a guard outside then rejoined the group at the table. "I have sent for him. Even if ye dinnae wish to begin the marriage process today, he will mayhap give us an idea where yer holy accoutrements are from."

"I shall retrieve them." Phillipe rose and, placing a kiss atop Maggie's head, strode from the room. Alex gulped down the last of his wine then bolted after Phillipe.

Donal motioned to the table. "Eat, drink. My home is yers."

"Thank ye, m'lord," Maggie replied. "I find my appetite has been replaced by a swarm of *dirdy-flichters* which have taken up residence in my stomach." Her smile only managed to lift a corner of her mouth. "This day has produced many surprises. Forgive me."

The baron waved away her concern. "Och, 'tis nae every day ye come across a hidden treasure *and* accept a marriage proposal from a man scarcely known to ye."

"I have known him longer than I knew my last husband before we wed." She tried another grin with slightly better results. "I am a wee bit breathless over entering into matrimony, but only because I hadnae thought to do so ever again."

Maggie settled back in her chair, fingers ruffling Serkan's ears. The pup groaned.

"I find my decision to wed Phillipe a good one. He has shown me courtesy and encouragement, and is most agreeable to my opinions."

Donal plucked a dark red cherry from the nearly denuded tray. He held the fruit up as if inspecting it for flaws. "A good sight more than mutual respect is needed to create better than a polite marriage. I expect Phillipe to be courteous to any woman, regardless of age or relation." He slid his gaze to Maggie.

Heat rushed her skin. The baron smiled. "Of course, I would also expect Phillipe to choose a wife based on more than a pretty face." He popped the cherry into his mouth, spitting the pit into his hand before dropping it to his trencher where others lay. "Dinnae rely on the earl to have prepared ye for marriage to Phillipe."

Maggie raised a brow. "Shouldn't I be having this conversation with my ma?"

Donal laughed. "Fair enough. I raised the lad to be honorable, and his honor led to his death, but for the grace of Almighty God. I also raised him to be truthful, and he willnae hide himself from ye. He is nearly as much my son as is Alex. I wish only the best for him."

"I understand ye feel protective. But he has done naught to force us to wed. 'Tis of our own free will. Ye shall be content with that." Her brow arched higher. "The rest is nane of yer business."

"Good!" The baron brushed his hands together as if ridding them of more than the crumbs of his late dinner. "Ye are verra welcome in this family, Maggie MacLaren. Ask whatever ye will. If 'tis in my power to grant, 'tis yers."

Maggie lifted her chin. "I ask for help keeping the treasure secure, and in providing protection for the people of Hola. Phillipe and I will handle the rest."

"Done. Phillipe and Alex are excellent strategists and will devise a plan to provide protection without overburdening the isle's resources. If foodstuffs are required to supplement those on the isle, I am pleased to provide such."

Phillipe and Alex strode through the door. Alex set a large cloth bag on the table with a muted clatter, but Phillipe drew to a halt, his gaze on Maggie and the baron.

"Is aught amiss?"

Maggie smiled. "Nae. The baron is quite generous in both his praise of ye and in his offer of help." She crossed to his side and took his arm. "I am interested to see what the priest has to say about our trinkets."

Phillipe's hesitation spoke of his intent to question her further as soon as they were alone, but he returned her smile and patted her hand. "Let us see what we have. Light a few more tapers, Alex. The night is closing in."

The yellow glow of candles replaced the encroaching gloom of evening. Maggie and Phillipe unwrapped the silver flagon and the twelve small silver cups. Taking a quartered lemon, Maggie sprinkled it with salt then gently rubbed the surface of the flagon. A few minutes later, she cleaned it with a swipe of a cloth.

"My God! What have ye done?"

Maggie whirled at the gasp from the door. Phillipe gripped her wrist, yanking her behind him. She teetered off-balance a moment before she regained her footing. Stepping around Phillipe, she noted a slender man dressed in a simple brown robe, tufts of white hair sprouting from his head just above his ears, dark eyes wide. He gazed open-mouthed at the flagon in her hands.

"'Tis a bit of silver we discovered yesterday," she replied, voice low and soothing. "Do ye recognize it?" She glanced at the baron who gave her a solemn nod. Placing the flagon on the table, she took a step back, indicating permission for the priest to examine the piece.

He swept to the table, intent on the flagon. He reached out then drew his hands back. "Twelve cups—one for each apostle," he whispered. "The wine jug decorated with biblical scenes." His hand quivered as he finally touched the flagon.

"Ye know of this?"

He turned tear-filled eyes to her. "Aye. 'Tis the lost relics of Saint Donan who was martyred in the year of our Lord, six hundred and seventeen, along with fifty of his followers, on the isle of Eigg."

Maggie turned to the baron. "How far is Eigg from Hola?"

"I doubt 'tis as much as ten miles distant."

She'd known the flagon and cups were stolen—as was the rest of the treasure. But to hear Father Sachairi's words . . . .

"The silver is in too fine of shape to have been in the water for more than six hundred years. Are ye certain?"

"Have ye more? Mayhap a cross?"

Maggie exchanged a startled glance with Phillipe. He opened the second bag on the table and withdrew the metal cross. The blood drained from Father Sachairi's face, and for a moment, Maggie thought he might collapse. He inhaled deeply and stretched his hand over the cross.

"A ringed cross . . . typical, yet . . .." He gripped the cross in both hands and turned it over. "Aye. A hunting scene." Father Sachairi stared at the cross then lifted his gaze to Maggie.

Awe settled over the old priest's face. "I was a lad when I left Eigg to become a priest. ''Twas accepted by my family to do so, for my ancestors from Iona rebuilt the monastery on Eigg after Saint Donan and his *muinntir* were killed."

"'Twas a long time ago, Father," Maggie said. "Yet, it seems ye recall the tale well. Would ye tell us?"

He nodded. "'Twas a time when the isle was known as *Eilean nam Ban Mora.*"

"Isle of the Big Women?" Maggie's brow furrowed. "Giants?"

"Respected women. Women of consequence," he corrected. "The isle was ruled by Queen Moidart, and her warriors were Pictish women. 'Twas said Saint Donan arrived on Eigg, spreading the Christian faith among the Picts. Queen Moidart, who laid claim to the isle, was angered. Whether by his religion, his popularity among the islanders, or because he'd built his monastery on a prime piece of grazing land . . .." The priest shrugged. "Mayhap a bit of all of it. 'Tis said she ordered the islanders to rid the isle of Donan and his followers, but they refused. She then dispatched her warriors *in defense of the isle.*"

"The monks would have stood no chance against warriors," Maggie exclaimed.

"When the queen's forces arrived, they found the monks singing mass. Donan requested they be left to finish, and the respite was granted. As soon as the liturgy was finished, every one of the monks was slain, and the monastery was burnt to the ground."

Silence filled the chamber. Maggie bit her lip, holding back tears for men long dead. The priest had woven his tale well, making the horrific act seem as fresh as if it had happened only a handful of days past.

"That night," Father Sachairi continued, "at midnight, unearthly voices were heard chanting, and lights rose from the remains of the building. 'Tis said the women warriors, unable to resist, followed the lights up the path to the loch where they hovered just over an island in the middle of the water."

The priest's eyes flashed in unholy vengeance. "Every warrior tamely walked into the loch, eyes fixed upon the lights, and drowned."

Chapter Thirty

Firelight filled the tavern's room with a thick yellow glow, unable to penetrate the soot-darkened windows. Smoke hung low over the tavern tables, rushing in and out of the large chamber as the doors opened and closed. Pausing a moment for his eyes to adjust to the gloom, the Earl of Mar allowed his man servant to tug his rain-beaded cloak from his shoulders. He pulled his gloves from his hands, finger by finger, then set them atop the carefully smoothed wool in the servant's arms.

"Find the innkeeper and secure a room." The earl fished a small coin from the purse tucked inside the waist of his trousers and held it for the servant's taking. His gaze lit on a heavy-breasted tavern wench who cast a look in his direction then tossed her black hair over her shoulder in invitation. The earl settled the snug fit of his trousers and strode to an empty table, his two men-at-arms following at a discreet distance.

The girl sashayed near. "What'll ye 'ave, m'lord?" Her eyes flashed shrewdly, her manner welcoming as she rolled a shoulder enticingly. The neckline of her gown slid a notch closer to the tip of one full breast.

The earl's lips curled. Beneath the table, his cock swelled. "Yer sole attention for an hour, to begin with," he purred as he rolled a copper coin between his fingers.

"Och, 'twill take more than a copper to gie ye what ye're askin'. I risk me job if I'm gone from me duties too long."

"Ye dinnae make more than a copper with yer current duties," the earl scoffed. "And I'm offering to pay to touch what ye so obligingly display."

The girl bit her lower lip, clearly undecided. The earl added a second coin. She brightened.

"Ye'll find me in yer room, m'lord, at yer convenience. T'awd besom can find another lass to fill me shoes for an hour or twa."

Movement at the doorway caught the earl's attention. His brow lifted. *An interesting development.* He waved the girl away. "Bathe first. I'll be with ye in an hour's time."

The man at the door commanded the attention of the entire room as the noise level dropped to near silence and men shrank back to give him and his men space, clearly unwilling to present the man any cause for complaint.

His dark brown eyes shone with glints of gold in the candle and fire-lit room. Broad shoulders fell to a thick waist that the earl knew had naught to do with fat. The three men at his heels appeared cut from the same cloth; fit, brawny, and dangerous.

As if he'd been looking for the earl, the man's gaze pinned him, and he altered his path as he crossed the floor. Legs like tree trunks showed beneath the plaide wrapped about the man's hips. He reached the earl's table and inclined his head inquiringly to the empty chair opposite.

"May I join ye, Earl?"

The earl motioned to the seat. "'Twould please me to share my table, Lord MacDonnell."

The laird grinned as he sat. "But not the treat I saw ye send from yer side a moment ago, eh? Common enough tavern wench, though quite the handful—I'm certain ye know what I mean."

"Ye are, of course, quite welcome to engage her affections once I've finished," the earl demurred, shrugging one shoulder. He tilted his head. "Were ye looking for me? I havenae the time for a game of chance this eve. Mayhap another time?"

"My men told me ye were wont to come here betimes."

"Ye've had me followed? Why?"

MacDonnell's face darkened. "I want me isle back, Mar."

"I gave it to my last wife when I set her aside for not giving me an heir. I dinnae wish to return her dowry, yet I couldnae in good conscience send her home with naught."

"Dinnae wish to embroil the law, eh?" MacDonnell shook his shaggy head. "'Tis likely her dowry went to pay to have the marriage annulled."

The earl huffed. "If she'd only retired to the nunnery as a proper woman would, I wouldnae have given the isle to her. She dinnae know her place, headstrong lass that she is, and I'm well rid of her." He battled down his temper. "I received no monies from the islanders during the two years I owned the isle, despite yer assurances 'twas worth something. The isle and my wife both proved to be of little value."

"'Tis yer fine self what cost ye an heir, not yer wife," MacDonnell growled. "As fond of yer pleasures as ye are, ye should have a large number of bastards to choose from." He glanced pointedly at the corner staircase. "As far as I can tell, the wench awaiting ye in yer chamber willnae need to worry about breeding a bairn from ye, either."

Anger slid white-hot through the earl at Lord MacDonnell's slur against his manhood. "'Tis the woman's job to breed a bairn, mine to enjoy myself planting it. My current wife hasnae been in my bed long enough to show results."

"Ye wasted little time finding a replacement for the MacLaren lass. But I dinnae come here to discuss the merits of yer wives—past nor present. I want the isle back."

Drawing a breath slowly through his nose, the earl calmed. "Why?"

"As I mentioned at our last meeting . . .."

"When ye lost the isle to me," the earl interjected, pleased to see the laird scowl.

"Aye. When ye won the isle." He fumed silently. "It holds a bit of value to me and I want it back."

The earl shrugged, enjoying the MacDonnell's discomfort. "There are many small isles in the waters off the western coast, and ye lord of them all. Surely one of them will do as well?"

"The monks on Hola ferment a mead that pleases my palate. None have been able to recreate it." MacDonnell appeared fit to burst.

The earl allowed himself a small smile. "My friend, it would please me much if ye would take the isle. By as much force as ye wish."

MacDonnell grunted. "What shall I do with yer wife? My information states she and a handful of men-at-arms currently occupy the isle. 'Twillnae be a difficult battle, but there is the potential for bloodshed."

"She lives there? What a peculiar . . .." He leaned forward, forearms on the table. "Tell me, is this mead of yers of any value?"

"They sell half to Baron MacLean, and I receive monies from the sale—along with a tithe of the mead itself."

It was all the earl could do to contain his rage at his lost income. "Then, my dear Lord MacDonnell, take yer isle, its mead, and my un-lamented former wife. Teach her what happens to wayward women who lack the sense to spend their days under the supervision of the church in penance for their sins."

He rose. "Let me know what happens to her. I will be eagerly awaiting the news."

* * *

Lord MacDonnell paced the deck of his ship, impatient to be home. Clouds roiled overhead, presaging the storm on the horizon. Sunlight faded as swiftly as tossing a blanket over the sun. Wind roiled the seas and filled the ship's sail, sending it skudding across the water.

"Lower the sail!" The captain's shout whipped about the ship.

"Nae!" MacDonnell bellowed. "Run ahead of the wind. We'll round the point of Islay and be home before the rains hit."

With a scowl, the captain complied.

"In a haste to return to Finlaggan?" Hugh, Lord MacDonnell's second-in-command braced his feet against the pitch of the deck.

Lord MacDonnell glowered. "Ye will linger only long enough to supply one of the galleys. Twenty men will be enough to subdue the earl's former wife and her rabble. No need to sail a full crew."

Hugh nodded once, thoughtful. "Any thoughts on what ye'd like me to do with the lass?"

"Bring her to me. After that . . .." With a cold lift of a shoulder, MacDonnell consigned an ill end to Maggie's future.

* * *

Jeweled light from three stained glass windows lit the exquisitely carved pillars in the baron's chapel. Every available stone surface was carved, giving the small, private chapel the feel of being inside a flawless work of art. Maggie's gaze traveled from the gold-chased silver cross to the flagon and cups resting on the snowy white cloth draped over a low table. Someone had polished them to a warm glow, and they now resided in a place of honor, appearing quite at home amid the other items on the altar.

Beside her, Phillipe's tall form lent reassurance, filled her heart with joy. Father Sachairi's voice droned through the wedding mass, but she listened to none of it.

I dinnae know we'd found such wealth. Coins, jewels, and accoutrements to make a priest weep—and give absolution for Phillipe's past, and grant me permission to remarry with the church's blessing. The flagon and cross more than paid any penance which could have been set.

The Treasure of Hola was proving to be worth more than the value of its gold.

She stroked the reliquary she'd strung on a silver chain about her neck. The weight of the clasp had pulled at her gown's delicate cloth, and the chain solved the problem nicely, turning the brooch into a pendant. Peace settled over her with the thought she could achieve what she desired most. She sighed happily.

Phillipe squeezed her hand, his thumb drifting over the ring he'd placed on her finger when they'd exchanged their vows at the chapel door an hour earlier. The dark, heavy gold held a magnificent oval lemon-quartz stone the size of her thumb nail, encircled with cabochon rubies and diamonds. She'd never seen a stone so large and half-feared being given the care of it. She glanced at Phillipe, smiling to meet his amused gaze, jolted back to the ceremony by the approach of her father, mother, Uilleam, the baron, Alex, and his sister Arbela who Maggie had met only the day before.

Representing both families, the small crowd surrounded Maggie and Phillipe as the priest spoke his blessing over them.

"*Ego conjungo vos in matrimonium in nomine Patris et Filii et Spiritus Sancti. Amen.*" He placed a hand atop Maggie's and Phillipe's heads. "Go in peace and glorify God." He withdrew his hands and gave Phillipe a nod.

Phillipe's dark eyes met hers, setting up butterflies in her belly. "Ye are the bride of my heart. No matter what came before this moment, and no matter what lies ahead, 'tis ye and only ye who shall have my heart and my name, and possess my very soul for the rest of my life. It pleases me beyond bearing to name ye wife."

He lowered his mouth to hers, lips hot as a searing brand. A moan escaped Maggie. Her arms wound about his neck and she pressed against him, feeling the impediment of clothing between them. Her heart pounded so, she could scarcely think. The kiss ended and she braced her forehead against Phillipe's chest, letting the delicious fog of wanton abandon settle over her and slowly dissipate. The scent of the hot beeswax tapers on the altar blended with Phillipe's own scent, smoky and beguiling.

"Ye are as light to my eyes, as bread to my hunger, and the only joy to my heart," she replied. "I pledge my love to ye and will honor ye above all others. Ye are, from this moment on, my true husband."

A rousing cry filled the room and Maggie's face heated. Phillipe pressed a quick kiss to her temple then faced the crowd, Maggie's upraised hand in his. A yip and answering shout cut through the congratulations.

"Serkan! Get by, dog!"

Alex's bellow did not halt the pup's headlong rush through the crowd. The lightning-fast ball of fur bolted across the room then slid to a stop at Maggie's side. She snatched her skirts aside, rescuing the embroidered velvet hem from mud-spattered paws.

Alex sent her an apologetic look. "It appears he dug out of his kennel, though how he got inside the keep I dinnae ken."

"'Tis also apparent I have competition for my wife's favors, already," Phillipe laughed.

The crowd milled about them, feeding slowly through the chapel doors where they were guaranteed a festive meal and entertainment in the great hall. Alex hoisted his young son onto his hip, then grabbed his sister's step-son by the hand and marshalled the MacLeans from the room. Janeth MacLaren blinked tear-filled eyes and joined her husband and son as they followed Alex and his family. Someone slipped a thin rope over the pup's head and led him away—under protest. The last to leave, Balgair cuffed Phillipe's shoulder and sent Maggie a broad wink.

The voices faded from the room, echoing from the main hall then fell to silence as the door closed. As though he awaited the click of the latch, Phillipe pulled Maggie into his arms. His hungry kiss eclipsed the warmth of the binding one only moments earlier. Possessive, demanding, teasing, he told her how impatient he was to be done with the formalities and have her to himself.

Maggie plundered his mouth, filled her hands with his hair, returning his passion.

A low growl slipped from Phillipe. "Now's our chance to flee to our chamber before we're missed."

"We leave for Hola on the morning tide," Maggie breathed. "We will have little privacy once aboard the ship."

Phillipe ran his hands up Maggie's arms and she shivered. "I am beginning to regret this schedule we've chosen, howbeit, we've much ahead of us in the weeks to come."

"Then, let us leave the others to their merry-making. I find the idea of sharing ye with our guests for the next few hours not to my liking."

Phillipe stepped to the door, Maggie on his heels. A quick glance into the hall told her Balgair guarded the passageway into the hall, leaving the opposite direction exposed. Stifling a mischievous giggle, she slipped through the chapel doors and followed her husband's silent tread to the prepared chamber above.

Chapter Thirty One

Phillipe gazed at his new wife. "Ye should always wear rubies and roses, *mon coeur.*"

Maggie's pale skin blushed, the rosy hue reflecting that of the flower petals scattered across the silken gold brocade blanket and the glow of the ruby bracelets loaned to her for their wedding day by Arbela, her new sister by marriage.

Her fingertips brushed the stones crowding the delicate filigree surrounding her wrist. Phillipe dismissed the sultan's ransom worth of jewels, preferring the bare skin of his new wife who lay beneath him, his cock still buried inside her. Fascinated, he watched the rise and fall of her breasts as she caught her breath from their first, passionate exploration.

Discarded clothing littered the floor without regard for the costly items. Even Maggie's burgundy gown hadn't been proof against the heat of their passion as they'd locked and barred the portal against intrusion. One fluttery sleeve still hung limply from the door latch, not deemed worthy of stopping their urgent need to be alone together.

Phillipe gave her a half-grin. "I did not mean to fall upon ye as soon as we closed the door."

"Hmmm," she murmured, ending on a sigh. She stretched languidly. "I dinnae recall complaining."

"Ye said a number of things. *Halt* was not among them." Phillipe's grin widened, feeling immensely pleased. Despite their rather disrespectful flaunting of the proper wedding rituals, he'd been right to bring her directly to bed. Lingering among the bawdy rabble would only have allowed old memories to surface. Maggie's eager participation in consummating their vows was worth any amount of ribbing he'd endure on the morrow.

He nibbled along her shoulder, making his way to her neck. Her skin tasted of roses, smelt of heaven. And a bit of salty sweat. Divine—and worth exploring further. He trailed his tongue across the soft skin. Maggie gasped and rolled her head to the side, exposing more creamy flesh. He suckled one breast, then the other, cupping them to exquisite fullness in his palms.

234

"Ye are beautiful," he whispered.

Maggie flushed deeper and stilled, the soft lines of her body hardening against his words. "I am too tall, too sturdy to be anything but merely pleasing to the eye."

Phillipe propped his weight on one elbow then ran his fingers slowly through her hair, drawing the flaming curls out to the side to better view the firelit strands.

"I will tell ye every day ye are beautiful, and ye will never disagree with me." He pulled locks of her hair forward to drape over her shoulders and curl over her breasts. Lowering his face to hers, he kissed her, infusing the truth into the caress until her body yielded the argument.

Maggie's moan against his lips sent Phillipe's passion spiraling. The warmth of her enveloping his flagging cock hardened him again. She wrapped her legs about his waist, answering the slow questioning circling of his hips. Her breath quickened then caught as her fingers bit into his shoulders. With a cry, she arched her back, fitting her body perfectly to his.

His own release struck hard. He shouted her name, arms shaking as he poured himself into her. Dragging air into his lungs, he lowered himself to the down-filled mattress, unsure when he'd move again.

Winded, he pulled her against his chest, drawing great draughts of air through her scented hair as he tucked her buttocks against his groin and slid one arm beneath her neck.

"I have never been so complete."

"'Tis beyond me, as well," Maggie murmured, pressing a kiss to the inside of his elbow. His skin pebbled at her touch, but he was beyond rousing—at least for the next half-hour or so.

He woke some time later to find the silken blanket about his shoulders and the sheets next to him empty. Groggy, he sat and wiped a hand over his eyes before casting a glance about the room. Maggie sat upon a folded blanket next to the hearth, one corner pulled over a shoulder as she prodded the peat block into a low flame. The flickering light cast her body in gold relief, outlining every curve, framed the long lines of her arms and legs, and glimmered through the veil of her hair.

Urgency possessed him. He slipped from the bed and crossed to her side. She glanced up, lips rounded softly in surprise.

"I dinnae mean to wake ye."

Phillipe held out a hand. "Ye are welcome to wake me any time, *mon coeur.*"

Her eyelids fluttered and a satisfied smile curved her lips. She grasped his hand and rose from the hearth to lean against him. Heat exploded through him as her hardened nipples pressed against his chest. She hooked a foot behind his ankle and tugged, forcing him slowly to the thick rug before the hearth. Phillipe obligingly sprawled on his back, hands spread invitingly. Maggie straddled his hips, ran her fingers through the hair of his chest.

"My turn."

* * *

There was naught to do but face her fears. One hand clasped firmly in Phillipe's, the other nervously fingering the fine wool of her soft green gown, Maggie strolled into the great hall as if she hadn't spent most of the previous day closeted with her new husband, determined to withstand the ribald jokes certain to greet her after Phillipe's and her precipitous departure following the wedding mass. After waking too late to meet the ship at the dock, Phillipe had sent word they'd not be taking the *Mar* on the morning's tide. The lateness of the morning hour hadn't resulted in an empty hall.

"They linger because they're hung over, not because they wish to bandy words with us," he chuckled.

Phillipe's whispered assurances did not help, though they appeared to be true. Bleary eyes blinked at her from drawn faces as she made her way to the head table, slippered steps hissing loud on the stone. A few people winced and turned away, cradling steaming mugs of some tisane the healer had likely made available to treat their infirmities. Or perhaps the glistening eels Maggie could see heaped upon platters would ease the symptoms of their over-indulgences.

She suppressed a grin and a shudder. Though she'd oft been assured of the eels' worth as a cure for such ailments, the thought of downing the slippery bits had gone a long way toward keeping her on the temperate side of inebriety. Not for a king's ransom would she insult an already abused belly with a helping of eels—cooked or not. She fingered the brooch dangling from its chain then sighed. She already possessed a king's ransom.

The mood of the room lightened as those who'd managed to avoid serious after-effects of the lavish feast, and who appeared to have slept well, drifted into the hall to break their fasts.

Balgair took a seat across from Phillipe, his smile peeking bravely through his whiskers beneath bloodshot eyes. He accepted a steaming mug from a serving lass, but shook his head gingerly at the offer of food.

A noisy trio of lads shot into the hall. Bram, Arbela's step-son and the elder of the two other boys by some five years, leapt about, holding a leather-bound ball in the air, out of the reach of the others. The two younger, scarcely more than toddlers, raced at his heels, squealing with glee. Two men at a far table scraped to their feet and stumbled from the room.

"I see ye've decided to grace the hall with yer presence," Alex said, giving Phillipe a clout to his shoulder. He gave the three lads a stern look then captured a chair next to Phillipe and set about buttering a bannock which immediately was preempted by the eldest boy.

"Ye've had yer morning meal," Alex protested. With a mock scowl, he picked up another bannock.

"Their bellies are naught but empty barrels." Arbela sighed as she sank into the chair across from Maggie. The small, dark woman carried a new bairn all but hidden beneath a sash over her shoulder and across her chest. Maggie had only met her two days earlier and found her straight-forward, kind—and immediately loyal to Maggie whom she hailed as her newest sister.

Maggie sent Phillipe a sidelong glance, wondering about his prior attachment to Arbela, but he joked with Alex, giving Arbela no special heed.

The woman who took a seat next to Alex, his wife, Annag, picked up the youngest lad and placed him on her lap.

Arbela quickly served up a trencher of cheese and bread and set it amid the clamoring lads, silencing them nicely. She dusted her hands. "There. That should do them until the noon meal."

She gave Maggie a conspiratorial smile. "Ye'd best have a limitless larder if ye have lads."

Maggie's skin heated. The conversation seemed odd to have with the woman who'd once held Phillipe's heart.

Could Phillipe be right? Was her barrenness due to the earl's inability to sire a child instead of something wrong with her? Could she conceive Phillipe's child? If not, 'twouldnae be for lack of trying—they'd gotten off to a fair start already.

Maggie cleared the last bit of smoked haddock, white pudding, and sautéed mushrooms from her trencher and reached for the porridge, ignoring Phillipe's grin. He'd eaten well, also.

Casting an arch look in Phillipe's direction, Arbela slipped a bannock from her brother's trencher and took a bite.

Alex shook his head. "She'd leave me to starve," he complained in mock despair.

"Nursing a child, dear brother," she mumbled through the crumbs. "Eating for two."

"Motherhood suits ye," Phillipe said. "I hope ye did not risk your health coming here."

A tender look passed between them. "I wouldnae miss yer wedding, Phillipe. I am pleased to see ye so happy." She tilted her cheek to receive her husband's kiss as he strode behind her. He patted her shoulders and took his seat with a genial nod to the rest of the group.

The exchange warmed Maggie's heart.

The hall began to clear as the last of the stragglers finished their meals and set off to whatever chores or duties awaited them. Servants quickly cleared the tables.

Maggie peered about the hall, looking for her parents. Uilleam slipped behind her and pressed a quick kiss to her cheek.

"Ye are happy, Sister, mine," he said as he settled in the chair next to her and set about piling his trencher high with the various offerings left on the head table. Clearly, he'd either limited his intake of rich food and wine, or had an excellent head for such extravagances. He set the platter of sausage aside and sent her a mocking look. "Though ye fair scandalized Ma when ye dinnae show up for yer wedding supper."

"I'll lay claim to the fault for that," Phillipe said, reaching behind Maggie to tap the back of Uilleam's head. "Don't tease your sister."

Phillipe's words and veiled threat eased Maggie's mortification. She had thoroughly enjoyed herself at her husband's hands, and could think of no good reason to be sorry for it. Especially when . . .. Her throat grew dry and she reached for her mug.

She took several gulps of cider before she dared speak. "I'm verra glad ye were able to come to the wedding, Uilleam. But Da doesnae look well."

Her brother deftly caught the leather ball winging toward his head. He tossed it back to the elder lad who stuffed it quickly beneath the table, flushing darkly beneath Arbela's indignant stare.

"I've heard Cook is looking for a likely lad to keep the birds at bay in the garden." Arbela's statement held a veiled threat, for it was clear young Bram would rather spend the day playing with his cousins than sitting on the edge of the kitchen gardens tossing rocks at unwary birds.

"Can we go play?"

The two younger lads nodded, casting adoring glances at Bram.

"I'll send yer nurse out to ye in a moment. Mind ye, dinnae stray from the yard, and dinnae go near the stables."

Wooden legs screeched against the stone as the boys flung themselves from their seats and bounded from the room. Alex rose, wiping his mouth on a bit of linen. "I'll find Una."

Annag stopped him with a touch to his arm. "Dinnae bother. I'll watch them."

She left the room, Alex's gaze lingering on her a long moment before he returned to his meal.

Maggie turned back to her brother.

"He hasnae been himself of late," Uilleam agreed, answering her concern. "Slow to rise of a morn, and pushing away his trencher." He took a large bite of sausage, nodding thoughtfully. "I heard him coughing the other morn. Ma willnae speak of it."

Maggie's heart sank. Uilleam was too young to remember their grandda's final days. His decline had started as a simple need for extra sleep and eating less than had been his wont, but within the year his legs and belly had become enormously bloated and his wracking cough could be heard throughout the keep.

She pushed away from the table, appetite gone, absently fingering the brooch at her neck. She took a deep breath as the heavy gold weighed against her breast, warm and comforting.

All will be well.

"Uilleam, take this." Maggie lifted the necklace from about her neck.

He eyed her askance. "I dinnae need a necklace."

"Shush. 'Tis nae just a pretty bauble. Within lies a bit of the true cross. This brooch is said to contain the healing powers of our Lord. Wear it or keep it close when ye are near Da. 'Twill help."

Uilleam wiped his fingers on his trousers and held out his hand. She placed the brooch on his palm. He stared at it. "A reliquary? Maggie, the setting alone is worth a fortune."

She nodded. "'Tis worth exactly Da's life."

Chapter Thirty Two

The sun still hovered well above the horizon when the *Mar* slipped from the dock at Morvern on the afternoon's high tide. Seagulls engaged in endless swoops and shrieks as fishermen on the far end of the dock finished sorting their nets and pots for a few more hours of plying the waters of the loch. The scent of fish, water, and wood warmed by the sun assailed Maggie.

She'd had little time to speak privately with her ma, and Janneth had flatly refused to speak of her husband's health. Lips flattened unremittingly as she'd held back tears glittering in her eyes, Janneth spoke only of Maggie's responsibilities as a new wife, her gaze lifted toward the heavens, her lips moving in what Maggie suspected was a short, silent plea that this marriage would be better than the first. Maggie had endured the lecture, sensing her ma knew no other way to express her concern, then escaped to seek a few moments alone in the chapel to pray for her family.

Uilleam stood next to Lady MacLaren on the dock, among those gathered to bid the newly-weds farewell, the brooch sheltered in his up-raised hand in silent promise to do all he could to see their da received whatever treatment needed. Maggie sent her brother a nod of thanks, recalling his assurance he'd send word soon.

People cheered as the Mar rode the tide into the Sound of Mull. The brisk wind of the Sound tangled Maggie's skirts against her legs and teased strands of hair from her braid. She closed her eyes with a sigh and raised her face to its caress.

"We may have a rough sail of it 'ere we reach Hola, if the clouds on the horizon are any indication."

Phillipe's voice in her ear sent shivers straight to her core.

She faced him, pulling a wisp of hair from the corner of her mouth. "Mayhap 'twill head out to sea and spend itself there."

"Mayhap. Alex says storms blow up all too often in the Sound. Hopefully, we will be ensconced in the longhouse, 'ere the rains fall."

"I fear we'll have little time to ourselves on Hola."

Phillipe pressed his hips against hers, his arousal evident even with clothing between them. "Asatrus and Igor snore loudly." He tilted his head, eyes twinkling. "As does Fraida, if memory serves."

Maggie swatted his arm playfully. "'Tis nae gentlemanly to remark on a lady's snores."

"Even my wife's?"

"I dinnae!" Heat flamed Maggie's cheeks.

"Oh, but you did, *ma belle*. Exhaustion dulled your senses, or I'm certain ye would have noticed."

"Our . . . loving dinnae tire ye out?" Maggie affected a pout, for she knew he'd slept deeply as well.

"I woke once or twice if ye recall." He shifted, putting slight space between them, then propped an elbow against the rail. "Ye are beautiful in your sleep. Like an angel."

She huffed but was unable to hide her grin. "Like a snoring angel."

He chuckled. "Like a snoring angel I am blessed to call wife."

Maggie leaned her head against his shoulder and sighed. "Ye are an easy man to love, Phillipe."

"Is that your way of saying ye love me?"

Maggie lifted her head and placed the palms of her hands against the linked mail he wore over his tunic. "Nae. This is how I say I love ye."

She leaned up on her toes, her breasts firm against his chest, and pressed her lips to his. His mouth softened, his arms surrounded her. His tongue tangled with hers and tremors sparked through her belly. With a sigh, she broke the kiss.

"Mayhap this should wait until we have a wee bit more privacy," she murmured regretfully.

Phillipe's moan rumbled in his chest as he tucked her back against his side. "Aye. Though everyone has thoughtfully turned their backs and are busy seeing the *Mar* through the Sound, I am enormously curious to see how ye say I love ye when we're alone."

The clatter of toenails on the wooden planks heralded Serkan's headlong dash across the deck. Sailors' curses rang out. Rigging snapped from their hands as they struggled to keep their feet steady as the pup raced past. A seagull squawked, taking flight as Serkan leapt to the rail. White and gray feathers burst into the air, no longer attached to the hapless bird.

The pup yipped then pranced to Maggie, a bit of down trailing from his jowls.

"Bad dog!" Maggie scolded. "Ye mustnae disrupt the men, and ye cannae chase birds." She turned to Phillipe. "I cannae have him around Colyn if he's a danger."

"I will spend some time with him," Phillipe said. "He needs to be shown what he can and cannot do. He has already abandoned his penchant for jumping on people." Phillipe nodded to the pup who sat at her feet, tail eagerly sweeping the boards. "He wishes to please."

"He likes me." She frowned. "I think I prefer horses."

* * *

The falcon's wings snapped like the sails of a ship against the wind. His cry shrilled, signaling frustration as he shifted his feet on the leather glove, his jesses held tight between Narfi's fingers. Svala clapped her hands, her pale hair bouncing, while Halle's lips thinned in disapproval.

"Let him go!" Sakki cried, shoving his fist into the air in his excitement.

Narfi shook his head. "The wind's kicking up too much. 'Twill bring us a storm soon."

"He's strong," Sakki argued. "I want to see him hunt."

"Nae a lot of prey out," Narfi said, nodding to the skies, empty except for the dark gray clouds roiling in from the sea. "Nae with a *sump* coming on." He peered at the cloud-heavy sky. "Freya insisted ye get yer exercise, but I have a wee mouse to fill yer belly. Nae need to hunt this day."

Narfi placed the bird on a boulder, his talons scrabbling against the rough stone. Turning his back as Maggie had taught him, Narfi scooped the dead rodent from the bag looped over his shoulder. He faced the bird.

"Here, *fálki*. Eat."

The falcon cocked his head then snatched the proffered meal from Narfi's glove. Pinning the body with one claw, he consumed the mouse with great relish.

"Ewww!" Svala covered her mouth and nose.

Narfi frowned. "I am happy to provide yer meat, but I dinnae have to watch ye shred it."

"Do ye think Freya would let ye keep him?" Sakki asked. "Ye've had the care of him this past sennight and more."

Narfi shook his head. "She doesnae intend to keep him past his first year. She wants him to be free."

"But, what if he dinnae wish to be free?" Sakki insisted. "Do ye think he's attached to ye?"

"I dinnae know. ''Twould be grand to keep him, but he isnae a pet."

He turned his attention down to the water's edge where seals crowded, barking as they jostled for position on the rocks. The cliffs provided the seals protection from the hunters' arrows and spears, for even if they killed one of the great beasts, it was the task of all the men to drag the carcass up from the beach. Waves crashed against the rocks beyond the cove, a proven barrier against those of Hola who sought the seals from the sea.

"I want to look for baby seals," Svala said, apparently forgetting the falcon's bloody display as she stepped to the overlook.

"Dinnae get too close!" Halle warned. "The edge is dangerous."

Svala wrinkled her nose and halted a few feet from certain disaster.

Halle joined her. "I dinnae see any pups yet."

"Soon. Then 'twill be truly noisy here." Sakki and Narfi came alongside the girls, peering over the rocks to the beach below.

"Watch out. Mayhap the pirates will return," Sakki teased. He gave Svala's braid a tug.

She shrieked and pulled away. "Dinnae say that! Ye're bad!"

Halle cupped the small girl's shoulders in her palms to steady her. Svala leaned against the older girl, a scowl half-angry, half-frightened on her face.

"Ye know better than to taunt her," Halle scolded.

"She's just a bairn. She doesnae remember . . .."

"I do, too! They made my ma cry." Svala snuffled.

Halle tucked the girl beneath her arm. "Leave off, Sakki, or I'll tell ma."

With murmurs of comfort, Halle led Svala away.

Tufted grass swayed in the freshening breeze. Sea spray peppered Narfi's cheek and he tasted salt on his tongue. "We should hurry. The storm is rising."

"Wait." Sakki touched Narfi's arm. "Look."

Bits of sandy soil rose in the air, driven by a sudden spiral of wind. Clouds lowered to mingle with the surf, and sheets of rain drove down upon the waves as the storm raced toward the shore. Narfi raised his arm to shield his face. "What did ye see?"

Sakki held silent as he peered through the swelling storm. Thunder rumbled overhead. "I cannae say. 'Tis vanished." He sighed. "I thought 'twas a pirate ship."

Narfi glanced over his shoulder. Heads bent against the wind, Svala and Halle hurried down the path. "Ye shouldnae tease Svala."

"'Tisn't about Svala. I thought I saw a sail."

"Are ye certain? Should we inform Asatrus?"

Sakki shrugged. "Nae one can land on this side of the isle. Mayhap I was mistaken. 'Twas only a glimpse. Ye are right. I shouldnae have said what I did to Svala."

"Nae. Ye shouldnae. But if ye saw a sail, we should alert the guards."

Large drops of rain pelted down. Sakki waved a hand. "Forget it. 'Twas naught. Let's go home."

* * *

Dawn sifted through the lingering clouds, casting them in pink, orange, and gold against a blue-gray sky the same deep hue of the choppy seas that had yet to give up the fury of the prior evening's storm. Waves crashed, spewing white foam in a furious roil against the rocks. Mist floated knee-high above the grass and muffled the normal early morning sounds.

Maggie's head nestled on Phillipe's shoulder, warm and relaxed. Her breath came in deep draughts, misting faintly in the cool air. A wool blanket kept the brunt of the mud and damp away, though he'd paid little thought to it until just a few moments ago.

The bark of a seal, softened by the fog, sounded below. A chill breeze wafted over the promontory. Salt scented the air. The hallmarks of Phillipe's new life.

"I am blessed." He drew the edge of his cloak over Maggie's thinly-clad shoulder and tucked it about her neck.

She stirred, turning her face into his chest. "I agree, but what makes ye say this?"

Phillipe smiled contentedly. "I have everything I could ever wish."

"Ye wish to make love to yer wife on a cold overlook, in the mud?"

He ruffled her hair. "I would make love to ye anywhere. Save, mayhap, the noisy, cluttered longhouse. The snores and proximity of the others kept my ardor at least cooled to a manageable level overnight."

Maggie shifted. "I dinnae care for the rocks." She reached an arm around and plucked a fist-sized stone from beneath her back. "Mayhap we should have retired to the abbey. Though if the mead turned sour or the apples dinnae make, we'd get the blame for desecration." She chucked the rock away and it clattered its way through the fog.

Maggie sat and stretched, her face upturned toward the sky. Her flaming hair pooled on the blanket around her hips. Her thin shift stretched across her breasts, teasing Phillipe as the cloth slid over her skin. He cupped one breast, the nipple firm against his thumb.

Maggie smiled and bent to caress him. "I love what ye do to me, how ye spark desire in me with the look in yer eyes. I love yer touch, the way ye fill me and hold naught back from me."

"Ye have given me your trust and your heart." Phillipe groaned as the stroke of her hand increased. "Naught could be better than this."

Maggie stilled. "Did ye hear a shout?"

"I hear my heart pounding in my ears, love. Naught else." He silently cursed the interruption as Maggie patted him absently, her head tilted in a listening posture. "Give me a moment whilst I look."

He rose to his feet and inhaled deep as his cock vied with his brain for attention. Slipping on his trews, he managed to get them seated properly, then slid his feet inside his boots. Awareness of his wife's approving appraisal of his still mostly-naked form did nothing to lessen the tightness of his breeches, yet her distracted manner concerned him.

Accepting his tunic as she handed it to him, he pulled it over his head, leaving the strings to trail untied at his neck, then strapped his sword belt about his waist. Once away from their shelter between two large boulders, the brisk air raised hen's flesh on his arms. Sunlight peeked from the thinning clouds and fog parted enough to see the beach below. Seals plunged about, sliding off their rocks with enough racket to raise the dead.

246

What on earth could cause such a ruckus? He stepped closer to the edge, urging the wind to sweep away the fog lingering over the water. His boots sank silently into the soft soil.

A flash of black, stark against the gray mist, caught his attention. Amid the barks of the seals came the creak of wood.

Asatrus assured me his boats could not sail into the harbor at the rookery.

Dread came over him. *Asatrus is not a sailor. Asatrus is a mazer.*

He spun on a heel to warn Maggie. A flash of steel winked above an instant before it struck his head and darkness ended the pain.

Chapter Thirty Three

Maggie gathered her clothing. Something was not right. The sky promised a beautiful day—eventually—with the sun peeking through clouds paling from pink to white. The mists had thinned, though they still drifted above the ground and fluttered from the crevices of the cliffs like shreds of funeral shrouds. Despite the sunshine and the flowers tended by busy bees, something dangerous lurked nearby. The nearby birds had fallen silent and the otherwise normal pleasantries of a late spring day could not dispel her worry.

She dressed quickly, pulling her kirtle and surcoat over her thin chemise. She slipped her dagger into the front of her bodice, wishing she had something more substantial with which to protect herself.

I wasnae thinking of my crossbow when we slipped out of the longhouse this morn.

The memory of what *had* been on her mind brought a flush of heat to her cheeks, but was not enough to settle her fears. Another wave of uneasiness swept over her and she glanced toward the edge of the overlook where Phillipe had headed . . . a dark silhouette, shoulders wider than Phillipe's, the height not as tall, stood over a crumpled form. Maggie hobbled to the edge of the sheltered area for a better look, one boot partially on, the other dangling from her hand.

Phillipe lay sprawled on the ground.

"Nae!"

The attacker stepped away, ignored as Maggie's gaze focused on Phillipe's unmoving body. Without a second thought, she lifted her skirts and charged across the field. Rough hands grabbed her from behind as she reached Phillipe, jerking her off her feet. She shrieked and reached behind her head, fingers stiffened, clawing at her attacker. He barked angrily as her nails caught soft flesh, and flung her away. Arms wind-milling for balance, Maggie landed on her feet in a crouch, wasting a scant second to adjust her weight before launching at the ruffian.

Fist closed, she put her entire weight behind a strike to the man's head. Pain shot through her knuckles as she encountered the solid bone of his cheek. He reeled back on one foot. Ignoring the agony in her hand, she pushed her advantage. Planting one foot behind his forward leg, she shoved hard against his shoulder. Caught off-guard, he tripped and fell heavily to the ground.

"Get back!" he shouted, raising his hands protectively.

Maggie fell atop him, one knee in his chest. His breath whoofed out in a great gasp. Fury riding her like a demon, she snatched her dagger from its sheath and forced it against his throat, burying it beneath the shaggy beard.

"If ye so much as breathe loudly, I will silence ye permanently."

His eyes widened. He slowly spread his hands wide. "I will do as ye say."

"I dinnae care if ye live or die." Maggie's heart pounded wildly in her ears. Her hands trembled. She shook her head as her vision darkened at the edges. "Who are ye and why are ye here?"

The man relaxed beneath her and a grin parted his beard. "I am Brandr Ottosen, and *we* are here for ye."

* * *

Phillipe sputtered awake, cheek against the sand. He gagged violently as he sucked salty water into his nose and throat. Disoriented, frantic for breath, he braced his hands on the sand and raised his chest from the waves. He inhaled sharply and water shot into his lungs. He choked then gagged again as more landed in his belly. His stomach protested the heavy brine and he vomited onto the sand, eyes closed against the sun and the misery shooting through his head.

Belly mollified, he lowered himself to the ground and rolled to his back, cautiously laying an arm over his eyes to blot out the sun. The crash of surf surrounded him, punctuated by the barks of seals. Memory of a raised arm and the heavy hilt of a sword ran through his mind. Who had struck him and why?

Maggie.

With a groan, Phillipe pushed to a seated position, opening his eyes determinedly against blinding pain. He felt gingerly along the side of his head and found the skin split, an area the size of the palm of his hand swollen and tender.

He gritted his teeth. *I must find her.* He rose but could not stand upright. Listing to one side, he staggered a few steps until he came to rest against a large boulder. He gripped the stone, struggling to keep his feet beneath him, unwilling to resign to the ground. He must find Maggie. Nothing else mattered.

"Phillipe!" Balgair's voice boomed from above.

Phillipe swiveled toward the sound, but his feet didn't respond properly and he landed, legs beneath him, on his butt in the sand. "*Fils de . . ..*"

"Eejit."

Debris clattered down in a shower of pebbles, sand, and grass. Instinctively, Phillipe raised an arm to ward off danger. The end of a rope dropped suddenly and coiled on the ground. A pair of boots topped by stout, hairy legs dangled above Phillipe's head. More pebbles and sand cascaded down as Balgair descended the face of the cliff. Landing on the beach, he dusted his hands and straightened the drape of his plaide. He peered at Phillipe.

"Ye look like hell."

"Where's my wife?"

"I dinnae ken, laddie. The morning wore on and since even I would have a hard time keeping it up that long, I came along to ask ye to join the rest of us as we've a lot to accomplish." He squared his jaw and his eyes hardened. "I havenae seen Maggie, only a scuffed area near the secluded bit on this overlook. Someone must have taken her, though it appears she put up a fight."

Phillipe groaned and held out a hand for assistance to his feet. "Maggie thought she heard something. I went to investigate and someone coshed me over the head. They must have tossed me off the cliff for good measure."

"Ye shouldnae be standing here talking to me, 'tis that great of a fall. Ye're a lucky bastard."

"'Tis clear the fates have a worse death awaiting me. I must find Maggie."

"We need to get ye back to the longhouse and get yer heid stitched and come up with a plan. I hate to say it, laddie, but she could be anywhere by now."

* * *

Maggie's kirtle and surcoat were filthy from the scramble down the cliff to the beach, torn from her frantic fight against her captors as they'd rolled Phillipe over the edge of the overlook. A tightly-bound rag had muffled her cries, a bit of rope tied her hands, leaving only her feet loose for walking. The pirates had quickly learned such measures weren't enough to keep Maggie subdued, and most had bruises to show for their mistake. They'd manhandled her aboard their waiting ship and kept watch over her with distrustful eyes during their short sail to a nearby isle.

The shallow cave they took refuge in reeked of smoke, whisky, and unwashed bodies. Four men made up her guard, one more or less tasked with keeping an eye on her, the other three congratulating themselves with a good amount of whisky for a job well done—whatever it was. With their accelerating raucous behavior, she was just happy to keep out of their notice.

She was also livid that she'd been captured, and frightened more than she'd dreamed possible, not knowing Phillipe's fate.

Her fingers twitched. She tested the rope binding her hands behind her. They had not loosened since the last time she'd tried, and the rough fibers bit into her wrists. Her right hand was swollen, knuckles likely cracked from hitting the brute's cheek. Damned hard-headed man!

I've earned their enmity twice over. I warned them—they simply couldnae stay away. Is it the mead that drives them? Or the legend of the treasure? Or, mayhap, something else? She shied from the thought she might have brought this to Hola. She was finished with the greed of men.

She pushed against the foul-tasting rag in her mouth with her tongue and discovered it had loosened. Shielded from her captor's direct view by the flickering shadows, she rubbed her cheek against her shoulder, shifting the rag further. A few minutes later, she worked it from her jaw and it fell around her neck. The relief was immediate.

"MacDonnell's man will be here anon," a man said as he slurped from the whisky flagon. Maggie caught the glimmer in his eye as he shifted his glance to her. "He'll give us the lass—when he's finished with her."

A chorus of belches and other bodily noises rose as if in celebration of—MacDonnell? The Lord of the Isles? Of the Southern Hebrides at least. The man the earl had bested in a game of chance to win the isle of Hola.

What could be his intent? Thank God it required her to be unmolested—at least until her use was at an end.

Her keeper swayed, eyelids at half-mast. Taking a risk he was too drunk to realize she'd dislodged her gag, Maggie nudged him with her foot. "What does MacDonnell want?"

The man eyed her blearily, but the use of the name seemed to claim his attention. "The isle. And the mead." He belched.

Maggie drew a sharp breath. "Ye accosted me, attacked my husband—for the isle and some mead?" Her voice rose and she bit her lip, hoping the others, seated several feet away, hadn't heard.

"Best mead. None like it. Lord MacDonnell wants his isle back. Since yer husband doesnae own it anymore, we got ye."

The somewhat garbled information told Maggie what she wanted to know, though she could scarcely believe the explanation.

Her keeper stood, stooping slightly to keep from bumping his head on the ceiling—or perhaps because he was hardly able to stand. He shuffled to the dim corner of the chamber which was less than half the size of the longhouse. Maggie could see no other entryways branching from the single room. Piles of shrubs filled the only access, blocking nearly all the sunlight, and likely disguising the opening from casual view. Snores ruffled from the three men who'd abandoned their drinking and apparently decided to await their lord and master by sleeping off their drunken spree.

The tinkling sound of water reached her ears and the man set to watch her sighed. He braced against the far wall with one hand, his other occupied beneath his plaide. He pushed away and stumbled back to his spot only a few inches from Maggie and collapsed.

Maggie watched the man with disgust as he fought against sleep.

He swayed, body drifting from side to side. Finally, his head thudded softly against the wall at their back. He sat, mouth agape, eyes rolled back in his head.

The hilt of Maggie's dagger lay stiff within her bodice. Maggie raised her hands, angling so her stiff fingers gripped the leather-wound steel. With extreme care, she awkwardly slid it from its sheath. Her heart raced, breathing deepened.

Propping the hilt between two stones, she placed the rope binding her wrists against the sharp edge. She worked her hands back and forth, wincing as the blade nicked her skin. The rope parted and the dagger clattered against the rocks. Maggie glanced quickly to her captor.

He snorted.

She froze.

With a muffled rumbling honk, the ruffian shifted his position against the wall. His eyelids fluttered then flew open wide. He scrambled to sit, but Maggie was on him in an instant, knife pressed to his neck, one thin arm wrenched behind his back.

"Dinnae so much as breathe loudly. Blink twice if ye understand yer life is forfeit if ye dinnae mind what I say."

His blink came without hesitation and rose to his feet at Maggie's gesture.

She shuffled quietly past the three sleeping ruffians, keeping the fourth silent with the prodding promise of her dagger. Her breath came shallow and rapid, consumed with escape. Thus far, the command from MacDonnell to merely restrain her until he came for her had held. Drunken fumes rose from the sprawled bodies on the floor of the cave. Sound judgement did not seem likely when they woke.

Fear of discovery choked her, increased the sound of feet against sand, magnified the pounding of her heart. She and the pirate stepped past the low fire. Maggie averted her face to avoid inhaling the trail of smoke winding its way through a narrow crack in the ceiling.

She flexed her fingers to relieve the cramp in her hand, wincing at the pain but relieved to find all the parts moveable—if uncomfortable. Her grip strengthened on the dagger's hilt.

"They will come after ye," the pirate whispered. His drunken mien vanished and he shot a glance of hatred over his shoulder.

Maggie's heart raced. She squared her shoulders and gave him another prod. "Dinnae speak."

He cursed under his breath and pushed aside the brush hiding the opening to the cave. The rustle of dry branches sent signals of alarm racing through her veins. She hesitated, ears primed to any movement from the drunken ruffians. Satisfied they'd not been alerted, Maggie pushed the pirate ahead of her and stepped through the entry and into the sunlight. A fresh breeze caressed her face and she inhaled deeply. The rush of air caught in her throat and she quickly stifled a cough.

The pirate whirled, meaty palms catching her shoulders, trapping Maggie's hands between them. She grabbed the hilt of her dagger in both fists then shoved the weapon forward with all her strength, burying the blade deep within his belly. She jerked her hands upward and felt the tip of the dagger jar against something hard. Blood gushed hot over her hands and she released the hilt as though stung. She stared at the pirate, frozen in shock.

He gasped. His hands flew protectively to his stomach, body doubled over as Maggie backed away.

"Ye've kilt me!" He stared at her, eyes wide with disbelief. He glanced down. Bright blood glistened on the sand at his feet. His gaze returned to hers and his legs trembled. With a thud, he fell to the ground.

A disgruntled voice echoed behind her in the cave. Maggie threw a panicked look over her shoulder. Her legs quaked and her stomach dropped. She'd killed one pirate, but she stood no chance against three. A single blow from a meaty fist would fell her. Anger rose, battling her fear. She knew what these men were capable of. What fate awaited her. She would not allow them to capture her. She snatched the dagger from the dead pirate, jerking it free of its gory sheath.

Sounds from inside the cave died away. How long before they realized she was no longer there? Brush partially hid the opening, but sunlight fell through the bits which had been pushed aside. It would eventually be noticed. And mere shrubbery would not prevent their pursuit once her escape was discovered.

Driftwood lay strewn about the beach. Hands trembling, she swiftly gathered an armful and placed it at the entry to the cave.

They arenae too drunk to chase after me, but mayhap they willnae be so quick to dart through flames. But to obtain the embers needed to set the driftwood ablaze, she must enter the cave again. She quailed. *I cannae.* She shook her head. There was no other option.

Head pounding, she swallowed the nausea rising in the back of her throat. She eased inside the cave, holding her breath as she listened, allowing her eyes to adjust to the firelight once more. A man tossed from one side to the other with a rustle against the sand, throwing one arm against the man next to him. With a muttered curse, the second ruffian shoved back.

"Keep tae yerself," he grumbled.

Giving him the space of two breaths to settle, Maggie shifted her attention to the fire. Her leaden arms and legs weighed too much to move, but she edged closer to the glowing bits of wood. She pulled a partially burned brand from the coals, her trembling hand knocking the wood from its arranged pile. The embers hissed and popped. Muttering an *Ave Maria* beneath her breath, she eased back through the entry. Kneeling, she inserted the burning stick within the wood and blew it into fiery life.

Smoke billowed as the fire licked the damp driftwood, then lapped hungrily at the dead shrubbery shielding the opening. Lingering a moment as the flames blazed, Maggie flinched at the scrambling sounds and cries that rose beyond the fiery curtain.

Taking to her heels, she fled across the sand to where the pirates' birlinn lay beached half in, half out of the water.

Keening cries raked through the air. Maggie glanced back to the cave. A man raced in a circle a short distance behind her, arms waving frantically, clothes aflame. Jolted by fresh fear, Maggie increased her pace across the beach.

Her hands shook as she hacked at the rope tethering the ship to a large rock. Strands frayed then parted swiftly. Tucking the dagger into her bodice, she hiked her kirtle above her knees then retied her belt to keep the skirt out of the surf. Digging her feet into the sand, hands on the prow of the ship, she pushed it into the water. Turning the boat to face the open sea, she climbed aboard. Using the rudder, she sculled away from the beach, into the waves. The ship rocked beneath her feet as the sea gained control of the ship.

Her mind went blank. She stared at the ropes, trying to remember sailing with Uilleam on the loch. Which ones raised the sail aloft? How did she tie it off?

Tears flowed. She would not be bested by a damn boat. She *would not* be at the mercy of the pirates again. Maggie wiped her sleeve across her eyes and stared challengingly at the sail. *I will master ye.*

The yard. It holds the sail. Raise the yard and the sail will follow.

Uilleam's voice came as clear as if he stood beside her. Maggie's tremble eased and she stepped confidently to the mast and untied the lines holding the sail in place. As if in league with the pirates, the wind whisked the halyard from her grasp, dangling it just beyond her reach over the edge of the birlinn. The ship tilted, angling back toward the beach. Exasperated, she pulled back her skirt and placed a foot on the wet rail. The rope flapped out of reach.

Be careful, lassie. If it isnae safe, find a better way.

She glanced about and spied a long slender rod with a rusted hook at one end. Mindful to keep her weight canted inside the boat, she leaned over the rail and snagged the errant rope with the metal hook.

Do ye ken where ye're going?

Several yards now distanced her from the beach as the current tugged the birlinn toward the open ocean.

"Nae. I dinnae," she whispered, despair rising once again. "Wait. 'Twas morn. The sun was in my face. We sailed *east*, away from the harbor, then south, rounding Hola's eastern point." She peered at the sky. The sun dipped a few degrees toward the horizon to her left. *West. That's west. Hola must lay ahead.*

Taking a deep breath, she pulled the halyard and raised the black sail a few feet, arms straining as wind filled the cloth. Though she sacrificed speed, handling the boat was easier with the shortened sail, and it would also make her less visible from a distance to other boats she might encounter.

The ship leapt across the water, dancing before the wind, heading east. She tried to bring it about with the rudder, but the birlinn bit the waves like a fractious horse champing at the bit. She lowered the sail a bit more, sighing with relief as the birlinn settled.

She risked a glance at the beach behind her, a brush of pale gold against the sea, backed by low fields and flowers. Beautiful—and nearly her undoing. Yet, she had escaped. She'd killed a man outright, saw another burn who likely would not linger long with his wounds—if he still lived.

She glanced at her hands, firm on the rudder, one swollen and bruised, both stained rust-brown with dried blood. Memory swamped her. The firm feel of her dagger against the pirate's belly—the sudden give of flesh against the blade. Blood, hot with life, gushing over her hands. Her stomach roiled. She lurched forward, landing on her knees, vomiting on the planks as horror washed over her.

I killed him. With my own hand, I took his life. Plunged my dagger into his belly, watched his eyes widen in shock, fade into death.

She retched again, tears mingling with the yellow fluid which was all her stomach now contained. Breathing deeply, she calmed, then eased back to the bench and took the rudder again to correct the birlinn's course. It answered with a bone-jarring dip in the trough of a wave, but Maggie guided it determinedly toward the black cliffs that rose in the distance.

She was going home.

Chapter Thirty Four

With Balgair's help, Phillipe reached the top of the cliff before he passed out. He woke to darkness and a slight pressure on his brow. He raised a hand and encountered a pad across his eyes. The heavy cloth was removed, and the fuzzy image of an old woman, gray hair lying about her shoulders, smiled at him.

"How do ye feel?"

Phillipe squinted, just barely able to discern a bead of light outlining the shape of a door. The cover flapped, bringing sunshine and a fresh breeze into the chamber before it swung closed again.

"I want my wife." The words emerged, a cross between a rasp and a wheeze. Phillipe winced at the swollen, ragged sensation in his throat.

The cloth over the doorway moved again and a figure darkened the portal. Balgair dragged a stool across the dirt floor and settled on it next to Phillipe.

"I've a bit of news for ye. First, ye've been here a brace of hours or so and 'tis past the noon hour. Ye took quite a blow to yer heid, and being tossed from the cliff dinnae do ye any favors. Fraida has stitched ye up nicely and has some manner of noxious brew for ye now ye're awake."

The woman held out a steaming mug. Fighting the frustrated urge to throw the mug across the room, Phillipe allowed Balgair to help raise him enough to choke down the tisane. It was as noxious as Balgair'd promised.

His friend grunted as Phillipe passed him the empty mug. "Here's what I've learned. It seems yester eve, just before the storm hit, Narfi and Sakki were on the overlook with yer wife's falcon. As they watched the seals and the storm rolling in, Sakki thought he saw something. He'd been teasing Svala about pirates—which he kens he shouldnae do—and decided 'twas his imagination, though he first told Narfi he thought he saw a sail."

"*Merde*," Phillipe hissed. "Why were we not told this?"

"It seems they forgot in all the excitement of our arrival."

Phillipe swung his legs over the side of the cot, raising his head slowly against the roiling protests shooting arrows behind his eyes. He placed his feet on the floor and rose, palms braced against his thighs.

"Fraida says ye arenae to rise for at least a full day," Balgair offered as he reached a hand to steady his friend.

Phillipe glared at him, head tilted and bowed slightly forward. "I willnae lie abed whilst my wife is missing. We will set a watch on the promontory and on the beach, then send the *Mar* to Morvern and request ships to sail to all neighboring isles."

"I've already placed men all over the isle, even at the monastery in case the pirates have grown wings. Which reminds me, I saw a bit of trampled grass on the overlook when I was looking for ye, which means they likely made their way to the rookery then climbed the cliffs there."

"Then I'll be about finding Maggie."

He reeled at the onslaught of sunlight as he brushed aside the door hanging. He could see naught but bright light and vague dark lines that could have been people, boulders, or the frame the women used to smoke fish. Two forms approached. Phillipe shielded his eyes, fuming at his weakness.

"Sir, we havenae seen or heard anything." Asatrus' voice carried a thread of worry.

Phillipe waved his hand impatiently. "I do not want the boys punished, but there is now an edict that all sightings will be treated with utmost importance. All will report to whomever is in charge that day, and they will be taken seriously. I do not know what has happened nor how the pirates landed on the isle without notice, but it will not happen again. Am I clear?"

Asatrus bowed his head. "Aye, my lord. 'Tis clear."

Footsteps thudded up the path. Phillipe squinted his eyes, gratified to find the sun's assault lessening. The lad, Narfi, huffed to a halt next to Asatrus, grabbing his sleeve, eyes wide.

"I've come from the point," he panted, canting his head to the highest part of the isle. "Evan says to tell ye a ship's been spotted."

Balgair shouldered through the doorway. "What kind of ship, lad?"

"A birlinn, sir. 'Tisnae like the pirate's ship. This one has a black sail."

Phillipe turned to Narfi. "Get Callan. Have him bring three men with him and meet me on the beach. I want him here before that ship docks."

The lad scampered off, leaving Asatrus and Sakki staring expectantly. MacLean men and islanders clustered near.

"Sakki, get my mail from inside."

As quick as an otter sensing danger, Sakki disappeared inside the longhouse. A moment later, he returned, Phillipe's chain mail flashing beneath the lowering sun. With Balgair's help, Phillipe dressed, patting his sword and each sheathed dagger in a pattern long since committed to memory as he checked the placement of each. With swift movements, he tied his cloak about his shoulders.

"The rest of ye, follow me."

Ignoring the wavering images and throbbing pain in his head, Phillipe strode to the beach, men fanned out behind him, Balgair and Asatrus at either side. Slanting rays of sun turned the sea to gold, penance for the previous day's storm.

The birlinn eased into the harbor, sail reefed to half its size though the wind was calm.

Maggie.

He pushed thoughts of her from his mind. He could not allow distractions to what could become a battle once the ship docked.

The birlinn inched closer. Phillipe squinted against the sun, trying to determine the number of people aboard the small ship, but the black sail disguised the silhouettes. The ship's oars were not in evidence, leaving the birlinn at the whim of the wind and rudder. It slipped against the dock with a gentle creak of boards. The spar tilted and the sail drooped against the mast, losing the wind.

"They willnae make a quick escape," Callan noted, slightly out of breath from his race from his vantage point. Paden, Dawe, and Gunn joined him.

Phillipe grunted his acknowledgement of Callan's observation. Whoever commanded the birlinn clearly did not envision a swift departure from the harbor. Yet, he still saw no evidence of warriors or war trappings. Was the ship's captain that bold? Or that ignorant?

"There." Callan pointed to the bow of the ship. A figure stepped across the prow to the dock, back bent, hands splayed for balance at the rail—skirts playing about her ankles.

Phillipe shot forward as red hair flamed against the sky, shrugging off Callan's restraining grip.

Maggie.

Maggie straightened, hand gripping the rail. A bonfire on shore told her the birlinn had been spotted. Men lined the harbor, but from this distance, Maggie could not put names to any of them.

Where is Phillipe? Has anyone found him?

Shouts rang out.

"M'lady!" Callan's voice.

She stumbled forward, catching her gown on a splinter. With an impatient jerk, she freed the hem, ignoring the tear as the cloth gave way.

"Phillipe?" Her voice caught. Tears blinded her. So close. So close to the people she knew and cared for—who cared about her. A few more steps and the pirates would be a memory. A few more steps and she would know . . ..

Hands gripped her shoulders. She ground her teeth, fighting the instinctive urge to fight free. She inhaled sharply, swallowing a shriek.

"Maggie." A man stepped close. "*Mon coeur.* I am here."

She whirled.

Phillipe. Her heart raced. "I saw . . .. I saw ye fall . . .."

The grip of his arms belied any injury, but in the instant before he crushed her to him, Maggie caught a glimpse of a long wound, freshly stitched, on the side of his head. The pallor of his skin bespoke pain, the quiver of his muscles matched her own as her body rejoiced in his touch.

Gradually, her heart settled to its normal rate and she pulled reluctantly from his embrace. Still within the circle of his arms, she gently brushed his hair aside, tilting her head as she viewed his wound.

"Ye have a penchant for head injuries. Should this worry me?"

His quiet snort of laughter was a balm to her heart, one she'd thought never to hear again. Tears sprang to her eyes again. She cleared her throat and sniffed.

He smiled. "I believe ye know my tale, and 'tis a short one. Balgair found me at the bottom of the cliff and brought me back." He searched her head to toe and back. "Are ye wounded? How can I care for ye?"

"There is naught a bit of salve and time willnae cure," she replied, indicating the nicks and burns on her wrists, the swollen knuckles of her right hand. She flexed her fingers, the pain slowly lessening. "They were commanded not to molest me—and to await their leader."

Phillipe's gaze darkened. "We will speak of their leader."

Maggie did not ask what would be done. Her husband's eyes spoke death.

He smoothed windblown hair away and cradled her face between his hands. "Will ye come tell us all of what happened to ye?"

She nodded. "Aye. We must decide what needs to be done."

Chapter Thirty Five

Phillipe led Maggie to the longhouse. Benches had been moved outside where space would accommodate them all. Islanders, MacLarens, and MacLeans hovered near. Ingrida handed Maggie a mug, steam wafting from the surface of the fragrant mead. Encircling the cup with both hands, she held it without speaking for several moments before taking a sip.

She glanced at Phillipe, anguish in her eyes. His heart twisted. *Ye did not sit and await your fate. Thank God ye did no*t. He placed a hand reassuringly on her forearm and waited for her to gather herself. A weak smile flitted across her lips.

"I saw ye fall. I ran to ye . . .." She shook her head. "A man grabbed me. I fought, but three more came. They took me to another isle not too far distant and hid me in a cave."

She fell silent and Phillipe scooted closer to her on the bench, offering comfort with his touch.

"I escaped . . .." She shook her head and Phillipe did not push her for details. "Their boat was on the shore. 'Twasnae much different from sailing on the loch, and I sailed it home."

"Why?" he asked, struggling to keep his voice level. "Why did they take ye?"

"They said they were to await Lord MacDonnell's man and turn me over to him when he arrived." Maggie scowled. "MacDonnell wants the isle back."

Noises of disapproval rumbled through the crowd.

MacDonnell hasnae proven loyal. Alex's words ran through his mind.

He placed his palm on Maggie's shoulder. "We will not give it to him. Whatever it takes, MacDonnell will not regain Hola."

The crowd dispersed, following Balgair, Asatrus, and Master Carpenter Munro to their tasks.

The weight of Phillipe's hand seemed to press upon Maggie. The need to tell him the truth of her escape filled her.

She touched his leg, gaining his attention. Her breath came short and shallow as memory rose. "Phillipe, I killed him. I plunged my dagger into his belly, felt him sag against me, his blood on my hands."

"Tell me," he invited as he wrapped her in his arms, his voice low and soothing.

Maggie took a deep breath and told him of her escape.

"I am truly sorry, *mon coeur*. I was not able to save ye. The knowledge will always be with me, though I will be forever grateful ye are strong enough to save yourself.

"I want to be the one who protects ye, keeps ye safe—not because I believe ye are weak, for ye are not—but because I love ye, Maggie, and ye are important to me. Beyond the need for my next breath."

She leaned her head against his shoulder.

"I killed men with my crossbow when they attacked Narnain Castle and suffered no qualms. But this . . . I took his life with my bare hands, and I watched another burn because of my actions."

"Let your mind empty, Maggie. Fill it with things which are good. Because of your actions, I am holding ye, not mourning your loss."

She raised her head and he shifted on the bench to face her. His kiss warmed her, banished her fears. He held her as she cried, murmuring words whose meanings she did not understand. Her heart ached to consider how close she'd come to never hearing his voice again.

Her breathing at last eased and she rested against him. His fingers stroked her hair.

"Though I would like naught more than to continue to hold ye, there is much to be done if we're to best a pirate."

With a nod of agreement, Maggie ducked inside the longhouse and exchanged her muddy and torn gown for a clean kirtle and surcoat, quickly scrubbing her face and hands with a damp cloth before dressing and returning to Phillipe's side.

She strode with him to the beach, sending him a searching look to ensure he wasn't about to fall down, for she didn't like the wobble she thought she saw in his step. He should be resting after a blow to the head necessitating several stitches, and a fall from the cliff. He likely wouldn't appreciate her pointing out such facts, though it was difficult to remain silent.

Balgair passed his end of a large log to another man and dusted bits of bark from his hands. "Whilst ye were away seeing the priest about being wedded, we set fire watches on the promontory and the cliff overlooking the abbey." He frowned. "We'll have one on the overlook as well by this afternoon, now we know the bastards can maneuver boats off the rookery."

He waved a hand over the activity near the beach. "We have labored steadily this past sennight, though without haste, and 'twas nearly our downfall. The lads are back at work, and I have a few ideas that may work as temporary defenses until the isle is secure."

"We'd like to see what ye've accomplished," Phillipe said.

Balgair tilted his head thoughtfully. "Can ye walk the trail to the abbey? Yer heid took quite a blow."

Maggie glanced at Phillipe. His brow lowered. "Don't be daft. There's no time to waste."

Balgair's grin reappeared. "Come with me."

Maggie kept an eye on Phillipe, but her attention soon turned to the changes she saw almost immediately. Her heart soared as they strode the narrow trail between the low ridges to the abbey. Rocks had been removed, the pathway widened where possible then cobbled with enough rounded stones to keep the trail from becoming a quagmire ever again. The path darkened as they reached its end. Overhead, trusses formed a walkway of timbers fashioned to protect those who stood above the trail, yet with openings wide enough to aim a crossbow bolt.

Maggie flashed Balgair a grin. "This is defensible."

"Yer lad, Narfi, borrowed yer crossbow—at my insistence—and I taught him to use it—him and a couple of others. The lad's clever. He absorbs knowledge faster'n a sponge soaks up water. Betwixt us, we determined the spacing and width of the bolt holes. He's been right good with yer wee falcon, as well. He'll be about with him shortly."

Her cheeks warmed. "I should have asked about Colyn sooner." Her gaze darted to Phillipe. "Much has happened since we arrived."

"Nae worries, m'lady. He's glad of the honor." Balgair moved to a sturdy wooden gate bound with iron bands and studs. He pulled a chain hanging over the top of the panel. The click of metal indicated he'd released the latch, and he pushed the heavy gate open.

"This allows us to open the gate from this side, though the chain can be pulled to the opposite side should we need to keep an enemy at bay."

They entered the open field where the abbey lay. Clusters of wind-stunted trees framed the meadow, the hives at their feet swarming with busy bees. On the far knoll stood the abbey, apple trees waving gently above the walls. Gone were the ragged bits of wall and roofing. Piles of stone sat ready to be added to the repairs. The garden at the foot of the wall was gone and clumps of dirt lay scattered about. Scaffolding and cranes rose high into the air. A curved, cobbled path led them to the massive double doors.

She gestured to the walls. "Ye've not only increased the height, but the width as well. And dug up the garden."

"'Twas necessary, *mon coeur*," Phillipe said. "The added height increases the weight, and the broader base helps keep the wall from leaning."

"We're able to build atop the stone of the isle itself with verra little digging, which helps as well," Balgair added. "We harvested what was ready, but will likely have to rely on foodstuffs from the mainland this winter."

He gestured to the abbey. "The men have also completely cleared the rooms which had become cluttered with debris, and will whitewash the interior walls once all repairs are made. The rooms will be yers to finish soon."

Maggie's gaze traveled the length of the abbey. "Ye've accomplished all this in little more than a sennight? Well done!"

"I'd nae have the baron's men sitting idly about." Balgair grinned, her compliment clearly pleasing him.

A volley of barks announced visitors. Serkan bounded up the path. Narfi and other children followed, the falcon on Narfi's wrist.

"Colyn can hunt, freya!" Narfi announced, his face beaming with pleasure. "I dinnae let him fly when the weather was bad. But he hunted a wee bird right from the sky a few days ago. He's a rare one!"

"Ye dinnae ken how proud I am of ye, Narfi, and how grateful for the care ye've given Colyn whilst I was away. My mind was eased to know he was with ye."

Narfi's face reddened and he glanced away, but the smile on his face broadened.

"May I ask ye to continue with yer care—for a time, at least? Phillipe and I will be verra busy with the work here and at our new home on the peninsula. 'Tis important his training continues without interruption."

Narfi's eyes glowed. "Aye! Ye can count on me, freya! And I can care for Serkan, as well. He's a good dog and will help Gerdur with the sheep one day."

"Ye have an excellent hand with the animals, Narfi. I thank ye for yer help."

Maggie turned back to Phillipe and Balgair. "I am verra pleased with the progress. 'Tis beyond my hopes, actually." She beamed, her heart full despite the lingering shadow of the pirates. "Beyond my wildest hopes."

* * *

Phillipe sent Maggie to bed with a lingering kiss and a promise to join her as soon as he could. His head throbbed, his neck and shoulders ached, and objects often appeared fuzzy or faded about the edges. But he was too worried to rest.

He paced before the watch fire, gathering his thoughts. "MacDonnell is their master?"

Balgair shifted his stance to follow Phillipe's gait. "Mayhap. He is lord over these isles and loyal to Norway." He glanced over his shoulder to the longhouse where Maggie and the other women had retired an hour or so earlier. "My guess is he sent them to kidnap Maggie, thinking her an easy target."

"Ye believe they were sent to only capture her?"

"If MacDonnell wanted her to hand over possession of the isle, he would have treated her well—at least until she capitulated."

Phillipe guarded the spurt of anger at the thought of Maggie as a pawn. "When should we expect MacDonnell's man to arrive?"

Balgair shrugged. "Mayhap a day—two at the most. He wouldnae leave her in the hands of drunken pirates long, lest they forget his orders."

Phillipe did not trust himself to respond. He increased his pace, noting the scent of brine and decay as his boots trampled deeper into the sand.

Balgair remained silent a moment, then turned from the fire. "It has occurred to me a chain across the harbor opening might deter ships from arriving unannounced."

"It might." Phillipe bit off the words, then changing direction abruptly to settle in the sand, his back against a boulder.

Balgair raised his eyebrows. "Ye are perturbed—beyond thoughts of yer wife."

"Maggie said the islanders fear the change we bring."

"They fear being protected?"

"They fear the violence of warriors who are strong enough to hold the isle. Fear how much of their way of life will attract the young men and turn them from their heritage of peace."

Balgair snorted. "Young men are attracted to protecting what is theirs, nae standing about whilst their fathers bow to the rapacious greed of pirates whose only claim to the isle is that they have swords."

Phillipe slid a questioning gaze to Balgair at his outburst, but the burly Scot shook his head. Silence filled the minutes as the fire crackled.

"We will proceed with the precautions ye and I discussed earlier," Phillipe said. "'Twill be no surprise to find MacDonnell on our shore in the next few hours. We must be prepared. Set a schedule, but work must continue through the night. Children below the age of twelve are exempt. Women will work alongside the men."

"This had to come to a halt sooner or later, ye ken. The pirates wouldnae have been satisfied with a mead tribute much longer. The slave trade escalates as tensions rise between Scotland and Norway. *Become one of us or lose yer life*. The caves made the islanders feel safe, but 'twould be too easy to smoke them out or simply kill them and take the isle. Ye have done naught to bring this about. Pirates were here long before ye set foot in Scotland." He paused with a low *harrumph*. "The islanders should be thankful to have men with our experience to provide for them."

Phillipe smiled, but without humor or happiness. "If I could leave Hola an idyllic isle with sheep the only blight on its hills, and the barks of seals the harshest sound, I would. I pray what we do is enough to give its people the opportunity to live in peace."

Maggie collapsed onto her pallet, exhaustion dulling the pain of muscles she knew would protest mightily in a few hours when she next rose. She hadn't wished to retire, but everyone clung to the schedule Balgair had set, knowing they needed rest as much as they needed to maintain the grueling pace.

Ingrida sank to the floor next to her. "Is it true ye and Lord Phillipe willnae remain here?"

Lord Phillipe? Such a change from the man who'd arrived on Hola with her less than a month prior. Maggie allowed herself a tired smile. If Ingrida only knew the real Phillipe.

"Aye. Baron MacLean has offered land and provisions on the northern edge of the Ardnamurchan peninsula. We are to provide a buffer against Lord MacDonnell's encroachment."

Ingrida twisted the wool of her kirtle between work-roughened fingers. "Will ye take Soren?"

"Who?"

"My son. The children call him Narfi because he is so skinny." She gave a low indulgent laugh. "Like his father." Ingrida drew a deep breath. "He is clearly enamored with yer falcon and wee dog. He is verra clever and has naught to look forward to here but raising sheep and making mead."

"Ye thought that was enough, last we spoke," Maggie reminded the woman. "Ye dinnae invite change."

Ingrida shrugged. "I have come to realize change will occur, whether I will it or nae. For generations, this isle was all our people knew. We were peaceful and traded occasionally with others from nearby islands. Then, the priests came, spreading word of their god. A few lingered and built the abbey, and then began making mead, changing Hola from a Viking outpost to a Christian settlement. The world is changing, freya, and our ways, while I still believe they are the best, willnae protect us from those who dinnae hold the same peaceful values we do. If Soren wishes to see more of the world, will ye take him?"

Maggie placed a hand on the troubled woman's forearm. "If he so wishes, he will have a place in our home for as long as he desires. But 'twill be his decision to make, not ours."

"Thank ye." Ingrida rose. "I have been neither fair nor honest with ye. Ye are a good woman, and Hola benefits from yer care. We should have told ye about the pirates sooner."

"Maggie. Wake." Someone shook her, whispering sharply in her ear. Maggie blinked and tried to sit, but her muscles groaned in protest. She wobbled then pushed to a seated position and shoved her hair from her eyes.

Phillipe's gaze met hers. The skin around his eyes was dark, bruised-looking, utterly exhausted. "A ship has been sighted. We believe it belongs to MacDonnell."

Panic drove Maggie to her feet. She stared at her husband, noted the mail beneath his cloak. Without a word, she sought her weapons, sheathing the daggers before laying her crossbow over her shoulder, quiver filled with bolts.

"We must be in place before the ship docks." Phillipe turned, but Maggie caught his shoulder and pulled him back.

"Naught is more important than this." She leaned forward and kissed him, all of her longing, fears, and trust, bundled into the brief caress.

He caught his arm about her waist and pulled her close. "I love ye, *mon coeur*. Never doubt it. We will see this through together."

Chapter Thirty Six

A longship rounded the point like a ghost against the pearly morning sky. The pristine sail flapped gently against the mast. Oars visible in the ports appeared locked in place, allowing the breeze to push the ship down the channel to the dock. Three men stood at the prow, but Maggie did not doubt many more sat below the row of shields lining the rail.

Dressed in trews and a thick tunic, Maggie stood next to Phillipe at the edge of the water, careful to remain a step beyond a stack of small rocks marking the range of arrows from the dock which had been determined the day before.

At the alarm from the promontory, the women and children had been sent ahead to their appointed places. Those capable of handling rocks and crossbows settled about the defensive positions, while those too infirm or young had fled to the abbey. The small number of islanders and MacLaren soldiers had been greatly increased by Baron MacLean's generous support, though the *Mar* had departed with a skeleton crew at dusk the day before. Maggie shuddered to think of the two dozen untrained islanders facing alone whatever the ship brought to their shores alone.

The three men climbed over the rail to the dock then halted. Their gazes swept the shore, populated with fewer than ten men, though all were warriors and carried their weapons in plain view.

One of the men took a step forward. "Ahoy, the shore!"

Phillipe mirrored the movement. "What brings ye here?"

The man spread his arms wide, his cloak sweeping clear of his sword hilt. Metal-studded leather bands encircled his wrists. A thickly-woven plaide draped his waist, falling to his knees. Two braids framed his face, the ends blending with his close-cropped beard.

"I seem to have misplaced a birlinn." He tilted his head at the black-sailed boat. "Much like this one. Permission to come ashore and discuss the errant crew?"

"The three of ye only," Phillipe concurred.

Within moments, the trio stood a few feet away. A gull swept overhead and a sheep bleated in the distance. Tension on the beach rose. Hands drifted to sword hilts, caught in the nick of time, then lowered.

Phillipe eyed the man directly before him. "Ye are . . .?"

"I am Hugh MacDonnell on behalf of the Lord of the Isles. And ye?"

"Phillipe of clan MacLean."

Hugh's eyes narrowed as if the information puzzled him. "And the woman next to ye?" His gaze raked Maggie head to toe and back. "Ah, such hair. She could be none other than the lovely Maggie MacLaren."

Maggie bristled.

"She is my wife." Phillip's voice hardened.

"Yer wife? The earl dinnae mention she'd remarried." MacDonnell raised a brow then shrugged his thick shoulders. "It matters not. I came to recover something which was lost. Do ye have knowledge of the men sailing this birlinn?"

Maggie stepped to Phillipe's side. "They are dead."

"Indeed? How is it ye come by such knowledge?"

"I killed them."

Hugh glanced at his men then back to Maggie. "'Twas a bit harsh, m'lady, was it not? I wished to meet with ye, 'twas all."

"I dinnae like the way they asked."

"Lord MacDonnell would like to regain possession of this isle. We would prefer ye be in agreement."

"Nae."

Hugh swore under his breath. "Sign over Hola or I will take it by force."

Maggie stiffened. "Ye can try."

His gaze swept the beach. "A handful of men willnae divert me from my path." He faced Maggie. "Nor a willful wench who doesnae know her place."

"Ye will speak to Lady MacLean civilly or learn better," Phillipe warned, his gaze narrowed, jaw set.

"My most abject apologies, m'lady," Hugh effused, eyes glittering with malice. "Yer former husband was less than kind with his opinion of ye, and words do have a way of lingering." His thin smile stole no warmth from the baiting glint in his eyes. "In fact, he is the one who suggested we send ruffians to bring ye to heel before I spoke with ye. A terrible thing, to be certain, and no less than I'd expect of a man who discarded such a lovely as ye."

"Ye are finished. Do not speak to my wife again," Phillipe growled.

Maggie caught her breath. He'd never looked so dangerous.

Phillipe's brow lowered. "Not even to ask her blessing with your dying breath. Your time is up. She will not surrender title to the isle, and if ye do not depart immediately, ye will be killed where ye stand."

Hugh gave a dismissive wave of his hand. "I dinnae fear such as ye."

Balgair stepped forward, beard bristling. "Mayhap answering to Baron MacLean is more to yer liking?"

A feral grin spread across Hugh MacDonnell's face. "Once ye are dead, what difference does it make?"

Movement at the pier caught Maggie's attention. She touched Phillipe's arm. "Men. Coming ashore."

Phillipe's slight nod told her he'd noticed. "The *Mar* was dispatched yester eve, sending word to Baron MacLean of the troubles on Hola. He will not take kindly to the mistreatment of his new daughter by marriage."

Hugh frowned. "Baron MacLean's son is Lord Alex. He's been at Morvern three years and more."

"I am Baron MacLean's other son. I've just arrived."

Phillipe dropped his hand to Maggie's shoulder. "Go!"

She whirled and darted up the path to the abbey. Two MacLaren warriors followed at her heels. Three MacLean men stood poised, heavy swords in their hands, as MacDonnell pirates waded ashore. At a shouted signal, the MacLeans hacked at ropes not easily visible by the invaders, and a section of sewn together fishing nets stretching across the flattest portion of the beach snapped into the air, strung taut on the frames used to dry fish.

Men cursed as the nets and ropes fouled their legs and dumped them into the surf. Hugh MacDonnell advanced on Phillipe and Balgair, sliding his sword from its sheath.

"Ye shouldnae have involved yerself. For this, ye will die."

Balgair grinned, clearly enjoying himself. "This day 'tis as good as any other."

As rehearsed, Phillipe and Balgair closed on the three, engaging them to give the rest of the MacLeans and MacLarens time to retreat to the abbey. Swords clanged. Small stones rolled treacherously beneath their boots. Pirates freed from the nets charged up the beach. With a final parry, Phillipe and Balgair sprang to the trail in Maggie's footsteps. At Balgair's shout, Narfi and his band of archers loosed a round of crossbow bolts. Most landed on the ground between Phillipe and the MacDonnells, but a few found more deadly marks.

Shouts of *huzzah* lifted in the air. Now exposed to the pirates against the wind-swept slopes, Narfi and the archers joined the others fleeing up the path to the abbey. Their unexpected volley gave the men precious seconds to pass the protected bridge spanning the trail. Agile as mountain goats, the lads sped to their next line of defense.

At the head of the trail, Phillipe whirled to a halt. "Now!"

At his shout, burly carpenters pulled against ropes attached to timbers supporting old doors scavenged from the abbey, topped with dozens of boulders plucked from the isle. With a groan, the supports gave way and the boulders flew down the hillside, some partially occluding the path, others bouncing in a deadly melee over the pirates who followed too close.

Another cheer rang out.

Phillipe motioned impatiently at the carpenters. "Hurry! Join the others. Balgair and I will support the lads on the bridge."

He and Balgair raced up the trail and through the gate. They quickly engaged the latch, then leapt up the hastily carved steps to the shielded bridge above. Narfi and the others awaited, eyes wide, crossbows at the ready. Maggie stood in their midst. Phillipe caught her gaze and grinned.

"We shall hold them here. We will not remain beleaguered long."

Maggie's tense composure relaxed and she gave a nod before turning her attention to the apertures in the wooden barbican. Peering through the slits, she and the others watched as the pirates approached.

The familiar excitement of battle raced through Phillipe as he waited. *Closer, wait, wait.* His motley band of archers needed no prompting. Either through obedience or fright, they remained motionless as the enemy drew near.

"Now." His single command released four bolts. Two struck true, felling the pirates in the lead. Two struck the cliffs on either side and ricocheted through the crowd, inflicting damage. With a bellow, Hugh MacDonnell ordered his men back.

Excitement raced through the archers. The pirates, anticipating closer combat, were armed only with swords and daggers.

A swift conversation took place, then a handful of pirates disappeared down the path. Silence stretched. Phillipe knew they likely sought a path over the low cliffs. The way was difficult but not impassable. Though they must pass the men stationed at the watch fires at the overlooks first.

Had he placed enough men there? Could they defend themselves against the pirates? He waited impatiently for one of the drums—newly made with cured seal skins stretched over a rough frame—to sound, indicating siting of the *Mar*.

"Look!" Maggie touched his arm.

He glanced through the aperture. Something glowed on the trail, rapidly approaching.

"They think to burn us out."

"*Fils de* . . .." He gestured to the archers. "Do not let them close. Spare your bolts for sure hits. Shoot only as commanded."

He and Balgair took up positions on either end, adding to the archers' numbers. A mark blazed on the stone on either side of the cliffs.

"Steady. As they pass the mark . . .."

Four bolts sped down the path. One struck the lead pirate, three thudded the path at their feet. The archers stepped back to reload their bows, the others moving into place.

The sequence became a deadly dance. Shoot. Retreat. Reload. Over and over. Pirates fell, but more replaced them. They built a fire on the path, fueling it with the brands from the bonfire on the beach. As it flamed, green shrubs were added and smoke built along the trail and wafted toward the wooden barbican.

Phillipe's eyes began to water. He tore a strip from his tunic and tied it about his nose and lower face, commanding the others to do the same.

A boom echoed faintly. The drums! The archers glanced at each other. Excitement lit their faces above their masks. The *Mar* had been sighted!

The pirates hesitated.

Breathless, Maggie peered through the bolt holes. "They've turned back!"

Narfi and his archers cheered, fists pumping the air.

"Give them space," Phillipe ordered. His eyes crinkled betraying the grin beneath his mask. "I'd like to chase them back to their ship, but they still out-number us. Do not be hasty."

Maggie's fingers lightly tapped the stock of her crossbow, impatient. Another boom reverberated. The *Mar* was in the harbor.

"The path is as deadly for us as it was for the pirates, should they conspire to trap us at the far end," Phillipe cautioned. "Balgair and I will go first. Follow at a measured distance."

Maggie nodded, though anticipation rose with cold fingers up her spine. Phillipe exited the barbican and repeated his instructions to the warriors guarding the gate. He disengaged the latch then led his force toward the beach. Callan and Dawe walked before and after Maggie, lending their swords to her protection.

They reached the top of the rise which opened to the harbor below. Men fled across the beach, heading for the MacDonnell ship. Maggie and the others raced in their wake, skidding to a halt at the shore. The *Mar* rocked on the gentle swells, a length from the pier.

A man stood at the bow, black hair waving in the wind.

"Lady MacLean! How may we help?"

Maggie grinned, recognizing Alex's voice. "Ye've been a great help already. Many thanks, Sir!"

"The might of Clan MacLean is ever at yer service."

Mirth bubbled up inside Maggie. "Send them on their way. We dinnae need the likes of them scouring our isle."

Obligingly, the *Mar* tacked in the small space, giving way before the birlinn.

"MacDonnell!" Alex shouted. "This is MacLean land, held by Maggie MacLean. Dinnae forget it."

There was no reply as the birlinn slid oars into the water and pulled out of the bay.

Alex met Maggie and Phillipe at the pier once the other ship gained open water.

"He willnae be happy about his defeat here. Da has sent warriors and will supply a warship to guard the harbor until we are certain Lord MacDonnell has regained his senses." His sharp gaze slid from Maggie to Phillipe. "Ye have sustained nae lasting harm?"

"Nae," Phillipe replied. "Though my head would not object to a few hours' sleep."

Asatrus stepped to the pier. He inclined his head. "Our thanks, m'lords, m'lady. We are in yer debt."

"There is nae debt," Maggie said. "Ye are our family, now, and we protect our own. As soon as the threat has diminished, we will recall most of the warriors and mayhap leave only a small ship in the harbor to remind any who come here with malice that ye and yer families are much valued. We will see ye are left in peace to grow yer orchard and brew yer mead."

Others joined them on and around the dock, faces wiped clear of worry, filled with wonder and relief.

Maggie surveyed the small crowd. "Ye fought well today. Not just the pirates, but yer own fears. I am proud of ye."

Cheers rang out. Phillipe turned Maggie to him and kissed her soundly.

The roar of approval rose. After a long moment, Maggie raised her hands. The noise subsided.

"Let us feast and toast our victories!"

Epilogue

April 1226
Ardnamurchan Peninsula

The *Saorsa* sailed north along the edge of the Ardnamurchan Peninsula where the westernmost lands of Scotland stretched into the sea, welcoming them with vivid blue waters and white sands. Rocky crags skipped from the shore into deeper water and tufts of wiry grasses waved in the wind. Low, grassy plains dotted with early spring flowers swept up from the beaches to the mountains.

Porpoises breached the waters on either side of the *Saorsa*, leaping playfully in the froth parting beneath the bow. Otters floated near the shores.

Serkan raised his paws to the rail, tail wagging gently. Nose to the air, he sniffed, then barked.

Maggie leaned over the bow. "Look! Puffins!"

The cheeky birds waddled on bright orange feet over the rocks and grass. Some dove into the sea, others taking wing to soar over the water in search of fish.

"Excited?" Phillipe grinned broadly, eyes shining.

Maggie bumped her shoulder against his arm. "Aye."

He hugged her against his side. "It has not been quite a year since we chose the site for the castle and approved the design. Though 'twill be many more months before 'tis completed, I am looking forward to seeing how it progresses."

"I could live on the ground floor for now," Maggie commented with a sigh.

"Tired of being a guest at MacLean Castle?"

"Mmmm. A bit. Though having the leisure to spend time with ye *is* lovely. I know demands will increase once we have our own demesne to oversee." She gave a wistful smile. "But I am ready for *our* home."

The coast undulated off the starboard bow, each cove seemingly more beautiful than the last. They finally reached the bay which sheltered a hidden harbor between a sweeping, narrow peninsula to the west, and a broad curve of sandy beach to the south and east. Waves crashed against a skerry of black stone a short distance to the north, making entry into the harbor dangerous under all but fair weather.

Two small birlinns, built for hauling merchandise—or, in this case, tools and men for building the new castle—wallowed gently as waves rushed beneath their hulls to sweep against the shore. A stone pier had been built for ease of off-loading supplies. A cluster of tents and other, more stable housing filled the space between the sandy beach and the slope to the foot of the mountain, housing the many artisans and craftsmen.

They disembarked amid shouted greetings. Phillipe waved the men back to work, a smile on his face. Maggie stepped ashore as Serkan loped past, nose to the grass. He made a wide arc through the field then returned, sitting at Maggie's feet as she absently patted his head.

Her awed gaze was drawn to the fortress sweeping up from the rocky crag as if it had been carved there when the earth began. The curtain wall, towering some thirty feet above the harbor, rose and dipped with the land. Two sides neared completion—the north wall and the one facing the sea. In the center stood the keep, scaffolding soaring above the vaulted ground floor, walls raised to the third storey. Piles of wood, stone, and mortar lay on the ground, the ring of chisels answered by the creak of ropes and pulleys.

"It rides the ridge, powerful and—och! I have the name. *Donansgeir.* 'Tis Norse for *Donan's rock.*"

Phillipe gazed at her solemnly. "Donansgeir Castle. In honor of the priest whose articles we found in the caves. 'Tis a fine name ye give our home, *mon coeur.*"

Maggie nodded and fingered the neckline of her gown, bringing to mind the brooch still in Uilleam's possession. "A fitting place for the reliquary someday." She smiled, serene. "Da is better."

Phillipe dropped a kiss to her forehead. "Thanks to the relic, your stubborn brother, and the healer who became God's hands."

Maggie swallowed back a sigh. She wasn't ready to lose a parent.

Phillipe tugged her hand. "Come."

Eagerly, she climbed the road to the castle, pausing twice to catch her breath. "Too much easy living," she remarked with a smile when Phillipe voiced concern. His eyes narrowed, but he waited without comment until she was able to continue. She placed a hand on the slight curve of her belly once his attention was engaged with the activity at the castle.

'Tis been nearly a year. I dinnae believe . . ..

Warmth swept through her. She would need to stop. To think. To count. She could not remember her last courses. Had it been two, even three months ago? Why had she not noticed? The possibility she was pregnant left her speechless.

Phillipe called to her from the entry to the keep. "The stairs reach our chambers. Come! Look at what's been done!"

His excitement was irresistible and she abandoned her thoughts as she hurried to join him. Two doors made of boards eight feet long and almost two inches thick, crossed with iron bands a hand's width apart, lay propped against the wall, waiting to be installed. The massive hinges protruded from the door frames, built into the rock.

"Look up," he urged. "What do ye see?"

Maggie leaned her head back to stare up the wall. "'Tis nae finished. A section is missing. They've another storey and the roof before they're finished."

Phillipe grinned. "Let me show ye."

They climbed the spiral staircase at the far corner of the great hall to the third storey. Sunlight lit the entire floor, the ceiling naught but beams set in place to support the next level. Phillipe led her to the front wall where stones rose on either side of a wide aperture.

"What do ye see? Beyond the keep."

She peered over the wall. In the distance, the sea swept into the harbor in jeweled colors ranging from cobalt to turquoise, rolling green and white upon the sands. Birds wheeled overhead. The flower-filled *machair* spilled at her feet.

"'Tis beautiful," she whispered. "I believe I might see Hola from here. On a clear day," she amended.

"We will place a window in this wall." Phillipe motioned to the edges of the open space. "'Twill be divided into three parts, each arched at the top and set with pierced stone. The view will be spectacular!"

Maggie opened her mouth but formed no words. Could anything be more splendid? "I dinnae know what to say. I never imagined . . .. Phillipe, 'tis wonderful!"

His gaze met hers. One corner of his mouth tilted up. "I wanted to surprise ye. I hope ye like it."

Maggie's breath hitched and she fell in love with him all over again. She took his hand and placed it on her belly. "My love, I believe I have a surprise, as well."

The End

MORE BOOKS by Cathy MacRae

The Highlander's Bride series

The Highlander's Accidental Bride (book 1)
The Highlander's Reluctant Bride (book 2)
The Highlander's Tempestuous Bride (book 3)
The Highlander's Outlaw Bride (book 4)
The Highlander's French Bride (book 5)

De Wolfe Pack Connected World

The Saint
The Penitent
The Cursed

The Ghosts of Culloden Moor series

(with LL Muir, Diane Darcy, Jo Jones, and Melissa Mayhue)

Adam
Malcolm
MacLeod
Patrick

The Hardy Heroine series

(with DD MacRae)

Highland Escape (book 1)
The Highlander's Viking Bride (book 2)
The Highlander's Crusader Bride (book 3)
The Highlander's Norse Bride, a Novella (book 4)

The Highlander's Welsh Bride (book 5)
The Prince's Highland Bride (book 6)

About the Authors

Cathy MacRae lives on the sunny side of the Arbuckle Mountains where she and her husband read, write, and tend the garden—with the help of the dogs, of course.

You can visit with her on Facebook, or read her blogs and learn about her books at www.cathymacraeauthor.com. Drop her a line—she loves to hear from readers!

To keep up with new releases and other fun things, sign up for her newsletter!

Other ways to connect with Cathy:

Facebook: Cathy MacRae Author
Twitter: @CMacRaeAuthor
Instagram: cathymacrae_author
Pinterest
Book bub

DD MacRae enjoys bringing history to life and considers research one of the best things about writing a story! With more than 35 years of martial arts training, DD also brings breath-taking action to the tales.

You can connect with DD through www.cathymacraeauthor.com. It's always exciting to hear from readers!

A Note from the Authors

We sincerely hope you've enjoyed this inventive re-telling of Phillipe of Antioch and how he and Maggie found their happy-ever-afters. As always, we strive to bring you the best mix of history and fiction. If you're interested, we've included some of our notes for The Prince's Highland Bride below.

Phillipe of Antioch: As you may realize, the real Phillipe shows up in Wiki and elsewhere as having died of poisoning after marrying Isabella, the child-queen of Cilicia (or Little Armenia), and falling into disfavor with the people. That's the short version, and one we took as solid truth until we uncovered a nugget of information suggesting he was well-loved by his young bride who genuinely grieved his death and refused to remarry (though she was eventually brought to heel and forced to marry Baron Konstantin's son, Hethum. She reportedly refused to consummate the marriage for many years—she was, still, a child when they wed—but appears to have eventually borne eight children to Hethum). Her actions didn't sound like those of a queen disenchanted with a consort she hadn't chosen, so we dug deeper.

All sources agreed Phillipe made a good initial impression on his subjects, even hailed him as a savior in troubled times after winning a victory over the attacking Turks (the original reason the queen's regent, Baron Konstantin, sought an alliance with Phillipe's father, the powerful Bohemond IV of Antioch), and bringing peace to the beleaguered country. However, he soon fell into disfavor when he refused to adhere to the rites of the Armenian Church and was seen as spending too much time in Antioch. His time in Antioch was possibly the more dangerous of his actions, as he was young and very much influenced by his father. The nobles of Cilicia feared their country would soon become a mere outpost for Antioch. Their differences with the Roman Catholic church also kept them at odds with the 'intolerable' situation with their young king.

285

A conspiracy soon formed among the high dignitaries of Cilicia, led by Konstantin of Barbaron. They realized they'd lost their power when Phillipe and Isabell (Zabel) married and became rulers of Cilicia despite her young age (she was six or seven at the time). Faced with the loss of their influence, they decided to put an end to Phillipe's reign by the most expedient way possible—death. One source suggested Phillipe was joined by Zabel on many of his trips to Antioch (causing even more strife, for if both king and queen became enamored of Antioch's ways, Cilicia was, indeed, doomed), and suggested he was arrested as he and Zabel traveled by night to Antioch—making a case that they were fleeing Cilicia at this point. He was accused of stealing the crown jewels of Cilicia. Was this code for the young queen? Were they actually accusing him of stealing her or her affections away from Cilicia? Or was he accused of stealing a king's ransom in stones and gold?

Whatever the truth, Phillipe was imprisoned in the fortress of Partzerpert, near Sis, the Cilician capital, where he remained for several months while his father appealed to Baron Konstantin. Bohemond's petitions were in vain, however, and Phillipe was poisoned in prison in 1225. Bohemond was enraged, but his plan to avenge his son was thwarted when his ally, the Sultan of Rum—who had raided Cilicia in 1225—switched to the side of the Armenians.

We decided Phillipe had been dealt a bad lot. He'd been portrayed as an arrogant, overbearing man who had married Zabel strictly for political reasons, and who despised the Armenian people. But Zabel's actions both before and after his death suggested otherwise, and soon we wondered, *what if . . .?*

Margaret Ellen MacLaren: Known as Maggie to her friends, she was a dutiful daughter who reluctantly agreed to marry the Earl of Mar according to her da's wishes. Bitter after the earl abandons her, she decides she's had enough of men ordering her life, and refuses to retire peaceably to a nunnery to live her life in penance for not bearing a child. She returns to her childhood home on Ben Narnain (mountain of iron) near the banks of Loch Lomond, though she doesn't find peace there.

What if she met a man whose was struggling with his past as much as she? Could she reach beyond her hurts and sorrows—and stubbornness—and allow a relationship to form? Both characters would be outside the favor of the Church, an institution as powerful as the monarchy. We wanted to explore this unique situation while attempting to stay true to the rules and influence of the Catholic Church at that time.

Known as *freya* to the people of Hola, Maggie sets out on a journey that will, at last, set her free to love again.

The Earl of Mar: Richard de Moravia is a fictional character, though the title has been in use in Scotland since at least 1014 AD.

Avril: In The Highlander's Crusader Bride, we introduced the Turkoman Horse, aka the Akhal-Teke. By the time of this story, Arbela's horse Voski has stood at stud and produced a number of beautiful, sure-footed foals, of which Avril is one. The Akhal-Teke is unique in that its coat has an almost metallic sheen, and is one of the oldest surviving horse breeds on the planet.

Serkan: Phillipe's puppy, named for the Turkish word for 'chief', brings back memories of the Aidi dogs Arbela brought to Scotland. More of a livestock protector, fearless and strong, the breed also has quite a good sense of smell. Serkan was a mix of what would eventually become the Border Collie (Coley), and the Aidi.

Saint Martin's Abbey on Hola: St. Martin is the patron saint of beggars, vintners, equestrians soldiers, tailors, innkeepers, alcoholics, and geese. He is known for his gentle, unassuming nature, and his ability to bring warmth and light to those in need. In this imagined abbey, the monks developed a tasty, potent mead which was much sought after.

Saint Donan: (also Donnan) The tale Father Sachairi relates about Donan of Eigg is true. Or, as true as can be said of a tale of such age. It was curious that, while we find most other subjects are more or less cut-and-paste repeats which vary little from website to website, the story of St. Donan and his death on Eigg did have some interesting differences. We discovered scholarly, ecumenical, oral tradition, and incidental recountings of the story which we blended for Father Sachairi's tale. Quite fascinating, really, and of course, the mention of warrior women employed by the Queen Moidart caught our attention.

You may recognize his namesake, Eilean Donan (Donan's Isle), and many other places in Scotland. He also lent his name to the Kildonnan Cross, at least ten churches in Scotland, and the Kildonnan Monastery on Eigg.

The Treasure of Hola:
What, exactly, were we likely to find on a small isle in the Hebrides? The answer was, pretty much anything. So, after digging up vast quantities of information on Pictish treasure, the Traprain Law Hoard, St. Ninian's Isle hoard, baubles a Crusader may have brought back from the East, and gold and silver coins, we added a brooch you may recognize from the book, *Mhàiri's Yuletide Wish*. Keep watch for it in other Yuletide tales.

To the best of our knowledge, there is no lost treasure of St. Donan, though the descriptions of a ringed cross with a hunting scene engraved on it are from the Kildonnan Cross, discovered in the graveyard at Kildonnan Church which now occupies the site of St. Donan's monastery. It is a pinkish slab with a Pictish hunting scene engraved on one side and the Christian cross and key pattern on the reverse.

Peregrine Falcon:
Colyn's inclusion was prompted by Cathy's visit to Dunrobin Castle where a falconry exhibit and demonstration was enough to encourage her to spend hours researching the how, when, and why of raising a hunting falcon. And, of course, the young chick became a great way for Maggie and Phillipe to meet.

Poison: What did Phillipe actually drink? It is likely he would have ingested an extract of aconitum, though the actual mixture remains a mystery. It was rather interesting to find the name, aconitum, possibly came from the village of Akonai in Turkey. The village doesn't exist today, but was thought to be near a cave said to house the entrance to Hades and guarded by Cerebus. The Chinese were said to have smeared a paste made of aconitum on arrow shafts as well as their tips, in the hope that anyone attempting to remove an arrow from a wounded warrior would also absorb the poison. It is easily absorbed through broken skin and open wounds, and there have been cases of people feeling unwell after working with the plant.

Hola: The isle was based on the Isle of Muck, but we wanted an isle we could manipulate as needed for the story, and so, Hola does not exist beyond these pages.

Weapons: We included a mix of weapons including the Kilij, a single-edged curved sword or scimitar which originated in the Middle East. This is a light saber excellent for using from horseback.
The crossbow was Maggie's weapon of choice. It was relatively lightweight and quite easy to use. It's only drawback was the slow firing rate of about two bolts per minute. However, it required little training to use, and little strength to operate—at least, the use of a foot-based method (stirrup) of pulling the string leveled the playing field quite a bit.

Narnain Castle (castle of iron), Maggie's childhood home, was a motte and bailey castle. Laird MacLaren was transitioning the walls from wood to stone, but lacked the men and coin to make this a priority.

Mead: We discovered orchards were first planted on a notable scale in Scotland during the 12th century, and primarily maintained by various religious orders. Without firsthand knowledge, though we have a friend who makes his own mead with modern methods, we decided the Pippin apple would be a good choice to add to honey, spring water, and exposure to air—as yeast had not yet been discovered. The 'blessing stick' used to stir the honey was actually the means by which yeast was introduced to the honey so it would ferment. The monks did not know this was happening, only that it worked.

Bridei Keep: The name is ours, but it is based on the keep—a motte and bailey castle—at the site of the Pictish church established in 581 by King Bridei I of the Picts. Kildrummy Castle was built (1250) on the site and was the home of the Earl of Mar.

Eels: Raw eels were a favored cure for a hangover in Medieval Europe. A more modern Scottish cure would have been a bit of corn starch (aka corn flour) stirred into buttermilk, heated, and seasoned with salt and pepper. However, corn was not available in Europe until after the arrival of explorers in North America in 1492.

Acknowledgements

This story wouldn't be complete without the support of our critique group. Dawn Marie Hamilton, Cate Parke, and Lane McFarland are hands-down the most amazing group to work with. Thank you all for your help, suggestions, and even the hard questions. We're very glad to be working with you.

Thanks also to the amazing Dar Albert for the cover. It is exactly what we wanted!

Manufactured by Amazon.ca
Bolton, ON

20247995R00169